# MOON'S PROMISE

## THE LAST RIDERS, #11

## JAMIE BEGLEY

Young Ink Press Publication
YoungInkPress.com

Edited by CD Editing &
Diamond in the Rough Editing
Cover Art by CT Cover Creations

*Connect with Jamie,*
*Facebook.com/AuthorJamieBegley*
*Instagram.com/authorjamiebegley*
*JamieBegley.net*

# PROLOGUE

"It's time to go, Riley, Eric. Say bye to Devon. You won't see him until we get settled."

The three children sat huddled on the couch, hugging each other. Devon held his tiny three-year-old sister on his lap as she sobbed into his chest while he hugged his young five-year-old brother closer to his side.

"Why can't Devon come with us?" His brother raised his tear-stained face from his shoulder to ask.

His stepfather glowered down at them at the question he had answered repeatedly since Vance told his mother he was moving away to live with another woman. "Because he doesn't belong to me. I can't make his mother let me take him. I'd go to jail if I tried to take him. Do you want me to go to jail?"

Vance's harsh question had both his brother and sister trembling in his arms.

"No," both Riley and Eric sobbed out their answer.

Devon remained silent instead of yelling out *yes* like he wanted to. If he did, Vance wouldn't keep his promise to bring Eric and Riley to see him once a month.

He might not have said anything, but his stepfather easily read his hate-filled expression.

"Come on; grab your shit," Vance ordered the clinging children. "I want to be out of here before Kiko comes back."

Devon watched as his brother and sister reluctantly left his arms to go to their bedrooms to grab the two backpacks they had worn in from school. Vance had already packed their belongings while Riley was in daycare, and Eric was at school.

Walking to the door as Vance pushed his sister and brother to the doorway, Devon picked up his little sister.

"Don't cry," he tried to soothe Riley. "Vance will bring you to see me."

Riley gave him a tearful nod.

Carefully, he handed her over to Vance and hugged Eric.

"Make sure you keep practicing your timetables. I have something special for you if you can tell me the sevens."

Eric's somber expression switched to excitement. "What is it?"

Devon gave him a gentle smile. "You'll have to wait and see."

"Okay"

"Bye ..." Devon told them miserably.

Before he could say anything else, Vance grabbed Eric's hand and led him out the door. Devon wasn't surprised that Vance hadn't bothered to say goodbye. As he held the door-knob in his hand, he had never felt so much hatred for anyone in his life as he did for Vance.

Devon waited to close the door until Vance's red truck pulled away from the curb before he returned to the living room and sat down on the couch. He was still staring blankly at the television screen when his mother came home.

Placing her purse on the end table, she sat down next to him.

"You okay?" she asked hesitantly.

"No."

His mother released a sad sigh as she laid a comforting hand on his arm. "I'm sorry. I wish you had stayed at school the way I wanted you to until I could get off work."

Devon shrugged away from her touch. "I wanted to say goodbye to them."

"Are you blaming me for them leaving? It's not my fault Vance wants to be with another woman."

"You could have been here to tell them goodbye. They cried when you weren't here."

His mother's eyes brimmed with tears. "I know my weaknesses. If I had been here when they started crying, I would have broken. I am not strong like you, Devon. They are my babies, yet I have no legal right to them—I am not their mother. I didn't trust myself not to beg him on my knees to stay. I couldn't do that, Devon, not even for Riley and Eric."

Devon saw the anguish on his mother's beautiful face. No, his mother would never lower her pride to bring herself to her knees. Vance had tried many times to accomplish that humiliation but had never succeeded.

"Do you think he will keep his promise to bring them to see me?"

His mother smoothed her tears away. "I wouldn't count on it. Vance promised to marry me when he talked me into leaving Hawaii. He didn't. He promised to let me adopt Eric and Riley. He didn't. He promised to treat you and me well. He didn't. Vance hasn't kept any promises he's made to me. Maybe you will have better luck."

Devon didn't hold out hope.

Seeing his mother's proud face break into tears made him feel bad. She was hurting as badly as he was but had been hiding it to appear strong in front of him.

He hugged his mother, manfully holding back his own tears.

"Don't cry. It'll be all right."

"He took my babies from me ..." She sobbed into his shoulder. "No one ever keeps their promises to me. Your dad promised me he wouldn't reenlist again. Vance promised never to leave me. Why can't they keep their promises?"

"I will. I'll keep any promise I make."

"Swear to me, Devon. Don't be like other men. When you make a promise, keep it."

"I swear."

---

Two Years Later...

evon sat in his mother's car, waiting for Vance's truck to pull into the garage he managed. It had taken him two months to find the bastard after he stopped by to take Eric and Riley out to a movie and lunch. The hatred between them had only grown over the last two years.

He had applied for his driver's license the day he turned sixteen. As soon as he earned it, he drove to see Eric and Riley and take the option out of Vance's hands to bring them to see him.

He had only seen them six times during the last two years. Vance had tried to prevent him from seeing them, but one benefit of him getting older was his size. Vance was a small man, barely five-four, and if Devon was to guess, he weighed less than one-twenty. He, on the other hand, was six-three, and working out with the football team had developed his body into a muscular build which Vance noticed gradually becoming more aggressive each time they saw each other. The bastard couldn't bear someone he still considered a boy not being afraid of him.

Devon gave a sarcastic snort in the silence of the car. He hadn't been afraid of Vance since he was fourteen and caught his swinging fist before it could land on his back. Vance had a bad habit of waiting until his back was turned to drill a fist into him when his mother hadn't been home. When he swung around and caught Vance's fist then pinned him against the refrigerator, Devon had seen the fear in his eyes.

"You're not going to touch me again," Devon told him as he placed a restraining forearm against his neck to hold Vance in place. "Got it?"

Vance glared back at him. "Got it."

"Good." Devon released him, and neither of them had mentioned it to his mother.

Two weeks later, Vance had come home and told her he was leaving her. The son of bitch was a coward, and they both knew it. If Vance had stayed, it would have only been a matter of time before the arguments between them became more physical.

Seeing Vance pull to the side of the garage, he got out of the car to intercept him before he could reach the garage bay.

Vance noticed his approach. "What do you want?"

"Where are Eric and Riley?"

"None of your fucking business. Get out of here before I call the cops on you for trespassing."

Devon didn't move. "Call them. Neither of them are answering the cell phone I bought them. I checked with the bitch you were living with. She doesn't know where they are since she kicked your sorry ass out. They're not in school and too young to be left alone, so unless you found another woman to keep your ass up between jobs and she's watching them, which I doubt"—watching Vance's expression as he talked, Devon carefully scrutinized his features for any telltale sign to indicate his brother or sister had been hurt—"I might be able to convince them to check it out to make sure they are being taken care of."

Vance gave him a gloating look.

Devon's heart sank. Whatever Vance had done to Eric and Riley, he knew it was going to hurt.

"I'd tell them they're with their mother." A cruel smile played on the bastard's lips. "When Carole threw me out, I didn't have any choice but to call Marie. She came and got them. They're in Georgia. I threw the phone away. You're not a blood relative of theirs. You keep bugging them, I'll press charges on you for stalking." Vance laughed at the expression he wasn't hiding. "You're a little too interested in children much younger than you. It's in Eric's and Riley's best interest to live with their mother. You're not a blood relative; it's none of your fucking business where they are." Vance gave him a curt lift of his chin. "Get your ass out of here before I call the cops and have you arrested."

Devon stared at Vance, unmoved by the threat. "I'm going to check on them and make sure they're okay."

"What you going to do if they aren't? You're a kid; you can't do a fucking thing ..."

His mocking laughter didn't have the desired effect Vance wanted.

"If you hurt them, I'll kill you." Devon returned his threat with one of his own. "That's a promise."

"Oh ... I'm so scared. Get your punk ass out of here."

More mocking laughter followed him back to the car.

At home, he convinced his mother to accompany him to the police station. Luckily, they were assigned to a female officer who didn't brush off their concern.

"You two go home. I'm going to send a couple officers to Mr. Laughlin's place of work. Then I'm going to call the school and find out if Riley and Eric have been there before

I'll drive to the address you gave me of where they've been living." Officer Campbell gave him a comforting smile. "I'll also do what I can to find out their mother's address and send officers to check on their welfare. I'm sure the children are fine," she assured them.

Devon and his mother left. He dropped her off, then went to his part-time job at the grocery store. He was stocking canned corn when the manager told him his mother had called and it was important he called her back.

He dialed the number and held the receiver with a sweaty hand. Devon heard her crying on the other end the moment she answered.

"Mom?"

"Devon … it's Riley and Eric … they've been found."

Devon couldn't understand the words coming from his mother because she was crying so hard.

Dropping the phone, he ran out of the manager's office. His chest was heaving by the time he was able to get behind the wheel. He squealed out of the parking lot and was driving home when he changed his mind. Doing a U-turn in the middle of the road, he drove to the house his brother and sister had been living in.

He jerked to a stop when he came upon a police car blocking entry into the neighborhood, quickly got out of the car, and tried to run past the yellow tape, but a police officer caught his arm.

"Stay back. You can't go this way. You'll have to move your car."

"My brother and sister live down there!" he yelled, trying to break away.

"Let him go." The officer he had spoken with at the station got out of a car sitting at the curb.

The officer released him, and Devon walked over to Officer Campbell. "Where are Riley and Eric?" Looking away from policewoman's grim visage, Devon glanced toward the house that had police cars sitting out front while officers came and went from the backyard.

"Devon, I'm going to call your mother and have her come here."

He shook his head. "Don't. She's too upset to drive. Just tell me. If they're hurt, I want to be with them," he started to beg.

She stared at him sympathetically. "There isn't anything you can do for them, Devon. There isn't anything any of us can do for them anymore. I'm so sorry."

Devon felt as if a switch had been flicked inside of him. A darkness encased him in such a deep coldness that he was surprised his body didn't break into a thousand pieces when the policewoman laid a hand on his shoulder.

"I'll have one of the officers drive you home."

"Are they in the ambulance?"

Frowning at him, she stared where he was looking. "Yes, they are about to be taken to the coroner's office."

Devon stared at the ambulance containing his little brother and sister with deadly calm. "I want to ride with them."

"I'm afraid that isn't possible."

He nodded. "I understand. I'll follow behind them in my car, then."

"Go home, Devon. There is nothing you can do."

Without arguing, he got back in his car, moved it to face the other way then pulled up to the curb to wait. When the ambulance drove past, he pulled out to follow.

As they drove through town, he fixedly stared at the ambulance door and stopped a few feet from the vehicle when it arrived at a large building. Watching as the driver went into a garage until the automatic door closed behind them, he still felt eerily emotionless.

While he hadn't seen them more than six times over the last two years, he had taken the part-time job at the grocery store to pay for their cell phone so he could talk to them every night before going to bed. He remembered the last time he talked to them. He had promised to be at all of Eric's baseball games when they started in a month and read a bedtime story to Riley despite having an English paper due the next morning. After he finished, he'd ended the call the same way he always did.

"Love you. I miss you."

"Love you back," they had told him sleepily.

Hearing their voices in his head, Devon felt as if the switch inside of him had been turned back on, bringing with it a rush of emotions that had his shoulders shaking as the painful sense of loss struck him. He didn't know how long he sat there, crying, his head on the steering wheel, before he could gather himself and drive home, leaving the tender part of him behind that had been ripped from him.

At home, his mother hugged him, crying out her grief into his arms. He made no attempt to hug her back, making an excuse to go to his room, where he sat on the side of the bed and stared out the window, the moon shining down on him.

Envying the moon being untouchable from the cruelty people could commit on each other, he promised himself never to let anyone take anyone he loved from him again.

A Year and Two Months Later...

Devon took another glance around his bedroom, making sure he hadn't missed anything. Then he picked up his duffle bag and slung it over his shoulder before heading into the living room, where his mother was sitting on the couch.

As she lifted her composed face, Devon saw she was fighting back tears.

"Did you forget anything?" she asked.

"No, I double-checked." Dropping the duffle bag onto the ground, he went to the couch to pull his mother to her feet.

"Are you sure you want to do this?"

"I'm sure, Mom. I've always told you I was going into the military when I graduated high school, just like Dad."

"Yeah … and how great did that turn out for him?" Tearfully, she stared up at him, her eyes pleading for him to reconsider.

Devon gave her a cheeky smile. "He met you, didn't he?" Laughing at her glare, he gave her a tight hug before releasing her to pick up the duffle bag. "I have to go. I called for a taxi."

"I was going to drive you," she protested.

"No, I don't want you driving back home upset. It's better this way."

The sound of a horn honking from outside had him going to the door.

"I'll call when I can."

"You better," she threatened tenderly, and then her expression grew serious. "I'll write to you about what's going on with Vance's trial."

"Do that," he said offhandedly. "Love you, Mom."

"Love you back."

Hearing the familiar words, and the sound of the horn again, he walked away from her.

He got into the taxi and rolled the window down to wave at his mother as the car moved away.

"You heading to the airport?"

Devon glanced at his watch. "I need to make a quick stop

first." He gave him the address of the grocery store where he had worked until graduation, then reached for the money he had tucked into his jacket pocket. He leaned forward when the taxi came to a stop in front of the store and handed it to the driver. "I'll be about fifteen minutes. Wait for me."

"I can't wait. Call the dispatch when …" When Devon started peeling apart the bills, his eyes widened. "I'll wait."

Leaving his duffle bag behind, Devon stepped out of the taxi.

He waved at the cashier who had replaced him on his way to the manager's office. After knocking on the door, he went in and closed it behind him.

Joel rose from his desk, went to the window, and opened it. Sticking his head out, he then quickly pulled his head back inside before giving him a nod.

Devon carefully maneuvered himself out the window without shaking the shelf containing several trophies. Dropping down to the ground below, he felt the switch move inside of him, leaving him cold and emotionless as he traversed the dark back streets. He ran at a loose jog until he came to the house he wanted, then stopped behind a fence. Glancing around, he made sure no one was close before he lithely climbed the fence. Then, sticking to the shadows, he snuck toward the back door, where he silently jimmied the lock and slid inside the house.

As he quietly moving around the place, he heard the sound of a television playing from somewhere. Carefully maneuvering himself closer, he pressed against a wall. When he heard the click of the television channel being switched, Devon came out of hiding to stand at the door.

It took the man lying on the bed several minutes before he realized Devon was standing there. Rising upward into a sitting position, Vance glared at him angrily as he reached for

11

the phone sitting on the nightstand. "What in the fuck are you doing here—"

Devon rushed forward, snatching the phone with his gloved hand and gently placing the receiver back down on its cradle. He stood, outlined in the moonlight coming in from the window. "Keeping my promise."

Four minutes later, Devon slid out the back door then over the fence. Jogging unhurriedly, he made it back to the grocery store with time to spare.

Joel reached a hand out to help him.

Devon dropped down next to him, then reached out to straighten a picture that had been knocked down. As he gazed at the picture, he felt the switch turn back on as emotions rushed back in.

Swallowing down the heartache at seeing his brother's image, he turned back to his manager. "Thanks. I don't want to leave the taxi waiting any longer," he forced out croakily.

Joel reached out his hand, and Devon shook it. "Stay safe."

"For sure. I have another favor to ask." Releasing his hand, Devon removed an envelope from his pocket and gave it to the manager. "Pay the entrance fees for the kids who can't afford theirs. I bagged up my bats and gloves; told Mom you would stop by to get them."

Joel's compassionate gaze caught his. "I can't take those; you bought them to practice with Eric."

Devon clenched his jaw, the pain easing in his chest. "Take them. They aren't doing any good sitting in a closet."

Joel nodded. "I'll stop by tomorrow."

"I put extra in there for you to buy the kids snow cones when they win their first game. Eric loved snow cones."

"Devon, you already did so much for the kids last season. I don't expect you to keep doing it every year. You need to get on with your life."

"From the moment I handed Eric his first baseball, that's

all he wanted to do. He would throw that plastic ball until I got tired of throwing it back. It isn't possible for Eric to play anymore, but I think he would like it if I spent the money I would have given him to provide the same opportunity to another kid."

Joel nodded. "I think so, too."

Devon left the office and made it back to the waiting cab.

"I was about to leave." After giving him a harassed look, the driver turned around and put the car in motion.

"Saying goodbye was harder than I thought it would be," Devon explained, taking off his gloves.

The rest of the ride to the airport was accomplished in silence.

Handing over the rest of his cash to the driver and taking his duffle bag, Devon got out. He passed a trash can at the entrance and threw the gloves away before walking through the electric doors. He had barely enough time to make it through security and reach the gate before his plane called for final boarding.

Getting in line, he noticed two women in front of him turn around and do a double-take before turning forward again. When two ticket agents split the line apart to make it move faster, Devon maneuvered himself around the women as they searched for their tickets. Wistful expressions followed him.

Finding his seat with the help of a flight attendant who had left greeting other passengers to latch on to his heels, he put his bag in the overhead before sitting down.

"Can I be of any other assistance to you?" Suggestively leaning forward, she moved his hands away to latch his seat belt for him.

Uninterested in the overture, Devon turned his head to stare out at the dark sky. "No, thanks. I'm good."

Not moving his eyes away from the window as the other

passengers boarded, he felt someone take the seat next to him.

"Hi!"

A breathy voice had his head turning. It was one of the women who had been in front of him in line.

"So, you're going to Chicago, too?"

"Unless I got on the wrong plane," he answered wryly.

Red flooded her cheeks but, undeterred, she kept trying to make conversation. "Were you visiting Carsen City?" Devon felt her eyes travel down from his face to his chest.

"No, I lived there," he replied shortly.

"That must have been cool." She sent a glance toward her friend, then looked back at him. "Castlena and I are on vacation." She nodded her head toward the woman sitting across the aisle from them. "Thought we would visit Chicago before heading to the Great Lakes."

"Great minds think alike."

"How long are you staying in Chicago?"

"A couple of days," Devon answered.

She let the tip of her tongue wet her bottom lip. "We should hook up for dinner tomorrow night. Then see what trouble we can get up to."

"Maybe. We'll see," he answered noncommittedly.

The women were gorgeous, but he was not in the mood to provide the entertainment they wanted.

"I'll give you my cell number before we get off the plane," she said as if their hooking up was a done deal. "I am Amanda, by the way. What's your name?"

His eyes shifted away from the moon he had been staring at and toward her. Reading the sexual interest left him just as cold and alone as the satellite he had been looking at.

Forcing a smile to his lips, he stopped thinking of leaving his mother, knowing he would never step foot in Carsen City again, that he wouldn't be there to visit Eric's and

Riley's graves every Saturday, and he would have to look over his shoulder for the rest of his life for the crime he had just committed. Joel had told him to move on with his life, and he was going to do that from now on.

"Moon. Everyone calls me Moon."

# CHAPTER ONE

L arissa watched the room full of women talking and laughing as if they were the best of friends and hadn't been trying to tear each other's hair out just an hour ago. Standing off to the side at the back of The Last Riders' club-house, she kept the length of the room between her and the two groups of women in case tensions rose again. If they started fighting again, she was out, and her two sisters could find their own way home.

Her younger sister must have sensed what she was thinking because she started making her way toward her. "I think the worst is over."

Larissa eyed the room of women doubtfully. "Then it's the perfect opportunity for us to be leaving. I'm ready to go, Priscilla. You can go get Lana and say our goodbyes. I'll be warming up the car." She started for the coatrack, where she had hung up her coat, when Priscilla caught her by the arm.

"She wants to stay a little longer."

Frustrated, Larissa bit her lip. She didn't trust these women any further than she could throw them. With their volatile behavior, Larissa was afraid a wayward comment would set off Sex Piston or one her friends.

"Listen …" Larissa hissed at her baby sister, "these women are wackos … We're damn lucky that bartender didn't call the police."

Priscilla's lips trembled in amusement. "About that … I found out why he didn't. Come to find out, the sheriff's a member of The Last Riders. Or"—Priscilla shrugged—"he used to be. Depends on who you ask."

"Oh my God … what kind of town have you and Lana talked me into moving to?"

Her sister's eyes twinkled. "In my defense, I just found out, too. You'll have to ask Lana if she knew."

"This isn't funny." Glaring at her sister, Larissa motioned to Lana to come to where they were standing, only to be ignored. Larissa knew damn good and well Lana had seen the gesture.

"I told you she isn't ready to go yet." Priscilla reminded her. "Lana is enjoying hanging out with Sex Piston and her friends."

"We're just asking for trouble being here." Larissa went back to eyeing the women warily. "I don't understand what's going through her head … We should have left them at the bar when they started in on that poor woman who tried her best to ignore them."

Lana sighed. "Maybe there's a reason they dislike her…"

"They acted awful to her."

"I'm not disagreeing with you, Larissa, but I'm trying to be understanding. Crazy Bitch was spoiling for a fight because of the bad news I gave her, and I guess she was taking it out on the woman instead of her friends. I'm not excusing her for the way she behaved, but she got paid back when her face was slammed by the door." Priscilla covered her mouth as she turned to give the rest of the room her back. "I thought I would die when Lily slammed that door on her."

Larissa couldn't help but smother her own laughter. "God, it was like she read my mind." Wiping the tears of laughter away, she hastily pasted an innocent smile on her lips when she saw Crazy Bitch and Sex Piston staring at them suspiciously. "Do you think they know I was happy when Lily whacked her?"

Priscilla made a face at her. "How wouldn't they? You were cheering them on."

"I was not."

Her sister arched an eyebrow at her. "You tripped Killyama before she could keep Ginny from pouring a beer on T.A. and moved the table out of the way so the other women could get Sex Piston."

Larissa grimaced. "I forgot about that."

"They won't." Priscilla gave her a stern look. "We are trying to build our business here, and we actually *want* people to like us, not want to kick our asses."

"They like you. I'll tell you what. You can have Sex Piston and her friends as clients, and I'll work with the leftovers."

Her sister didn't appear thrilled with the trade-off.

Giving a sigh, Larissa crossed her arms over her chest. "Fine. But Crazy Bitch is your client. I'll take Fat Louise. We'll draw cards on who gets Sex Piston if she gets pregnant."

"I think we're good there. Sex Piston said she's done having any more babies."

"Thank G—"

Larissa cut off what she was about to say when Priscilla gave her a reprimanding glance.

"I'll remind you of that when you're deciding which house you can afford to buy based on how our business is doing."

"Okay, okay. You win. We can stay a little longer."

"Good." Priscilla dropped her reprimanding tone, the twinkle in her eyes returning. "It's not like Lana was going to let us leave anytime soon, anyway. She's hoping the drop-dead gorgeous dude would come home soon after she found out he lives here."

Dropping herself down onto an overstuffed chair, Larissa caught her older sister staring at the front door for the third times in just as many minutes. "I still think it made more sense to stay at the bar where he was at versus coming here to wait."

"Blame that on me. I told Lana that Winter invited all of us back for a drink, and to make sure Crazy Bitch's nose was all right after Mick threw all of them out of his bar. I thought she would feel more comfortable talking to him here rather than hitting on him at the bar."

"So, you're the reason she's not ready to leave. Thanks, sis."

Priscilla sat down on the arm of the chair, placing an arm over Larissa's shoulders. "Please don't be mad at me, sissy."

Larissa grimaced at the childish voice Priscilla used. "I hate it when you call me sissy, almost as badly as when someone calls you Prissy."

Priscilla gave a mock shudder. "I hate it worse."

"I doubt that," Larissa said ruefully, allowing her sister to lay her head down on her shoulder as they both watched Lana glance at the door yet again. "We can stay another thirty minutes. After that, we're leaving."

Priscilla gave a sleepy yawn. "Deal." She settled her head more comfortably on her shoulder. "She's really attracted to him. I think he might be able to get her mind off Bennet."

Larissa bit down on her lip, her mind's eye going back to the brooding man who Lana hadn't been able to take her eyes off all night. An eerie chill went down her spine. He was the first man Lana had taken an interest in since she had been left at the altar. She really didn't want her sister to get her heart broken again.

"I don't know, Priscilla. Do you think it's wise for us to encourage her to meet a biker?"

"Well, Bennet stole her blind, and he drove a Porshe. I'm going to be positive and give him a chance. Besides, we both know she'll chicken out at the last second and probably won't talk to him, anyway. Lana will come up with another excuse why she didn't, and we can go home. It's a win-win for us. She would have at least taken a step in the right direction by thinking about another man, and we will support her in her endeavor to get laid."

Larissa wanted to laugh. Instead, she shrugged her shoulder, forcing Priscilla to raise her head.

"I think our dear sister is going to need our support a different way than getting a new man in her life," she said ruefully, noticing the expression and pallor on Lana's face.

Priscilla's eyes went to where she was looking. "Uh-oh."

"Oh yeah." Larissa's inclined her head in Lana's direction. "She looks like she's getting ready to blow a gasket."

"I warned her not to mix liquors." Priscilla turned her head to stare back down at her. "It's your turn ..."

Larissa immediately started shaking her head. "Nope. It's your turn. I'm the one who had to watch her binge on that wedding cake, then—"

Priscilla raised her hand to stop her. "Enough said. You win." Getting to her feet, Priscilla gave her a mock threatening glare. "You better not take off like you tried to when we were in the restaurant and leave us stranded."

Larissa pasted an innocent expression on her face. "Would I do that?"

Priscilla narrowed her eyes on her. "In a heartbeat."

# CHAPTER TWO

"Y ou ready to settle up?"

Moon raised blurry eyes from the glass of whiskey he had been staring morosely into. How was he spending another Christmas season without a wife and kids? He was the only one of the brothers who had wanted to find a woman to marry when they got out of the service and start having children immediately.

He was thirty-eight, and it seemed his dreams of having a family were getting further away instead of closer. Each passing year, he would say to himself, *This is the year I'll find the woman I can settle down with and start making babies.* Inevitably, by October, he knew another year would end with him being fucking alone. Like he always was.

He was sick as shit of being alone. Despite having the brothers, and a variety of women he slept with, none of them filled the void of having a family. The brothers' friendships were constantly on thin ice and threatening to crack open. Tired of his moody behavior, they bounced him from the clubhouse in Ohio to Kentucky. When he wore out his welcome in one, he would be shuttled back to the other.

Depending on the job they needed him for, he was on borrowed time until what they needed done was completed.

Viper or Wizard would run inference for him when he started making a nuisance with the other brothers. Invariably, he would start a fight with the brothers, then sit back and watch the fireworks, or do something which would bring down heat on the club. He hated watching television, nor was he really into video games or reading. What was left for enjoyment? Stirring shit up.

"Moon?"

Moon blinked, trying to clear his vision. "You say something?"

"You want another drink, or you ready to settle up?" Mick asked impatiently.

Draining the glass, Moon pushed it toward the bartender, who looked like the last thing he wanted to do was refill the glass.

"Why don't you go on home?" Mick picked the glass up but made no move to give him a refill. "I've had a long night. I'm ready to go home."

Moon stared at Mick through a drunken haze. "Why?"

Mick frowned at him in confusion. "Why what?"

"Why do you want to go home? You don't have anyone waiting for you to rush home to any more than I do."

Mitch gave him a steely look. "Brother, you don't know shit about my life."

Giving the bartender a sarcastic snort, he tapped the empty glass to be refilled. "I know you wouldn't work the hours you work—seven days a week without a day off for more years than I can count—if you had better options waiting for you."

"You're drunk off your ass. I'm going to call Knox to give you a ride home."

Mick's gruff assessment of the shape he was in might be

spot on, but Moon was unfazed at the threat of Knox being called.

"No, you won't. Greer is working tonight. Knox will just send him. We both know you'd rather shoot your foot off than have Greer walk in that door. What's his bar tab up to now, anyway?"

Mick stared at him in consternation. "Don't ask."

"That bad?" Moon was just drunk enough to feel bad for the bartender. There wasn't a person in Treepoint who hadn't been taken by Greer.

"Brother, I could buy myself a new bike with what he owes me. I need every dime I can get. The weather and the holidays have put a damper on business.

"You had to have had a good night—those bitches went through three bottles before I lost count."

The bartender, whose rough visage managed to keep his tough-as-nail customers from wrecking his place, gave him a stony look at being reminded of the women he had thrown out. "Those weren't bottles I sold them—they snuck them in their coats. The only drinks I made money on were the ones they suckered the guy with Jewell to pay for. Those bitches are fucking lunatics to go after Jewell like that."

"Every damn one of them," Moon agreed. "Every time they talked, they shriveled my balls to the size of skittles."

Mick laughed. "At least yours stayed attached to your body. Mine took off running when I threw them out of the bar. I'm hoping they're waiting for me in the parking lot—my balls, not the bitches."

Moon laughed along with him. "There isn't much that scares me, but, brother, I'm man enough to admit they scare the bejesus out of me."

"Same," Mick confessed. "I expected you to put a stop to the way they were treating Jewell."

Moon rolled his eyes to the ceiling and nearly fell off the

stool. "Why? Jewell saw them when she came in the door. She also could have left when they started goading her."

Mick's expression filled with understanding. "You think she wanted a fight?"

Moon looked at his empty glass then met Mick's eyes meaningfully.

Reaching for the whiskey bottle, Mick poured him a knuckle's worth then slid the glass toward him.

"I think Jewell wanted to let off some steam, and if Rory hadn't gotten her out of here, those bitches would be nursing more than a bloody nose."

Mick shook his head. "I don't know about that. I think the bitches would have wiped the floor with her."

Moon gave a sarcastic grunt. "You were never good a judge of women."

"You're a dick when you're drunk."

"I am even when I'm not." Moon shrugged.

"That's for sure." Giving him an aggravated glance, he started wiping down the counter around him. "Finish up; I'm locking up in five minutes."

Moon stared at the bartender balefully.

"Careful …" Mick warned. "You better remember who's the one who taught you fuckers to fight."

Moon picked up his drink and slung it to the back of his throat before he set it back down on the bar.

"You need a ride home?"

Moon considered the offer. "You have your car or bike outside?"

"My car."

"No, thanks."

"How you getting back to the club? Because you're sure as shit not getting on your bike."

"I'll walk."

"You'd rather walk than catch a ride with me?"

"I'm not getting in a car. The only way you'll catch my ass in a car is if someone puts my dead body in one."

Mick raised curious eyebrows at him. "You're still claustrophobic as fuck, aren't you?"

"No. I just choose not to ride in cars."

"Brother"—Mick plunked the bar towel into the sink before raising a disbelieving gaze to him—"there isn't anyone who would choose to freeze off their balls in this weather rather than drive in a heated car."

"I don't feel the cold."

"Yeah … that's because your ass is still sitting inside. Whatever …" Mick picked up the empty glass to put in the sink. "Let's go. I'll follow you in my car to make sure you get to the club okay."

Moon stood up. "I don't need you to follow me."

"Shut up. Either I follow you, or I call Viper and let him watch you walk back to the club, drunk off your ass."

Moon walked toward the door with lagging footsteps. "He won't care. Viper knows I'm like a cat—I always land on my feet."

Mick came out from behind the counter, shrugging into his leather jacket. "I wouldn't tempt fate, if I were you. Sooner or later, everyone's luck runs out."

Moon stepped out into the cold air, waiting as Mick locked the door. "Neither fate nor luck are responsible for me being alive." Moon gave him a half-wave then stepped away and started walking.

Mick took a step to the side of the bar then paused, turning his head. "What is it, then?"

"The devil protects his own."

Hunching his shoulders, Moon lowered his head so the bitter wind wouldn't hit him directly in his face. He reached into his pocket, took out his gloves, and slid them on as the limbs on the bare trees moved back and forth. His boots crunched on the snow-covered ground as he kept to the side of the road, seeing Mick's lights coming up behind him.

He wished Mick would go on without worrying about him. He actually enjoyed the dark quiet of the night. He preferred the night over daylight. Perhaps that was why he hadn't found a woman to settle down with. At night, women fought over who he would share his bed with. During the bright light of day, they ignored him until night rolled around again. They thought he was their plaything. He was sick of it. He wasn't anyone's plaything. The next time a woman used him as a yoyo, they would find out their plaything bites.

# CHAPTER THREE

Larissa watched as her two sisters disappeared into what she assumed was a restroom. Thank goodness it was Priscilla's turn. She had never been good at dealing with someone with a sick stomach.

Rising, she went to stand by the restroom door in the hall just in case they needed her.

"Lana okay?" Winter asked from the chair she was sitting in.

"I think so," Larissa answered.

Standing, Winter walked over to tap on the door. "Can I get you anything?" she called out.

"No. We'll be out in a minute," they heard Lana reply over the sound of wrenching from the other side of the door.

Both she and Winter made sympathetic faces at hearing how sick Lana was.

"Damn. I hate being sick to my stomach."

Larissa grimaced in agreement. "Me, too. Priscilla has a stronger stomach than me. If I were in there, I would be barfing up next to her."

As she talked, Larissa felt the cold air come in from the door but didn't turn because she could hear Lana start to cry.

"I'm so embarrassed."

"It's okay." Larissa pressed her face to the door so Lana could hear. "No one is listening."

Focusing on her sister, she didn't turn around to check who had come through the door. When no one walked around her, she just assumed one of the women had decided to leave.

Winter pressed her face to the door, too. "That's true, Lana. Most of them are in the same shape you're in. T.A. had to go to the other restroom downstairs."

At the sounds coming from inside the restroom, Larissa didn't think Lana was paying attention to them.

As she straightened from the door, an uncomfortable feeling struck her. Trying to ignore the pressing need in her bladder, she bit her lip, wishing Lana would hurry up while she looked around to see if she could spot T.A.

With the need becoming more urgent, she glanced at the door. "How are you doing?"

"She's still heaving," Priscilla answered for Lana.

Winter stared at her. "Are you getting sick, too?"

"No. I just need to use the restroom. I've been drinking water all night."

"Oh …" Winter's eyes turned to the group of women, and Larissa guessed she was searching for T.A. to see if she was back, also.

"Is there another restroom I could use?"

"Um …" Winter's gaze turned apologetic. "Sorry, but …"

Larissa gritted her teeth, feeling as if her bladder would explode any second.

Winter's gaze softened into compassion. "Sure. Come on; I'll show you."

Hurriedly following Winter up the steps, Larissa prayed

she would make it in time. *This is what you get when you put off going to the bathroom until your bladder is ready to burst,* Larissa scolded herself.

"Here you go." Winter opened a door near the end of a long hallway. Turning the light on, she moved aside so Larissa could enter.

A loud yell from downstairs and a crash had her and Winter staring at each other. Larissa recognized the woman's yell.

"That was Crazy Bitch …" Winter moaned.

"Yes … I think so, too."

"Viper is going to kill me."

Larissa wanted to know what happened downstairs, but she needed to use the restroom first.

"I need to go see what she did. Can you find your way back downstairs?"

"Of course."

"Okay …" Winter seemed to hesitate before moving out of the way so she could close the door. "Just make sure you come right back downstairs. Guests aren't allowed upstairs unless they have a club member with them," she explained.

"I won't be long."

"All right, I'll see you downstairs." Winter rushed off at another loud crash that Larissa could have sworn had the house shaking on its foundation.

Larissa closed and locked the door before she relieved her aching bladder.

Poor Winter. From her expression, Larissa surmised Viper was not going to happy about the impromptu party in The Last Riders' clubhouse. The way they had to wait in the car until Winter had come to the end of the porch and waved before everyone got out of their cars and into the house reminded her of the time her sisters and her had thrown a party when their mother was at work.

As she washed her hands, Larissa decided she would grab Lana and Priscilla if they were out of the restroom and leave. She really didn't want to get caught in the middle of an argument if Winter's husband showed up and found his club had been invaded by a group of women who were drunk off their asses.

When she left the restroom, she noticed one the doors along the hallway was open and the light was on. There was no way to get to the stairway without passing the open doorway. Remembering Winter saying no one was allowed upstairs without a club member accompanying them, she hoped to rush past and hit the stairs before whoever was inside caught her.

As she passed the open door, she cast a quick glance inside, nearly stumbling over her own two feet when she saw a couple inside having intercourse. The man was lying on his back, and the woman was grinding herself up and down on his shaft. The woman's back was toward her and blocking her sight of the man as she stood there, gawking at them.

The uninhibited way they were having sex shocked her. Plus the fact that they had left the door wide open, uncaring if anyone could see what they were doing. Since she had never been around any bikers personally, the only impressions she had of them came from the news, or books. Both conveyed they were wild, violent, and sexually easy, but Larissa, nor neither of her sisters, based their opinions on anything other than how they were treated. One thing was for sure: she would be giving Lana a heads-up before she went pursuing the man from the bar.

As she stood frozen in place, her heart lurched when she noticed a door next to the one she was staring in begin to open.

Blankly, she watched as the door started to open wider.

31

Then, like an anxious rabbit caught in a headlight, she reacted without thinking.

Frantically, she spotted a door on the other side the hallway that was partially open with the lights off, and she rushed inside and closed the door behind her.

Pressing her face to the door, she listened for who had come out the bedroom to leave so she could make her way back downstairs.

"Do me a favor and take my boots off."

Larissa barely managed to cut off the gasp of dismay with her hand at the low voice coming from behind her.

Frozen in place yet again, she lowered her hand from her mouth to the doorknob.

"Come on." His grave voice sent tingles down her spine.

Tightening her hand on the doorknob, she prepared to sling the door open and take off running in a ten-second dash.

"Fuck it. Just turn the light on, and I'll do it myself."

As she turned the knob, she heard voices outside coming from whoever was in the hallway. The low timber of two males' voices and a woman's plaintive cries of sexual ecstasy had Larissa wanting to melt in embarrassment.

"Are you going to turn the light on or not?"

There was no way she was going to step into that hallway, nor was there any way she was going to turn any lights on either.

Left with the only option available to her, she followed the sound of his voice, moving toward where she hoped he was. She bumped into what she assumed was his bed and ran her hand over the cover until her fingers felt denim and what she thought might be the hardness of his knee. Swallowing hard, all the while telling herself she was out of her ever-loving mind, she ran her hand down his denim-covered leg until she felt leather. She cupped her hand under the hard sole, then used her other hand to wrap around the back of the boot to pull it off. The boot slid off easily. Relieved, she searched blindly in the dark for his other leg. Her hand landed on a hard, muscled thigh underneath his jeans. Shakily, she slid her hand down his leg to find the boot.

"Hurry up, Ember. My feet are freezing. I should have worn thicker socks."

Desperate to get out of the room, she removed the boot then started to heave herself to her feet so she could make her escape. Surely, the couple across the hall would be finished.

As she started to straighten, the man wrapped his hand around the nape of her neck.

Bent over, she was so close to him that she could feel the warmth of his breath against her lips.

"Thanks. My feet are so cold I couldn't get them off."

She grew concerned despite wanting to get out of there, and her healing instinct wouldn't let her abandon him without making sure he was okay.

Going back to her knees, she found one of his feet. Whoever he was, he wasn't exaggerating. The sock was damp and freezing. Removing the sock, she searched for his other foot and removed that sock, too, then tucked a chilled foot between her thighs to warm it while she started massaging the chilled flesh of the other.

His hand tightened on her neck before she felt his fingers comb through her long strands.

"My bad, Echo. I thought you were Ember. You should have said something."

Remaining silent, she switched his feet out, rubbing the one which was between her thighs until she felt the warmth returning to the clammy skin.

"Is that why you're giving me the silent treatment?"

*Drop his foot and get the hell of here before he finds out I'm not either of these women,* she told herself frantically.

"How about I make it up to you?" His voice turned into a seductive timber that grabbed her by her ovaries, holding her still. The hand on her neck pulled her closer until his parted lips were pressing against hers. The tip of his tongue traced her bottom lip, sending her into a tailspin of desire she had never experienced before.

"Baby, how do you want me to warm you up?"

# CHAPTER FOUR

What in the fuck was he doing? The last thing he wanted was company tonight. He hadn't needed Echo to rub his feet. Who was he kidding? If he hadn't wanted company, he would have shut his door. Any plan of sending her away ended when she dropped to her knees. He'd always been a sucker for a woman who would do anything to please him.

He had never asked for a foot rub before, but damn, from the way his dick was aching, he'd been missing out. Who knew his foot had an erogenous zone?

Changing his mind about having company, Moon pulled Echo onto his lap. Covering her mouth with his, he lay back and, with a twist of his hips, rolled them over until she was under him.

There was something different about the way Echo was kissing him tonight, but he couldn't place what it was. He had fucked her numerous times, yet he had only kissed her maybe three or four. That was normal for most of the women he fucked. Usually, his mouth had better areas he preferred to explore and give pleasure to.

About to cut the kiss short and take her top off, Moon found himself delving deeper into her mouth at the unexpected, lush taste of her. It was the weirdest feeling he had ever experienced. What made it more confusing was that he had kissed Echo before, and he would have certainly remembered these sensations if he had experienced it with her then.

Lifting his head, he took a deep breath, filling his oxygen-deprived lungs. "Damn, woman, you nearly sucked my soul out with that kiss." Moon lowered his mouth back to hers. "Do it again."

Sliding his hands under her top, he moved up her ribcage then went around to her back to find the snap of her bra. Unhooking it with experienced fingers, Moon slid his hands downward to cup her ass, raising her pelvis flush to his.

A groan of satisfaction escaped him as he rubbed his crotch against hers.

"We're going to lose these jeans." Moon raised himself off Echo's sublime body to unzip her jeans before tugging them and her panties down in one quick movement. Removing a condom from his back pocket before unbuttoning his jeans, he shoved them off his hips. Then, kicking them off, he reached out a searching hand in the dark to find the heated warmth he knew would be waiting for his touch. "Then I'm going to fuck you like there is no tomorrow."

Finding the smooth skin of her thigh, Moon was taken aback when he realized she was trembling under his touch.

"Are you cold?"

Her reply came out a strangled whisper. "No."

He chalked Echo's unusual behavior up to his brain being fried after working nonstop for the last forty-eight hours on an assignment Viper had given him, then drinking for the last four hours to unwind so he would be able to sleep.

"I can turn up the heat if you are."

All he could see in the pitch-black room was her shadow.

Because he worked so many night hours, the window coverings were black-out shades.

Skimming her thigh, Moon stroked higher, finding the silken warmth of her pussy. He covered her body with his, then went back to kissing her, wanting her mouth as badly as he wanted her wet pussy. Gliding his tongue inside of her mouth, he palmed her pussy, rubbing it hard in a circular pattern, spreading her slick juices onto his hand.

"Feel good?"

"Mmm …" she moaned. "Mmm …"

He raised his hand slightly, then her leg until Echo's knee was bent. Using his shoulder, he laid her out, exposing her to his machinations.

He pulled his tongue out of her mouth and tantalizingly raised his palm from her pussy a few inches, then smacked it back down.

A startled scream escaped her mouth.

Using his thumb, he swirled her swollen clit, soothing the small sting. Then he stroked his tongue down her jawline to her neck, stopping when he felt her tremble when his tongue found a particular spot. Delicately licking the spot, he grazed his teeth over it. When her hips wiggled against the mattress, he knew he had found the erogenous zone he had been searching for.

Moon's breath hitched in his chest at the feeling of euphoria settling over him. It was if he were having sex with Echo for the first time, wanting to outdo any man she had fucked before, make her crave him more than any brother here, and lastly, never let her forget the earth-shattering, mind-blowing, never-ever-can-be-beaten experience of having sex with him. He lived for this shit—to make sex so awesome one of them would beg him to make them his woman.

Lifting his hand an inch higher, he heard Echo catch her breath.

"Soft or hard?" he teased. Waiting patiently for her answer, Moon rubbed his rigid cock against her thigh.

"Hard," he barely heard her whisper.

He gave her what she wanted, and his cock swelled at the sound of his palm hitting her wet pussy.

He smacked her pussy three more times, giving her the choice each time, until he couldn't stand the darkness any longer. He wanted to see the pink heat in the light.

"Damn, I'm going to turn on the light."

"Don't." Her startled murmur coincided with her suddenly pushing at his shoulder until he was flat on his back.

She pressed her hands on his chest, and Moon felt her knees settle between his thighs.

Her soft hands traveled down his chest and stomach until they reached his cock. When her luscious mouth settled over his cock, his hips surged upward demandingly. Sucking hard, Echo took more than half his cock in her mouth, which was an achievement for her. Echo was notorious about disliking giving blowjob, usually doing the bare minimum to get one of the brothers off. Tonight, she was going all out, as if she wanted to lick his cock and never give it back.

Groaning, Moon buried his hands in her hair as he bucked his hips upward, driving his cock deep into her throat.

When her hand started caressing his balls, he used her hair to pull her off. Then, using his free hand, he searched for the condom in the direction he had tossed it onto the bed. Finding it, he handed it to Echo. "Put it on me," he ordered, letting his hands move to her waist to get her in the position he wanted her. "Hurry up, or you're going to be sucking me dry instead of me fucking that wet pussy begging for me."

Moon heard her opening the condom in the darkness before he felt it being rolled onto his straining cock. Gritting his teeth, he lifted her higher in the air so the tip of his cock prodded at her opening.

"Soft or hard?"

"Hard," the choked murmur came out as her knees braced herself on each side of his hips.

He slammed her down, and his eyes nearly rolled to the back of his head at the imaginable pleasure of his cock plowing inside the tight inferno which threatened his control before they could get started.

"Goddamn …" Moon groaned. "Fuck me."

Echo started raising and lowering herself over his cock fervently, and he let her without trying to control her movements as he lay back, enjoying the passionate cries she was making.

When he gripped her thighs to keep her steady, something in his sleep-deprived mind teased him. Attempting to figure out what it was through the alcohol he had consumed while Echo was riding him as if the world was about to end, he did everything he could to not to come. It took more effort than trying to figure out what was nagging at him.

Small whimpers coming from her tore him from his thoughts.

"Baby, you're not getting there full throttle. Slow down …" Moon raised his hands from her thighs to her hips, not letting her raise herself from her downward stroke. "Try this …" He showed her the movements he wanted her to make, and Echo sank down further on his cock and started rubbing her clit against the hand he had slid between their bodies.

When her pussy clenched around his cock, he rolled to the side, lifting one of her legs over his hips. Echo's face burrowed into his neck as she shook in his arms. Aiming his cock in her sheath so she would get the most amount of her pleasure, he felt her small teeth suck his skin into her mouth. Usually, that was a big no-no with him. He never let any woman leave a mark, but when her teeth sank into his flesh, his mind blanked out in a red haze of lust.

Twisting his body, he started thrusting inside of Echo so hard he slipped and had to maneuver himself back in to finish the climax he thought was about to blow his skull off. As he shuddered in the aftereffects of his climax, Moon wouldn't have been able to spell his nickname.

His chest was still heaving, trying to achieve a full breath, when Echo suddenly pulled away, nearly ripping his cock off in the process.

"What the fuck?" All he could see was her shadowy movements and hear the sounds of her getting dressed. "You're leaving? I ..." Sitting up on his elbows, he could see her bend over then stand, and he heard the hiss of a zipper.

Fuck this. At least they usually waited until the sun came up to take off.

"At least turn on the fucking light so I can ..." Moon sat up, his hand moving to the nightstand to take out a towel to wipe him off with.

Gaping at her in the darkness, he saw her shadow form hurry toward the door. Then, instead of turning on the light for him, he saw the door crack open and her starting to slip out.

He lost his cool and didn't hold back. "If you see Ember, send her my way. At least she wears a man out. I see why you always prefer threesomes—you're lame as shit on your own," he snapped out harshly.

With her back to him, Moon saw her jerk as if she had been struck. Then, without saying anything, she slipped through the door and closed it behind her.

"Fuck ..." Regretting his harsh words, Moon shimmied across the mattress to turn on the bedside lamp. He jerked the twisted sheet off his hip as he took the towel out of the drawer, then wiped his pelvis off, seeing he no longer wore the condom. When had it come off? When she had jerked away from him? Moon tried to remember if it had slipped off his cock and couldn't.

"Fuck." Throwing the towel into the hamper next to the nightstand, he turned the light back off then lay back down. He was too tired to be worried about it tonight. The condom was just an extra safety measure all The Last Riders swore by to keep their lifestyle worry-free. All of the women in the club were on birth control, so he had no worries if the condom slipped off. There wouldn't be any unexpected consequences.

Spreading out on the bed, Moon bunched a pillow. "Fuck the holidays ..." he murmured groggily. "Fuck them all. I never got a gift I wanted, anyway."

He pressed his lips together and turned, reaching for another pillow to hold as the familiar loneliness settled back into the room.

A small hint of perfume wafted from the pillow, loosening the chock-hold keeping him awake and allowing his mind to finally let him drift off into a dreamless state where it didn't matter if he never woke up. No one would care.

# CHAPTER FIVE

C losing the door behind her, Larissa thanked every God in existence that the hallway was empty and the sprawled-out couple across the hall seemed comatose from their exertions.

Instead of using the opportunity to flee down the stairs, she rushed toward the restroom Winter had led her to before she had lost her ever-loving mind. Hurriedly closing the door, with fumbling fingers, she managed to lock it before leaning against the sink and staring at the woman she didn't recognize.

Shell-shocked eyes took in the tumbled hair she had taken over an hour to style before going out, her shirt had been stretched out and no longer clung to the curve of her neck, and worse than anything, her lips were puffy and swollen from the man who had pillaged her mouth as if he were on a mission to storm every defense she had to keep men at bay.

Frantically looking around the bathroom, she found a small door to the side—a linen closet—and quickly grabbed a hand towel before she went back to the sink.

She turned the cold handle on to wet the cloth and pressed it to her lips. Then, uncaring about the privacy of who lived there, she started opening drawers, searching for a hairbrush. When she couldn't find one, she tried finger-combing the thick mess without success when a thought came to her mind. Going to the shower, she pulled back the curtain to find a purple hairbrush hanging from a shower caddy. Seizing it as if were a bar of gold, she darted back to the sink and brushed her hair out so fast she felt the roots being ripped out.

A sudden tap on the door had her soul leaving her body, still so shaken by what she had done.

"Larissa?"

Winter's voice from the other side of the door had her running back to the shower to put the brush back.

"Are you okay? You were taking so long I thought I would come check on you to make sure you're all right."

"I'm all right." Quickly switching the washcloth to her forehead, she unlocked the door. "I'm sorry I took so long. I've had a headache. I was hoping the cold washcloth would help."

Winter gazed at her sympathetically. "I hate migraines." Stepping around her, she went to the mirrored cabinet beside the sink and opened the front to take out a bottle. "Here you go." After handing her the Tylenol, Winter turned expectantly toward the hallway.

Getting her silent message that she wanted her to go back downstairs, Larissa started walking next to her.

As she came down the steps, she noticed most of the other women had left. Only Lily, Beth, and her sisters were still there.

Her jaw dropped when she realized what they were doing. Closing her mouth with a snap, she could only shake her head at the sight of the heavy bar being turned over.

"We needed you to help right it again," Winter explained, moving to one end of the bar. "Lily, Beth, and I can take this side if you, Priscilla, and Lana can get the other."

Following Winter's suggestion, they took up their positions.

Larissa didn't think they wouldn't be able to right the heavy wooden counter. but after four failed attempts, they finally succeeded.

Moving the stool that had survived the crash back to the bar, Larissa, along with Lily, gathered the remains of the other two.

"Do you mind helping me put them in the dining room? I'll ask my husband to fix them in the morning."

Lifting one of the bent stools, she followed Lily to the dining room. She set it down next to the one Lily carried as one of the legs fell off.

"You sure we shouldn't have carried them to the dumpster?"

Lily frowned at the now three-legged stool. "I'm positive they can be fixed."

"Okay." Larissa gave her a crooked smile. "I'm a big believer in thinking positive, too, but I'm pretty positive these two would be more useful as firewood."

Lily laughingly nodded her head. "I think you're right."

"Will you girls get in trouble for the damage?"

A mysterious look crossed Lily's face. "Depends on if they find out."

"How did the counter get turned over?"

"Sex Piston bet Crazy Bitch all of them could stand on the bar."

"How many did it hold?"

"We'll never know. Sex Piston, Crazy Bitch, T.A., Fat Louise, and Killyama all climbed it at the same time. When they did, it flipped over."

"Winter didn't want them to stay and help put it back up?"

Laughter gurgled from Lily as they walked back to the main room. "They took off."

"Oh no." Larissa pressed her fingers to her brow. There had to be a full moon tonight, right? That was the only reason that could explain the absolutely bizarre behavior that had gone on.

Wanting to burst into grateful tears at finding her sisters standing by the door with their coats on, Larissa grabbed her own coat and tugged it on so fast that she slapped herself with the belt.

"Thanks …" Larissa came to a stop, not knowing what to thank Beth and Lily for. "For the invite," she finished lamely.

Ignoring her sisters' strange looks, she motioned them to open the door.

"We can't leave just yet," Priscilla explained. "We're waiting for Winter to get the guard watching the door to leave."

"There's a guard at the door?" Larissa asked stupidly.

"Yes, Winter told him her cat got out and asked if he would mind looking for it. She's going to let—"

The door snapped open.

"Nickel just went around the corner. Hurry." Winter waved them through the door. "Be careful—the steps are slick," she warned.

Larissa didn't care at this point if she slid down the fucking steps on her ass; she just wanted to get in her car and get the hell out of there.

Rudely brushing past her sisters, she rushed down the steps, ignoring Winter's warning. Her mind was still trying to come to grips with the stark reality of what she had allowed to happen in one of the bedrooms upstairs in a motorcycle club.

In the headlong rush, she congratulated herself for making it safely to the bottom when her foot hit a slab of concrete.

Fearful of being caught after Winter had gone to so much trouble keeping their presence a secret, she bit back a pain-filled scream.

She found herself in a crumpled heap and was still trying to figure out how she had hurt herself when Priscilla and Lana appeared by her side.

"What happened?" Lana whispered.

"I don't know," Larissa whimpered out.

"Let's get you in the back seat of the car. I'll check you out while Priscilla drives."

It took everything to not to cry out as her sister got her back on her feet. A rush of dizziness struck her when she tried to put her weight down on her right foot.

"I've twisted my ankle."

Priscilla supported her while Lana opened the car door, which she used to slide inside. As she closed the door, Lana rushed to the other side to slide in next to her. Larissa started crying when she heard the engine start.

The sound of crunchy snow was music to her ears.

"I'm going to check your ankle," Lana warned, bending down. "I'm so sorry you got hurt," she apologized. "You wanted to leave, and I ignored you."

Larissa was in too much pain to be angry, and she certainly couldn't be angry at her sister for wanting to chase after a man when she had done something so much worse.

"It's okay. Were you able to get a chance to talk to him?"

"No. Winter said he came in while I was in the restroom, barfing up my left lung."

Larissa frowned. "I'm sorry it didn't work out for you. He must have come in after I went upstairs to use the restroom."

A sinking feeling hit her in the gut. The man she had sex with had just come in from the cold ...

"Did you see him come in, Priscilla?" Larissa asked casually.

"Yes. He didn't talk to anyone. He just went up the stairs."

He couldn't be the man she had sex with, could he? Oh God ... she had a sinking suspicion he was.

Larissa started shivering, either in reaction to hurting her ankle, or for being such a stupid idiot for having sex with a man she wouldn't recognize if she sat next to him in a restaurant.

Wearily, she leaned her head against the window and stared out, then started laughing hilariously.

Lana's concerned voice drew her back to reality. "Why are you laughing?"

"It's a full moon."

# CHAPTER SIX

oon's eyes flicked open, instantly becoming awake. Groaning, he rolled over onto his stomach. All he wanted to do was go back to sleep the way his aching body was crying out for. Instead, he rolled back over onto his back, knowing it was useless.

For some aggravating reason, he had never been able to sleep longer than five hours, regardless of how exhausted he was. Once his eyes were open, he was up for the whole stinking day.

He released another irritated groan and sat up on the side of the bed, lazily rubbing his stomach. Damn, he was getting too old to drink like he had last night.

The sight of his crumpled jeans and T-shirt lying on the floor brought back vague memories of the night before. Fuck, he had drunk so much that the sexual encounter seemed more like a figment of his imagination rather than one that actually happened. If not for the pale ivory panties on the floor, Moon would have chalked it up to a horny wet dream. The images in his mind were more like a kaleidoscope of parts of the night.

He rose from the bed and gave a long stretch, extending his arms upward while twisting his back to the left then right as he pondered last night. He was pretty sure he owed Echo an apology. He wasn't sure, but he thought he might have confused her with Ember when she had come into his room.

He pulled a pair of shorts out of his drawer, then left his room to go the bathroom down the hall. In the shower, he rinsed off before he washed his hair. Done, he stepped out of the tub and wrapped a towel around his hips while heading to the sink to brush his teeth.

When he casually glanced into the mirror, he stopped brushing. Narrowing his eyes on his neck, he spotted something that better not be what he thought it was.

He spit out the toothpaste and cupped his hands to fill them with water so he could rinse out his mouth before letting his fingertips investigate the red spot of color on his neck.

Echo had given him a hickey. A fucking hickey. He hated them. The sight of one on his neck infuriated him. That showed just how fucking drunk he had been last night.

After he apologized to Echo, he was going to make fucking sure she knew he wasn't happy about it. All the women in the club knew hickeys were his pet peeves. Echo was the first one to have been given him one, and she was going to be the last.

Irritable, Moon opened the medicine cabinet in the search for the Tylenol. However, he came up short when it wasn't in its usual spot.

Snapping the door closed, he gritted his teeth. The day was off to a wonderful fucking start.

As he left the bathroom with the towel wrapped around his hips, the smell of bacon put him in a better mood. He dressed in fresh jeans and a T-shirt before combing his hair, then put the jeans from the floor in his hamper and picked up the cream panties, laying them on top of the closed hamper. He would tell Echo at breakfast where she could find them.

A flash of a memory of Echo getting dressed in the dark and not turning the light on came to him as he was heading down the steps. Had Echo been acting weird, or was he just thinking that because he had been so out of it?

Fuck if he knew.

When he pushed the door to the kitchen open, he only found Puck and Jesus inside. Both were sitting at the kitchen table, drinking coffee with a big plate in front of them.

"You fuckers have better saved me some food," he warned, moving to the counter, where he found enough to make himself a couple of plates.

Shoving a slice of bacon into his mouth, Puck commented to Jesus, "Someone woke up on the wrong side of the bed."

After piling his plate high, Moon set his plate on the table before going to the refrigerator to pour himself a glass of orange juice. Back at the table, he sat down and started eating.

Taking a sip of his coffee, he glanced across the table to see Puck and Jesus staring at him. "What?"

"You could've asked if everyone has eaten yet," Puck replied drily.

Moon shrugged. "You can make more if they haven't."

"I don't want to spend all day in this kitchen," Jesus complained.

Chewing on a piece of bacon, he shrugged again. "It doesn't bother you when I'm the one doing kitchen duty."

Jesus stared at him in consideration. Then, chagrined at being called out, the brother resumed eating while throwing him dirty looks.

Spreading jelly on his toast, Puck changed the subject,

seeing how well Jesus had fared at trying to make him feel bad about taking so much food. "You get up to anything good last night?"

"No." Moon gave a huff of irritation while pouring an excessive amount of sugar into his coffee. "This town is lame as fuck during Christmas."

"It's lame as fuck whatever the time of year," Puck replied, getting up to refill his coffee mug.

"I like it," Jesus gave his two cents. "At least I have a room here, and Viper doesn't hound me to divvy up to pay for what I drink. Wizard is a stingy bastard."

Moon had to agree with Jesus but didn't say it out loud. Puck or Jesus would forget that they had been the ones originally complaining about Wizard and tattle for bad-mouthing him.

Puck sat back down and stared at him curiously. "Heard the women went at it last night at Mick's."

"Wasn't much to it. It was over before it started. The best part was Crazy Bitch smashing into the door."

"I'm glad I didn't bother to get my ass out of bed, then, when Echo told me the women were going to make sure they had Jewell's back."

Moon sat back in his chair, finally full. "Echo didn't want to tag along?"

Puck gave him a satisfied grin. "She tried. I changed her mind. Jewell had enough women to take her back. I needed someone to massage mine. Have you asked her for a massage yet? If not, you're missing out."

Moon felt an unexpected jab of jealously. The emotion was so new he thought it was indigestion at first. He realized it was jealousy when he wanted to smash Puck in the face with his plate. "Her foot rub is nothing to sneeze about, either."

"Oo…" Puck's grin widened. "Guess what Echo will be doing tonight."

"Not if I snag her first again." Moon didn't know why he wanted to put a wrench in Puck's plans. He was still pissed about the hickey. Why did he give a fuck if Echo gave Puck a foot massage?

Puck gave him a confused frown. "When were you with Echo last night? We watched movies when I got back from Rachel's house. We stayed in my room the whole night. You mean this morning after I came down to start breakfast at six?" Puck nodded his head, as if he had answered his own question.

Moon frowned. "Echo was with you the whole night? Bro, I got news for you; she must have snuck away when you were sleeping because she came to my room in the middle of the night."

"Why would she have to sneak? If she wanted to go to your room, all she had to do was tell me."

Puck was right. She wouldn't have had to sneak into his room without telling Puck. The brothers were never jealous over which woman slept where unless they were claimed. Echo wasn't claimed. Hell, he didn't know why he was making a big deal out of it, anyway.

"Never mind. I could be wrong."

Puck and Jesus stared at him strangely.

"You good, bro?"

"Of course." That was the last time he got so wasted he mind-fucked himself.

"Cool." Puck stood up, his eyes traveling up from the table toward him.

Moon's lips tightened ominously when Puck sat back down and started laughing.

"Brah, is that a fucking hickey?"

"Can I get you anything?"

Using the heel of her good foot, Larissa turned, shuffling until she managed to back up until she felt the bed behind her. Pulling the crutches out from under her, she sat down on the bed. "A bottle of water, please."

"No problem. Lana, bring her a bottle of water when you bring the pillow," Priscilla yelled out.

Larissa gave her sister an exasperated look. "I could have yelled at Lana to bring me the water if I wanted to wake the whole apartment complex."

Priscilla gave her an unrepentant grin. "Sorry about that. Old habits are hard to break. Here, let me help you put your foot on the bed."

Larissa stopped her before she could bend down. "I need to go to the bathroom first."

"It would have been simpler if you had gone to the bathroom *before* sitting down."

"I thought of that, but I needed to rest. Those crutches hurt." Larissa hated that her voice sounded so weepy, but darn it, her foot hurt.

"What's wrong?" Lana asked, walking into the room. "Why's she crying?"

"I don't know." Confused, Priscilla sat down next to Larissa and started rubbing her back. "I just asked her why she didn't go to the bathroom before she sat down."

"What did she say?"

"I'm right here," Larissa reminded them. "I told her the crutches hurt."

Lana sat down next to her on her other side, taking her hand. "You'll get used to them," she soothed. "How's the pain?"

"Not too bad."

"Let's get you to the bathroom, and then we'll get you settled in bed. You'll feel much better after you get some sleep. I've scheduled an appointment with an orthopedic tomorrow. Once you get the temporary cast off, you'll be able to manage easier with a boot. I'll even spring a scooter for you, so you don't have to deal with the crutches."

Larissa had to sniffle back tears at how sweet Lana was being to her. "Can I have some tissues?"

"Of course." Lana reached out to pluck several tissues from the box on the nightstand.

Her sister waited until she blew her nose before both of them helped her hop into the bathroom. Leaving her on the toilet, they left her alone, closing the door after them. When she was done, she used the side of the sink to lift herself to her good foot, then held on to the sink as she stared at herself.

She was wearing two hospital gowns, both turned in opposite directions. Taking one of her sister's hair scrunchies, Larissa pulled her hair into a ponytail. Seeing herself in the mirror reminded her of doing the same thing several hours before. She covered her face with both hands and burst into tears.

"Hey!" Lana yelled, startling her. "Why are you crying?"

Unaware that her sisters had opened the door, Larissa dropped her hands to find them staring at her in dismay. "You could have knocked." Brushing her tears away, she tried to distract them from what she had been doing.

Priscilla and Lana frowned heavily at her. Then Lana moved from the doorway to place a hand around her waist. "Help me get her to bed, Priscilla."

Larissa let her sisters get her situated back on the bed, in a nightgown. Once she was sitting up against the headboard, and Priscilla had spread a comforter over her, Lana sat down next to her, retaking her hand.

"What's going on, Larissa? You've been acting weird since we left The Last Riders' clubhouse."

"It's just the pain. I'll be okay when the pain meds kick in." Larissa turned her face away from Lana's discerning gaze.

"Bullshit. I've seen you in much worse pain than this, and you never cried as if the sky was falling. Besides, you were acting weird before then. You ran down those steps as if the devil was chasing you."

Priscilla sat at the foot of the bed, careful not to touch her injured foot while listening with a concerned expression.

"Can you blame me with the way Winter had us sneaking in and out of the club? I've never been around bikers before. I don't know what they're capable of ..."

Lana paled. "I would have never accepted Winter's invitation if I had thought you or Priscilla weren't safe."

Larissa burst into tears again, feeling terrible about how Lana was taking blame for the way she was acting.

Lana scooted forward and wrapped her arms around her.

"Don't be nice to me. I don't deserve it!" she bawled out, covering her face with her hands.

Lana took her by the wrists and lowered her hands. "Stop it, Larissa, right now. You're scaring me. Something happened while you were there, and I want to know what it was—right now."

"Nothing ... happened," she stuttered out.

"Don't lie to me." She firmly reached for the cell phone on the nightstand. "The only time you were out of my sight was when Priscilla told me you had gone upstairs to use the restroom while I was in the one downstairs."

"That was the only time she was out of my eyesight, too," Priscilla agreed.

"So, something must have happened upstairs. What was it? Tell me, or I'm going to call Winter and ask her."

Larissa knew Lana would do exactly what she threatened.

"You're going to hate me," she warned.

"I could never hate you—you're my sister. I love you, and nothing you say or have done could ever change my feelings for you."

"I broke our golden rule," she confessed.

"Shit," Priscillia muttered from the bottom of the bed.

"Shut up, Priss," Lana ordered, turning her head to glare at their baby sister before turning back to her again. "You couldn't have broken the golden rule because I'm not dating anyone."

"No, but you wanted to." She gave a sobbing breath.

Lana's confused expression cleared. "You mean Moon?"

She couldn't help it; she broke into hysterical laughter.

"She's lost her marbles ..." Priscillia's frightened voice brought her back from La-La-Land.

"That's ... his ... name?" she managed through hiccupping sobs.

"I'd say that's his biker nickname," Priscilla replied, as if she were some sort of expert. "Is he why you lose it every time you hear Moon's name?"

"Yes, that's a ridiculous name. I mean, really ... who calls themselves Moon?" Her voice rose higher with each word she spoke.

"She's going to lose it again."

Lana turned around to glare at Priscilla. "Will you please nip it?" she snapped. "I'm trying to find out what's happened, and you're not helping."

"Sorry," Priscilla apologized. "I'll be quiet."

Both she and Lana stared at her.

Lana rocked her head back and forth in a huff.

"Well, I will."

"God help me." Lana reached for the extra pillow then smacked Priscilla with it. "You're going to make me lose my medical license because I'm about to strangle your ass. You say one more word, and I'm going to put honey on your hairbrush."

Priscilla didn't say a word, but Larissa could tell she wanted to.

"Try me," Lana warned.

When she didn't hear a peep, Lana focused back on her. "Let's start over. Why do you think you broke our golden rule? Did you kiss Moon upstairs? Is that what all this is about?"

Their golden rule was to never to kiss one of their sisters' boyfriends, regardless of if they were an ex or currently in a relationship.

Larissa rested her head on the headboard, tears streaking down her cheeks. "I did more than kiss the man."

# CHAPTER SEVEN

L ana and Priscilla sat as if turned to stone.

"Exactly how much more did you do?"

"I had sex with him."

Both of her sisters had entirely different reactions.

"Oh my God!" Priscilla shouted then quickly clapped her hand over her mouth.

Lana's eyes grew wide in concern. "Are you all right?"

"Yes."

"Did he make you…?"

Larissa hastily shook her head at Lana. "No, I … just lost my mind …" Larissa sniffed, not wanting to break into tears again. "I don't even know if Moon was the person I had sex with."

"Oh my G—"

"I swear, Priscilla, if you say that again, I'm going to make you go in the other room."

Priscilla hopped up from the foot of the bed, ran around it, and then jumped onto the empty side of the mattress, wiggling across to snuggle against Larissa's side.

"Careful ... you'll hurt her," Lana warned.

"Psst ... Larissa has enough pain meds in her system to Riverdance."

"It's okay. She didn't hurt me." Tired, Larissa sought to stop the budding argument.

"Fine, then." Lana threw Priscilla an exasperated glare at her gloating smile. "How do you not know who you had sex with?"

Larissa explained how she had seen the couple having sex. Then, from there, finding herself in the dark bedroom. "I didn't know what to do when he asked me to take his boots off. He thought I was a girl named Ember."

"I would have told him to take them off himself," Priscilla said matter-of-factly.

"I would have left," Lana reasoned.

"Of course, you would have. I was embarrassed by what I saw the other couple doing that I wasn't thinking straight. I thought I could get out of there, and he would just think it was Ember."

"Go on," Priscilla encouraged raptly. "When did the touchy-feely stuff start?"

Larissa felt herself blushing. "I took his boots off. Then he thought I was a girl called Ember. She must live there, too. Anyway, his feet were freezing cold, so I massaged them to get them warmed. They were freezing."

"You said all that already."

"I bet you warmed them right up," Priscilla joked, then had to arch her head away when Lana swung the pillow toward her.

Larissa jerked it away from her to put it behind her back then continued. "After that ... I was going to leave—"

"But you didn't."

Her shoulders slumped. "No, I didn't. He must have

figured out I wasn't Ember and thought I was mad at him because he had called by that name, so he started calling me Echo. Moon must have wanted to make it up to her really badly, because he started kissing me, and I mean really, really kissing me."

Opening her eyes wide, Larissa tried to explain with nonexistent words just how much effort Moon had put into kissing her.

Lana arched an eyebrow at her. "We get it, Larissa."

"Sorry…" If Larissa could stand, she would kick herself. She had as gotten carried away describing it as she had when it happened. Mentally smacking herself for being insensitive, she went back to recalling the night before. "Then, the next thing I knew, we were having sex … When it was over, he wanted me to turn the light on. I threw my clothes on instead, terrified he was going to turn the lights on himself and would find out I wasn't Ember or Echo. I would have died of humiliation. Thankfully, I was able to slip out before he did and ran back to the bathroom. I was still in the bathroom when Winter knocked on the door."

"Moon has no idea who he actually had sex with?"

"I don't think so." Lana put her hands up, as if she were going to give a lecture, then let them drop to her lap.

"At least tell me he used protection."

"We did."

"That's a plus," Priscilla said cheerfully. "I bet it was Moon. When I saw him at the bar, he seemed the type of guy who could sweep a woman off her feet."

"From what Larissa said, he's sweeping more than a couple."

"I don't know what I was thinking." Larissa stared up at the ceiling. "I hadn't even been drinking."

"He had been, though," Lana reminded her. "Was he drunk?"

"No, it was pitch black in the room, but he didn't sound or talk like someone intoxicated, which is why it never occurred me it could be Moon. He didn't have any trouble getting my clothes off, or his, either. I can't believe I had sex with him. I've never had a one-night stand." Larissa started crying again. "I'm sick with myself. Have either of you had a one-night stand?"

"Almost," Lana said soothingly, trying to comfort her.

"Almost?" Priscilla made a comical face. "I haven't, but you either have or haven't. So, which is it?"

Expecting Lana to shut Priscilla down again, she stopped crying when Lana started laughing.

"I wanted to, but my sister snagged him away."

Larissa couldn't bring herself to join in on the laughter. "What am I going to do if he ever finds out it was me?" Taking the Kleenex Lana held out, she wiped her damp cheeks.

"We don't know for sure if it was Moon. Besides, how is he going to find out?" Giving her a reassuring pat on the hand, Lana brushed the damp tendrils away from her face. "Did he ever see your face?"

Larissa shook her head.

"Did anyone see you leave his room?"

"No."

"Then we're going to pretend it never happened."

"That sounds good to me." Larissa didn't think she was going to forget how good it felt having sex with Moon anytime soon, but she was willing to give it a go.

"Do you mind me asking before we forget …" Priscilla tentatively asked, as if afraid Lana was going to yell at her again. "How was he? I mean … was he as good as he looks?"

She really didn't want to answer since Lana had been so interested in him.

Larissa licked her suddenly dry lips. She could have sworn she could still taste him.

"I'm so sorry I screwed that up for you."

"Literally!" Priscilla crowed.

Larissa lowered her lashes, turning toward Priscilla. "I'm going to—"

Priscilla held her hands up. "Okay, I'll stop if you answer my question."

"I'm not going to answer."

A wide grin spread across Priscilla's face. "You just did. If he was a dud, you would have said so."

She dearly loved Priscilla, but she could be such a pain.

"We need to let Larissa get some rest. Let's go." Lana stood, saving her from more of their sister's teasing.

Priscilla gave her a brief hug before sliding off the bed.

"Your cell phone is on the nightstand. Call me if you need help to the bathroom." Moving the crutches within her reach, Lana reached for the plastic bag that Priscilla had dropped on the bed when they entered the room. The nurse who cut off her jeans had put them in the bag at the hospital.

Lana opened the bag, taking out her jeans and top. "I might as well go ahead and throw the jeans away for you. I'll put your shirt in the laundry."

"Thank you. I would appreciate it."

When Lana opened the plastic bag again, Larissa couldn't understand what she was doing.

"What are you looking for?"

Lana looked in the bag again, then raised curious eyes. "Where are your panties?"

L eaving Puck and Jesus cleaning the kitchen, Moon went down to the basement to work out. He was still doing a series of warmups on an exercise mat when Echo walked down the steps, carrying a laundry basket.

"Morning, Moon, how's it going?" she cheerfully greeted him, setting her basket of dirty clothes on the floor in front of the washer.

"Morning." Swinging his leg back in front of him, he then raised his arm to stretch it behind his head.

"I wish Viper would spring for a new washer. This one is older than me." Opening the washer, Echo started sorting through her clothes before throwing them into the drum.

"If you're doing your lingerie, don't forget the pair you left in my room. I left them on the hamper."

Bent over the basket, Echo turned her head to look at him with a frown.

"*If* you had turned the light on like I *asked*, you might have found them before sneaking back to Puck."

Echo straightened, her face filled with confusion. "What in the fuck are you talking about?"

He had never been a person to beat around the bush when he was irritated, and the fugitive way Echo had acted last night irritated the hell out of him. "Since when do you have the need to sneak around to fuck me? Do you and Puck have something going and—"

"Moon, I have no idea what in the hell you're talking about. Why would I sneak around to fuck you? There's nothing more going on between Puck and me than any other brother in the club I have sex with." As she straightened from the basket, her expression turned uneasy, as if he had a screw loose. "The last time we had sex was two weeks ago, after the football game. We were upstairs in the TV room. Nickel,

Jesus, and Puck were right there, watching. How in the hell is that sneaking?"

Moon brought his arm back down. Was she shitting him? What mindfuck was she trying to play? "You're going to pretend you didn't come into my room last night and we didn't fuck?"

Echo's hands went to her hips. "There's no pretending. I didn't take one step inside your room last night. I didn't leave Puck's room all night, other than to go the bathroom a couple of times, and I didn't take a detour into your room. If I did, I wouldn't have to lie about it." Bending back down, she grabbed the rest of her clothes and shoved them into the washer. "I love it. You must have been so fucked you don't know who you fucked. I guess you can't tell us apart as long you get what you need."

Moon winced when she slammed the lid down on the washer.

"You lame-ass prick," she snarled. "You having trouble telling who's who? Try opening your fucking eyes!" As she sharply turned the dial on the washer, Moon heard Echo mutter under her breath, "Unbelievable." Then, turning back to stare at him from across the room, it was plain Echo was debating hitting him. Storming toward the stairs instead, Echo curled her lips in disgust.

Moon mentally prepared himself for what Echo would say next. Whatever it was wasn't going to be good. Echo was the most laidback of the women members. That he had made her so angry showed how much he had fucked up.

"You pull this shit on Ember, she'll rip your balls off. Not that you've noticed, you arrogant prick, but I don't wear underwear. And guess what?"

He was almost afraid to ask. "What?"

"Ember doesn't wear anything but thongs."

Fuck…

"Sorry. Let me make it up to you. I'll—"

"Forget it, Moon. I don't need you to make a damn thing up to me."

He felt like a gigantic ass when he saw the sheen of tears in Echo's eyes.

"Instead, I should be thanking you. You just showed me how low we women are in your estimation. Do the other brothers think that way?"

"Echo, I fucked up, okay? Don't bring the other brothers into this."

"Why not? I want to know. Do the brothers in Ohio think like this, too, or just the brothers here?"

Rubbing his fingers across his forehead, he tried to think of something to ease Echo's hurt. "I'm the only moron in both clubs. Okay? Wizard and Viper would say the same thing. Just let me ... make it up to you. I saw an Ulta magazine sitting on the table in the kitchen; you go pick anything you want, and I'll buy it," he promised.

"*Anything*?"

Moon recognized the glint entering her eyes.

"Anything," he confirmed through clenched teeth.

"I don't know if I could enjoy it if the other women can't pick out what they want, too."

Well, that was no subtle hint.

"Give them the magazine, too. Tell them each to pick out five things they want, and I'll make sure they get it."

"I want them to have everything they want." Echo knew she had him over a barrel.

"You're missing the point of me letting you have everything you want. I want to show *you* that *you're* special."

"Ah ... I must have missed that part. In that case, we can let them pick out *six* gifts apiece."

Where was the fucking *we* coming from? The only credit card number Echo would be using was his.

"Sounds good."

"Thanks, Moon! You're the best!"

Moon watched Echo's ass bounce up the steps eagerly. Waiting until she had gone through the door and shut it, he fell backward onto the mat to stare at ceiling. He had just made a costly mistake because he hadn't listened to Puck.

As he looked at the ceiling, another thought came to him.

If it wasn't Echo or Ember, who in the hell had he fucked last night?

# CHAPTER EIGHT

"Moon! Did you hear what I just said?"

Moon jumped at Viper's yell. "I heard."

Viper folded his arms over his chest. "Then what did I just say?"

Moon gave the brothers sitting in the den a look, hoping one of them would divert Viper's attention from him.

"Brother, you're on your own," Rider mumbled out of the corner of his mouth.

Clueless as to what Viper had been saying, Moon decided to wing it. "What? Are we in sixth grade again? Why don't you ask Rider if he was listening?" If the brother didn't want to help him out, then Moon had no compunction about throwing him under the bus.

At his flippant reply, Viper strode forward to where he was sitting on the couch and stared down at him imposingly. Moon was perceptive enough to know he was about rip him a new one.

"Maybe because Rider doesn't know the answer to the question I asked *you*."

"Sorry, Viper, I must have tuned out for a second. What did you ask?"

Viper wasn't mollified, but he did step back. "I asked you if you finished with the inventory at the factory."

"Almost. All I lack is the refrigerated section."

"Fuck. Shade's waiting for the numbers so we can compare to last month's figures. What's the holdup?"

Moon sat up from his relaxed position on the couch. "It's taking so long because those seed packets are a bitch to count. I've busted my balls for the last three days to get the inventory done for you. Sorry I decided to take a night off because all I could see was numbers when I closed my eyes."

Moon expected Viper to have at him again, but he was too tired to give a damn. If Viper wanted to give the job to someone else to complete, he could. Shit, he didn't need the money from the overtime pay that badly.

As the words floated through his mind, he remembered the promise he had made to Echo and knew he was fucked. He was going to need that overtime money when they came to him with their wish lists.

Viper began nodding toward Puck. "Puc—"

"I'll have the figures to Shade by six," Moon cut him off.

Viper turned back to him. "If not, Puck's getting the job, and he's going to get paid for doing the whole inventory."

Moon clenched his jaw to keep from smarting off to Viper. Viper paid enough that the brothers competed with each other as to who would get first pick of either taking the overtime or turning it down. Doing the inventory was easy, and he had jumped at the chance when Viper had offered it to him. He had to get his mind back on track and put last night on the back burner.

"I'll get it done."

Viper gave him a curt nod before he continued with club business. "When Shade has the numbers, we'll be able to compare them to the ones Wizard sent over and see if any of the changes we've implemented have made a difference in the losses we've been experiencing the last four months."

Moon met Viper's eyes. "I told you what I think."

"I know what you think—the losses are coming in transit. But the drivers have cameras mounted in their vehicles, both in the cab and cargo area. We have all looked at the footage. Unless you or anyone else is seeing something I'm not, then the losses have to be coming from the factories. Have you?"

"No." Moon shook his head. "It's a gut feeling."

Viper didn't dismiss the way he felt. Frowning, he rubbed his jaw, as if thinking, before he dropped his hand. "All right, then if the inventory comes back with another loss, we'll continue monitoring the factories using monthly inventories, and we'll give each delivery truck an escort of two brothers."

The brothers all groaned.

Viper ignored them and continued, "The Ohio brothers won't be pitching in to help with the delivery trucks from Ohio to here. I want to keep them in the dark as long as I can, other than Wizard, Puck and Jesus. He wants to wait and see which factory is losing more inventory.

Rider's boot dropped from the coffee table it had been propped on. "That's pretty damn convenient for him. We'll be the ones having to make the rides. You want two of us to ride all the way to and from Ohio with each delivery?"

"For a month," Viper confirmed.

"Damn. Why two escorts? One should be enough," Rider argued. "What's being stolen aren't high-ticketed items."

Viper's expression became grim. "Because the amount of losses we're experiencing has been increasing. Whoever is stealing from us is getting more confident. I'm not going to make the same mistake I made with Reaper. Each one of you will have backup, and you won't know which one of you will be riding until Shade gives you the go."

Reaper's coffee cup hit the table. "That's not going to work. I've got a wife who's expecting and a kid I can't leave at a moment's notice."

None of the brothers were happy about it, yet Reaper being Viper's brother was the only one brave enough to speak up.

Viper wasn't having it and gave Reaper a stone-faced expression. "You are the last person to complain. Ginny has seven brothers to stand in for you when you can't be there. The rest of us aren't as lucky. Everyone is going to pull their weight as escorts."

"*Everyone?*" Razer asked.

"Everyone," Viper stated. "That includes Knox, Drake, King, and me. Train, you and Killyama can follow along as escorts together in a vehicle if you want to include her."

Train shook his head. "Sorry, count Killyama out. With her expecting, we've both agreed she's going to stay close to Treepoint for the time being."

"No more riding to Jamestown anytime one of the bitches calls?" Cash joked.

Train wasn't amused. "I'm not worried about the bitches, but she can't help inserting herself in one of Hammer and Jonas' cases. The only riding I want her to do is on the keyboard. Killy's going to work with them remotely while she finishes her degree."

Cash raised a skeptical brow. "How'd you get her to agree to that?"

Train's face went impassive. "None of your fucking business, but she agreed, and she'll keep her word."

"Good luck with that." Cash still seemed unconvinced. "Killyama isn't going to be able to resist running to Hammer and Jonas anytime they call any more than Rachel does when her family calls."

Train's expression didn't change. "We'll see."

Cash just shook his head at Train. "Yes, you will."

Moon watched the byplay between the two men. "You two crack me the fuck up." He looked back at Viper. "Can we get back to the meeting? I'd rather be counting seed packets than listening to this. Where are the brothers I rode with who knew how to lay down the law on their women? You all just hand over your balls with those wedding rings? God Almighty, you don't want them to do something? Fucking tell them. They don't do it, divorce their ass. Move on. Simple. Problem solved. Can we move on, or are you going to be paying me that overtime, Viper, for the fucking time I've wasted listening to their horseshit?"

Viper's lips curled in amusement. "Brother, when you can practice what you preach, we'll take your advice. Until then, I wouldn't be spreading those pearls of wisdom."

Moon shrugged, uncaring if they took his advice or not. He would never find himself in their situation. "I'm just saying it like I see it. You'll never hear me saying 'we agreed.' My word will go. If not, then she can." Moon rose from the couch. "We done here?"

"We're done." Viper gave him a tight-lipped smile before gesturing to Shade and Rider to stay. "Train, I left my laptop on Jewell's desk at the factory; do you mind getting it for me?"

"No problem." Train walked out of the den with him as they headed to the factory.

"I'd be careful if I were you," Train said as they went out the front door of the club.

Moon gave Train a sideways glance. "About what? You don't want to take my advice about Killyama, then don't. I could give a rat's ass—"

"I'm not talking about your advice where our wives are concerned. You can't keep track of what woman you fucked last night, much less maintain a relationship long enough to get married."

Unwilling to show Train he had hit the mark dead center, Moon restrained himself from faceplanting the brother in the snowy mud. He needed to finish the inventory, not fight on the front lawn.

"I was talking about Viper. You've been pushing his buttons lately, and Wizard is just as fed up. They're not going to keep giving you special treatment much longer. If you don't chill, you're going to find yourself without a club."

He had been provoking both Viper and Wizard more than usual, despite telling himself to chill. He was unhappy with his personal life, and it was bleeding over to his club life. Last night wasn't going to help, either.

With both Echo and Ember taken out of the equation, that only left Jade and Stori. Jewell had been with Rory. Or maybe she hadn't? He would check with her first. If she got angry, she wouldn't go for his wallet—she'd go after his ass.

# CHAPTER NINE

M oon kicked the tire of his bike as he watched Stori and Jade come back from grocery shopping. Finally! They had left over three hours ago. He had been thwarted from talking to Jewell until he had taken the bull from the horns and texted her. Her response had been a no she hadn't fucked him, then she told him to fuck off.

"Need some help?" Moon called out, already walking toward them.

"Please." Jade gave him a thankful smile as she moved to the side so he could take the bags out.

Leaving the smaller bags for them to take, he fell in step with them as they went to the walkway beside the club instead of taking the steep stairs.

"Was the grocery store busy?"

"Not at all." Stori lightly swung the bag in her hand as they walked.

"What took so long, then?"

Both women looked at him at the irritation he hadn't been able to keep out of his voice.

"We treated ourselves to lunch at King's." Jade frowned. "I didn't realize there was a big rush for us to get back."

"There wasn't. I was just worried about how long it was taking."

Jade held the back door open for them to walk through. "Since when do you keep tabs on the amount of time we're gone?"

Dammit. He wasn't in the mood, but between Viper keeping him busy, running back and forth from Ohio, and working at the factory, he hadn't had the opportunity to talk with Jade or Stori. Either they were asleep, working, with one of the other brothers, or other people had been around. He wanted to know which woman he had fucked three weeks ago.

Moon was unable to explain to himself why it mattered. He only knew it did. The encounter preyed upon his mind, especially with the feeling that he hadn't been with the woman before was gnawing at him, yet the likelihood of that happening was between null and none. It had to be Jade or Stori, and he was going to find out which one it was before the clock struck midnight.

His hand went to the curve of Jade's ass. "Since I saw how fine your ass looks in those new jeans."

Jade turned from the counter, her arms wrapping around his waist to hook her fingers in his belt loops. "You should have said something before I left," she purred, rubbing her lush tits against his chest.

"I didn't want Stori to have to go alone." Catching Stori's arm when she reached for another bag on the counter, Moon pulled her to his side to kiss her. Holding on to both women, he started maneuvering them toward the sectional couch in the den.

Stori pulled her mouth away from the passionate kiss he

was giving her. "I should finish putting the groceries away," she protested halfheartedly.

"The only things left are cans; let someone else do it. You two deserve another special treat."

Jade giggled. "I suppose you consider yourself the treat?"

"You tell me." Pushing both women down onto the couch, he stood over them. "Let's me see who should go first." Rubbing his chin in pretend thought, he gave each woman a seductive grin. "Whoever should go first isn't the one I was with last. That way, it will be fair. Don't you agree?"

Stori and Jade both nodded.

"The problem is I've been so busy lately I've lost track of time. When was the last time we fucked, Jade?"

Jade reached for his belt buckle, enticingly unlooping it to pull it free. "Christmas Eve ..." Unbuttoning his jeans, she slid his zipper down. "We played naughty or nice. Do you remember?"

Hell, how had he forgotten that?

Because it had been unmemorable.

He had become so jaded where sex was concerned that one woman blended into another. The only woman who had stood out was a woman he couldn't put a face to.

"Of course." Moon leaned over her to tilt her head back and placed a passionate kiss on her mouth. His tongue dived deep as his hand slid under her low-cut top to cup her breast. He knew at the touch of Jade's lips that she wasn't the woman in his bed three weeks ago.

Slowly, he removed his mouth from hers, letting his tongue glide over her bottom lip before turning his attention to Stori.

She had wasted no time while he had been kissing Jade in removing her sweater and jeans.

"Ahh ... my little eager Stori." Going down to his haunches in front of her brought him to eye level with her glistening pussy. "I take it you already know who gets to go first."

"I do." She beamed. "We haven't been together since I came back from Thanksgiving."

"I remember," he lied convincingly, his mouth touching her knee before gliding up her leg. When he reached her mound, Moon homed in on her clitoris and pulled it into his mouth for a tongue thrashing that had Stori moaning. Pulling his mouth back, he gave Stori's clit one last lick before rising to his feet.

Moon sat on the couch between the two women to remove his boots. Then, standing, he got rid of his clothes.

"You get first choice. Do you want my mouth or my dick?"

Stori pouted, her lips puffy from his mouth. "I want your mouth. Jade and I can switch next time. That way, each of us gets the best of both worlds."

Damn. He'd had a long day driving back from Ohio, and it seemed it was going to be an even longer night.

"Jade?"

Her eyes were already eye-fucking the cock pointing up toward his bellybutton. "What's to complain about?"

There were a few things he'd like to complain about but didn't.

Having the women stand up, Moon gave Jade a condom before lying down on the couch. "Come here, Stori." He helped her sit on his face, his tongue finding the entrance to her channel, as Jade smoothed the condom over his cock before gradually lowering herself over him.

"Damn," Jade hissed. "I swear I think your cock gets bigger every time we fuck." Slowly, she started riding his cock as he tongue-fucked Stori.

The women's sighs and moans filled the room as he worked to satisfy both. Slowing the thrust of his tongue to tease Stori, he felt Jade's movements become fluid as she adjusted to his size and length.

He raised his arms up to place them beside his face and Stori's thigh, to keep her from strangling him, and used the opportunity to play with her breasts. Opening the front clasp, his fingers searched for the piercing he knew was there. Both of her breasts had piercings, as well as her bellybutton.

As he played with the barbell in her nipple, he heard her moans increase. Lowering his hand. he twirled the dainty money sign dangling from her bellybutton.

"Your tongue is fucking magic." she whimpered.

Moon felt Stori's stomach quiver under his hand as Jade ground herself down on his cock.

"His cock is no joke, either," Jade gasped out.

Moon arched his hips, driving his cock higher inside of Jade, while he stuffed his tongue and started thrusting inside of Stori's pussy. Sensing both women were close to coming, he used his teeth to tug at Stori's clit, sending her whimpers into full-fledged screams. He waited until he could feel the tremors slow, then Moon carefully lifted her over his head so he could place her on the cushion next to them.

Giving Jade his full attention, he raised her off his cock. Then he got off the couch and changed Jade's position until she was on her knees on the couch, facing the kitchen and back door. Sliding into position behind her, Moon made sure he hadn't dislodged the condom before thrusting back inside her wet pussy.

"Harder, Moon! Harder!" Jade screamed as her head fell to the back of couch. "I'm coming!"

Thrusting hard, Moon grabbed Jade by the hips to pull her back and forth on his dick. When he felt her pussy muscles clamping his cock, Moon finally allowed himself to come. He buried his mouth in Jade's neck and gave himself over to the climax rushing through him. He was still gasping for breath when he heard a loud gasp from the doorway.

At the sound, Moon raised his head to find Killyama and a woman he had never seen before standing in the doorway.

Moon had never been a man to be embarrassed easily, and from where Killyama and the other woman were standing, the only view they had of him was his chest. Jade and Stori were another matter. Jade's breasts were exposed, and it was obvious what they had been doing. Stori had moved to sit on the back of the couch, and her naked body was clearly visible.

Killyama was the first to find her voice. "My bad. Train was supposed to meet us. When he didn't show, I thought I mixed up where we were meeting him."

With his cock still buried deep inside of Jade, Moon considered his options. All of them were embarrassing for Jade, Stori, and the unknown woman. Killyama, on the other hand, seemed as if she had accomplished exactly what she had set out to do.

"Close the door." Moon felt his nostrils flare in anger. "Give us five minutes before you come back inside. We'll get out of your way."

"Take your time. We're in no hurry." Killyama turned toward the woman who had already turned and was rushing back out the door. "I'll send Train another text."

"That would have been a good idea before you came in here," Moon gritted out, furious Killyama had so blithely brought a stranger into the club at this time of day.

He didn't know what game Killyama was playing with Train, and he didn't give a fuck. She had broken a club rule, and she was going to be held accountable.

The club had gone through a series of transitions since some of the brothers had married, and he had adjusted through them, but Killyama's blatant disregard of the rules pissed him the hell off. Whoever the woman was should have never been allowed inside at this time of the day, and the members who lived here would be made aware that an outsider had come inside. Killyama had broken two rules at the expense of Jade, Stori, and the unknown woman. He wasn't even including himself, as furious as he was.

At least Killyama had the sense to realize she had gone too far and had left, closing the door after her.

Detaching himself from Jade, he quickly gathered her and Stori's clothes and handed them to them.

"I bet she got an eyeful." Stori laughed, not bothering to put her clothes back on. "At least you two were mostly behind the couch."

Jade only tugged her top back on, leaving her bottom half uncovered. "It doesn't matter. She's used to seeing women's bodies," she casually remarked.

Moon tugged his jeans on then pulled his T-shirt over his head. "You know who that woman is?"

"I don't know her name, or which one she is, but Killyama mentioned at lunch today that she would bring her by."

Moon grabbed his boots in one hand. "Who is she?" he asked Jade since she seemed to know more than Stori.

"Killyama's doula."

"Her name is Doula?"

"No, she's a doula."

Moon frowned. "What in the fuck is a doula?"

"She provides emotional support for Killyama and Train during their pregnancy and having the baby."

His jaw clenched, still furious. "That's a thing?"

"Oh … yes. It's getting more and more popular."

"I'm glad Killyama is going to have emotional support; she's going to fucking need it."

# CHAPTER TEN

"You're not going to believe this!"

Larissa dropped the book on her lap as Priscilla stormed into the living room. Lana closed the kitchen cabinet and moved to the counter to listen as Priscilla dropped her coat and purse on a chair offset the couch.

Larissa hesitated to ask what had Priscilla so fired up, aware of who her last scheduled appointment of the day was with. Lana, on the other hand, had no such hesitation, giving her a worried frown.

"What aren't we going to believe?"

"I just want to say ..." Priscilla glowered at both of them as she raised her hands, emphasizing how furious she was with the both of them. "I want to know how you two were both taken in by a man who has the morals of an alley cat."

Larissa felt a heated blush creep up her cheeks. "Are you talking about Moon?"

Priscilla karate chopped the air. "Who else would I be talking about?"

Placing another pillow behind her back, Larissa raised herself higher on the couch. "I didn't pick him." She tried to keep her voice level and calm, even though she was fighting not to raise her voice. "I didn't know Moon was even back at the club."

Leaving the kitchen, Lana went to the couch to pick up the coat and purse, which had been tossed aside, and hung both on the coat rack. "I accept full responsibility." She took a seat on the chair she had cleared. "Both of you were ready to go home. I was the one who wanted to stay at The Last Riders'."

Priscilla sighed, losing steam at Lana's unhappy expression. "I'm sorry. I shouldn't have gone off." She shot each of them an apologetic glance. "It's just ... he's such a ... dog."

Larissa couldn't help but smile. "A second ago, he was an alley cat. Why don't you tell us what he did, so we can cast our vote?"

"Ugh..." Priscilla grimaced. "You know I was meeting Killyama and Train at five thirty?"

Larissa nodded. "I should. I'm the one who scheduled it for you." With her foot being in a cast, she was confined to the office until the weather turned warmer so she wouldn't have to fear another tumble.

"Train was late, and the later he was, the angrier Killyama got. I offered to leave and reschedule their appointment. She wasn't happy with that option at all." Priscilla rolled her eyes. "Instead, she looked at the consultation sheet, which is what we would have done if Train had been there. Killyama suggested she show me around their house, if they decide to go ahead with a home birth, that since you're out of commission for the next four weeks, I could give insights if they decided to have a water birth."

Larissa frowned. "I know she was going back and forth about whether she wanted a midwife or a doula, but she never mentioned a water birth. We would have gone over that during the consultation, of course. But she should have waited for Train. Many fathers' doubts need to be addressed."

"I told her; she wasn't listening. So, you know Killyama is going to be a nightmare to work with." Priscilla gave the air another karate chop. "She's going to be worse than Roxanne."

"Ouch." Lana winched. "That bad?"

"Worse." Priscilla scowled. "She wouldn't stop asking about the water birth, so I gave in and told her that you have to set up a birthing pool at their home before the delivery due date. Boy, was that a big mistake ... she said there was a whirlpool at The Last Riders' clubhouse and she could use that. I told her you would have to take a look at it and give your opinion. That's when she was determined for me to check it out, that if it wouldn't work, there would be no need for you to come out. During all this, she's texting Train, and I could tell she's about to blow a fuse." Priscilla's shoulders slumped. "I gave in, which was an even bigger mistake."

"You went to the clubhouse?" Lana prompted.

"Oh, yes ... there was no stopping Killyama. We went in through in the back door." Priscilla's face went deadpan, and she shook her head. "It was like walking into a porn scene. I actually looked around for the cameras."

Larissa made a conscious effort not to gape like Lana was, biting her bottom lip to keep her jaw closed. "You're joking?"

Priscilla kept shaking her head. "I wish I were. I kid you not, Moon was having sex on a couch with a woman, and another naked woman was watching them. I think it was a threesome."

She would have laughed at Priscilla's scandalous tone, but the sick feeling in her stomach told her it was no laughing matter.

"And let me tell you something else ... neither of you stood a chance with Moon. The woman looked like she was a pin-up model. She even had staples in her and everything."

Lana frowned. "You mean, like medical stitches?"

"No, like they went through her nipples, and one was dangling from her bellybutton."

"You mean piercings?"

"Whatever." She nodded. "The women were gorgeous. I don't want to hurt your feelings, but neither of you would stand a chance of getting that man's attention. Not with those centerfolds as competition."

Larissa was tempted to throw her book at Priscilla.

"Moon would have been lucky to have gotten Lana."

Her older sister sent her a shaky smile.

"Then why did you steal him away from her?" Priscilla asked.

The book went flying. "I did not steal that jerk away from Lana! I didn't know who he was!"

Priscilla caught the book and set it down safely on the coffee table. "Whatever. I was just saying neither one of you should be feeling bad. He's obviously a hound dog, and since neither of you are into threesomes …" Priscilla raised a curious brow.

Larissa narrowed her eyes on her baby sister, who was getting on her last nerve.

"What do you think?" Lana snapped.

"I don't know … I wouldn't have a one-night stand, either …"

Larissa reached for her crutches.

"Behave, Priss," Lana reprimanded their sister.

Priscilla got off the couch to sit on the couch next to her. "I'm sorry. I think I'm still shellshocked. I hate to admit it, but wow, if that dude was on a calendar, I would buy it."

"Are you going to throw it in my face for the rest of my life that I accidentally had sex with Moon?"

"Probably," Priss admitted.

At least Priss was honest.

"How did Moon act when he saw you?"

Priss made herself comfortable, putting an arm around a pillow. "He was angry but watched his language more than I would have. He told Killyama to leave and give them five minutes, then we could come back in."

"What happened after that?"

Priss picked up the crutch she had dropped and placed it within reach. "I was so embarrassed I told Killyama that it might be better for Train and her to make an appointment to come into the office."

"What for? Train is obviously resistant. That's why he must have missed the appointment. Train probably told her no, and she made the appointment, anyway."

"Exactly, Killyama doesn't accept no. So, I'm giving you the opportunity of being the one to break the news to her, not me."

Larissa and Lana shared a troubled gaze.

"We can't pass taking Killyama on as a client," Lana told Priss.

"We're going to need every dime we can to fight to get the Certificate Of Need for the birth center we've dreamed of opening. That's why there aren't any freestanding birth centers in Kentucky—people run out of money fighting to get them in the courts. Thanks to my stealing ex-fiancé, we're down several thousand dollars."

"Thankfully, he only had access to your personal accounts, not the account with our savings for the birth center. We'll get the money back from him somehow," she promised.

Lana shook her head. "I deserve to lose it. I should have never given him access to my account. I thought because he put me on his that ..." Lana made a painfilled face. "Anyway ... stupid me wasn't smart enough to check out how much he actually had in his account. If I had, I would have found out sooner it had been closed due to insufficient funds."

Larissa gave Lana a fiery glance. "You call yourself stupid again where that lying thief is concerned, I'm going to make Priss get up and bop you!"

Lana gave her trembling smile. "I won't."

"So, what we going to do about Killyama if she calls?" Priss asked with an unhappy expression.

"You know, now that I think about it"—Lana gave her a cheerful smile—"we can give her a pass. I've never known a better candidate for a hospital birth. We'll refer her to Dr. Price."

# CHAPTER ELEVEN

**W**ould *he just hurry the heck up!*
    Larissa stared at the obnoxious man holding the line up, preventing her and the others from moving forward.

The jack-hole at the back, who was holding the door open until the line moved, wasn't helping either. Cold air was blowing inside, making the whole experience of getting her Kentucky license painful, as if going to the DMV wasn't painful enough.

Staring a hole into the man's back was useless, or he would have moved forward by now. She really hated confrontations, but she hated being cold even worse.

"Excuse me; do you mind moving forward so the person at the back will close the door?"

The man in front of her just turned his head to the side, only giving her the profile of what he looked like. "He should have waited outside until there was room for him to come inside."

"He should have, but he didn't," Larissa agreed, still trying to be polite. "If you took a few steps forward, he would be able to close the door."

"There's a line that says do not step forward until called. I'm up to the line."

"I'm sure they won't mind if you go over a few inches."

"It's the DMV. They care." The jerk turned his face forward again.

Running her tongue along the inside of her cheek instead of snapping at the rude man, Larissa promised not to say another word. Surely, someone in the back would say something to the man holding the door open.

Neither of the men moved to alleviate the problem, the office grew colder, and if the woman behind her with the stroller bumped her crutch again, they were going to have a problem.

To heck with this. She'd wait to transfer the license. It wasn't like she was able to drive, anyway, and it wasn't worth creating a scene in a town she was still unfamiliar with, especially with the people who lived here.

"Excuse me; will you let me pass?"

The man in front of her must have been texting, because when he spun around, his cell phone was in his hand. His outflung hand struck her crutch, jerking it out from under her. She lost her balance and started falling backward.

"Watch out! My baby!" the woman behind her yelled as she yanked the stroller to the side.

In a split second, Larissa felt herself lifted into the air by the man who had almost knocked her down.

"Why didn't you tell me you were on crutches?" Brownish eyes, which were so dark they almost appeared black, glowered into hers.

"I don't know … Maybe because I thought you could see them," she snapped.

"If I did, I would have let you go in front of me."

"Okay," she said, giving him a disbelieving look.

He became angrier. "I would have."

"Huh! Yeah right; you wouldn't even take a couple of steps forward. All this could have been prevented if you had just done what I asked. I'm probably going to have pneumonia because of you."

The man still holding her looked over her shoulder. "Nial, shut the fucking door!"

"I can't—it's jammed!" Nial yelled back.

"Then why didn't you say something?"

"I was going to when it was my turn!"

Larissa's head went back and forth as the men yelled at each other.

"He didn't shut the door because it was broken," he said, giving her a smug grin.

Balefully, Larissa stared at him. "So I heard."

"So, it wasn't my fault."

"Yes, I got that, too. Do you mind putting me down, please?"

Despite his irritation at her, he set her gently down on her good foot and held on to her until he returned her crutch. "There you go. How's that?"

"Fine. Thank you."

"Next!" the clerk called out.

Looking her over, as if gauging she had her balance, the man turned and walked toward the clerk.

Would it have hurt him to let her go first? She was fuming. Any thought of leaving had disappeared. She was going to stay in line until her foot rotted off, she was so angry. At least what he needed done didn't take long, and it wasn't long until he was striding out without giving her another glance.

That dude was so conceited she was surprised little blue jays didn't fly out of his ass when he walked.

Thankfully, she had the required paperwork and transferring her license didn't take long, other than a quick vision test.

Hobbling out the DMV, she decided to grab some lunch before returning to her office. There really weren't many choices. The food at the diner consisted of hamburgers and fries, and King's Restaurant was more expensive but offered more variety. Not wanting to call Priss to broaden her choices, she bit the bullet and headed toward King's.

The restaurant was packed. She guessed everyone else in town was sick of hamburgers as well.

Larissa was happy the hostess found her a small table. She ordered a diet soda and browsed the menu, only lifting her gaze when she heard someone being seat at the table next to her.

When the hostess moved away, Larissa found herself staring at the rude man from the DMV.

Could she catch a break today?

Self-consciously, she hurriedly bent her head over the menu. She really didn't want them staring at each other as they ate their meals at their respective tables. If it weren't so obvious, she would leave. Concluding she would order the food to go rather than be uncomfortable, Larissa waited for the waiter to come.

"I'll take the pork chops and a baked potato, with asparagus."

As she was about to order it to go, a couple took the empty chairs at DMV dude's table, fortunately blocking her view. She changed her mind about eating there and took out her cell phone to check for messages.

Unable to help herself, she peered through her lashes at the couple who had sat down. The older man had caught her eye. He was striking, with a chiseled jaw and broad shoulders dressed in a suit. There was something about him that struck a chord of fear inside of her without knowing why.

It was apparent the man and woman were a couple by the way they spoke to each other, and the arm placed over the back of her chair was a clear sign of possession. The scary man was giving the conceited jerk a warning.

Larissa almost wished she had a better view of their faces.

She lost interest in the other table when her attention was diverted by her waitress.

"I'm sorry. We're out of pork chops. Would you like to choose another entrée?"

Choosing a strip steak instead, she forced herself to go through her messages. She dealt with those which couldn't wait and was electronically paying her storage unit when she noticed the food arrive at the other table. No wonder there weren't any pork chops left. All three people had ordered them.

Irritated, she set her phone down as her waitress arrived with her food.

She told herself not to say anything when the waitress asked if there was anything she could get her, but Larissa wasn't able to help herself.

"I have a quick question. How is it that I ordered before the table next to me, yet they all were able to get the pork chops when I wasn't?"

Larissa wanted to slink under the table when all the occupants at other table looked in her direction.

"The owner of the restaurant placed the order before you sat down," her waitress explained. "May I get you something else?"

"No, thanks. I'm good."

Humiliated with the people still staring at her, she started cutting her steak.

"Sorry, I don't mean to interrupt your meal. My friend texted me that he was coming, and I placed the order, not realizing we were taking the last. I apologize."

"No, no, there's no need to apologize. I shouldn't have said anything to begin with." Larissa took a bite, hoping the woman would turn around and continue with her meal.

The pretty redhead smiled. "Let me make it up to you. I'll have Valerie give you a gift certificate. Your meal will be on the house."

Swallowing her bite, she forked another piece of steak. "No, that's completely unnecessary."

"Eat your food, Evie. Can't you tell she wants to be left alone?" the man from the DMV told the woman.

Hoping the woman would take the advice, she raised the steak to her mouth. It was delicious. If she had two good feet, she would kick herself.

"Moon, I'm trying to make a customer happy ..."

Larissa's eyes flew to the table at the same time she tried to swallow the bite of steak. Immediately, she regretted the action when she felt it go down the wrong way. Raising her napkin to her mouth, she tried to cough the steak up.

"You want to make her happy? Quit talking to her."

"I will ..."

She felt the steak sink lower in her throat. She dropped the napkin and clutched her throat, feeling herself turning red ... She couldn't breathe ...

"Where are you going?" the woman asked.

"To keep your customer from choking to death."

# CHAPTER TWELVE

Moon didn't hesitate to rush toward the woman who was choking. He jerked her out of the seat, and his hands went into position for the Heimlich maneuver. At least she was smart enough not to fight him as he applied quick thrusts between her bellybutton and ribcage.

At the third thrusts, the bite of steak she had taken came out to land on her table.

He released her and stepped around her so he could make sure she was breathing freely. "Are you okay?"

The woman shook her head. "I'm all right." Giving Evie, King, and him embarrassed glances, she sat back down. "Thank you for your help."

Moon tried to return to his chair, but Evie blocked his way.

"Are you sure? Can I get you anything?"

"I'm fine," the woman assured her. "Other than dying of embarrassment."

Evie's serious expression lightened. "Don't be. There isn't anyone in this restaurant who hasn't been embarrassed at one time or another." Evie held out her hand. "I'm Evie, and this is my husband, King."

The woman reached out to take Evie's hand then took the one King had extended.

"I can see why the pork chop was so important to you, if you react like that to steak."

Laughter bubbled from the woman at King's humorous remark. "My mother did warn me to chew each bite twenty times before I swallow. Thankfully, she's not here, so I don't have to hear *I told you so*," she said wryly. "It's nice to meet you both. I'm Larissa."

"It's nice to meet you, too," Evie responded smilingly then turned to Moon. "I forgot to introduce you to Moon. He's a friend of ours."

Moon extended his hand at the introduction.

Larissa stared at it for several seconds before lifting hers to shake his. No sooner had his palm met hers than she was pulling it away.

The unusual way she shook his hand drew his notice. Until then, he really hadn't paid any attention to her, his mind too occupied with trying to find out who had slipped into his room the night he got drunk. It wasn't like there was anything about her that would have diverted his attention. Her brown hair was shoulder-length, her eyes almost the same shade as her hair, and with an average figure, there was nothing about her which would have given him a wow factor.

His interest in her piqued at her unusual behavior, then waned.

"Perhaps we should let her finish her meal before it gets cold," he suggested. "It's nice to meet you." He gave her a nod before he moved around Evie and King to resume his seat at the table. Picking up his knife and fork, he went back to eating his food, his mind once again on who had slipped into his room.

He hadn't taken Echo's word that Ember didn't wear underwear and had gone to her room to check out her drawers. She didn't own one pair of underwear he could find.

"That was rude," Evie said as she and King sat back down.

"I saved her life, didn't I? You expect us to become BFFs now?"

Evie gave him a killing glare. "Lower your voice. Why are you being such an ass?"

Moon sighed then set his fork and knife on the plate. "I didn't mean to be. I just have something on my mind that's driving me nuts."

Evie raised her brows at him. "Anything I can help with?"

"Nope, I'll figure it out."

"Let me know. I might not live at the club anymore, but I still count you as a friend."

"Same." Moon smiled at Evie, ignoring King's watchful gaze.

His lips quirked up in a smile. Regardless of how long King and Evie had been married, he never let her eat alone with him when he stopped by to catch up with her.

Putting his plaguing thoughts behind him, he relaxed to enjoy their lunch.

They were still chatting when the woman who had been choking rose from the table. Her wince caught his attention, and when she would have passed by their table, Moon stood up to block her.

"Did I hurt you when I did the Heimlich?"

"I'm just a little sore. I'm sure it will go away."

Moon frowned when Larissa took a step away so fast she bumped into a chair someone was sitting in.

"Excuse me," she apologized then turned back to him.

"Maybe you should go by the ER and get checked out," he suggested, staring at her.

Why was she acting so jumpy? Her reaction to him made no sense. He might have acted like an ass at the DMV, but he couldn't understand why she had jumped back when he moved close to her. Did she think he was going to examine her?

"I'm good. Thank you. It's only natural I'd be a little sore."

Inexplicitly, Moon felt a spurt of concern for her. "You should be checked by your doctor. I could have hurt you."

"I would know if you damaged anything."

"Not unless you get checked out by a doctor. You may need an X-ray—"

"I don't need an X-ray. I'm breathing fine."

"I'd feel better if you saw a doctor," he insisted. Next time, he would mind his own business. What if she sued? "I'd be willing to pay for you to be checked out by a professional."

Moon knew he had fucked up when the woman's eyes narrowed on him. He had just talked himself into a lawsuit if he had hurt her.

Before he could retract the offer, Larissa set her to-go container down on the table and pressed her fingers to each side of her ribcage. Then she took deep, strong breaths.

"There you go. All done." She picked up her container again. "I'm good to go. Nothing is harmed. I'll probably have some bruising, but nothing that will keep me from performing my normal activities."

Moon gaped at her then started to get angry. Was she making fun of his concern for her?

"Now you have your medical opinion, free of charge. May I please get past you?"

Moon sat back down, his hands itching to turn her over his lap to administer a spanking he reserved only for women who had had been intimately involved with him and who had the wherewithal to know they had pushed him to give them the punishment.

Thankfully, the woman moved away while he was still debating whether it would be worth it to be arrested for assault.

Evie's soft laughter drew his gaze.

"What are you laughing at?"

"You." Evie used a napkin to wipe the corner of her eyes. "You're dying to spank her, aren't you?" She nodded to his hands on the table, where his fingers were rubbing the underside of his palms. "That's always a dead giveaway."

Flattening his hands on the table, he glanced toward King, who he could see wasn't appreciating the turn in conversation. "You can quit giving me the death glare. I've never spanked Evie. Give your wife some credit. Evie is smart enough not to bring it up if I had."

King's clenched jaw loosened when Moon saw her hand move under the table to rest on King's thigh.

"I was only an observer when Moon handed his punishments out, never a recipient," she told her husband. "My question is: what got you upset?"

"She was mocking me," he ground out.

"Ah ... and you didn't like that."

"I was concerned for her."

Evie tilted her head curiously. "Why?"

"People are getting sued for everything; if she had gone to the doctor, it would be documented that I didn't hurt her. She could say some crazy shit, like that I attacked her for no reason."

"I see." Evie shrugged. "You have nothing to worry about if she does." Evie's free hand came up to gesture toward the cameras on the wall. "What you did was caught on tape, from two different angles."

"I still don't appreciate her mocking me."

Evie laughed. "That's the part I don't get. Usually, you just blow off someone showing you attitude."

Moon sighed. "You're right." Raking a hand through his hair, he told himself to get a grip. "I've been uptight lately. Once I'm confronted with a problem, only solving it will take that weight off my mind."

King's lips curved into smile. "Maybe, or maybe not. From the way you're acting, your problem involves a woman. Solving the problem could entail more than you bargained for. I didn't bargain on falling for Evie."

"Aw …" Evie leaned over to kiss King.

Moon rolled his eyes at the PDA.

"I need to head out." He took out his wallet despite Evie shaking her head. "It's my turn to pay. You haven't let me pay the last three times I've come to eat." Hell, the only times they had let him pay was when he managed to catch them gone from the restaurant.

"We don't want your money." King pushed the money back to him.

The way he said it made him glance at Evie.

"You told him."

"King's my husband; he deserves to know."

"I would have never told him."

"I still owe you."

"You don't owe me jack shit. I've told you—"

"It doesn't matter what you told me; you won't let me give the money back to you. At least let me pay you back with a meal every now and then. Okay?"

Moon pressed his lips together. "Give Valorie the money as a tip, then."

Evie didn't argue.

Telling them goodbye, he strode out of the restaurant. The downcast day didn't lighten his dark mood.

On his bike, he drove to the convenience store around the

block. He parked and went inside, returning in less than three minutes to sit on his bike and open a pack of cigarettes, something he had quit six months ago. He tore the package open, pulled out a cigarette, and flicked the new lighter he had purchased. Drawing the poison into his lungs, he let loose a vicious curse, startling a man walking into the store.

When he waved that he was good, the man continued inside.

"You've got to get your shit together," he muttered to himself. Moon knew what was bugging the piss out of him was the only alternative to the women who lived in the club —those who had been there the night he got drunk were the wives. Had one of the brothers' wives been the one he fucked? How was he going to find out if he had?

After smoking the cigarette to the nub, he stomped the butt out.

*That's going to be me if I did.*

## CHAPTER THIRTEEN

Moon stuck his head inside Nickel's open bedroom door. "Hey, you got a minute?"

Nickel pulled his gaming headset off. "Yeah. What's up?"

He moved further in and closed the door behind him. "I checked the logs; do you remember guarding the door the night I walked home?"

Nickel grimaced. "How could I forget? I damn near shot your ass—appearing out of the dark like that. Why?"

Moon nodded to the headset. "You have anyone listening?"

Nickel turned the computer game off. "No." Rotating more fully toward him in his computer chair, he gave him a curious look.

"I'm in a predicament, and I need your help."

Nickel frowned at him. "How?"

"Will you keep it just between us?"

"No." He turned back to his game.

Moon swung his chair back to face him. "Brah, it doesn't involve club business."

Nickel folded his arms over his chest. "Go ahead, but I'm not making any promises."

"Cool. Just hear me out." Moon raked his hand through his hair. He needed to get the shit cut; it was driving him crazy. "Do you remember who was in the club when I came inside? The only person I remember is Winter, because she was standing outside the bathroom. The rest is a mother-fuckin' blur to me."

"Why does it matter?"

"That's all you're getting unless you promise not to repeat what I tell you."

Nickel shrugged. "I don't need to know that badly." His face turned thoughtful. "Lily, Beth, and Killyama were there." Nickel stopped, as if he were still thinking. "Ginny was there ..."

"Anyone else?" Moon prodded.

"Hmm ... I think that's it, but I remember thinking they were louder than normal. Winter was bugging the piss out of me that night. Had me searching for Aisha's cat a couple of times."

"Anything else?"

"Nope, that's it."

"If you remember anything else, let me know."

"Sure thing." Nickel turned back to his game. "Later."

Moon left Nickel's room, shutting the door after him.

"Fuck, fuck," he muttered. "Fuck, fuck ..."

"Ah ... no, thanks."

Moon spun around to find Nickel behind him.

Nickel looked at him like he had a screw loose. "What are you doing?"

"Nothing, just deciding if I want to eat now or later."

His expression cleared. "I'd eat now. Beth made chicken, gravy, and biscuits. They aren't going to last long."

Walking downstairs with Nickel, Moon saw Lily and Beth serving behind the counter. He took a plate and got in line.

"How you doing tonight, Lily?" Giving Lily a friendly smile, he held his plate out to her.

"I'm doing good." She smiled back at him.

"I'll take a breast or a leg; I'm not particular."

Moon caught her eyes when she handed his plate back with a chicken breast and a leg. Lily's translucent skin blushed as her gaze shied away from his.

Moving along the counter where Beth was standing, he handed her the plate. "Your night going good, too?" he asked conversationally, bestowing another smile on Beth and catching her eyes in the same trap he had Lily's.

Beth wasn't as flustered. Frowning, she gestured to the potatoes and green beans. "Yes, thank you. What would you like?"

"I'll take both."

Beth filled his plate, keeping her eyes turned to his side, where Puck had gotten in line behind him. "What can I get you, Puck?"

Moon moved aside to make himself a salad next to where Beth was dishing out the vegetables.

When neither Beth nor Lily looked in his direction, Moon found a spot at the kitchen table. Pouring salad dressing on his salad, he noticed Viper eyeing him. He had thought the coast was clear with his back to the table and neither Razer nor Shade being around.

Shoveling a forkful of lettuce into his mouth, he ate as usual while his stomach was doing flips.

*You got to play it cooler than this. You want to get your ass killed?*

"Where's everyone at tonight?"

"Jesus and Train are sleeping. They just got back from Ohio. Shade and Razer are on their way to Ohio."

"Hmm …" Moon mumbled around a mouthful of lettuce and onion.

Viper crinkled his nose at him. "You have enough onion shoved in there?"

"Onions are good for you."

"If you say so." Viper continued eating his food as he listened to Rider talk about a new car he had bought.

Moon ate slowly, taking his time.

After Rider finished his meal, Moon expected Viper to leave as well, when his plate was empty. Finally, Viper stood up to leave, taking his plate and coffee cup to the sink. When he came back with a brimming coffee cup, Moon got up to make another plate after putting the first one in the sink. He headed around to the front of the counter and handed the clean plate to Lily.

"Could I get another piece of chicken?"

"Of course." Lily placed a chicken leg and a thigh on his plate. "Here you go."

Beth's hand was already outstretched to take his plate. She filled it, then handed it back.

Going back to the salad, he forced himself to make another huge serving. When he sat back down, he saw Viper eyeing his plate.

"You're hungry tonight, aren't you?"

Moon poured the salad dressing over his salad. "I've been eating out so much lately. I miss having homecooked food. What has you here tonight?"

"Winter has a meeting. She should be here anytime. Aisha is spending the night at Rachel and Cash's, playing with Emma. I'm getting ready to go pick her up."

Moon stabbed a cherry tomato with his fork, pretending as if he didn't care if Viper stayed or left.

Viper checked his watch before finishing his coffee. "I need to leave."

Moon nodded. "Later."

"Brother, I would ask what you're up to, but I have a feeling I don't want to know. I'm going to be back in ten minutes, and your ass better be upstairs. Got me?" Viper's menacing voice got his meaning across loud and clear.

"Got you," Moon replied, stabbing another tomato.

Viper rose to put his cup in the sink before leaving out the back door.

He glanced at the counter, seeing what he had been waiting for—Lily and Beth were both making their plates. Turning his head back to his plate so they wouldn't notice him looking, he pretended disinterest when they took chairs at the table. He made sure to continue eating to get them to lower their guard. He had felt their tension when they first sat down.

He had hoped when he got in line and caught their eyes, one of the women would reveal something that would remind him of the woman he had fucked in the dark. The calculated risk had backfired—both women had been staring at him distrustfully.

"Not many here tonight." He started to try to ease their guard.

"Most of them went to a movie. We're going to put the leftovers in the oven. Nickel and Puck offered to clean up for us once their game is over," Beth told him.

Moon looked at his watch. Viper would be back in five minutes.

He placed his fork on his plate. "I haven't seen much of you girls since the fight at Mick's. How's Crazy Bitch's nose?"

Beth and Lily shared a secretive glance.

"Much better," Beth said, buttering her biscuit.

"You girls seemed to be having a good time when I came home."

The sisters shared another glance. This time, Moon caught a glint of fear in their eyes.

"Yes, we did." Beth laid her butter knife down. "You seemed to have a good time while you were out, too."

Moon shrugged. "Just so-so. I noticed one of the barstools is fucked up. It's off kilter. Another one is missing."

Looking at Lily, Moon saw she was playing with her food, and Beth wasn't making any headway with hers, either.

"That's not surprising; they're pretty old. I'll mention it to Viper tonight. We wouldn't want any of the men falling on their asses, would we?"

Moon stiffened as Winter walked into the room. How long had she been listening behind the door?

"No, we wouldn't," Moon agreed, picking his fork back up.

"Any food left?" Winter asked, moving behind the counter to get a plate.

"Plenty." Lily started to rise from the table. "Can I get you something?"

Moon pinned her in place. "Finish eating. Winter is capable of making herself a plate."

Lily gave him a defiant look. "I'm finished. I need to get home so Ember can come and eat."

She carried her plate to the sink after she emptied her plate in the trash, then took off out the back door.

Winter set her plate down with a hard thud before getting herself a glass of ice water. "Proud of yourself?" she asked as she took the chair Lily had vacated.

"I don't know what you mean."

"Bullshit, you don't." Winter gave him a stern glance, as if he were one of her misbehaving students. "Viper knows we had a party that night, so if you think of trying to blackmail us—"

Moon started laughing. "You've been watching too many movies. Blackmail was the furthest thing from my mind."

The women looked at him disbelievingly.

Moon dropped his fork to the plate. "Damn. Thanks. Show me what you really think of me."

Winter wasn't fazed. "Then why all the interest about that night?"

He needed to tread carefully. Wanting to find out who had snuck into his room was his priority, but he didn't want to out the wife either, indirectly saving his own life if he had fucked one of the brothers' wives.

"Killyama came barging in the other day after the hours outsiders are allowed. Jade, Stori, and I were having—shall I say a good time? She killed the moment. The point I'm getting at, you wives aren't allowed upstairs afterhours without your husbands. Did one of you come upstairs?"

Moon felt the hair on his arms stand up at the nervous tension hitting the room.

Winter took a bite, looking at her food. She was no longer meeting his eyes. "What makes you think that?"

"Killyama came upstairs, didn't she?"

Winter's gaze flew back to his. "Of course not."

"I don't believe you." Moon narrowed his gaze on Winter. "One of you came upstairs."

"Fine. You're right. I went upstairs. *Whoopee*. Give Moon a star. I went upstairs to use the restroom. You can run and tattle to Viper if you want."

Moon stared at Winter searchingly. Taking his mind back to that night, he thought about the fact that she did have the right length of hair. Without being obvious, he tried to gauge Winter's size. He thought the woman he had been with might have been her size, but Beth wasn't far off from her weight, either. Lily was the slenderer of all the wives.

Winter started talking to Beth, asking her about her day.

Moon decided he had pressed his luck enough for the day. He carried the dirty dishes to the sink.

Going out the back door, he took a seat on the picnic table to light a cigarette. While smoking, he replayed the conversation with Winter. He had heard the ring of truth in her voice about going upstairs. That part, Moon believed. Had she decided to take a detour on the way back downstairs? He couldn't tell from her reaction. One thing he knew for damn sure was she was hiding something, and he was going to find out what the fuck it was.

# CHAPTER FOURTEEN

Moon was still sitting outside when Winter and Beth walked out.

Winter stopped when the concrete path curved to lead to Beth's house. "Good night, Beth."

"Night, Winter."

Watching through the smoking haze as Beth hesitated leaving Winter, Moon took out another cigarette. "Night, Beth."

Beth gave him a sharp nod, leaving Winter to walk toward her house.

"When did you start smoking again?"

"Tonight."

"Why?"

"I felt the need," he said meaningfully.

Winter frowned. "Is that supposed to have some kind of hidden meaning? Because you left me in the dark."

"Like you left me?"

"Moon, I have no clue what you're talking about."

He gave an internal sigh. Whoever had slipped into his bedroom wasn't Winter.

"I see that." Moon pierced her with his eyes. "But you're not being truthful. You weren't the only woman who came upstairs that night. Who else was there?"

"What's the big deal? Why does it matter so much?"

A footfall on the path had their heads turning to the side as Ember came walking down the path from Lily's house.

"It's a little chilly to be standing out here this late at night," Ember said when she was within hearing distance.

"I'm about to go home," Winter told her. "Moon and I were just chatting."

Ember wrapped her arms around his, blatantly pressing it against her breasts. "I put the order form on your bed, Moon. The girls are so excited for their extra presents."

"I'm glad they're all happy."

"You want me to make you a plate?" she offered. "It's the least I could do."

Moon pulled his arm away from Ember. "I've already eaten."

Pouting at Moon, she left to go into the kitchen.

"What made you so generous all of a sudden?"

Moon shrugged. "I can be generous when I want to."

Winter raised dubious eyebrows. "You're the least generous person in the club. You gave a whopping ten dollars to the toy fund for Christmas."

"Lily caught me before payday."

"Okay, I've had a long day, and I'm tired …"

Did Winter really think she would be able to distract him then slip away?

"You never did answer my question. Who else went upstairs?"

Her expression turned stubborn. "No one that I know of. You're really being obnoxious, and that's saying a lot for you."

Flipping his cigarette toward the firepit, he told her, "Whoever went upstairs left a memento behind."

A frown furrowed her brow. "What kind of memento?"

"A size-eight pair of panties."

Winter started laughing. "Do you know how many times I've gone into that bathroom to find panties in there?" She rolled her eyes at him. "I'd take it up with the women who live up there to quit leaving their underwear lying around."

Moon cocked his head to the side. "She didn't leave them in the bathroom. They were left in my room."

Moon could tell Winter was floored by the information. It wasn't often he had seen her speechless. The silence didn't last long.

"Your bedroom has a revolving door—"

"Actually, it doesn't. Haven't been in a mood for company the last couple of months, and before you can come up with another excuse, she was wearing them when she came into my room. I was the one who took them off her."

"I don't understand, then. Why are you pressuring me about who went upstairs?"

"I was lit, and the room was dark. She pulled a Cinderella act and disappeared before I could turn the light on. So, do you still want to stick with the story that you were the only woman who went upstairs?"

"No, I don't think I do."

"Then who was she?"

"I have no idea."

Moon's expression turned frigid. "You're lying."

One second, he was standing there. The next, he was flying through the air, hitting the side of the gazebo.

Managing to catch himself before falling to the ground, Moon spun around to see which motherfucker had tossed him through the air.

"Are you calling my wife a liar?"

Moon didn't shy away from Viper's gaze. "Either she's

lying, or I have something that belongs to her. Which is it, Winter?"

Bracing himself to be tossed off the side of the mountain, he raised his hands, preparing to defend himself.

Winter caught the back of her husband's shirt. "Stop it, Viper!"

"Brother, you better explain yourself!"

"I'll leave it to Winter to explain. Maybe she'll tell you the truth, because she isn't telling me jack shit."

Viper grabbed him by the arm when he would have walked into the house. "I expect you to be in the office first thing in the morning," he snapped.

"I'll be there."

Jerking his arm out of Viper's grip, he slammed into the house to see Ember running back to the counter.

"You get an eyeful?"

"Sorry, I couldn't help it when I heard you and Viper arguing outside."

"Next time, mind your own business."

Storming out of the kitchen, he took the steps two at a time. He hit his bedroom and shut the door with his foot. Staring around the room, he wanted to tear it apart. Instead, Moon sat down on the side of the bed and buried his head in his hands.

The room felt like a cage to him. He wanted his own damn home. Something with a big backyard so he could throw a ball to his kid. He'd had his backyard designed since he was twenty-five years old.

Raising his head to look around the small room, he felt it closing in around him tighter each day.

He was losing it, and Moon knew he was losing it. Why else would he have goaded Winter to answer his question, other than he was losing his fucking mind? He couldn't understand why it mattered so fucking much to him who had slipped into his room. Maybe one of the club women had come up with the idea, thinking it was a game to spice the sex up. They had been successful, if so.

The woman had taken over his thoughts so much he had lost his fucking mind enough to insult the club's president. He'll be lucky if Viper didn't give him his marching orders.

Rising from the bed, he threw off his clothes, deciding to go to sleep. Turning the light off, Moon grabbed a pillow as he rolled onto his stomach. He thought he wouldn't be able to sleep, but the early morning sun woke him when he rolled over.

Yawning, he stretched out, looking toward the clock on his nightstand. Damn, it was only five a.m. It would be several hours before Viper would be at the office at the factory. No one else would be awake, either. And he didn't feel like working out so early in the morning.

After showering and dressing, he went downstairs to make himself a cup of coffee. Echo and Jade were already looking at the coffee machine, blurry-eyed, as if something was wrong.

"You forget how to make coffee?" he joked, moving to where they stood.

"We're out of coffee," Jade said, as if he could make coffee materialize.

"Sorry, I don't keep a spare bag on me."

Neither woman appreciated his humor.

"Could you run to the convenience store in town for us?"

"I can."

Jade smiled at him. "Thanks. We were dreading going out."

"I'll be right back."

Moon left the women working on getting breakfast started. Going to the front closet, he grabbed his thicker jacket and took out the stocking hat he kept in the pocket.

He grimaced as the freezing air hit him when he opened the door to Domino, who moved aside to let him exit.

"You're going out early."

Moon closed the door. "It's cold as a witch's tit out here," he observed, drawing his gloves on.

"Not too bad today. Yesterday was worse. Where are you heading so early?"

"Puck must have forgotten coffee when he went to the grocery store yesterday," Moon told the new prospect.

"I'm out of cigarettes; you mind picking me up a pack?"

Moon reached into his pocket and handed him the smokes. "I'll grab me another pack. Text me if you want anything else."

The icy steps were no joke as he went down. And if he hadn't been awake when he straddled his motorcycle seat, he was when he sat down.

"Motherfucker," he hissed. "I need to get another life. I'm getting too old to freeze my balls off."

At least the roads were in good shape, and he made it to the gas station without a problem. Parking at the gas pumps, he fueled his bike before heading inside the convenience store.

Finding the coffee on the shelf, he decided to grab a ready-made cup as the tantalizing aroma filled the store.

He grabbed a lid after making a to-go cup, then went to the front of the store. There was a woman already in line, checking out. Recognizing who it was, he almost decided not to get in line behind her.

*Fuck me*, he inwardly groaned at seeing the woman from the day before.

"Your advice came in handy last night. I had dinner ready for Mandy after she got off work and did the dishes without her having to ask," the cashier was telling the woman. "She didn't cry once before going to bed."

"That's good to hear. Being a first-time mother is over-whelming. She needs all the help you can give her. Parent-hood is a partnership. It's not fair to put all the responsibility on her."

"Yes, ma'am. I'm going to do better. I don't mind telling you it shook me up seeing her crying like that."

"Pretty flowers and a night out would do wonders, too," the woman suggested.

"I'll do that," Joel told her.

Jesus, breakfast would be over before he could get back to the club with their jibber-jabbering.

"You mind giving Joel marital advice after I check out?"

The woman turned her head, a strange expression crossing her face when she recognized him. "Excuse me. I didn't realize someone was behind me. I'll get out of your way." She picked up a plastic bag and a cup of coffee then maneuvered away on her crutches, out of the way. "I better be going, Joel. I'll talk to you tomorrow."

"Have a fantastic day, Larissa!" Joel called after her.

Balefully, Moon stared at the cashier.

Turning red, Joel started ringing up his purchases. "Any-thing else?"

After adding two packs of cigarettes, Moon paid after Joel gave him the total. Taking his items, he started to leave, but then Moon raised an eyebrow to the cashier. "You aren't going to tell me to have a fantastic day?" he mocked.

Joel turned a brighter shade of red. "Sure... have—"

Shaking his head at the embarrassed man, Moon walked to the door. He would kiss Joel's ass if the fucker had actually cooked and did the dishes for his wife.

Mandy worked at the factory and had just come back from maternity leave a couple of days before. He had heard her talking during their lunchbreak, complaining about Joel.

Moon didn't need to be a psychic to see a divorce in Joel's near future.

Coming out of the door, he raised his cup to his lips to combat the cold, which was about to attack him.

"Watch where—"

Startled at the female voice directly in front of him, Moon started to lower his cup at the same time his body came into contact with the woman who had just left.

"What the fuck?"

The force of their bodies coming into contact had his coffee tilting toward her before he could stop. In a split-second, he had to decide to keep the coffee from spilling or saving her from falling on the crutches. If he let her fall, she would trip over the step and hit her head on the corner post right behind her. He had just tasted the lukewarm coffee; she was better off getting wet.

Moon let the coffee cup complete its trajectory when they bumped together, then grabbed her by her forearms to steady her.

Gaping up at him through a sodden clump of damp hair, she jerked her crutch back under her arms. "Dude! What's your problem with me?" she snarled at him. "Either you're trying to take me out, or you're the world's biggest klutz. Which one is it?"

# CHAPTER FIFTEEN

"Y ou're blaming me?"

Larissa gaped at him. "You think this is *my* fault?"

The big jerk's eyes widened, as if he couldn't believe she wasn't accepting responsibility.

"I'm the one who you've almost bowled over twice!"

"How was I supposed to know you were on my ass yesterday? I was going out the door when you came barging in. You're obviously looking down at the ground instead of watching what's ahead."

"I'm the one not watching? You turned around yesterday without looking, and when you came out of the store, you were too busy sucking that coffee cup to care that anyone was coming inside!"

"I was watching where I was going," he argued.

"I was watching where I was going, too," she countered.

"Why were you coming back inside?"

"I was coming back inside because, when I was getting into my car, I found a cell phone on the ground and was bringing it inside." Realizing she must have dropped it when they bumped into each other, she looked down at the ground. "There it is." Larissa pointed to where the cell phone was lying next to the newspaper machine. She could tell from his surprised expression whose phone it was.

"It must have slipped out of my pocket when I went up the step," he admitted with a pained expression.

When there was no thanks forthcoming, Larissa hopped on her good foot to start back toward her car.

God, why on earth had she had sex with that man? The sex voice, which had lured her toward the bed, was missing, for sure. She didn't have to be told he wasn't attracted to her; his treatment of her made it glaringly obvious. She bet, if she looked like one of the women Priscilla had told her about, he would have gone down on his knees to beg her forgiveness.

Opening her car door, she glanced in his directions as he picked the items he had purchased off the ground. Moon's total disregard for her feelings had anger flowing through her veins.

Bracing her hand on the roof of her car, she let her fury fly. "I just moved to Treepoint, and if you're an example of the men who live in this town, I feel sorry for the women. You are so full of yourself, no wonder you can't see where you're going—your *big* head won't look down."

The big jerk gave her a mean stare, which she returned in spades.

"You don't scare me. I've taken on bigger and badder, believe me. You want to know what I found out about them?"

"Not really."

"The bigger the ego, the smaller the dick."

"As you're never going to get near my dick, I guess you'll never know, will you?"

His sarcastic remark didn't faze her. It was everything she could do not to tell him she could tell him what size his dick was, but she wasn't that far gone.

"Thank God!" she yelled at him.

"Amen!" he shouted back at her.

She got in her car before saying something regrettable and drove out of the parking lot, calling Moon a litany of names.

Her being the first one in the office allowed her enough time to cool down before Priscilla arrived. Going to her desk, she pulled up today's calendar. Her first appointment wasn't until eight.

Larissa was about to click onto another screen when she saw the small notation at the top corner. Frowning, she pulled up last month's calendar, hoping she was wrong.

Closing her eyes, she ran her fingers over her forehead.

*You're just late*, she told herself as she pushed her computer chair back from the desk.

Her stomach churned as she went to the treatment room next to her private office. After opening the drawer with the pregnancy tests, she went to the restroom.

With shaking fingers, she opened the pregnancy test. Then, making sure the door was locked, she took it.

Deep down, she didn't need to see the result before the positive sign appeared. She was never late.

Carrying the test and wrapper back into the treatment room, she disposed of it before returning to her office.

She closed the door and laid her head on her desk.

She detested Moon. He would off himself if he found out she was having his baby. He couldn't stand her any more than she could him. Would he even believe it was his child? Probably not, and she didn't want to find out. There was no way she would let that conceited oaf anywhere near her baby.

Pulling a tissue from the box on her desk, she wiped her eyes before taking her purse out. She repaired her makeup, then went to the breakroom to find a snack and grabbed a juice.

Forcing herself to eat despite the food tasting like cardboard, she took the last bite when her appointment arrived.

When she was finishing up, Priscilla walked in.

"Good morning."

Larissa forced a cheerful smile to her lips. "Good morning," she returned her sister's greeting.

"How are you doing, Ginny?"

"Fine, thank you."

"The baby healthy and happy?" Priscilla grinned at the expectant mother.

Ginny gave her a rueful smile. "From the way she's dancing on my bladder, a little too happy."

"You still think you're having a girl?"

"Yes, at least until the baby comes out and proves me wrong," she joked.

Larissa laughed. "I admire your restraint. I wouldn't be able to help myself from asking during the ultrasound."

"All I care about is if she's healthy. Whether it's a boy or girl, I really don't care."

"I'm surprised Gavin didn't come with you today. He hasn't missed any of your appointments so far," Priscilla commented.

"He's out of town, on business," Ginny explained.

"Tell him we missed him, then," Priscilla said as she took off her coat and hat.

"I will. Bye."

"Bye. See you in four weeks."

"You're early," Larissa said once Ginny had left.

"I thought I would get caught up on some paperwork before my appointment arrives."

"I'll be in my office if you need me. I want to check in with Eryn. She missed her appointment yesterday."

Priscilla frowned. "That isn't like her."

"I know. I'm concerned. I called her yesterday when she

missed her appointment, but she didn't answer. I left a voice-mail, and she hasn't called back. Maybe something came up and she hasn't had the time to respond yet? I'll feel better once I've spoken with her."

Priscilla nodded. "Keep me updated."

"I will."

Larissa returned to her office to make the call. Still receiving no answer, she left another voicemail. Then, biting her lip, she went to the front office to wait for her next appointment. Once she finished the appointment, she'd have a two-hour break.

She Googled Eryn's address and saw it was twenty minutes away. Plenty of time to go check on Eryn and be back before she was needed. Should she, though? She had only seen Eryn twice. Could she have changed her mind about using her as a midwife and didn't want to tell her? It wouldn't be the first time a patient had dodged her calls.

She was still indecisive when her next patient arrived. Clearing her mind. she greeted them.

The appointment took an hour, as she needed to go over Mrs. Terrell's medical history and the folder she had put together for her, which gave her all the information to talk through with her husband to help in their decision-making. The next step would be for the couple to decide if they preferred to use Priscilla, her, or give both of them a pass.

Before Mrs. Terrill left, Larissa introduced her to Priscilla. Then, after she'd escorted her to the door, Larissa turned back to her sister.

"She seemed nice."

"I agree."

Priscilla leaned on the side of the front desk. "How'd it go?"

"I couldn't tell." Larissa shrugged. "She seemed interested in both options. I guess we'll know in a few days."

Larissa went back to her office to call Eryn again. Hanging up the phone, she looked up as Priscilla walked in.

"Still haven't heard from Eryn?"

Making up her mind, she went to the closet to take out her coat.

"Where are you going?"

"I'm going to drive to her house and check on her."

Priscilla frowned. "How far away?"

"About twenty minutes. I'll be back before my next appointment."

"I'm not worried about that. I could do the appointment for you. I just don't want you going by yourself. Wait until my appointment is over, and I'll go with you."

"You have two appointments back-to-back; I don't want to wait."

"No, then I'll cancel my appointment and go with you."

"You can't. It's Crazy Bitch. She would have already left her house. In all likelihood, she just doesn't want to use me and didn't want to tell me."

"Was she still having issues with her husband?"

"I don't think so. She told me he had agreed to a divorce and was giving her space to think it over."

"Call the sheriff's office and ask them for a welfare check on her. I really don't feel good about you going."

"Eryn told me Dennis threatened her the last time she called the police on him. I don't want to start an argument if they did decide to get back together. I'll take my phone and call you before I go in. You can hear the whole thing."

Taking her phone out of the desk, Larissa walked from her office to the front just as Crazy Bitch arrived for her appointment.

"Hey, honoree bitches. What's shaking?"

Larissa laughed. "You're in a good mood today."

Crazy Bitch came sashaying into the office as if she felt

like a million bucks. "Why wouldn't I be? I've been keeping my man busy this month. You're going to give me some good news today, aren't you?"

Larissa and Priscilla shared worried glances. The way Crazy Bitch was acting, she was practically warning them that the pregnancy test she was about to take better be positive.

"Yes ... we'll"—Larissa cleared her throat—"hope for the best. You can go into the treatment room, and Priscilla will be right there."

"Where you going?" Crazy Bitch's expression turned turbulent. "Don't you want to be here when I get the news?"

"Of course, I do," Larissa hastened to assure her. "Unfortunately, I need to go check on a patient. Priscilla will call me when she has your results."

"Won't be the same without you here."

Larissa reached out to take Crazy Bitch's hand. "I wouldn't leave if I didn't have to. Priscilla can put me on speaker phone right after you take the test. I'll still be driving. I might not be here in person, but I'll be with you when you find out. Will that work?"

"I guess it'll have to. But if the test is negative, I'm going to wait here until you come back and break your other foot."

"Having you as a patient is such a joy," Larissa told her.

Crazy Bitch narrowed her eyes at her. "You're kissing up to me, aren't you? Because you're making fucking bank off me, aren't you?"

"Totally," Larissa teased her.

"Works for me." Crazy Bitch nodded at her. "Keep it up."

Larissa shook her head at the woman. "Call me when you're ready," she told her sister, heading for the door.

Priscilla held the door open for her. "I wish you would wait."

Larissa wished she would, too, but the sick feeling in the pit of her stomach was prompting her to go.

"I won't be long," she promised, maneuvering her crutches through the doorway.

Thankfully, the weather was on her side, and it was turning out to be a sunny day, brightening her spirits. *Eryn's fine*, she told herself. At least with her going, she'd be able to assure Eryn that there were no hard feelings for her deciding to go the other route with the birth of her baby. Yeah … it was going to be fine with Eryn. Who she really should be worried about was Crazy Bitch. She wasn't exactly one hundred percent positive the wild woman wouldn't break her only good foot.

# CHAPTER SIXTEEN

Viper was talking to one of the workers when Moon came through the door. When he saw Viper gesture toward the office, Moon walked inside to wait.

Hearing the door close, Moon turned seeing Viper eating the distance between them in furious strides.

"Before you say anything, I admit I fuck—"

Moon wasn't able to finish his sentence before Viper grabbed him by the neck and lifted him into the air.

"Don't open your fucking mouth until I ask you to speak. You motherfuckin' hear me?"

"Yes," Moon managed to croak out.

He found himself flung backward against the wall. The filing cabinet shook, sending the files on top sliding toward him. He managed to catch them and balanced them back on top. Then Moon warily watched Viper take a seat behind the desk.

"You better have a damn good explanation about what happened last night." Viper shot him a dangerous glance, which if it had ammunition, he would be dead. "Because, right now, it's taking everything I have not to beat your ass to

Kingdom Come, and that would be if Shade and Razer left me a piece of you. Don't think I didn't see the way you looked at them last night. Do you have a fucking death wish?"

"I know I handled last night badly."

"You think?" he snarled. "What in the fuck got into you? Have you been sniffing glue?"

Moon guessed the question was rhetorical because Viper didn't give him a chance to defend himself.

"It's the only thing I can think that could possibly explain how asinine you acted. Winter told me you seem to be under the mistaken belief"—his voice rose with each grated word out of his mouth—"that my wife snuck into your bedroom the night they got in a fight at Mick's bar."

Moon battled back the embarrassment filling him as Viper repeated what he had said to Winter. Shit, he didn't have to be a rocket scientist, which he clearly wasn't, to know Winter, Lily, and Beth now thought he was a first-class douchebag after last night. He had acted like a fucking asshole toward some chick in town because it was easier to take his frustration out on a stranger than on someone you had to live with.

Coming to a conclusion, he decided he might as well come clean and see if Viper could help solve the riddle of who the woman had been, as he was making zero progress on his own.

"Someone came into my room that night, I fucked her, she left. I have no idea who she was. I didn't fuck air, nor was it a wet dream. I've ruled out all the club women—it wasn't any of them. I asked Winter who had gone upstairs that night, and she told me the only person who went upstairs during the party was her ..." Seeing Viper's expression darken, he hastened to add, "So, going by what she says, I either fucked her or she's lying."

Moon took a hasty step back from the desk when Viper rose from his chair to lunge toward him.

"Call her a liar again, and I'll rip out your tongue." Viper snarled, straightening after the failed attempt to grab him.

"You're president of The Last Riders—be fucking impartial for a fucking minute and hear me out. Wouldn't it bug the piss out of you if the shoe were on the other foot? Take Winter out of the equation and be open-minded. I don't think it was her, but she's protecting someone. I want to know who it is."

Viper's grim demeanor didn't relax. "You're always managing to get involved in some stupid shit! I'm fucking sick of your bullshit nonsense. Wizard is, too. Hell, the whole club is." He sat back down on the chair behind the desk. "You've crossed the line with Winter."

Moon's jaw clenched. "I know … but this shit … it's driving me nuts."

Viper wasn't sympathetic. "Maybe so, but you should have told me and asked me to talk to her. Don't think I don't know why you decided to confront Winter instead of the other women. If she knows, the other women know as well. You want me to play referee to keep yourself alive before you press your luck with them. Brother, you're going down a slippery slope testing those women. Shade will kill your ass if you say the wrong thing to Lily. Razer will, too, but it will be more painful. And we both know you don't want to fuck around and find out with Reaper."

Obstinately, Moon stared at Viper. "I'm not going to let it rest."

"I know you're not … Fuck!" Viper picked up a stapler to throw it at him.

Moon tilted his head to dodge the flying missile.

"You're leaving. There's a truck heading out this afternoon. You, Jesus, and Puck are going to be escorts. You three can stay at the Ohio chapter. I don't need you here anymore. You'll be more useful there, anyway. Seems like most of the thefts are happening there—the missing orders are being logged out of here but coming up short on the other end. Wizard can deal with your bullshit."

Moon was about to argue that he wasn't leaving until he found out who had slipped into his room, but Viper's chilly expression stopped him cold.

"I'll find out who in the hell she was, and maybe I'll let you come back then."

Moon gritted his teeth, sitting down in the chair next to him. "I'll go, but only because I respect you, brother."

"Don't do me any favors."

Viper's sarcasm caused Moon to wince. When Viper wanted to cut you down, he didn't need a blade.

Aware he was skating on thin ice, he moved toward safer ground. "Brother, I realize I'm a pain in the ass." He ran his sweaty palms down his jean-clad thighs. "I swear I don't go looking for this shit to happen to me. I didn't expect Dream to go off the rails and start lying about me, and I damn sure didn't expect for someone to sneak into my room, other than who normally comes in there. Just figure it out for me—fast."

"I'll do the best I can." Viper eyed him challengingly. "I love you, brother. I've put up with you for a long time, but you're coming close to insubordination. It was your decision to step down as president of the Ohio chapter." He sighed. "There comes a time the disadvantages of you being a Last Rider outweigh the advantages." Viper rose from behind the desk to study him, as if debating to rip him apart or throw him out of the club.

"I've seen you fuck six women in a row and not give a flying fuck who they were. Why are you suddenly willing to get thrown out of the club over this one?"

Moon wasn't stupid; he had seen brothers thrown out for

a lot less than he had done when a member caused turmoil within the club. Viper's patience wasn't infinite, and he had gone past where other brothers had ventured.

"I have no fucking clue." Moon fidgeted in his chair. "Whoever she is felt different to me than other women I've been with. She's stuck in my head."

Viper placed his hands on the desk as he leaned back. "Like I said, I'll do what I can to find out who she is. Until then, do you think you can go back to Ohio without starting shit there, or maybe you should take a break from the club? When's the last time you went to see your mom?"

"It's been a few," Moon admitted. "I don't want a break. I'll keep out of everyone's hair."

"I'm taking your word on it, Moon. Next time, I won't give you the option."

Moon reluctantly nodded.

"Make sure you apologize to Winter before—"

The phone on the desk rang, interrupting him. Viper went back around the desk and answered the phone.

"Yes, Knox?"

Moon couldn't hear what the other brother said as Viper listened. He started to rise to give him some privacy but sat back down when Viper motioned him to stay.

"I'll take care of it," Viper said before lowering the phone, disconnecting the call.

"Knox needs someone to do a wellness check on a woman. The woman is pregnant and isn't answering her calls. The person who reported the woman missing called to say her midwife is on her way to check what's going on, but she is worried because of a past history of domestic violence and doesn't want her to go alone. Knox is on his way but wants some backup. His other deputy is working an assault, and he has to leave the other one in town in case of an emergency."

Moon rose. "Text me the address. Did Knox say who called in the report?"

"The midwife's sister. Get started on the way. I'm going to send Nickel, too."

Hurrying out of the office, Moon made his way to his bike.

He started his bike then checked the address Viper sent him.

"Fuck."

He wondered how long of a head start the midwife had on Knox as he pulled out of the parking lot. Depending on where Knox was when they had called in, he could beat him there. Thank fuck he had adopted the habit of always keeping his weapon on him.

He deliberately gauged his speed despite the sense of urgency, which was increasing with each mile. The area of the address was off the main road. He would be surprised if it even had a paved road.

When he had first come to Kentucky, he discovered homes had been built in the dense woods, making it nearly impossible to reach. It still amazed him how the home-owners managed to get in and out unless they were on foot.

Slowing, he looked at the GPS, checking for the turnoff. When he sighted the break in the trees, he held on to the handlebars as he gradually turned into the rutted dirt road.

"Dammit," he swore. If the road got much worse, he would be better off parking the bike and making his way on foot.

He was about to say to hell with it when large pieces of gravel almost sent him flying over his handlebars. Only the sense of urgency kept him going.

Where in the fuck did this chick live?

A small creek ran along the dirt road, which he could see through the dense trees sporadically. As he went over a small

bridge, which seemed barely wide enough to get accommodate a car, he gritted his teeth when he had to return to even
more gravely road. Seeing it was winding up the side of the
mountain before it disappeared from sight, Moon decided
he'd had enough.

He found a clear spot off the road and parked his bike.
Then, taking off, he started sprinting upward. When he
reached the top, he was given a full view of the house he was
trying to reach.

"Holy shit!"

# CHAPTER SEVENTEEN

"**A**re you still there?" Larissa softly asked Crazy Bitch through the speaker phone as she drove.

"I'm here."

"I wish I were there with you."

"You're better off where you are."

Crazy Bitch's rejoinder didn't frighten her.

"Anna-Kate, I wish there were something I could say that could make the disappointment easier. There's no magical way to conceive a baby, except time. You've had all the tests done, and Calder's sperm has been analyzed. What you're going through, thousands of other women have gone through. Cherish this time you and Calder are spending alone. Enjoy it while you can. Once you have a baby ... believe me, there won't be any alone or couple time for years. Make the most of it instead of looking at it as a negative. Follow the diet I gave you, continue taking the vitamins, and for God's sake, quit stressing yourself out. You and Calder should take a week off and fly somewhere with plenty of sun. Have a bunch of randy sex not because you want a baby but to have a mind-blowing orgasm. Take making a baby out of the mix and just have sex for the pleasure of being close to that damn good-looking man you're married to."

Larissa faintly heard a sniffle on the other end of phone.

"You want my man, don't you?"

"It wouldn't do me any good. Calder only has eyes for you."

"It's not his eyes I'm worried about."

"A baby isn't going to keep a man from cheating," Larissa told her. "Nor will it make him stay if he wants to go. Don't borrow trouble where there isn't any. Go on vacation, lotion Calder up with sunscreen, and let nature take its course."

"Fuck it, I will," Crazy Bitch snapped. "But if I'm not knocked up next month, I'm going to beat your ass."

"You couldn't harm a fly," she teased. "Can I talk to Priscilla?"

"I guess. By the way, she called the cops on you."

"What did you just say?" Larissa was listening to the call from her car speaker. Had she heard Crazy Bitch wrong?

Priscilla's voice came on "Are you still there, Larissa?"

"Yes. Did I hear Crazy Bitch right? Did you call the police?"

"I didn't want you going alone," Priscilla said unapologetically. "You know the statistics as well as I do. IPV increases when a woman becomes pregnant. Dusty has a restraining order to stay away from Eryn."

"Eryn told me she was going to drop it. He has a girlfriend in Tennessee. I called him before you; Dusty doesn't want anything to do with her. He said he's moved on and hasn't talked to or seen her."

"Dusty could be saying that to give himself an alibi."

"He could be, but I don't think so. Hang on; I need to concentrate. I'm trying to find her turnoff."

She would have missed the turnoff for Eryn's house if she hadn't memorized the directions before leaving the office. When she had taken Eryn on as a patient, the first step was to go to the home. Using the excuse that her husband worked nights and Dusty slept during the day, the home visit had been delayed. Then, when they had broken up, Eryn had come up with various excuses to put her off. She had been about to give her an ultimatum if she had come yesterday that she wouldn't be able to be her midwife if she didn't schedule the home meeting.

The rutted road had her Jeep bouncing as she followed the directions. Then she held her breath when she went over the small bridge, which seemed ready to collapse under the weight of the Jeep.

"Wow," Larissa breathed out a sigh of relief.

"What's going on?" Priscilla voice came from the speaker anxiously.

"Nothing," Larissa reassured her. "It's a good thing I did come out. There's no way I can be her midwife unless she comes to the hospital. An ambulance wouldn't be able to get to her if there's an emergency."

"Why didn't Eryn say something?"

"I have no idea, but I'm pretty sure that's why she put me off on the home visit."

Driving forward, she climbed the nob of the mountain, then went down the slope on the other side. The house she was searching for had finally become visible. Eryn's home sat on top of another rise, with several vehicles sitting to the side of home.

"I see several cars outside." Larissa held the steering wheel for dear life as she went down the steep hill. "It looks like she has company, which is probably why she missed the appointment and didn't answer my calls."

As she drove closer to the home, Larissa debated turning around, but the trees were too thick and the rise to Eryn's house was so rocky there was no way she would make it to the top if she weren't driving her Jeep.

She parked next to a jacked-up black truck and released the death grip she had on the steering wheel. "I'm here. And since I'm here, I might as well check in with her. I'll call you back when I get back in the car."

"Are you sure it's safe?"

"There are at least six trucks here, and three men and a woman are sitting on the porch. I'm good. I would turn around if there weren't so many blocking the way. I'll have to ask a couple of them to move. There's no way I'm going to back down this hillside."

"That bad?"

"I don't understand why they made it so steep. I thought I was going to get a nosebleed for a second. All righty, I need to hang up to get out and go talk to Eryn."

"Make sure you take your phone," Priscilla insisted.

"I will. You can call the sheriff back and tell him everything is okay." Larissa detached the cell phone from the holder as she got out. Juggling it, she started to pull her crutches toward her. "Wait—I see the sheriff coming up the hill. He's not going to be happy you dragged him out—"

She leaned her head back into the car when she heard her cell start to lose the connection. Then Larissa unconsciously gave a startled scream. A burning pain on her shoulder had her releasing the cell phone as she dropped to her knees to hide behind the door.

"What are you doing shooting at me!" Larissa yelled out. "I'm Eryn's midwife!" She placed a hand on her shoulder at the stinging pain and felt blood seeping through her fingers.

"What are you doing here?" a loud male voice yelled back.

"Eryn missed her appointment yesterday. I wanted to check on her!" Larissa yelled without raising her head.

"If that's true, why are the police with you?"

"For the same reason—because Eryn was missing."

"She ain't missing. She's right here. You all are the feds, wanting to see what's in the house!"

"I don't care what's in the house. I was worried about Eryn!"

"You better get your ass out of here!"

Another shot rang out, hitting the door she was hiding behind.

"I was going to!" she screamed at them wildly. "I wanted you to move the trucks so I could turn around!"

When she heard several shots being fired, Larissa hunched herself into a ball. She barely lifting her head but saw the sheriff's vehicle slowly coming to where she was parked. Gaping, she watched as the sheriff maneuvered himself across the front seat to the passenger's side to fling the door open. Throwing himself to the ground, Knox then aimed his pistol toward the house.

"You can't shoot. There's a pregnant woman inside!" Larissa yelled at him.

Knox didn't take his eyes off the house.

"She worth dying over?" he snarled loudly.

Larissa pressed her hand to her belly. Eryn wasn't the only one pregnant. She had a duty to her own child to survive. Knox was a husband and a father; he deserved to go home to his family, too.

"Eryn, make them stop!" Larissa screamed at the top of her lungs.

"Stop it, Tanner!" a woman yelled. "If you had taken her to the hospital when I told you, none of this would have happened!"

"I'm not going back to jail because of that bitch!"

Larissa and Knox stared at each other as the man and woman yelled back and forth.

"Tanner, what are we going to do?" another male voice whined.

"All of you, shut the fuck up!" a man yelled over them, who Larissa assumed was Tanner.

"Woman, can't you count? There's only two of them, and there's eight of us. We'll take care of them, then clean the house out. Jay—"

Larissa felt her heart drop when she could no longer hear what he was saying. From the flurry of movement on the porch, she reasoned they had been sent out to surround them.

Frightened, she gave a whimper. Not wanting to appear like a wimp, she pressed her knuckles against her mouth.

When she raised her eyes, she saw Knox's deadpan face looking at her.

"How in the hell did you manage to stumble into a drug house in Bumfuck, Egypt?"

She lowered her hand long enough to mutter, "Luck, I guess."

Knox didn't seem to appreciate her humor.

"What are we going to do?"

The sheriff pressed a button on his shoulder pad before he turned his eyes back to her. His face turned grimmer as Knox started giving her the stark facts.

"The way they graded this hillside, and the house looking down on the road, right about now, I'd start praying for a miracle."

Larissa swallowed hard. She'd never been so scared in her life.

"Isn't there something you can do? Like call SWAT?"

"You've been watching too many movies. I get enough funding to hire three deputies, bullets, and an occasional uniform. The nearest SWAT team is thirty minutes away. Besides, I have a better idea."

Hearing a shuffle of footsteps, Larissa pressed her hand to her mouth, terrified.

"On the count of three, I want you to shuffle over here, next to me."

Nodding, she prepared herself.

"One … two … three."

Larissa shuffled over the rocky ground to Knox's Bronco, holding her screams back when a barrage of bullets hit their vehicles.

"Fuck," Knox hissed, hunkering back down.

"What?" she gasped.

"They took out my motor. They knew what I was going to do."

Larissa looked at him blankly. "What were you going to do?"

Knox looked at her like she had marbles for brain neurons. "Get the hell out of here and let others deal with this shitshow when they get here."

As his Bronco was blocking her Jeep, their only option left was to try to make it to the trees. On foot, she would become a liability.

"You should go; get to the woods. You don't happen to have another gun in your car, do you? I could cover you."

Knox's eyebrows rose. "You expect me to leave you here to face them alone?"

"There's no sense in both of us dying," she replied practically, even though she was terrified.

"Do you know how to fire a gun?"

"I do." She nodded. "My dad taught all three of his daughters how to shoot a gun. Do you have another?"

"In the back of the Bronco."

"I can climb inside—"

Knox was already shaking his head. "Look at the seats in

136

the front—they're torn to ribbons. You wouldn't make it to the back seat."

"I could try."

Knox suddenly raised his gun to fire next to her.

Shaking, Larissa turned her head to find a man lying on the ground next the Bronco's bumper.

"I told you, you wouldn't have made it."

"I see that," she whispered hoarsely.

The dead man's blank stare was directly in front of her.

Hopelessness filled her. How many times had her sisters warned her that she reacted without thinking? Hadn't having sex with Moon a big enough wakeup call? No, she came running out here, placing herself and the baby in danger. All she'd had to do was call the sheriff and let him handle it. Instead, she was going to die.

Knox looked at her curiously when she started to bow her head. "What are you doing?"

"Taking your suggestion—I'm going to pray." Larissa pressed her hand over the tiny child she was carrying. "Psalm 18:2. 'The Lord is my rock and my fortress and my deliverer, my God, my rock, in Whom I take refuge, my shield, and the horn of my salvation, my stronghold."

When she raised her head, she saw Knox studying the group of trees behind them.

Sure the men from the house were there and were about to release a spray of bullets, she placed a hand on his forearm. "Would you like me to say a prayer for you?"

"No need. The answer to my prayers just arrived."

# CHAPTER EIGHTEEN

"Holy shit!"

Taking one glance at what was going on, Moon hunkered down as he ran toward the thick trees. Hopefully, the people who had Knox and the midwife pinned down hadn't noticed him on the crest of the hill.

He took out his gun, cocked it as he made his way in the direction of Knox's vehicle, then called Viper.

"How bad is it?"

"You already know?" Moon asked, making sure to keep his voice whisper soft.

"Knox pushed the panic button." Then Viper asked, "Which level?"

"Red. Seven. Knox is next to his vehicle with the midwife. SUVs a foot before crest. Split right, left." With that, Moon disconnected the call and silenced his phone.

Stealthily making his way forward, he heard the sound of gunfire. He maintained his focus and kept a steady pace as he moved through the trees, carefully trying to step over limbs and looking for trip wire. With the firepower being leveled at Knox, he wouldn't be surprised if they had them.

The break of gunfire felt deafening in the woods.

Looking around the tree he was hiding behind, he saw Knox and the woman behind the door of the Bronco.

Moon pulled his head back. How was he not surprised that woman had managed to be there? She was clearly becoming the bane of his existence.

Looking around, he found two men cautiously maneuvering themselves closer to Knox through the trees. Seeing one already dead by the bumper, Moon's eyes went to the other left side of the road. There were two in the woods and another making his way across the opposite side of the Bronco.

Slightly moving where Knox could see him while the two closest to him couldn't, he signaled him with a sweeping hand movement, pointing toward him then two pointing to the right then himself.

Waiting for Knox's nod, Moon raised three fingers, dropping them one by one. At the end, he pointed his gun at the two closest to him, taking them out before they could shoot a single bullet.

He quickly glanced back at Knox. He was lying on the ground then rose up after shooting the man on the other side.

Taking out his cell phone, he saw the brothers were close.

He put his cell phone away again, then unzipped a pocket on the sleeve of his jacket and pulled out a red bandana to tie it around his skull.

The bandana might be easily seen by their opponent, but it was worth taking the chance. Anything without a bandana would be neutralized without a second hesitation.

Knox signaled Moon to hold, and Moon repeated the signal to Reaper and Viper, who were now on the other side of the road. Rider, Train, and Cash were already spreading around the area he was in.

"You still there, Tanner?" Knox yelled out.

There was no reply.

"Tanner's woman, can you hear me?"

"I'm not his woman!" the woman shouted from inside the house.

"Is Tanner the one who calls the shots?"

"He was. He's the one you killed."

"Who's next in line?"

"Benie," the woman answered.

"What's your name?" Knox asked.

"Cielle."

"Benie, can you hear me?" Knox shouted out.

Benie remained silent.

"Either Benie's dead or he's not answering; which is it, Cielle?"

When Cielle didn't reply, Moon assumed the fucker was still alive. Knox did, too.

"Benie, you're surrounded. There are only two ways this is going to end. Either you can come out with your hands up, or you're going to die along with the rest of the men with you."

"Go fuck yourself!"

A shout was then heard from inside the house.

"You try to come in here, you'll set this whole mountain on fire. I bet you don't want to be responsible for killing two women, and one of them pregnant, either!"

Knox gave a harsh bark of laughter. "You bet wrong, motherfucker. They're nothing but collateral damage to me. Their deaths are going to be on your conscience, not mine. You think I'm going to lose sleep over some pissants polluting my town? Fuck no! The only reason I'm giving you a fucking chance to save yourself is because I left the camera on in my vehicle. If I hadn't, you'd already be dead. In case you haven't noticed, I'm not alone anymore, you stupid fucker, so come out, or the next thing you're going to feel is your body being blasted to hell."

Did he just see the midwife give Knox a reproachful glare? If he were Knox, he would have …

Moon took a steadying breath. Why did that woman get under his skin so fucking badly?

"We're coming out!" Benie yelled out. "Rob, Miller, come out!"

Moon and the brothers stayed in hiding until all the men came out, and one of the women.

"Is that all of you?" Knox roared.

"Yeah!"

"Where's the other woman?"

"She's in the bedroom. Eryn's in too bad of a shape to come out," Cielle spoke up. "You might need to call an ambulance now that she doesn't have to protect that son of a bitch." The woman disdainfully glared at the body lying beside Knox's Bronco.

Out of the corner of his eyes, Moon saw Larissa use the Bronco door to lift herself to her feet. She then hobbled over to the other vehicle and pulled out a crutch.

He was amazed as she navigated herself around the men and rocks to reach the porch. Then, seeing what she was about to do, Moon rushed toward her, managing to block her path before she went in the door.

"You can't go in there until it's checked out."

Determined, she didn't back away. "I'm going inside to check on Eryn. Get out of my way."

"Give me a couple of minutes." He tried to get her to think rationally instead of with her heart.

"I don't know what condition she's in; a couple of minutes might be all she has, so move!"

Moon didn't bother arguing with her.

"Rider!" he called out.

Rider stepped forward to lift her away from the door. When she would have tried to rush forward, Rider blocked her.

"Stay here until Moon comes back."

Moon didn't wait to hear Larissa's answer. Going room to room, he checked the large, two-story house out.

When he heard footsteps, he came out of a back room on the first floor to find Reaper and Viper conducting their own search. He had already retied his bandana around his mouth. The stench of rotting food had him ready to lose his breakfast. From their expressions, the smell was just as offensive to them.

"I'm surprised they didn't give themselves up rather than stay here."

"Goddamn," Viper swore as he tied the bandana around the lower part of his face. "I won't be able to eat for a year after seeing that kitchen. Why in the hell would they live in this filth?"

Moon's and Reaper's eyes met.

"To distract us from other smells," Reaper answered.

All three moved upstairs in unison. As they reached the top of the stairway, Moon turned left while Reaper moved right. Viper remained in the middle, ready to back up who needed him first.

When he slowly opened a door, an unmistakable scent hit him. His first instinct was to open a window. Instead, he went to where they were cooking their meth, making sure everything was turned off.

"Fucking hell," he swore out loud, carefully turning the nozzle to turn the gas off where they had jerry-rigged it to the stove. Then, striding toward the window, he opened it before moving to another in the room, where he stuck his head out to breathe in fresh air.

Pulling his head back in, Moon started to leave the room

to check the next when he stopped. Had he heard a faint sound? He stayed still but didn't hear anything and was about to move again when he heard the faint rustling sound again.

Frowning, he looked around the room. There wasn't a closet door where anyone could be hiding. The floorboards? Not finding anything amiss on the floor, Moon looked up and noticed the attic door.

Leaving the room, he started walking toward Viper and saw Reaper carrying an unconscious woman down the steps. Glad the pregnant woman was out of the filthy house, he put her out of his mind.

"Perp hiding in the attic." Moon nodded his head toward the room he had just left. "It's going to be risky as fuck to get them out."

Viper nodded. "I'll do it."

"I'll do it. I'm going to need something to stand on."

"Check the other bedroom. Maybe there's something there you can use," Viper suggested.

Both men turned as Reaper came back up the steps. Then Moon and Reaper split up again to continue searching the house.

Wanting to close the door as soon as he opened it, it took all his willpower not to go outside and shoot the other men.

Moon gave two whistles before he went farther into the room.

There were a crib and a playpen in the filthy room. He walked up to the crib to see a baby about a year old lying in a curled-up position. Slowly, he put out his hand to touch a soft cheek. At his touch, the baby opened her eyes.

Hearing footsteps behind him, Moon gently lifted the baby into his arms and handed her to Train.

He saw Rider lift a small boy from the playpen and continued searching the room. There were several boxes stacked against a wall.

Moon waited until Train and Rider had left with the children before kicking the boxes until the stack tumbled down. Opening a box released a wave of odor that caused him to gag.

He moved away from the boxes and managed to search the small closet before leaving the room. Outside the door, Moon doubled over, breathing in gulps of air, trying not to vomit.

"You okay?" Reaper came to his side.

Moon gave a shaky nod. "Don't go in there. The sons of bitches were too sorry to throw the dirty diapers away."

"Probably didn't want anyone to know there were any kids in the house," Viper said grimly. "Were you able to find anything to stand on to reach the attic door?"

"The crib is on wheels. We can roll it into the other room, and I can stand on it. Are the other rooms clear?" Moon asked.

"Yes," Reaper told them.

"Let's get it done." Viper gave him a pat on the back as he and Reaper passed him to go into the baby room.

Moon remained stationed in the hall as they wheeled the crib out.

"They had the window nailed shut." Viper's face was filled with fury as they walked out. Reaper was stone-cold hard, which had a chill sliding down his back.

Rolling the crib down the hall, Moon promised himself when they flushed out the fucker hiding in the attic, he was going to bury some motherfuckers in the same boxes they had used for the dirty diapers.

He placed the crib under the attic hatch and lowered the side to climb on top of the mattress. Reaper and Viper raised their guns toward the ceiling.

Holding his gun with one hand, Moon pushed the hatch upward with a hard shove, sending it to the side.

The three men remained motionless, listening.

Moon placed his gun at the small of his back, then gripped the wood above his head, preparing to pull himself upward and get his fucking head shot off. Just as he heaved himself upward, however, someone jumped down on him, sending him falling backward and onto Viper.

Rolling to the side while simultaneously trying to catch the fleeing person darting out of the room, Moon collapsed on the floor, completely out of oxygen.

"Reaper!" Viper yelled out to his brother when his attempt to catch the fleeing figure bolted out of the room was just as ineffective.

Viper managed to get to his feet first. Moon consoled himself that it was only because the air hadn't been knocked out of him.

Gasping, he used the crib to heave himself into a sitting position. Slowly, the oxygen started to return to his lungs.

"Wha …?" he gasped. "What in … the fuck was that?"

Viper was bent over, holding his thigh. "I think it was a girl."

# CHAPTER NINETEEN

Larissa was about to use her crutch to make the man blocking her move.

"I really don't want to hurt you, but if you don't move—"

A tall man stepped out of the door, holding Eryn.

"We need to get her to the hospital."

Larissa looked around, searching for a vehicle they could use. "Someone find the keys for one of the trucks!"

The man holding Eryn laid her down on the porch then took off.

"She needs the hospital!" Larissa ordered, lowering herself to the ground.

"Who has the key for the tan truck?" Knox's sharp voice rang out.

"They're in Tanner's pocket," one of the men sitting on the ground in a group spoke up.

Larissa started examining Eryn, finding her pulse dangerously low.

"Eryn, can you hear me? Eryn?"

Her eyes opened. "Larissa?" she whispered.

"I'm here. We're going to get you to the hospital. Are you in pain?"

"No, I'm just cold … I tried to get Tanner to turn the heat on, but he said we're out of oil."

"We'll get you warmed up." Larissa took off her coat to place it over her.

"I've got the keys," Knox said, bending down to lift Eryn into his arms. "Shade, you drive them."

Larissa hobbled after Knox and Shade toward the large tan truck. Shade opened the back seat door for Knox then hurried to the other side to help slide Eryn along the seat. Before he could shut the door, Larissa tried to climb up.

"*Oof.*" Larissa found herself sitting in the back seat and the door slammed shut next to her before she could draw another breath. Immediately, she began examining Eryn as best as she could while being jostled when the truck started moving.

"I'm going to die, aren't I?"

"You're not going to die," Larissa assured Eryn, despite her doubts.

"I screwed up so bad. Dusty found out I was having an affair with Tanner, that the kids weren't his, and he left me. He and Tanner were friends. He swore he'd never tell Dusty, but they got drunk, and Tanner let it slip. I don't even know why it mattered to him. He didn't care about them even when he thought they were his."

"It's okay. Don't worry about any of that now. Just think about holding this precious baby."

"Don't. I'm not stupid. They won't let me keep any of my kids when Knox tells them what Tanner was doing in my house. Once Dusty left, Tanner moved in with his buddies and turned my home into a lab. I didn't try to stop him. I didn't want him leaving me like Dusty."

"Was that why Tanner wouldn't let you come into your appointment yesterday?"

"No, he wouldn't let me leave because he knew I would have called the sheriff on him for not letting that woman leave."

"The woman in the house?" Shade asked from the front seat.

"Dusty quit making house rent payments. Tanner wouldn't give me the money to pay it because he was waiting for a buyer to come today to buy his merchandise. He said we would clean the house out after the buyer left, and he would buy me my own house. The woman showed up yesterday, said she had bought the property and would give me time to pay the rent." Eryn gave a sobbing cry, clutching her stomach. "I guess I felt that, huh?"

Larissa swallowed hard, seeing tears slip out of the corners of Eryn's eyes.

"It won't be much longer. We're almost at the hospital."

"Tanner was high and thought the buyer had sent her to scope out how many men he had. He was always paranoid about someone stealing his stash. He wouldn't let her leave and locked her in one of the bedrooms upstairs. He promised me he'd let her go today after the buyer came.

"Last night, I was in bed when I woke up to hearing her screaming and went to the room where she was locked inside. Tanner was trying to rape her. I started hitting him, and she got loose and started running down the stairs. I got away from him and went to the kids' room to get my baby. He caught up with me at the top of the stairs, and we started fighting. He didn't mean to make me fall down. His buddies caught the woman and brought her back before she could get out of the house. Benie told her if she tried to escape again, he'd kill me and my babies. She stayed even when the shooting started, despite me not calling the police when

Tanner wouldn't let her leave." Eryn started crying harder. "I hurt so bad …"

As she talked, Larissa took Eryn's pajama bottoms off to examine how far dilated she was.

"I know you do."

"How many children are in the house?" Shade asked, bringing the truck to a stop in front of the emergency entrance.

"Three."

Shade put the truck in *Park* and slid out of the truck with his cell phone to his ear as he hurried inside the emergency room.

Larissa opened the truck door and was sliding herself out when the sliding door opened and Lana and two orderlies came rushing outside with a gurney.

Lana's eyes flew to hers. "I've been worried sick," she snapped as the orderlies maneuvered Eryn out of the truck.

"I'm fine," Larissa assured her. "We'll talk about it later."

Lana's anxious gaze switched to Eryn.

"She's eight centimeters dilated. Her pulse is slow and thready," Larissa started rattling off Eryn's stats as they went through the sliding door. "She fell down a flight of stairs yesterday. We need to get an ultrasound—"

"I've got this," Lana stopped her from entering the triage room. "You have to let me handle it from here."

"I'm her midwife. I can be in there," she argued with her sister.

"Not after holding you hostage. Anything goes wrong, you could lose everything you've worked for. Dr. Price is on his way down from the second floor. Once he's here, he'll take over for me. Go wait in the waiting room. Priscilla is on her way."

Larissa stepped and had to watch as the door closed behind Lana.

She went to the restroom, where she washed off, her mind still on Eryn. Leaving her was hard to do, but knowing Lana wouldn't handle over Eryn's care until Dr. Price got there was assuring.

The waiting room was empty except for Shade, who was standing by the front door, talking on his cell phone. Taking a seat, she leaned the crutches against the wall.

When Shade finished the call, he sat in the seat in front of her.

"I thought you had left," she said uncomfortably. There was something about Shade that always made the hair on the back of her neck rise.

Shade shrugged. "I thought I'd stick around until the others arrive."

"What others?"

From what she had witnessed, everyone shot at Eryn's needed a coroner, not a hospital.

"My friends are bringing Eryn's children to be checked out."

She had been so focused on Eryn that she had forgotten about the children. "I should have called Knox." Angry at herself, she asked Shade, "How are they?"

"Knox thought they seemed okay, despite the conditions they were living in."

Larissa frowned. "Their living conditions?"

Shade's expression made her stomach plummet.

"How did I let her fool me so badly? I should have—"

"How could you have known? Knox is the sheriff, and he didn't. Unless a report is made, no one would investigate. Usually, they pick out-of-the-way places to remain unnoticed, get regular jobs, and mingle with people in town so no one will grow suspicious of where their money is coming from. Treepoint's been clean the last few years. They were good; they sailed under Knox's radar."

"Eryn told me they just moved to town about eight months ago."

"Makes sense, then." Shade's eyes dropped to her shoulder. "You should get that wound taken care of."

"I will after Lana comes out."

Her sister was going to be furious she had been grazed by a bullet.

Looking down at her shoulder, she saw the black color of her sweater had hidden the bloodstain. How had Shade seen it when her sister hadn't?

The door slid open, and a group of men walked inside. Moon was carrying a baby wrapped in his jacket. Viper was holding one who was chewing on her fist.

Their young age made her emotions swirl. She liked Eryn, had felt them growing closer with each of the appointments.

A door opened, and two nursers came out to take the children back to the emergency room.

As the emergency room door opened again, Knox walked in with a girl who appeared to be fifteen or sixteen. The girl's appearance had Larissa's hand going to her mouth. Long brown hair was in total disarray, she was more dirty than clean, and the clothes she wore hung off her tiny frame. It took her several minutes as Knox talked to a nurse and the girl sullenly listened, refusing to give her name each time Knox or the nurse asked, for Larissa to realize what was off about the girl. She was barefoot.

When the nurse tried to take the girl's arm, she jerked away and tried to run out of the door.

"Leave me alone!" she screamed frantically.

Seeing Knox was about to stop her, Larissa spoke up.

"Come sit by me."

The girl spun in her direction.

Larissa patted the hard plastic chair next to her.

Looking caged, the girl glanced at the door, which the men had moved to stand in front of, then looked back at her. Slowly, she started toward her, giving her a suspicious look as she sat down two chairs over from her.

"I want to leave," she said with hostility.

"From the way things look, I don't think that's going to be an option."

"Are they going to take me to jail?"

Larissa gave her a gentle smile, despite the girl glaring at her. "I'm guessing not."

"Is Eryn okay?"

"They're working on her right now."

"Then she'll be okay. Doctors can fix anything," she said assuredly.

She hated to disillusion the girl, but she had a terrible feeling it would be a wasted effort.

"Is Eryn your mom?" Larissa asked her curiously.

"No, she's my aunt."

She pressed her lips together and didn't respond. Larissa didn't want to press her, since her legs were shaking under her thin pants.

"Larissa," Priscilla called, walking in from the entrance with Crazy Bitch and Ginny. They rushed toward her.

"Are you all right?"

"I'm fine."

"You're bleeding."

"It's just a nick."

Priss started to reach for her sweater.

"We'll take care of it later." Larissa nodded her head to the young girl, who was watching Ginny as if memorized. "Priscilla, Crazy Bitch, Ginny, this is Eryn's niece ..."

Put on the spot, the girl looked shyly toward Ginny. "My name is Lennon."

"It's very nice to meet you, Lennon." Ginny smiled at her, holding her hand out.

"I've seen you on TV." Awestruck, the girl's tough veneer disappeared into a gushing teen.

The women all sat down. Ginny sat next Lennon, soothing her when Knox approached to talk to her.

"Ah … to be that young again," Priss observed.

Larissa rolled her eyes. "It's not been that long." Turning toward Crazy Bitch, she became more somber. "I'm sorry."

"I guess I'll let you off the hook this time since you got all shot up and shit."

"I appreciate your understanding." She grinned.

Knox finished talking to Lennon, then went to talk to Viper and Moon, who were standing just a couple of feet away.

"I'm going to have to call Child Services," Knox told Viper. "They'll have to find a placement for all three of them. Going to be hard to find someone for all three, especially with two being so young."

Moon looked at his watch then at Viper. "You got this? I need to hit the road unless you've changed your mind about me leaving?"

"No, you can go. We've got this. Thanks for your help."

Eavesdropping despite telling herself to stop, Larissa tuned out what Priscilla was saying. She watched Viper fist-bump Moon and Shade ignore the same gesture when Moon moved his hand in his direction.

"You talked to Wizard since Viper told him you're moving back to Ohio?" Shade asked Moon.

"Not yet. I thought I'd wait to get his reaction when I get there."

"He's not happy," Shade informed him chillingly.

"I'm not either."

*Moon is leaving Treepoint?* Her hand unconsciously went to her belly. *Should I tell him?*

Licking her dry lips, she stood undecidedly for a second then made up her mind. She couldn't, in good conscience, keep the information from him.

She took a step toward them and prepared herself to face the most humiliating experience in her life.

"I'm sure it won't be long before Viper lets you come back," Knox joked, breaking the tension between the two men, hitting Moon on the back good-naturedly.

Larissa changed her mind and took a step back. There was no need to rush. She had eight months to let Moon find out he was going to be a father.

# CHAPTER TWENTY

W hen she stepped back next to her sister, Crazy Bitch caught her eyes.

"You hear what they're saying, too?"

There was no way she could deny it since Crazy Bitch had seen her. She racked her brain to come up with a viable excuse. Crazy Bitch sent her pulse racing.

"It bothering you as bad as me?"

"Uh ..." Had Crazy Bitch figured out what had happened upstairs at The Last Riders' the night of the party? She didn't think one of her sisters would have snitched. Had Winter found out? Was Crazy Bitch telling her she should confess to Moon it was her?

"I feel terrible about it."

"Good ... then you'll put a good word in for me with Knox?" Crazy Bitch gave her a please smile.

"Huh?"

"Tell him I'll take care of the kids. All three of them."

It took a minute for Larissa to wrap around her mind what Crazy Bitch wanted her to do. She had been so focused on Moon, it took her a second to comprehend Crazy Bitch must have been listening to the conservation between Knox discussing Eryn's children with The Last Rider's. When it finally clicked what she was referring too, she laughed nervously.

"Of course … I'd be happy to."

Priscilla gave her a strange look at the way she was acting. "Are you sure you're all right? You haven't lost too much blood?" Priscilla then muttered under her breath, "I don't think that would be a good idea."

Crazy Bitch gave her a threatening glare. "What you got against me taking care of a few kids? You don't think I can handle changing a few dirty diapers?" Crazy Bitch snapped her fingers in front of Priscilla's stunned face. "I could take care of fifteens kids and run circles around you while I'm at it."

Priss hastily shook her head. "I meant, I think Larissa's original suggestion about you and Calder going on a vacation is a much better idea." Priscilla gave her a warning glance. "Isn't that right, Larissa?"

"Uh … yes."

What was it going to take to snap her out of the fixation on Moon? The moment Crazy Bitch came up with the idea, she should have never agreed so readily.

"You should take a few days to think it over. Give yourself time to get over your disappointment, spend some alone time with Calder to discuss taking in foster children, then I'm sure Child Services will be happy to process your application," she said, giving Crazy Bitch the reasonable answer she should have given her in the first place.

"Fuck that!" Crazy Bitch stepped around them to barge toward Knox, Shade, and Viper.

Larissa couldn't help but watch as Moon went to the other men standing around before leaving out the door without a glance back. She could strip naked, and he wouldn't give her a second glance.

Turning her attention back to Crazy Bitch, she tried not to notice the sympathetic look Priscilla sent her.

Knox was attempting to explain to Crazy Bitch that she would have to get approval for state care of the children before he could hand them over to her.

"Don't talk that mumbo jumbo to me when we both know you can do whatever the fuck you want. At least be a man about it and admit you don't want me to."

"That's not what I'm saying," he denied. "I'm not going to lose my badge because you don't want to wait a couple of days to get approval."

"Who's going to take them in the meantime?" Crazy Bitch asked, her body tense as if she could change Knox's mind by sheer force of will.

"I don't know yet. I haven't made the call. I was waiting for the doctor to come out, so I know if the two young ones need to be hospitalized. I wanted to talk to the mother as well, to see if she has any relatives who could take them. I was trying to buy some time before notifying CPS. If a relative is willing to take them in, they might not have to go into foster care."

Knox looked at Larissa. "Did Eryn give you emergency contacts?"

"Yes." Larissa nodded. "Her husband, Dusty. You could contact him maybe."

Knox shook his head. "He's going to be under investigation for manufacturing and distributing drugs. A couple of the men I arrested say Dusty was involved, too. I won't have all the facts until I have the opportunity to interview them, but that isn't going to help the kids out until I finish my investigation."

Crazy Bitch folded her arms across her chest, tapping her foot impatiently. "I'm standing here. I can take them."

"Lennon says"—Larissa nodded her head toward the young girl sitting to the side—"Eryn is her aunt. That could be a possibility you could look into."

"I can't get her to talk to me."

"Maybe I can find out more if I talk to her," Ginny suggested.

Knox shrugged. "At this point, anything we find out could be helpful."

The door opening from the treatment area drew everyone's attention. Lana walked over to where they were standing.

"Dr. Price is about to move Eryn to the maternity ward. The baby is being checked out, but so far, his stats look good. She wants to talk to you," Lana told her.

Larissa immediately started toward the door. She entered the emergency room and found Eryn sleeping.

Not wanting to wake her, Larissa started to leave.

"Larissa."

She moved to Eryn's bedside and took her hand. "How are you doing?"

"I've been better," she replied wryly. "This isn't exactly how we planned for me to have my baby, is it?"

Larissa studied her seriously. "No, it wasn't."

"I always manage to screw everything up, despite how hard I try not to."

"Sometimes, life gets out of our control."

Eryn turned her head away on the pillow. "Then sometimes, we end up in the bed we deserve."

"Don't say that. No woman deserves to be hurt by their partner."

"I knew Tanner was bad news for me." She gave a bitter laugh. "I just couldn't stay away from him. Everything got out of hand after Dusty left. Tanner might have been better in bed, but Dusty had the brains. Everything went to shit when he took over. He wanted us to leave Treepoint. He said the only reason they hadn't been caught was they weren't selling to anyone in town. I gave him the excuse to leave when Tanner told him about us, but I knew he was terrified of The Last Riders. He kept saying they would kill us if they found about us."

Larissa's heart had started pounding when she'd mentioned The Last Riders.

"That's a harsh accusation for him to make. Did he say why he was so scared of them?"

"No. Some things, he would tell me about; others, he and Tanner kept it to themselves."

"I'm sure he was doing whatever to keep you safe."

"I don't know anymore." Eryn looked down at where she was holding her hand. "I figured you wouldn't want to talk to me after you found out all the lies I told you."

"I promised to support you through your pregnancy and afterward. I take that promise seriously. I'm here to be your cheerleader, not judge you."

"I'm sure there's going to be plenty of that in my future."

Wishing she could relieve her of that fear, she held back her assurances, not wanting to lie.

"It's okay. I'm not stupid, even though you'd never know it from the mess I'm in. That's why I wanted to talk to you. Your sister said Knox brought my kids here."

"Yes."

"I'm going to lose them."

"Temporarily." Larissa had to be honest with her. "You can get a lawyer."

"I've lost them. I knew the moment Tanner wouldn't let that woman leave. She was trying to give me a break, and he even fucked that up for me. I won't be getting out of prison anytime soon, and even then, my kids will be grown, and it won't matter, anyway."

"Would your niece's parents be able to take your children, or are there any other family members who could?"

"That worthless bitch is in worse shape than me. She's pulling thirty years for armed robbery, inflicting great bodily harm. We're both going to be old and gray before we get out. Her father was killed during the robbery. There isn't anyone else." Eryn's eyes pleaded with her. "You've always done me right; that's why I wanted to talk to you. I'm not asking you to take care of a handful of kids who aren't blood-related to you, but could you check on them every so often and make sure they're in a good place? Like you did me? They deserve to be in a better home than I can give them. Some place pretty would be nice, too. I'm not going to fight to get custody back. I've been a crappy mom so far, and they deserve better than I can give them."

"Eryn, you're just emotional right now—you just had a baby. Maybe a lawyer could get you a deal if you testify against them."

"You don't get what I'm saying … I'm saying I'm not going to fight to get them back. I'm going to sign them over. I'm going to give them a better chance than I got handed. Just check on them for me, okay? That's all I'm asking you for. I'm not going to be able to do it myself locked up. It'd be nice if you'd send pictures every now then, but you don't have to. Can you do that for me?" Eryn's tired eyes pleaded with her.

"I can do that," she answered huskily.

"Thank you." Eryn's body seemed to shrink under the white blanket. "You're good people. I knew that the minute I met you."

Larissa wanted to break down in tears at the woman's defeated expression.

A sound at the doorway heralded the arrival of an orderly to transport Eryn to the maternity ward.

"I'll come and visit you tomorrow," she promised, stepping away from the bed.

"You don't have to, but it'd be nice if you did."

Larissa nodded. "I'll have Knox keep me updated on your children, too."

Following the hospital bed out of the room, she found Knox standing just outside the door.

They remained silent until Eryn was farther away.

"She isn't as stupid as she thinks she is. She's smart enough to know she's in a shitload of trouble. Did I hear Eryn right? Is she willing to sign her kids over?"

"Yes, but she's emotional right now."

Knox's expression was harsh. "Save it for the jury. She's doing them a favor. You didn't look inside that house; I did."

"You're going to call CPS?"

"I have to, unless you have a better idea?" Knox said fatalistically. "Your sister is going to admit them to the hospital for tonight. That'll give CPS time to find a couple of homes for them."

"They'll have to go to different homes?"

"Most likely. There aren't a lot of foster homes in Treepoint. Shame Eryn doesn't have any relatives she could her sign rights over to. The wheels move faster when they try to keep kids within the families."

"How long does it take to become a foster parent?"

"Depends on who you know." Knox raised a questioning eyebrow. "You thinking of taking them in?"

"I would if I could, but my sisters and I are sharing a one-bedroom apartment right now; there's no room. They're also going to need someone who can spend time with them."

"Then who are you thinking of?"

"I'm thinking Crazy Bitch has a pretty big house."

# CHAPTER TWENTY-ONE

## TWO MONTHS LATER...

Larissa tiredly let herself into the apartment they were still sharing. The time was rapidly approaching where she was going to have decide about staying in Treepoint or moving back to Bowling Green. How many times had she regretted letting her sister convince her to come to Treepoint? Too many to count.

Her heart did a downward turn at finding Lana and Priss still awake.

"I thought you would both be in bed." She hung her jacket on the coatrack and passed them sitting on the couch, going over paperwork spread out on the coffee table.

Opening the refrigerator, she took out a pitcher of water to pour herself a glass.

Lana stretched her neck from side to side, straightening from leaning over. "I thought I would help Priss figure out who this new client is."

Larissa walked into the living room to curl up on the recliner. "I never go in your desk without asking, so why did you feel the need to go in mine?" She was going to tell them once she had made her decision of staying or going.

"My pulse oximeter wasn't working, so I borrowed yours. The file was right underneath it. I didn't remember the client making a appointment."

"You could have waited to ask me when I got home instead of bringing the file home for Lana to look at."

"You know why. I recognized the name on the chart. It's the same name you said you were going to name your baby when we were growing up."

There was no sense arguing with the truth, so Larissa set the glass of water down on the table and said, "I was going to tell you both when I decided if I was going to stay in Treepoint or move back to Bowling Green."

Lana started putting the paperwork back in the folder. "What have you decided?"

"As much I want to go back to Bowling Green, I'm going to stay here, at least until I talk to Moon."

Priss and Lana looked at each other before turning their gazes back to her.

"Are you going to tell him you're pregnant with his baby?" Lana asked.

"He deserves to know." Larissa looked down at her shaky hands.

"You're scared, aren't you?" Priss asked intuitively.

"Terrified," she admitted.

Priss came to sit on the arm of the recliner. "How are you going to be able to tell him? Moon lives somewhere in Ohio now, doesn't he?"

"I was going to ask Crazy Bitch for help getting his number when I went by her house tonight, but I got distracted. Her husband is friendly with The Last Riders."

"How did you get distracted?" Lana asked.

"She was giving the kids baths, and I was dragged into being her assistant."

"How's she adjusting to having a full house?"

Larissa had to force herself to concentrate on answering Lana's question. She was so tired she felt it in every bone in her body. The stress of telling Moon they had sex and that he was going to be a father weighed heavily on her conscience. The longer she put it off, the more weight it added, until she felt as if she could break at any second.

She'd always prided herself for being the most logical one in the family. How her life had gotten so out of control frightened her. What if she was a terrible mom? Her mother had set the board high, and failing miserably so early in her pregnancy didn't bode well for the months and years ahead.

"Crazy Bitch is freaking amazing. She's aged me twenty years just watching her. I have never seen a woman so in love with being a mother. Everything is organic in her refrigerator. Calder brought home a pizza after work, and she threw it away and made him eat the salmon dinner she cooked."

"Ouch, I bet that hurt." Lana smiled laughingly.

Larissa shook her head. "That man is in seventh heaven. Crazy Bitch bathed the children, I dressed them for bed, and Calder was reading to them before bed. Then they put them in bed together. They're so happy."

"How's the older one adjusting?"

The happy glow of witnessing the happy family dimmed. "She isn't. Crazy Bitch is trying to form a relationship with her but isn't making any headway. The more she tries to include Lennon, the more she retreats to her room or goes outside to sit until it's dark.

"Eryn said Lennon always preferred being outside. I wonder if it's because she prefers the outdoors or if the outside became her safe space from what was going on inside the home," Larissa reflected out loud.

"That's going to be a hard habit to break," Priss said, standing to stretch. "Tell Crazy Bitch if I can do anything, just let me know. I better get to bed. I have an early appointment."

"Good night," Larissa told her.

"I better go, too. Do you need anything?"

"No, thanks. I think I'm just going to take a shower and get some sleep."

Lana stood and moved to where she was sitting, bending over to give her a tight hug. "Congratulations. I always wanted to be an aunt."

Larissa blinked away the sudden tears that sprang to her eyes. "Thank you. You're going to make a wonderful aunt."

"I'm giving you fair warning; I'm going to spoil her like crazy."

"Could be a boy." She laughed.

Lana clicked her tongue at her. "Bite your tongue. No boys are allowed in our girl club." She gave her another comforting squeeze before she left to go into the bedroom.

Sitting quietly for several minutes, Larissa gained enough momentum to shower and change into pajamas.

She brushed her hair as she went into the living room, then came to a stop. Either Lana or Priscilla had gotten the bedding out the closet, opened the pull-out couch, and made the bed for her.

Placing a loving hand on her barely swollen belly, she smiled. Being pregnant was going to have its perks.

---

Larissa locked the car before she started walking toward her office building, then went inside as the elevator opened.

Recognizing Winter as she came out, Larissa wanted to rush past her as if she didn't recognize her. Winter didn't give her the option.

"Morning, Larissa. How are you doing?"

"Doing great. How are you?"

"Today's Diamond's first day back at work, so I wanted to stop by and drop off some doughnuts before I went to school."

"That was nice of you. I haven't met her yet. I'll have to stop by and introduce myself."

Winter looked troubled. "You might wait a couple of days. I think she's only going to do a half-day."

"I'll wait, then." She nodded. "I'll look forward to meeting her. It's good seeing you." Hoping to bring the conversation to an end without mentioning the night they had last seen each other, Larissa started edging toward the front of her office.

"Larissa ..." When Winter glanced around then embarrassedly cleared her throat, Larissa's heart plummeted. "I ..." Winter cleared her throat again. "Do you remember the night you came to the clubhouse?"

Larissa prayed she could keep her face expressionless. "I do. Did you get in trouble for the chairs being broken?"

"No, but ..." Winter grimaced. "I hate to bring this up but ... did you *accidentally* leave the bathroom and *accidentally* go into one of the men's bedrooms?"

God, she wanted to lie so badly ... but couldn't.

"Perhaps we should talk in my office."

Winter nodded and followed her inside the office. Priss had come in earlier, and the exam room was closed.

After she opened her private office door, they went inside, where she motioned for Winter to have a seat. Larissa sat down in the chair next to her.

"I have never been so embarrassed in my life," she admitted shakily. "I don't know what got into me that night. I used the restroom, and I was going back downstairs when I heard a noise from a bedroom and looked ... I saw a couple having sex. I was so embarrassed that all I wanted to do was hurry back downstairs, but before I could move, I heard another sound. I didn't want to be caught watching the couple, nor did I want them to see me, so I thought I would hide in the room behind me and then come out when the hall was empty." Larissa was so nervous she could hear her voice quivering. "The room was dark. I didn't think anyone was there."

"There was, though, wasn't there?"

"Yes ... Moon. I didn't realize it was him until I went back downstairs. I thought he was still at the bar. He heard me come into the room and thought I was a girl named Echo, or Ember. I don't remember which. One of those two. I pretended that I was her because I was too foolish to admit why I didn't want to be caught out in the hall." Larissa twisted her car keys in her hands nervously. "From there, everything just snowballed, and I ... we had sex," she finally finished in a rush of words.

"He knows." Winter's expression didn't reveal her thoughts.

Larissa felt the color seeping out of her face. "He does?"

"Oh, not that it was you exactly," Winter relieved her fear. "But that he had sex with a woman whom he hadn't been intimate with before."

"I want to tell him. I'm just not sure how. I mean, I've only talked to him a few times, and neither of those times were the best opportunity to introduce myself as being the woman he had a one-night stand with, which he didn't know he was having."

Winter burst into laughter. "Moon's pride would be wounded if you considered it a one-night stand."

Larissa bit her lip. "He's going to kill me, isn't he?"

Winter tilted her head to the side. "Why would you believe that?"

"From the few interactions I've had with him in town, we didn't exactly hit it off. I think it's safe to say neither of us like each other."

"Yet you had no difficultly the night you had sex with him?"

"He didn't talk much."

Winter laughed so hard she reached for a tissue from a box on the desk. "Moon is nicer the less he talks." Wiping the corner of her eyes, she finally managed to stop laughing.

"I'm going to tell him. I was going to ask Crazy Bitch to get his number from Calder."

"I can save you the hassle." Winter asked for her phone number then texted Moon's to her. "I don't envy you that phone call."

"I've been working up my courage," she admitted frankly. "I'll do it this weekend."

"Look on the bright side. Maybe his reaction won't be bad. He might want a repeat."

"There won't be a repeat." Larissa made an exasperated face. "I've asked myself this question a million times: why did it happened in the first place?"

"You come up with any answers?" Winter asked as she rose from the chair.

"Other than insanity? No."

"You wouldn't be the first woman who had that same thought where The Last Rider men are concerned, myself included."

Larissa rose also. "I'll keep you posted on how it goes after I talk to him."

"I hated to ask, but Moon figured out it was someone in the group I had there that night. So far, he still thinks it was only club members, and I know who went upstairs. A heads-up would be nice so I could get my ducks in a row."

"Will you get in trouble?"

Winter grinned. "Don't worry; it won't be the first time, and I'm sure it won't be the last."

# CHAPTER TWENTY-TWO

Moon sat on his bike, watching the brothers unload a delivery truck from Ohio. He could clearly see them under the bright lights Wizard had installed. Shade and Train had already gone inside the club, hoping the thief would fuck up, assuming they weren't being watched by the older members.

"I thought you would be asleep by now," Moon said as the silent figure came up behind him.

"I couldn't sleep." Train's low voice blended into the symphony of crickets and frogs living in the long grass of the empty lot next to the club. "I'm tired of this bullshit."

Moon gave a sarcastic snort. "Shit, I was fed up with it a month ago."

"When they find out who's stealing, I'm going to ..." Train gave a ragged sigh, taking a joint out of his pocket. "I'm flying back. I'll sell my motorcycle before getting back on it for a week."

"Brother, you are tired."

"My ass is either numb or on fire, and I lost my left nut

riding through Corbin. Jesus, how long is that fucking road construction going to go on for?"

"You could hit up Viper for me to come back. I don't mind the ride."

Train gave him a sarcastic glare, which he could barely see when he took a hit of his joint. "I'm ahead of you. I went past asking a month ago. Hell, even begging him hasn't worked. I warned you ..."

"Yeah, yeah." Forestalling the I-told-you-so crap he knew was coming, Moon took the blunt Train offered him. "I don't see Viper stopping the escorts anytime soon. The thefts have stopped, so they're working. Stands to reason it has to be the drivers, so why not replace them?" Moon said more to himself than Train.

"Beats me. You'll have to ask Viper yourself."

The vibrating of his phone drew his attention. He handed the blunt back to Train and took it out. Raising his eyebrow at the name on the screen, he put it to his ear. "Yeah?"

"Moon, this is Ginny."

"Hi." Drawing a blank as to why Reaper's wife would be calling. he shrugged at Train's curious look.

"I'm hoping you could do me a favor whenever you have a spare hour."

"Sure. What you need?"

"I want to give Gavin a new watch for his birthday. Nickel told me you used to date a woman who works at the jewelry store in town. There's a watch I want to buy him. but she says it's on hold for another buyer. She told me if he didn't come to buy the watch last Friday, she'd sell it to me. When I went in Saturday, she said he called and would be able to purchase it in a couple weeks."

"Ah ... you want me to get that watch for you?"

"I would appreciate it. I feel bad taking it from that man, but I really want Gavin to have it. I'm even willing to buy the other customer another watch of his choice with the same value."

"You must really want to give that watch to Reaper."

"I do. I'll even throw in a watch for you," she offered.

"Consider the watch yours. I'll be in touch." Ending the call, Moon tucked the phone back in his pocket.

"What was that about?"

Moon gave Train a smug grin. "Brother, that was my ticket home."

---

Holding the jewelry bag as he left the store, Moon didn't remember the last time he had been in such a good frame of mind.

Hungry, he thought about eating at the diner, but the owner was a dick from hell, and as much as he loved the burgers, it wasn't worth the grief.

When he arrived back at the clubhouse, he went to the kitchen to make himself a sandwich. Shade and Train came in just as he was about to put the ingredients back.

"Either of you want a sandwich?" he offered. "I don't mind making them."

Train and Shade looked at each other as they were about to pour themselves coffee then turned to glance at him.

"Who are you asking?"

Moon frown. "You two."

"Are you sick or something?" Train asked. "You've never offered to make shit for us before."

"Jeez. You're killing my vibe. You want one or not?"

Shade gave him a critical stare. "Viper have anything to do with this change of attitude?"

"Never mind." Moon started putting the ingredients back in the refrigerator. "Make your own fucking sandwiches."

Train started laughing as Shade and he took a seat at the kitchen table. "That's more like it. My world is back to normal."

Balefully staring at the two men, he sat down at the table with them. "Fuck you."

Shade's chiseled brow showed his curiosity. "How did you manage to talk Viper into letting you come back?"

"My winning personality, of course." Moon gave them a smug grin.

Train pretended to gag on his coffee.

Moon picked up his sandwich and decided to ignore the fuckers.

Grabbing his cell phone, which he had laid on the table next to his plate, he checked the time. He wasn't really listening to the conservation Shade and Train had started, his mind elsewhere as he waited for time to click away.

"Moon?"

Shade calling his name dragged him back to awareness.

"What?"

The two brothers gave him weird glances.

"I asked what you thought of the thefts stopping so suddenly," Shade said.

Moon shrugged. "I think the thieving bastard knew he was about to get caught."

"I don't know ..." Rubbing his thumb against his jawline, Shade seemed to be thinking. "I think they would have slowed down, become more careful, not just stopped cold turkey."

Moon looked questioningly toward Train, silently asking if he felt the same way.

"I may have to go with Moon on this one, Shade. The escorts probably put the fear of God into them."

"Could be." Shade still didn't seem convinced.

"You don't think so?" Moon asked, taking the last bite of his sandwich.

"No, I don't."

The kitchen door swinging open had all three men looking to see who entered. Moon stood up when he saw it was Ginny.

"Hey."

When she gave them a smile, Moon could understand how she had been able to drag Reaper from the depths of hell that his soul had survived.

"Hi, Ginny, how are you doing?"

"Fantastic, thanks." Her hand went to the growing mound around her waist. "The baby is being good today."

"I wish Killyama could say the same thing. She hasn't been able to keep anything down. Her doula's going to come by after she finishes with another patient."

Moon had picked up the bag he had left on the counter as Ginny was talking to Train. Moving toward the door, he waited for her.

"Let me know if there is anything I can do."

"I will."

Moon opened the door for Ginny as she walked toward him, then let her go first before following to close it.

"You got it?" She beamed at him when he swung the bag in front of her.

"I did."

"You don't know how much I appreciate your help..."

When she reached out to take it, he lowered it back to his side. "Enough to give me a piece of information I need?"

Ginny frowned at him, her excitement dimming. "What information?"

"Do you remember the night you girls got in a fight at Mick's bar?"

"Yes. So?"

"Do you remember coming back to the club afterward?"

Moon had to give Ginny credit. If he hadn't seen the troubled glint in her eyes, her expression would have fooled him.

"I mean, it's not etched into my memory, but I remember hanging out here for a couple of hours."

"Let's see if you remember this part. Who went upstairs while you were here?"

When Ginny opened her mouth to speak, Moon held up his hand.

"Before you say anything, I want to warn you not to lie to me. I can easily sell this watch to someone else."

Ginny folded her arms over her chest. "One thing I do remember is you're the person who suggested giving Gavin a watch for his birthday."

"I want to know who it was," he said firmly.

"Why?"

Expecting her to be angry at his manipulation, he was puzzled why she wasn't.

"That's a private matter."

"It's not private if you're involving me."

"Who was it? Lily? Killyama? You?"

"I've changed my mind about the watch. I'll bake him a cake."

Realizing he wasn't going to get an answer from her, he lifted his hand with the bag to give her the watch just as a sharp, needle-like pain sank into his calf.

"What the fuck!"

Ginny, who had started for the door, swung back, and the unexpectedness of her action caused the bag to hit her face.

Moon looked downward to see what was attacking him then jerked his gaze back up when he felt the bag connect with Ginny.

"Fuck! Did I hit you?" Moon yelled sharply, seeing the evil

cat who had caused the mishap scatter away at his raised voice.

The back door slammed open as Reaper, Shade, and Train came barreling outside.

"Did you hit my wife?"

Moon froze.

Ginny, who had been holding her cheek, reached for Gavin, unwittingly exposing her cheek. Moon was sickened at the red welt that was already appearing.

"Gavin, it was an acc—"

"The cat jumped on my leg. I didn—"

His explanation was cut short as an *oomph* of air whooshed out of him when Reaper threw himself at him. Moon found himself fighting for his life at the barrage of fists Reaper threw at him.

Stunned at first, Moon started fighting back. There was no reasoning with Reaper in a rage. It was either defend himself or die.

"Stop him, Shade!" Ginny screamed.

"I thought you went to see Lily and Beth." Moon heard Shade asking Ginny as he was momentarily rolled away from Reaper.

"We were talking."

"About what?"

"He was asking whether Lily and Killyama went upstairs—"

Finding himself jerked to his feet by Shade, Moon was able to take a quick breath.

"Let me answer any questions concerning Lily."

Shade's fist struck out, hitting him square in the stomach. Already having the air knocked out of him from Reaper, Moon stumbled to the side. He managed to keep standing by sheer force of will. He had taken their hits while holding back his full strength, but when he realized they were out for blood, Moon decided, unless he gave as good as he got, he was going to be using handicapped parking for the rest of his short life.

Rushing toward Shade, he tried to gut punch him, only to miss his target when Train stepped in between them.

"Brother, it's three against one." Shade told him when it became clear Train had blocked the punch so he could take his own shot at Moon.

Train stonily glared at him. "I'm good with that."

"Then bring it on!" Moon shouted angrily.

Before Train could react, Moon rushed him, shoving him into Shade. Then, about to punch Train, Moon found himself swung around to face Reaper.

Moon blocked the blow Reaper aimed at his jaw, then clenched his hand into a fist to kidney punch Reaper. The fucker didn't seem to feel it, throwing a punch to his jaw and connecting. Moon saw stars exploding behind his eyes.

"Gavin, stop!"

A hard left coming from Train caused Moon to taste blood. He used his elbow to Reaper's face, then raised his foot to prevent him from hitting him again. Out of the corner of his eye, he saw Ginny take off down the side path to the parking lot.

Taking advantage of him being open, Shade came after him next, giving him his full attention. Sticking out his feet, Moon tried to swipe Shade's legs out from under him. When he smashed, his fist into Reaper's chin, he felt a spurt of satisfaction when the fucker stood there, blinking at him as if stunned.

"That rock your world, motherfucker!" Moon shouted. He tried the same move on Shade but only managed to clip him before he had to parry his move with one of his own.

Spitting blood, Moon flipped Train over his shoulder when the bastard tried to put him in a head lock. Shade barely managed to escape being Train's landing pad. Pity. Putting that mean fucker out like a light would have been nice.

As the men circled him, Moon swiped blood away from his mouth, getting ready to knock two heads together and pounce on the other one.

When Viper found out about him getting in a fight the first day back, he was going to be thrown out of the club, anyway. If he had to leave the club, Moon decided he was going to fuck these fuckers up one last time. He wasn't going to be the only one applying for handicap parking.

# CHAPTER TWENTY-THREE

"Y ou knuckleheads, stop!" Viper roared, pulling Shade off him.

Moon lay on the ground, blinking up at sky, not knowing how he had fallen. Lowering his eyes downward, he found Reaper standing over him. "I'm going to kill you," Moon groaned, trying to move into a sitting position. It took a second before he was able to comprehend Reaper had a foot on his chest. "Get off me, you ugly bast—"

"Reaper, I'm not going to tell you fuckers to stop again."

Thankfully, Viper shoved his brother off him.

He sat up with a groan, holding his ribs. Moon glared vengefully at the three brothers staring down at him, also vengefully.

"You want some more?" he egged them on, using his free hand on the ground to boost his ass up. "Let's go. Which one of you sons of a bitches wants to make a widow out of your wife? Don't worry; I'll make sure they won't get lonely."

The backyard turned into a free-for-all. Razer, Viper, and Nickel had to hold Shade back, while he and Reaper went in for the kill ...

L arissa heard shouts as she approached the back of The Last Riders' clubhouse. The backyard was filled with men having a massive brawl. Gaping at the viciousness taking place in front of her, she didn't know whether to run away or wait until it ended to help those who needed medical aid.

Seeing Moon pop up in the men gave her such a start that she took a backward step. Hearing the words he shouted out about making widows of his friends' wives and saying he would make sure they wouldn't be lonely was reprehensible to her.

*This* was the father of her child? The man who, if she told him that he was going to be a father, would have a part in his life? Hell no. There was no way she would let a child of hers be anywhere near this type of environment.

Disappointed, she watched Train grab Moon, put him a headlock, and from the way he was holding Moon, he seemed to be purposely trying to break his neck.

She was battling with herself about whether to call 911 now or wait until Moon was dead, then made the call. If anyone had the nerve to say she didn't go above and beyond for her clients, she would tell them about this situation. Train couldn't be his wife's birthing partner if he was locked behind bars.

As she reluctantly made the call, she watched the fight become more vicious when Train and Shade ganged up on Moon, all three of them stumbling into the gazebo behind them. The gazebo crumbled on top of them. From the shaking wood on top, Larissa guessed the fighting hadn't stopped.

"What's your emergency?" a male voice answered the call.

"I'd like to report a fight in the backyard of The Last Riders' clubhouse. Do you know where that is?"

"Yes. Who's involved in the fight?"

"Who isn't? They all are. You need to send ambulances, too."

"What is the injury?"

"I can't see from where I'm standing. They're under a gazebo."

"You can't see under the gazebo?" the calm male voice asked.

"No, I can't. The gazebo collapsed on top of them."

"I'm on my way."

"Please hurry. One of the men was trying to strangle Moon before the gazebo went down. I don't know if he succeeded."

"Who was strangling Moon?"

"I have no clue who it was," she lied. *Killyama, you owe me one.* "His back was turned. I couldn't see his face."

"What's your name?"

"I prefer to remain anonymous." God, did she ever.

"You know I'm equipped with caller ID, right?"

"Then why did you ask?" she snapped.

"To see if you would tell me."

Larissa pulled the cell phone away from her ear to glare at the object. Did she hear humor in his voice?

"I don't find this funny," she said once she had put the phone back to her ear.

"Sorry, I didn't mean to laugh."

Whoever it was didn't sound sorry.

"Who am I speaking with?" she asked sharply. She was going to report the operator to the responding officer.

"I'm the sheriff."

"Oh … that's good, then." Larissa wanted to smack her

forehead at how lame she sounded. "I'm going to leave now," she told them.

"Good idea."

She ended the call, then took a last look at the fight. It had calmed down somewhat. They were still fighting, but they were moving slower. Turning, she hurried back to Killyama's house.

She gave a quick knock before she entered the house, seeing Killyama had moved from the bedroom to the living room.

"Are you feeling better?"

"Yes, at least I didn't throw up for the last thirty minutes." Her eyes went behind her. "You didn't find Train?"

"No, I couldn't find him."

Killyama frowned. "You knock on the back door like I told you and tell them Train wasn't answering his messages?"

"I couldn't make it to the back door. Everyone was fighting."

Interest piqued in her eyes. "What were they fighting over?"

"I don't know."

"Why didn't you ask one of them?"

"I couldn't. They were all fighting. It wasn't safe for me to get too close."

"You mean, they were physically fighting or arguing fighting?"

"I mean they were physically fighting, with their fists," she elaborated.

"Damn, and I missed it." Killyama picked up her cell phone. Larissa assumed she was texting to find out what was going on.

Larissa looked at her own cell phone. "I hate to leave you alone. Is there someone else you can call besides Train? I have another appointment in thirty minutes."

"I'll call T.A. She lives about ten minutes away. You can go ahead and go."

"I'll wait until you make sure T.A. can come," she said firmly.

Ignoring the irritated stare-down, Larissa folded her arms over her chest stubbornly.

"You're a pain in my ass," Killyama told her.

"I will be for the next several months, so get used to it."

"I must be crazy …" Killyama broke off. "Bitch, get your ass over here. Larissa won't leave until someone is with me." Killyama listened to what T.A. was saying, her expression turning more irritated. "Bitch, I don't know where that fucker is, but when he comes home, I'm going to give him a piece of advice his ass will never forget. You coming or not?"

Nodding, she ended the call without a goodbye. "She's on her way."

Relieved, Larissa took a seat on an armchair across from where Killyama was sitting.

"Do you mind getting my nail file from my bedroom? It's on my nightstand. I meant to bring it out here with me and forgot."

"Perhaps it's better off in the bedroom."

Killyama laughed. "You think I'm going to use it to hurt Train?"

"Of course not," she denied, but that was exactly what she thought. You didn't get a nickname like hers without a damn good reason. "I just don't believe in putting temptation within reach."

"I'm not going to hurt my man, as mad as I am at him. I broke a nail."

"Let me see."

Killyama hit the arm of the couch she laughed so hard. When she finally stopped, she gave her an admiring look. "I like you."

Larissa smiled. "I like you, too. Would you like some toast?"

"Dab some peanut butter on that bitch—I'm hungry."

She went to the kitchen, made Killyama the toast, and poured her some water from the refrigerator.

She had settled a tray over Killyama's lap when T.A. walked through the front door without knocking.

"The cavalry has arrived," she said jokingly.

Slinging the bag she carried with her equipment onto her shoulder, Larissa told the women goodbye.

When she didn't hear any shouts, she assumed the sheriff had broken up the fight, as his squad car was still in the parking lot. Getting in her car, she hurried to put the key in the ignition. She didn't want to be here in case the sheriff wanted to talk to her about witnessing the fight. If he came looking for her, she planned to lie like hell. There was no way she was going to get dragged into court as a witness.

Her first plan of action when she got back to the office was to make plans to get out of Treepoint. The second was to forget how she had conceived her baby.

<hr>

After she saw her client out the door, Larissa immediately went to Priss' office.

"Are you busy?"

Priss looked up from her computer. "I'm free. What's up?"

"I'm going back to Bowling Green."

Her sister's jaw dropped. "Why?"

Larissa told her what she had seen at The Last Riders'. "I can't raise a child with that man. He's too violent."

"Maybe it wasn't as bad as it seemed. They're all friends. They could have been roughhousing. We didn't grow up with brothers, so of course it looks scary."

"There was blood, Priss. Train was trying to break Moon's neck."

"You can't leave." Priss began to look panicked. "What about your clients?"

"Lana can take over for those who don't want to use your services. I can't stay, and I have to leave before I start showing."

"Are you still going to tell him you had sex with him that night?"

Larissa started chewing on her bottom lip. "I don't know. I told Winter I would. If I leave without telling him, Moon might be angry enough to find me. I certainly don't want him finding me after I start showing. I want to go back to Bowling Green. Mom is there. I should have never left. I don't want to live my life on the run, afraid he'll find me if I don't. I think it would best to go ahead and tell him then move away. I can tell my clients that Mom has become ill."

Press rolled her eyes at her. "The same mom we're constantly bragging about acting like she's twenty years younger than her age?"

"I'll come up with some excuse. We can talk about it tonight and decide which would be the best way to go."

"Okay ..."

Priss' cell phone ringing had her lifting it from the desk.

"Hi. Are you ready for me to bring your lunch?" Priss' mouth snapped closed. Then she laid the cell phone back on her desk, and Lana's voice came over the speakerphone.

"I won't have time to eat it. The emergency room is full. There was a huge fight. I'll be lucky to get off by midnight. I'll grab something from the cafeteria. Moon's here with a dislocated shoulder and cracked ribs. He looks like he's been put through a meat grinder. We had to call in extra security. They're still trying to kill him."

Larissa and Priss stared at each other as Lana filled them in, unaware that Larissa had seen it firsthand.

"What started the fight?"

"From the little I've heard, he hit Ginny. He must have done something to Lily and Killyama, too, because their husbands are the ones I had to call security on. Anyway, I just don't want you wasting your time bringing me lunch. Bye."

After the call ended, they sat in silence, taking in what Lana had told them.

Priss' expression became determined. "Run."

# CHAPTER TWENTY-FOUR

M oon heard Viper finally getting the brothers to calm down, or the doc had given them something to slow their roll. Knox had placed him in a curtained-off room next to the door in case he and his deputies needed to get him out quickly. He had shuffled him into this room to hide him from the others when he returned from getting X-rays. The brothers still thought he was at the other end of the emergency department.

Adjusting the strap of his sling higher on his shoulder, he heard the sliding door of the emergency room open where the ambulance used to transport patients.

"Viper," he heard Winter say right outside his curtain.

"What are you doing here?" Viper's voice became clear, as he must have walked closer.

"Killyama called me. She said you were in a fight?"

"I wasn't fighting. These idiots were. Moon set them off. He's out as soon I can have a church meeting." Viper showed he meant business this time.

"For heaven's sake, what did he do?"

"He hit Ginny. He swears it was an accident. Ginny does,

too. Ginny said she asked Moon to buy a watch for her for Reaper's birthday, and then he wouldn't give it to her unless she told him some information about the night when you and the girls hung out at the club. The fucker has lost what common sense he had over whoever it was," Viper finished grimly.

Moon had to agree he had lost his mind over a woman whose identity still remained unknown. And thanks to the fist-fest he had caused, he might never find out.

"This is all my fault."

Moon's heartbeat quickened at how stricken Winter sounded.

"How in the fuck is this your fault?" Viper asked.

"You can't throw Moon out when he wouldn't have been put in this position if I hadn't broken the rules."

"What did you do?"

"I invited more people back to the club that night than I told you about," Winter confessed in such a low voice that Moon could barely hear her. "I sneaked them in when Nickel wasn't looking. I'm so sorry. I'll take any punishment the club gives me … We were just having a good time—"

"You know who went into Moon's room?" Viper cut her off.

"There was only one person who went upstairs. I showed her to the restroom, and I waited outside. But then Killyama, Sex Piston, T.A., and Fat Louise turned over the bar, so I left to see what happened. When I went back upstairs after she still hadn't come back downstairs, she was still in the bathroom. She said she had been sick."

"Who was she?"

"She's going to call Moon," Winter hesitated. "I talked to her. She's nervous about telling him."

Moon held his breath, praying none of the nurses or the doctor came back before he could find out.

"Winter"—Viper's voice turned harsh—"who was she?"

"Killyama's midwife."

Moon gritted his teeth. The woman who had seen him on the couch with Stori and Jade was the woman who had his stomach twisted in knots?

"You should have told me."

"I know. I'm sorry—"

"Excuse me. I need to get by …"

Moon was already unsteadily getting to his feet when the nurse opened the curtain, exposing him to Viper's and Winter's view.

The color washed out of Winter's face. "Moon, I should have—"

"Save it," Moon gritted out, taking the release form from the nurse. He then achingly walked toward the door, every single part of his body hurting. "Do you know where she is?"

Winter shot Viper a concerned glance.

"Tell him," Viper told her coldly.

"She has the first-floor office space in Diamond's building. But, Moon, wait … Don't say anything you'll regret. She didn't deliberately go into your room. Let her tell you how it happened."

He was so angry he forced himself to hold back words only out of respect for Viper.

"Don't say another word," he managed to grit out through a jaw that hurt so badly he felt as if it was going to fall off.

"I'm not going to tell you not to go, but you should wait at least until you have time to cool off."

"I'm cool," he lied, walking out the emergency door exit, only to come to a stop. With his shoulder, he couldn't ride his bike, even if it were in the parking lot, which it wasn't.

Frustrated, he turned around to find Viper standing behind him.

"Need a ride?"

"You offering?"

"I asked, didn't I?" Viper grinned.

Moon carefully maneuvered himself into Viper's SUV, his skin breaking out in a cold sweat.

"Leave your prescriptions. I'll get them filled after I drop you off. I'll swing back and pick you up when I have them."

He refused to thank him, still furious because of Winter. She could have been upfront from the beginning.

"I'm not excusing that Winter didn't speak up," Viper said. "She was trying to keep everyone out of trouble."

"Herself included. She broke the rules."

"She'll be punished." Viper assured him.

"Good."

"Moon, there hasn't been a rule you haven't broken, so come down off your high horse. Let's be real about what has you so mad."

"Tell me, old wise one," Moon smarted off.

Viper braked the SUV to a hard stop. Then, turning in his seat, he grabbed him by the shirt. "I have fucking had it with your attitude. You need to deal with your issues before they deal with you." Viper released his shirt. "We both know you were counting it being one of the women who belonged to the club or one of the wives who, in your crazy imagination, secretly wanted you. Someone you stood a chance of having again. This chick—whoever she is—didn't come looking for seconds, and it has you pissed off. The shoe is on the other foot, and you can't stand it."

"That's not it," he denied heatedly.

"That is it." Viper turned forward again. "You're not going to listen. You're going to go in there and destroy any chance you have, just like you always do. Moon, you're the only one responsible for not having the happy ever after you've been searching for. You think you don't deserve it because of your brother and sister."

Moon thrust open the door. "I'll walk."

"Suit yourself. I'll text you when I'm back outside," Viper said imperturbably.

As he walked away from the vehicle, his anger mounted with each step. Viper was right about one thing. He didn't stand a snowball's chance in hell of the woman wanting a repeat performance. Not after she had seen him the night she came to the club with Killyama. If she had seen him there just watching television, would she have told him? Did she even know he was the one she had fucked?

Moon came to a full stop, wishing he had asked Winter that question before storming off. He took a deep breath then wished he hadn't when fire streaked through him. The pain nearly blinded him.

Seeing the building in front of him when he cleared his eyes gave him renewed vigor. It didn't matter that he hadn't asked Winter; he was going to ask the woman his own damn self.

# CHAPTER TWENTY-FIVE

They were still going over the pros and cons about the wisest course of action when Priss' phone rang again.

"You forget something?" Priss answered on speakerphone.

"Get out! Moon is on his way there. He knows!" Lana screamed through the speaker.

They both jumped out of their chairs, and Priss didn't waste time ending the call.

"I'll get my purse." Larissa ran toward the door as Priss grabbed hers.

"I'll lock the front door. We can sneak out the back."

Larissa looked at Priss and saw the frightened expression on her face then realized she was shaking.

"It's going to be okay." Larissa didn't know who she was trying to reassure—Priss or herself. "You go ahead. I'll stay and talk to him—"

Priss pushed her through the door. "You are not going to stay here to deal with that maniac."

As they were rushing through Priss' doorway, Larissa knew Priss wouldn't leave her to deal with Moon alone.

"I'll get my purse."

She had just made it to her door when the main office door opened, and Moon walked through. Terrified, they both froze in place.

"Can I help you?" Priss asked unsteadily, trying to play it off.

Moon's eyes narrowed on Priss.

Feeling as if her knees were going to give out from under her, Larissa watched as Moon strode toward Priss. Then her breath stopped in her chest when Moon's hand came out and he bent down to kiss Priss, who didn't fight him, standing still as Moon kissed her. The kiss ended almost as soon as it had started. Then Moon lifted his head to stare down at her. "You're not the one I fucked."

Shifting, he turned to face her, his infuriated expression changing to fury. "Oh... hell no."

Larissa barely managed to swallow the fear down that had her threatening to break into tears as he started advancing on her.

"Let me explain ..." she began.

Moon covered her mouth with his, sweeping his tongue inside, replaying the night she had gone inside his room. Stiffly, she kept her arms down, trying not to push him away, sensing any movement would send a tidal wave of fury crashing over her head.

"Leave her alone!" Priss' yell had Moon lifting his mouth.

Realizing he had backed her against the outer wall of her office, she tried to slide to the side to escape and go inside to give herself more breathing room.

Moon's fist hit the wall next to her head, preventing her escape, and his body effectively blocked her from sliding the other way, leaving her no choice but to stare up at him warily.

"I swear I didn't mean for anything to happen," she tried to explain again.

Moon turned his head to glare at Priss. "Leave."

Priss' shoulder reared back. "I'm not leaving you with my sister!"

"It's okay, Priss." Larissa nodded toward her office. "We can talk in there."

Relieved when Moon stepped back enough for her to enter her office, she gave Priss a reassuring glance, who wiggled the phone she was holding. Larissa felt somewhat reassured as she closed the door between them.

Her heart was fluttering so wildly as she walked to her desk that she was afraid she would pass out. Thank God, she managed to sink down in her chair before she did.

Lana's description of Moon looking as if he had been put through a meat grinder was being kind. His eyes were almost swollen shut and were beginning to turn an ugly purple shade. His nose was swollen, and his lips were split where you could tell he had taken hits. He wore his arm in a sling, walked with a limp, and favored his right side with the way he was lowering himself into the chair in front of her desk. Knuckles on both of his hands had been bandaged and wrapped. From all the amount of injuries on him, she was surprised he wasn't wearing a neck brace.

Once he was settled, Moon's eyes traveled over her, making her feel as if he were stripping her blouse off her.

"I …"

"So, do you normally sneak into men's bedrooms who don't know you, or were you just looking for a thrill by fucking a biker?"

Larissa stared, aghast at the conclusion he had drawn.

"No! I've never done anything like that before in my life," she replied adamantly. "I was only there because my sisters wanted to go. I tried to talk them into going home." There was no way she was going to tell him that Lana had been the one who wanted to get up close and personal with him.

"For someone who didn't want to be there, you sure made yourself at home."

Larissa winced at the snide way he was talking to her. "I didn't know it was you who … I …"

"You fucked?" he finished for her.

She felt red flood her cheeks. "Winter took me upstairs to use the restroom, and I was coming back down when I saw a couple having sex in a bedroom. I was embarrassed and didn't know what to do—"

"Walk on by and mind your own business would have been my suggestion," he offered snidely.

"I was going to. Then I heard a door opening and ran into your room to hide. I didn't want the couple or the person coming up to see me outside the door," she explained. "The room was dark. I didn't even know you were inside until you spoke."

"You could have easily just left."

Larissa tucked a stray strand of hair behind her ear. "I could have," she agreed. "In both instances, I was so focused on not making a fool of myself I made bad decisions."

"That's a fucking understatement." Sarcasm dripped off his tongue. "You misrepresented yourself by acting like two of my friends."

"I did," she acknowledged, embarrassed. "There's no excuse I can make. I still can't understand why I did it." Giving him a perplexed expression, she sought to make sense out of it. "I can't explain something I don't understand myself." She laid herself bare, attempting to make amends.

"If you wanted to be fucked so badly, all you had to do was ask. Let's put that shit aside for now … what really pisses me off is you not owning up to what you did. Hell, I would have given you a whirl if you had asked."

Her teeth snapped together at the suggestive way he was looking at her. "I would have thrown myself over the staircase if I'd known it was you." Insulting him, she stared back.

"I just had the fucking hell beat out me trying to find out who was in my room that night, so excuse me if I'm not coming across as a gentleman. *But what the fuck?* We saw each other in town a couple of times after that—"

"Three."

"Three times after that night." His glower made her wish she had remained silent. "And it didn't dawn on you once to at least give me a hint that it was you?"

"It did," she admitted. "I was just too embarrassed to say anything."

"You should be." Moon used his good hand to brace himself as he rose up from the chair.

Larissa felt the burning sting of tears at the back of her eyes. "I'm sorry."

Contempt filled his expression. "That's the same fucking thing Winter said to me. Deceptive people are always sorry when they're caught. All you had to do was be upfront and honest." Moon gave her an insulting look. "I could have rocked your world."

Each word felt like a knife shredding her pride into tattered strips. She had to tell him.

"There's something you should know …" Her heart beat in her throat.

"I only want one word coming out of your mouth —goodbye."

Huskily, she gave him what he wanted. "Goodbye."

With that one word, Moon walked out the door and out of her life.

Bursting into tears, Larissa laid her head on the desk.

"Are you okay?" Priss comfortingly rubbed her back.

She didn't raise her head. "He hates me," she sobbed.

"Does it matter if he does?"

"I didn't want him to hate me."

"What are you going to do?"

Larissa raised her head to brush the tears away.

"Give him what he wants."

# CHAPTER TWENTY-SIX

## THREE MONTHS LATER...

Moon peeled Ember's thigh off his hip so he could get out of bed. He rose and lazily rubbed his stomach as he went to the dresser to get clothes before showering. A snore coming from a hanger-on who would make an appearance every other Friday had him returning to the bed to shake her awake.

"Time to leave."

"Come on; let me stay. I can't move," she complained sulkily.

"You didn't have any problem moving an hour ago. You've been partying here long enough to know the rules." Moon bent down to pick up her clothes strewn on the floor, tossing them to her on the bed.

"Why does she get to stay, and I don't?"

"Ember belongs here; you don't. I'm not going to argue with you, either. Get your ass in gear, or next Friday when you come to play, you won't get in the door."

Pushing herself off the bed, she dressed before sliding thin sandals on. "Next time, I'm choosing Nickel. Maybe he'll let me stay the night."

"I wouldn't count on it, but give him a go." Unfazed by her threat, he motioned her out the door. "I'll walk you to the stairway."

She slipped her arms around his neck and kissed him passionately. Unmoved, he pulled her arms away.

"Do you always have to be such a hardass?"

Once, he would have taken exception for being called a hardass, believing himself to be one of the more laidback Last Riders. As the years had passed, it was hard to deny the change in his personality.

After escorting her to the stairs, he watched as she reluctantly went downstairs and out the door. Hell, she had been coming for the last three months, and he still hadn't made the effort to find out her name.

He went to the bathroom to shower, removing any trace of the women's scent on him. Why did they have to cover their bodies with numerous scents? He had yet to find any he liked or thought any suited them.

Moon looked at himself in mirror as he brushed his teeth. *Don't lie to yourself. You liked the way Larissa smelled.*

He had liked the smell on his sheets, and on her panties, until the vanilla scent could no longer be detected.

Rinsing out his mouth, he placed his toothbrush back in the cabinet before heading downstairs. He expected the kitchen to be empty so early in the morning, but Moon passed Shade sitting at the kitchen table.

The silence in the room became tangible as he went to the cabinet to take out a box of cereal and a bowl. Pouring the cereal, he then went to the fridge to take out the milk. He put the milk back in the fridge and grabbed a spoon before he headed to the kitchen table, where he scrolled through the news as he ate.

"How long are you going to keep up the silent treatment?" Shade asked.

Moon didn't look up from his phone. "You're never up this early after a Friday night anymore. Say what you have to say so you can go back to bed."

"Cool. I can play it your way. Was trying to do you a solid." Shade got up from the table to rinse out his coffee cup then put it in the dishwasher.

Moon watched him casually walk toward the door, his instincts telling him not to let Shade leave. The brother had maintained a stony silence for the last three months, so there had to be a reason he was breaking it now.

Despite his misgivings, he let Shade leave.

He finished his cereal and put the bowl in the dishwasher before getting started on breakfast. Starting the two pots of coffee, he had just placed the bacon in the oven when the kitchen door swung open, and Ember groggily walked toward the counter.

"I'm getting too old for this shit."

"Right there with you." Closing the oven door, he took the eggs out of the fridge.

"Did you hear Diamond has decided to close her office?"

"No, I didn't," he answered, carrying the eggs to the counter, where he had placed a large bowl.

"Knox is going to take a leave of absence for a month, and they're all going on a vacation to her island." Ember went to check on the bacon. "She doesn't want to represent clients anymore."

"I can't say I blame her."

"Shit, me, either. Knox came by to ask if anyone would be willing to come and help clean out her office this morning."

"Any takers?"

"I think Nickel, Shade, and Viper told him they would."

"I'll text him. I can help after breakfast."

Was that what Shade was going to tell him? About Knox

needing some help? Moon didn't think so. How would that involve doing him a solid?

Texting Knox, he told him he would swing by Diamond's office after breakfast.

He gave Ember a harassed look when he smelled the bacon burning, then put both Shade and Knox to the back of his mind.

---

As he went through the entrance of Diamond's building, he couldn't help but glance in the direction of Larissa's office. Why in the fuck was he still thinking about her? There had never been a woman he had fucked who he hadn't been able to forget about. What made her so different?

Moon found the brothers in Diamond's office, taping up boxes. They had already removed the office furniture. An eerie feeling struck him at how stark the space had become.

Knox lifted a large box into his arms. "You mind cleaning out Dimond's desk? She was supposed to do it. Brink was running a fever, and I told her I would take care of it."

"Sure." Moon took one of the empty boxes and carried it to the desk. It didn't take long to clear out the odds and ends. Placing a pair of black shoes on top, he carried the box to the other room as Knox and Shade walked back into the office.

"You can take that to my car," Knox told him. "Shade and I can get the desk when Viper gets back with the truck. Thanks for the help. I think we can handle the rest."

"You sure you don't need my help with the desk?"

"Yes, it's not heavy. Shade and I could probably do it on our own."

"All right, then. Catch you later."

"Later."

Moon left with the box, deciding to take the elevator instead of carrying the overstuffed box down the steps.

As he stepped off of the elevator, he had a clear view of the ER doctor and the woman who had been in the office the day he confronted Larissa.

There was a shopping bag on the front desk, and the doc was holding up a baby's sleeper. He stopped cold when he read the word scrawled across the material.

*Auntie's Little Angel.*

There was no fucking way. He had used a condom. *One of them must be pregnant*, he assured himself, despite his eyes telling him neither of the two women he could clearly see were expecting.

He had almost convinced himself until the one he had mistakenly kissed glanced toward the door. Moon thought the woman was about to pass out when she found him standing there. The other woman turned her head to see what she was staring at, and her face showed an almost identical expression.

Terror.

The box dropped from his hands. He strode toward the door and jerked it open.

# CHAPTER TWENTY-SEVEN

M oon stormed forward, yelling loudly, "Larissa!"

The doctor who had worked on him in the E.R. recovered quickly from seeing him. "Lower your voice. My sister isn't here."

"Where is she?" Moon managed to lower his voice despite the fury surging through him.

"Larissa is none of your business." The doctor's chin rose haughtily.

Moon jerked the baby sleeper out of her hand, waving it in her face. "This makes it my business."

"You are aware my sister is a doula and buys clothes for her clients' babies as gifts, right?"

Moon wasn't buying the bullshit she was trying to sell. He gave a curt nod to the woman standing by the doctor's side. "What's your name?"

"Priscilla."

"Priscilla, do you normally give your clients' sleepers for their babies that say, 'Auntie's Little Angel?'"

"All the time." She was brazenly lying to him.

"Where. Is. She?" he gritted out.

"She moved away after you came here." Priscilla lifted her chin higher than her sister had. "She didn't want to chance running into you again in town."

"Because she didn't want me to find out she's pregnant with my baby?"

Condescendingly, she glared at him. "Because you told her to leave, remember? *All I want from you is goodbye*," she mimicked him perfectly.

"I didn't mean she had to leave Treepoint, just to stay out of my way."

"How's she supposed to know that? She gave you your wish, so don't come in here, complaining to us."

"Is she pregnant?"

"You'll have to ask her that question."

Priscilla might have appeared to be the meekest of the three sisters, but she had no trouble taking over once she got warmed up.

"I will when you tell me where she is."

She folded her arms over her chest. "That's not going to happen."

Moon looked at the doctor for the answer to his question.

All that one did was raise a lofty eyebrow at him.

"Okay ... I see how it's going to be." He gave them an unconcerned shrug. "Your family is going to regret screwing me over."

The doctor curled her lip in disgust. "I believe my sister already regrets screwing you," she said bluntly. "You can leave before I call the sheriff."

Moon opened his mouth then snapped it closed. He would find Larissa, and she would regret not telling him about the baby.

As he marched to the door, he heard Priscilla's parting shot.

"GOODBYYYYE!"

B lade took one look at his face when he stepped onto the porch before he quickly opened the door for him. Moon didn't spare him a glance as he went inside, intent on regaining his equilibrium.

Feeling as if he had been thrown for a loop and was yet to regain his bearings, he grabbed a bottle of whiskey to pour himself a glass while disregarding Train and Rider as if they weren't sitting at the bar, drinking beer.

Under their scrutiny, he drank a hefty amount of whiskey then poured himself another generous amount. The brothers broke off from their conversation and eyed the nearly empty whiskey bottle.

"Who pissed in your cereal?"

Moon turned a deaf ear to Rider's question to focus on Train.

"Killyama's midwife, where is she?"

Train's disdainful expression showed he wasn't ready to let bygones be bygones.

*Fuck!* He hated to admit that holding a grudge with the brothers for so long was biting him in the ass. They had all attempted to breach the gap he had placed between them, except for Reaper— that mean fucker couldn't care less—but he had held on to his anger.

"Why should I tell you jackshit?"

There was nothing on earth which would get him to lower his pride, except one thing—his child.

"I think I knocked her up," he stated, pouring himself another splash of whiskey.

Train raised a surprised brow. "You don't know?"

Moon lifted the glass to his lips and slung the whiskey to the back to his throat. "Her sisters won't tell me where she is," he admitted in a choked voice.

"Then I don't know what to say. You could go ask Killya-ma," Train suggested with an evil smile. "I'll even go with you."

What the hell? Did he have *sucker* stamped on his fore-head? "I'll call."

Train's smile grew wider. "Good choice."

Moon took out his cell phone and scrolled through his contact list before he found Killyama's name, then pushed the call button.

The phone rang several times before it was answered.

"What in the fuck do you want?" Killyama snarled.

His balls clenched in fear. "Hello ... This is Moon." He winced at how lame he sounded.

"No shit. Tell me something I don't know, like why in the fuck you're calling me?"

Moon shifted, trying to jiggle his balls loose. "I was ... I need to get in touch with your midwife. Do you happen to have her address or phone number?"

"I sure do." Killyama's voice dripped honey.

"Could I have it?"

"No problem," she replied sweetly. "As soon as you walk barefoot to east of Bumfuck, Egypt and come back, I'll get that information to you. Until then, fuck off, you pecker-head."

Setting the phone down on the counter, Moon poured what was left of the whiskey into his glass. "Your wife is a bitch."

"I should kick your ass for saying that, but she is."

"Why is she so fucking pissed at me? Hell, you barely had a mark on your ass."

"Dude, seriously?" Train gave him a disappointed look. "I knew you were self-centered, but you needing me to tell you that takes you to another level. Killyama wanted Larissa as her midwife. I've been arguing with her about having a midwife because I want my kid born in the hospital. Killy doesn't. You actually did me a favor by getting her to leave, which I will deny saying if you repeat it. I was losing the argument because I told her I wanted a doctor in the delivery room. Killyama waited until I opened my big mouth to tell me Larissa is not only a licensed midwife; she's a doctor."

"She's a doctor?"

"A doctor. From what I found out from Killy, Larissa worked on becoming a certified midwife while helping putting the oldest sister through college. When Lana graduated, she decided to become a D.O. She also helped pay for the youngest one's education. If I remember right, Priscilla is a doula, but she's working toward becoming a certified nurse midwife. When you went to their office and confronted her, she was humiliated, and rather than taking the chance of seeing you in town, she decided to move away. Therefore, no home birth for Killy, which puts you on her shit list."

Moon eyed him. "But you didn't want Killy to have the baby at home."

Train nodded. "I didn't, but Killy was counting on me caving in. You took it out of her control. She doesn't like that. She especially doesn't like you since you were the person who put an end to their dream of opening a birthing center here in Treepoint. Seems they have been scraping by, living together in a one-room apartment, watching every dime they spent, trying to afford a lawyer to help them in their fight to get legislation passed so they can open a birthing center. So, not only did you run Killy's midwife out of town, but a lot of other women in the county who wanted another option for giving birth to their babies are shit out of luck."

Moon's hand clenched around the empty whiskey bottle. "Or she could have left town because she had no intention of telling me I'm the father."

Train's eyebrows rose. "And that's a shocker? Larissa witnessed the fight. Then Killy sent her after me when I didn't see her texts the day she was sick. Larissa saw and heard it all. Then you come to her office to humiliate her? I would be more shocked if she had stayed."

"I'm more shocked he was able to nail her," Rider said cuttingly, taking a swig of his beer.

"Fuck you."

Rider grinned. "No, thanks."

Moon was tempted to grab another bottle of whiskey. Instead, he opened the drink fridge for a bottle of water.

Train got up from the stool and moved around the bar to throw his beer bottle away. "Since you've managed to snub anyone who could find out where she is, I guess you're on your own."

"I don't need anyone's help. I can find Larissa myself."

Rider handed his empty bottle to Train to dispose of it for him. "You mind handing me another?"

Train gave him the beer.

Twisting the lid off, Rider raised the bottle as if to toast him. "I love being able to sit back and watch someone else fuck up beside me. For what it's worth, I would be kissing everyone's ass for help if she were carrying my baby around and I didn't know where she was."

"Well, it's not your baby, is it? I'll find her, and when I do, she's going to regret fucking me over not once but twice," he promised.

"Yeah, that's right." Train shook his head at him. "You go ahead and really fuck yourself over. Then, when you're crying into your beer that your kid is calling another man daddy, I can really tell you *I told you so*."

"I can promise that will never fucking happen," Moon swore vehemently.

Rider gave him a sad smile. "Brah, you've made an art of

fucking up. That's why Viper and Wizard shuffle you back and forth. As a brother, we've all been able to count on you when we needed jobs done. You would have laid your life on the line for several of us, but brother, when it comes to personal life, it's like we're dealing with another person who takes a dump on everything. You've got the club to the point that having you as a brother isn't worth needing to cleaning up all the crap. Larissa isn't a member of the club who has to take your shit, nor does she have to clean up after it. She did the right thing taking her ass out of Treepoint, just like Jo walked away from me."

Rider's face turned reflective. "It took her walking out that back door for me to realize what I did, and I didn't have a kid in the picture. Your next move is up to you, but I suggest you get your ducks in a row before you do anything. I would start mending fences because, even if you do find her, she's going to slip right back out."

Moon felt each of Rider's words like a punch in his gut, so much so the dark side of him switched on, taking control of the pain.

"When I ask for your advice, I'll take it. Until then, keep it to yourself."

"Fair enough." Rider lifted the beer bottle to his lips then stood, carrying the bottle to place it in the container for recyclables. "You ready?" he asked Train. "Nickel's bike isn't going to get fixed with us trying to pour sense into a lost cause."

"I'm ready."

Both men walked around the bar.

"Have fun."

Moon frowned. "Doing what?"

"Cleaning up your own mess."

# CHAPTER TWENTY-EIGHT

oon sat in the shadows of a tree, watching a small house across the street from where he was hiding. In three hours, it would be dawn, and he would have to change his hiding spot to remain unseen.

Dodging the fucking cameras on the surrounding houses made it hard to switch positions. He had been staking out the house Larissa's mother lived in for the nearly two weeks and, so far, he hadn't caught sight of Larissa.

He had been able to use his own skills to find Larissa's past addresses, and those of her relatives. It hadn't taken long to find out her family was small, consisting of her mother and her two sisters. Her father had died when the girls were in grade school. An Army veteran, he had served overseas to come home to become a firefighter. He had lost his life when a home caught on fire and he risked his life trying to save a child who had become frightened and hidden in a bathroom linen closet. Neither had survived.

Moon had to harden his heart. Just because the father was a hero didn't mean the same qualities he possessed had rubbed off on Larissa.

Keeping his eye on the sky as it grew lighter, he started his move. He had already come to the conclusion that Larissa wasn't in her mother's home. What he was waiting for was the opportunity to sneak into her mother's house to search for anything that could provide a clue as to Larissa's whereabouts.

Every Tuesday, her mother went to the grocery store and was away for approximately an hour and a half to two hours. Ignoring his cramped legs, he waited for Kendra Griffin to leave. When she did, he had to practically crawl before he could stand. How in the fuck did Shade manage to walk after waiting for his targets? He felt as if he were a ninety-year-old man. If someone called the cops on him for sulking around the neighborhood, he would have to give up before the chase could begin. The way he felt, a turtle could outrun him.

Slipping into the backyard without being spotted took longer than he'd expected when he was nearly caught by a fucker taking out his trash. He had already determined his entry point. So, moving toward a kitchen window, Moon carried a deck chair and placed it underneath. Using his knife, he then managed to raise the window and slide inside.

He dropped inside and sat on the floor until he got his bearings before he used the kitchen counter to rise to his feet, cursing. He was getting too old for this shit.

Looking at his watch, Moon got on the move. He barely had thirty minutes left before Larissa's mother would return.

He moved from room by room but couldn't find anything that would shed any light on where Larissa was. If there weren't several pictures of her and the sisters, he would have thought he was in the wrong place.

Moon closed a desk drawer in Kendra's bedroom before he glanced around the room, rubbing his jaw thoughtfully. There wasn't a speck of dirt, the dishes were all done and put away—hell, even the coffee pot had been cleaned to a sparkling shine. Either Larissa's mother had OCD, or she had been expecting him.

He climbed back out the window, then returned the deck chair to the same position he had found it in. But instead of going back to his hiding spot, he returned to where he had left his motorcycle three blocks away in a parking lot.

---

L arissa's mother had made sure there wasn't a scrape of information he could use. Either it was deliberate, or she was a clean freak. He was done wasting his time.

He grabbed a bite to eat at a drive-thru, ate, then rode to the house he had been watching. Parking in the front, Moon strode toward the door, knocked, then waited for Kendra Griffin to ask who he was.

The front door opened to show a woman who appeared much younger than her age.

"Hello, Moon."

His fake smile nearly slipped. Holding on to it purposefully, Moon was aware of her gaze sweeping over him critically.

"Since you used my nickname, mind if I use your name, Kendra?"

"Not at all. Would you like to come inside?"

"Thank you. Yes, I would."

Kendra stepped aside to allow him inside. He followed her into the living room, where he took the chair she motioned him toward.

Larissa's mother didn't mince words. "If you came here expecting to find Larissa or for me to tell you where she is, you're going to be disappointed."

"Would you at least give me a number so that I can talk to her?"

"No, I'm sorry. My daughter would have given you a way to contact her if she wanted you to have it."

Moon kept his tone friendly despite his anger. "Do you know why I want to contact her?"

Kendra nodded. "Lana and Priscilla told me you believe Larissa is pregnant."

"Is she?"

"Larissa hasn't told me if she is or isn't, nor have my other daughters. I'm terrible at keeping secrets." She shrugged. "If they don't tell, there is no tea to spill."

"I deserve to know the truth."

"I agree, which is yet another reason they won't share the information."

"If you agree I should know, the least you can do is give me her number so I can talk to her." Moon gave her a concerned look. "As a potential father, I'm worried sick something could happen, and I won't be there. As a parent, surely, you can understand my dilemma?"

Her eyes narrowed on him while her friendly manner appeared to mirror his. "I understand. There just isn't anything I can do about it."

They were playing each other.

Moon rose to his feet, his smile disappearing. "I will find Larissa. Until then, you can give her a message for me. Come back to Treepoint, so we can talk amicably." Moon had to contain himself from saying what he really wanted to say. "I never meant for her to move away from Treepoint. I lost my temper, which I regret. There's no reason we can't coexist in town, whether she's pregnant or not, and I hope she'll give me a chance to apologize in person."

Her eyes searched his. "I will relay your message to my daughter."

"Thank you."

"I'm relieved to hear you want to apologize and want

Larissa to move back to Treepoint. My daughters are close; that's why Larissa moved to Treepoint after Priscilla and Lana did. Hopefully, Larissa will reach out, and you two can put the past behind you."

"I hope so, too."

Moon left the house and got on his motorcycle. He had gassed it before he ate, so he rode through the city limits toward the interstate, Ohio was closer to the part of Kentucky he was in, but he took the exit heading back to Treepoint.

After he talked to Larissa's mother, his instincts were yelling at him to get his ass back to Treepoint. Each club had its pros and cons, but he used to be closer to the brothers in Treepoint ... until the last few months. His behavior had created a wedge he hadn't attempted to breach. On the other hand, the brothers in Ohio were generally more laidback under Wizard's way of running the club. Wizard might be more lenient than Viper in some respects; in others, Wizard wasn't as forgiving as Viper and could be more ruthless in doling out punishments when the brothers inevitably made mistakes.

Jesus, he was tired. He hadn't had a good night's sleep since he didn't know when. Years?

Merging onto the interstate, he rode into the wind while fighting to hold his bike steady as a semi moved over into the passing lane, blaring his horn at him.

Moon didn't feel an ounce of fear for his safety. It was his super power, or his biggest weakness. He hadn't even felt the emotion until he had to take psychological tests when he was in the Navy to qualify for the assignments he had wanted. Inevitably, it was why he had never been able to increase his rank. The Navy wouldn't give him command when his profile showed he didn't feel a normal level of fear, making him an extreme risk taker. Viper, as his supervisor, had been aware of the findings and made allowances both in the service and once they were out. He had never asked Viper if he told the other brothers. He just assumed he did, and that was why they made allowances for him.

A sudden thought struck him. What if Larissa was pregnant? What if his risky behavior was genetic? The baby's grandfather was also a vet, who had become a firefighter, who rushed into burning buildings for a living. What if Larissa passed that gene on to their child?

*Fuccccck!* Why in the hell hadn't he locked his bedroom door?

# CHAPTER TWENTY-NINE

"How much longer are you going to sit here, twiddling your thumbs, rather than ask for Shade's help?"

Moon didn't take his eyes off the window that was giving him the view of the building where Larissa's sister worked to answer Evie's question. "As long as I have to."

"You're being ridiculous, Moon." Evie sighed, sitting down at her desk.

After talking to Kendra Griffin, he had banked on one of the sisters leading him to where Larissa was living. He had managed to break into Priscilla's office and the apartment they shared but found diddly squat. Larissa wasn't working, as far as he could find, so where in the fuck was she?

If they were so close, it stood to reason that Larissa would be within driving distance with her being pregnant, didn't it? He thought so to the extent that he was keeping tabs on both women.

"I have to do payroll this morning. If you want to go grab a few hours of sleep, I can call if she leaves," Evie offered.

His lips quirked up into a smile. "You trying to get me out of your hair?"

She stared at him seriously. "Yes, you've put yourself in this position."

"Ahh … you sympathize with Larissa. Why? You don't even know her."

"I don't have to. I know *you*."

"I'm cut to the quick." Moon put a hand over his heart while making a comical face. "I have been nothing but a friend to you."

Evie nodded. "Which is the only reason I've let you in here. Go take a break and give me one."

"Cool. I need the sleep anyway." He rubbed his tired eyes as he moved away from the window. "You need anything while I'm out?"

"You could grab me some burgers from across the street. King would kill me if he saw me walking in there."

Moon grinned. "I'll bring enough for both of us. That'll really piss him off."

Evie rolled her eyes at him. "Get out."

He gave in and rode to the club, determined to get some sleep. He had been burning the candle for so long that he nearly rear-ended a car at a red light when it stopped instead of going through the yellow light.

He was about to go upstairs when his growling stomach made him change trajectory, and he headed into the kitchen to grab a protein bar to tide him over instead.

Nickel was behind the counter, talking on his cell phone as he placed dishes in the dishwasher.

"I can take care of that for you. No problem. I'll see you when you get back."

Choosing a peanut bar, Moon opened it as he watched Nickel. "What's up?"

"Nothing much," Nickel answered. "How about you?"

"Going to take a nap. Someone needing help?" he asked,

taking a bite of the bar as he moved to the fridge to get a soda.

"Train needs someone to pick up a part for him before the auto store closes. He's in charge of the factory today and can't leave. He said Killyama was supposed to pick it up when she came back from Jamestown, but she called and told him she wouldn't be back before the store closed."

"What's she doing in Jamestown? I thought Train told her he didn't want her making the drive without him?"

Nickel laughed. "When has Killyama ever listened to anything Train said?"

Moon chewed on the bar reflexively. Jamestown was a short distance from Treepoint, but it was a twenty-minute drive before she would be near any emergency aid if she went into labor.

"She went by herself?"

"No, Beth's with her. They're both having lunch and spending the day with Sex Piston."

"You're going to get the part?"

"Yes."

"If you can't, let me know. I can."

"Will do."

Moon left the kitchen with Nickel doing the dishes. Rather than going upstairs as he had intended, he went outside to get on his bike. A ride to Jamestown was probably going to be a waste of time, but it was worth a shot. There were only three cities somewhat close to Treepoint—Jamestown, Rockcastle, and Wattford. Mistberg was between Treepoint and Rockcastle, but it was practically non-existent with many of the residents either dying out or moving away from the dreary town.

When he had returned from seeing Larissa's mother, he had scouted out each of the small towns and found no trace of Larissa being there. In each of the towns, he had put out feelers for a new woman moving there, and he was using his connections to let him know if Larissa was sighted.

When he reached Jamestown, Moon took out his cell phone to call Stud, one of his connections, to ask where Killyama was having lunch but then decided against it. He didn't want to humiliate himself more than he already had. Jamestown was only slightly larger than Treepoint, so the restaurant options were limited. There was a barbeque spot, a steakhouse, a burger joint, and a family restaurant.

Picking the restaurant he was closest to, he rode toward the family restaurant, finding it busy, but didn't see any familiar faces. Next, he rode to the burger place, which only had a handful of customers, who gave him curious glances.

"Can I help you?" a pimply-faced teenage boy asked.

"No, I'm good."

He retreated to his bike and tied a bandana around his head when the wind kicked up, blowing his hair against his face. *Fucking hell, just go back to Treepoint and ask for Shade's help*, Moon castigated himself. Stubbornly, he started his bike.

Train himself had said how upset Killyama had been when Larissa moved away, yet he hadn't heard about Priscilla coming to Train's house to take her sister's place. Had she decided to give in to Train's wishes to have the baby in the hospital?

Moon didn't think so.

He kicked up his kickstand then rode to the barbeque spot. The parking lot was crowded as fuck with the line coming out the door. Moon parked his bike and ignored the dirty looks he got from the crowd outside who were waiting. Sticking his head between two people in line, he was finally able to see where the customers were sitting.

His eyes traveled down the line of women sitting at a long middle table. He recognized every single one of them, including the one he had been searching for over the last several months.

He started to slip through the gap between customers only to find his T-shirt grabbed from the front and bumped out of line.

"Get your ass to the back of the line." Angry gray eyes dueled with his.

"I'm not here for the food. I'm just trying to get past."

"You don't have 'excuse me' in your fucking vocabulary?"

Moon wanted to pound the fucker into Neverland but decided he had more important shit to deal with.

"Excuse me, may I get past?"

The man, who was eye level with him, took a step back, allowing him space to walk through.

Giving the stranger a curt nod, Moon walked toward the table.

Larissa's eyes widened when she spotted him. Killyama and Sex Piston, who were sitting on opposite sides of Larissa, scooted their chairs closer to her.

He didn't miss Larissa folding her arms on the table, blocking the swell of her belly from view, but forced a polite smile on his face. "Larissa, I haven't seen you in town lately." Moon greeted her as if it was pure happenstance that he was there in the crowded restaurant. "How have you been doing?"

"Well," she said in a strangled voice. "You?"

"Good." Moon didn't let his gaze drop. "You living in Jamestown now?"

"I ..."

Moon could read in the fear in her eyes as she decided how to answer.

"I..." she continued to stutter.

"You mind leaving, Moon?" Sex Piston spoke out sharply.

"We're trying to have a girls' day out, so beat it. No dicks allowed."

"In that case, I wouldn't want to disturb your ladies' meal. Larissa"—Moon gave her a determined smile—"we can catch up after your meal. I'd like a few words outside when you're finished."

Sex Piston glared at him. "What in the fuck don't you get? A girls' day out means the whole fucking day. Besides, she doesn't want to talk to you, anyway, do you?"

Larissa's fear-filled eyes switched from his to Sex Piston, who must have given her the reassurance she needed.

"No, I don't."

"Larissa, look at me."

Slowly, she turned her gaze back to his.

"We need to talk."

"All right, give me your number, and I'll call you later."

"You have my number. I gave it to your mother." His eyes dared her to lie about her mother giving her his number.

"I meant I don't have it with me. I can call you when I get home."

"And exactly where is that?" he asked in a pseudo-sweet tone.

"Jet!"

Moon felt the floor move as heavy footsteps came up behind him. It was the man who gave him beef about cutting the line.

"Yeah?" he asked Sex Piston.

"This motherfucker won't leave us alone."

Jet turned to face him. "You going to leave, or are we going to have a problem?"

Moon glanced around the restaurant. Everyone was watching, thanks to Sex Piston's loud-ass mouth.

"I'll leave. I'll wait outside for you, Larissa. Like I said, we need to talk. There's no reason to make this difficult, is there?" he asked meaningfully.

"Jet ..." Sex Piston growled out.

Moon saw Jet's hand moving toward him. "I let you touch me once and let you get away with it. Touch me again, and I'll take you out."

Jet dropped his hand. Then, leaning slightly forward, he muttered under his breath, "You really want to start a fight where two pregnant women could get hurt?"

Moon's jaw clenched. It went against his grain to back down, but he did.

"I wouldn't count on me doing this again," Moon warned him.

Jet gave him a look that told him he had received the message.

"I'll be outside, Larissa." Moon left the restaurant. He got on his bike, rode around the door, then positioned himself on the side where he could see into the restaurant where Larissa was sitting.

Lighting a cigarette, he decided to give her until he finished his cigarette before going back inside. He would send Jet flying out the fucking window ...

As he smoked, he planned exactly how he was going to do it when the roar of motorcycles could be heard coming down the street.

Moon narrowed his eyes to find Stud, the president of the Destructors, riding lead in front of his men. One by one, they rolled into the parking lot, stopping in front of him.

Looking past Stud, Moon could see Sex Piston's gloating smile through the window.

The bitch had just raised the ante.

# CHAPTER THIRTY

"Stud."

"Moon."

"I guess I don't need to ask why you're here."

"I guess not."

"All I want to do is talk to her."

"She doesn't want to talk to you."

The back and forth was getting him nowhere.

"Larissa took off without telling me she was pregnant."

Stud leaned a forearm on his handlebars. "Brother, I feel for you, I really do." He nodded his head toward the restaurant. "Unfortunately, Larissa is under the protection of the Destructors, which means if she doesn't want to talk, she doesn't have to."

"You're giving her protection? Why?"

"Not that I have to explain shit to you …" Stud placed his other forearm on his handlebars, giving the impression of being laidback, but Moon wasn't stupid. "Larissa is Killyama's midwife, she did a solid for Crazy Bitch, and my old lady likes her. So do I."

"Enough to go to war over her?"

"The question is: is she worth going to war when there are much easier ways to get what you want without leading to a conflict between our clubs?"

Moon put out his cigarette with the heel of his boot.

Stud had fought his way to become the president of the Destructors. His brother was president of the Blue Horsemen and was considered an ally of The Last Riders. If he started a fight with Stud, it could be Viper's final straw to throw him out of the club.

"I'll leave, but I want to talk to her first. We can talk out here, in front of you, but I'm not going until she does."

Stud took out his cell phone.

Moon remained sitting on his bike while Stud talked to his wife.

"Bring her out. All he wants to do is talk, then he'll leave."

From Stud's expression, Sex Piston was giving him hell.

"Bring her out *now*." Stud disconnected the call, pocketing his phone as he gave him a harassed expression. "You sure you don't want to take off while the going is good? Brother, sometimes, they aren't worth the headache."

Moon gave a hiss of air through his teeth. "I have already found that out," he agreed.

Sex Piston and her crew all filed out of the restaurant, glaring at him. Larissa walked out last, next to Sex Piston. She said something to her before she left Sex Piston's side. Moon was surprised Larissa approached alone without the women.

Stopping in front of Stud's bike, she stared at Moon cautiously. "You wanted to talk?"

Moon's eyes dipped to the swell of her belly. "The kid is mine."

"Yes."

His eyes bore into hers. "I wasn't asking."

Red flooded her cheeks. "Oh ... I thought you were—"

"You have some misconceptions about me that we need to clear up," he stated coldly. "I'm not some kind of patsy you can play games with then make me out to be the bad guy. You've fucked me over twice. You know that, right?"

Larissa's bottom lip began to tremble. "I didn't mean to."

Moon hardened his heart. "You know I was at the clubhouse when you left town?"

"Yes, I did—"

"Then you meant to," he cut her off again. "All you had to do was come to the clubhouse and tell me you're pregnant. That's it. That's all you had to do. We could have worked out an agreement where we could have shared custody of the kid. I'm not a selfish man; I would have been reasonable. On the other hand, from how you reacted by deliberately leaving without telling me, then when I talked to your sisters and mother, you still didn't call, that shows me you have no intention of sharing. I'm afraid that won't be acceptable to me."

His hands were hanging loosely on the motorcycle's handlebars. Now, raising one lone finger, he pointed at her belly. "Enjoy having the baby with you. Cherish the time you're going to have together, because I'm making a promise right here and now that once that baby comes out of your womb, it's mine."

"You can't do that—"

"Watch me." Moon let his expression show just how serious he was.

"No judge in their right mind would give you custody of a child."

"Why not? My record is clean. I served in the military. I have a steady job. You might think I'm a loser, but I'm far from one."

"I was at the clubhouse when you were fighting in the backyard. They said you hit Ginny."

"Ginny will just have to testify that it was an accident. The fight with the brothers was just a misunderstanding. They'll even testify on my behalf." At least, he thought they would. "I have enough saved that I'll be living in my own home by the time the baby comes. Will you be able to say the same? Do you have your own place now?"

Indecision was written all over her face. "I'm still deciding where I want to live."

"At least one of my kid's parents has his shit together."

Moon saw her wince.

"Here's how it's going to be. You've got my number; you're going to text me where you're living. I will find you a place to live in Treepoint and pay the rent and all the bills. Every doctor appointment, I want the date and time so I can be there. Text me your information, and I'll take care of the medical bills."

As he talked, Moon saw anger replace the fear in her eyes.

"You don't get to tell me what to do. I'm not moving back to Treepoint." Her chin jutted out stubbornly. "I didn't tell you that I was pregnant because I thought you would make a terrible father, and you haven't shown me anything to change my mind. I'll put my reputation against yours any day of the week. I hope you do call The Last Riders to testify for you. They'll have to admit you have sex with multiple part-ners where anybody can see—my sister will testify to that."

Moon laughed at her. "Jealous?"

"No, I'm not jealous." Her lips curled in disgust. "Con-cerned for my health, yes! I'm getting extra tests done just in case I caught something from you."

"I used a fucking rubber; don't play the blame game on me," he snarled. "A word to the nitwit—get on birth control the next time you decide to sneak into a man's bedroom to get laid."

Moon knew his target had been hit when a hurt look crossed her face.

"You are so mean, I …"

Larissa's hand suddenly went to the swell of her belly, and Moon immediately jumped off his bike.

"Are you okay?" He laid his hand next to hers, feeling his child kicking underneath.

Distracted, Moon didn't notice Sex Piston storm forward until she pushed him away from Larissa.

"What in the fuck do you care?"

Moon stiffened at the aggressive way Sex Piston had shoved him.

Stud stood up, placing himself in front of the two women.

"You've said your piece. Now it's time for you to head back to Treepoint," he said stonily, his laidback façade gone.

Moon's lips twisted into a grim line. Tilting his head to the side, he saw Larissa softly rubbing her belly.

"Is the baby okay?" he asked.

"Yes, he was just kicking."

"He? Is that a guess or a fact?"

"Guess. I don't want to know the sex of the baby."

"I want to know."

"I'll have Lana text you."

The reminder that the three sisters had plotted to keep him from finding out about his baby made him return to his bike.

"Don't forget to text me the information I want. I'll be in touch."

He started his bike and returned Stud's glare until he gestured for the Destructors to move back.

He was risking Larissa taking off again, but it was a chance he was willing to take. Stud had given her his protection; why leave when she was safer where she was? He would find a place for her to live, and when he did, she would move where he could watch every move she made.

Stud was depending on the friendships between the clubs to prevent an all-out war. Whether The Last Riders took his back or not, until Larissa had his child, he didn't give a blazing fuck if an army of men was there to protect her from him. She belonged to him.

# CHAPTER THIRTY-ONE

Moon parked his bike next to Shade's, then checked his messages and saw Viper hadn't responded to the one he sent when he'd fueled his tank before leaving Jamestown.

He got off his bike, noticing a recruit coming down the steps from the clubhouse.

"Static," Moon called out, "have you seen Viper?"

"He's in a meeting at the factory." Static's long-legged stride covered the distance to his bike in three steps. "Going on a beer run; need anything?"

Viper hadn't told him about a meeting today.

"I'm good."

Making his way to the factory, he walked inside to find Viper, Train, Lucky, Cash, Reaper, Rider, Knox, and Razer involved in a discussion. The moment they spotted him, they stopped talking.

Moon walked further inside. "I must have missed the invite to the meeting."

"Since when do you care?" Viper asked him sharply.

He deserved that cut. For the last few months, his head had been everywhere but the club.

"Is that what this meeting is about? You're voting me out?" Feigning unconcern, Moon folded his arms over his chest.

Viper stared at him in disbelief. "You're shitting me, right? You come in here, interrupting a meeting, which is important, and instead of standing there and keeping your mouth shut, you assume it has to be about you?"

Viper's words lashed out effectively, showing him how much of an ass he had become.

Moon dropped his arms to his sides. "Sorry." Raking his hair back, he made the overdue apology. "I've never understood why you have tolerated my bullshit. I wouldn't blame you if you did vote me out. I deserve it."

Shade narrowed his rapier blue gaze on him. "I find it interesting you had ample opportunity to make it right with us, yet we haven't heard one fucking word from you until now."

The emotionless way Shade talked showed the brother wasn't buying he felt any remorse about his behavior. Ignoring Shade's attempt of making peace was coming back to bite Moon in the ass.

"Or does this change of heart have something to do with the reason Stud called Viper?"

If the brother was expecting an argument, Shade was going to be disappointed.

"No, it doesn't. I can be an ass most of the time, I admit, to you annoying fuckers. After the fight and finding out it was Larissa who came into my room, you all tried to apologize. I should have apologized for the way I handled it, but to tell the truth, I was pissed the hell off. At least one of you fuckers could have been on my side."

The brothers all blinked at him. All except Reaper, whose grim façade wasn't appeased.

Reaper straightened from leaning against a desk to ask Viper, "I don't have a fucking thing to apologize for. Are we done here?"

"Sure." Viper motioned toward the door. "The rest of you can leave, too. Moon, stay."

Moon didn't budge out of Reaper's way with a mail cart and a desk preventing him from going around. The two men came to a standoff.

"I didn't expect you to apologize. I was in the bad, using the watch to get the information I wanted from Ginny. I've never hit a woman, and I'm sick to my gut I did Ginny. It was an accident that shouldn't have happened. I've apologized to Ginny; she accepted it, and I believe her. I wanted to give her the watch, but she refused."

Reaper still didn't seem appeased. "No shit."

"I swear, brother, I didn't realize Ginny was so close to me. It was like I moved my hand, and the next thing I know, I had hit her." Unaware his confusion was visible as he relived how the strange circumstances had occurred for the hundredth time, Moon still couldn't understand.

Reaper frowned. "What did you do with the watch?"

"Nothing. I still have it. I told Ginny I'd keep it in case she wants to exchange it for the IOU I gave her."

Reaper's gaze sharpened. "You gave her an IOU?"

"Yeah."

"Did you offer it, or did she ask?"

"I told her I'd buy any watch or something else. Ginny said I could give her the IOU while she decided, so I did."

The unapproachable way Reaper regarded him eased. Moon reasoned out it must be the IOU. Reaper must have taken it as a sign he wanted to make amends to Ginny, which he did want to do.

"You want one, too?"

"I think you're going to have your hands full paying Ginny's back without adding mine."

Moon exhaled. "Then we're good?"

"No, but I'm not planning on burying you in an unmarked grave anymore, either."

"Hell, that's progress." Moon grinned, moving so Reaper could get by.

The other brothers who had hung around to listen started dissipating, leaving him alone with Viper.

Viper waited until the last of the brothers left before he started talking. "Stud wants you to stay out of Jamestown."

"Larissa is under the Destructors' protection."

Viper didn't mince his words. "I'm not going to intercede with Stud. You're on your own there."

"You're not going to order me to stay away?"

"No, she's carrying your kid." He turned off the lamp on the work desk he was near. "Do what you feel you need to do, but you're going to do that regardless."

Moon gazed at him suspiciously. "Why are you looking at me like that?"

Viper's lips curled mockingly. "Brother, I'm done giving you unsolicited advice. It goes in one ear and out the other. Besides, it would be useless. You have fucked yourself over so bad with that woman she hates your guts."

"Ask me if I care," Moon snapped out through clenched teeth.

"Why ask when it's pretty evident you don't?" Viper's hand went to his shoulder as he rolled it tiredly. "You don't care for her or the kid," he stated matter-of-factly.

Moon's head reared back as if he had been struck. "I didn't mean that I don't care about my kid!" His voice rose incredulously.

"You need to be real with yourself." Viper stared at him

mockingly. "Put yourself in her place. You aren't coming across as father-of-the-year material. What in the fuck were you thinking to start a fight with one of Stud's men in the restaurant?"

"I wasn't the one who started it. I wanted her to—"

"Jesus." Viper snapped his mouth closed. "Listen, I said I wasn't going to do this, and I'm not. Good luck getting past the Destructors." He turned to the side to switch out another lamp then walked into the office.

"I can handle the Destructors." Moon raised his voice so Viper could hear him.

Mocking laughter sounded from the office.

Moon saw the lights go off before Viper came back out.

"They aren't The Last Riders. Stud and his men won't have any loyalty toward you. You fuck with someone under their protection, they are going to come at you hard. That's why Stud called me—to give me the heads-up." The mockery in his expression died. "I owe him too much to pit the club against him, and I'll tell you straight up—I won't. He rode with me for months to catch Raul. I owe Killyama for saving Winter's and Aisha's life, which I won't ever be able to repay —ever. Same goes with the Blue Horseman. You know what Calder did for Reaper. I can't repay that, either."

Moon stared at him, deadpan, not speaking the words he wanted to say. He didn't have to; Viper knew what he was thinking.

"I repaid my debt to you when the brothers wanted to vote you out every fucking week."

"I've got this; you'll see," Moon said confidently, striding toward the door.

Viper walked out with him, turning to lock the door as Moon started to head toward the clubhouse.

"Moon," Viper stopped him before he could move away. "You've been a loyal soldier, and I don't think you're going to be able to get yourself out of this fucking shitshow when you realize you care more about that kid than your pride. If it were me, I would be kissing Shade's ass to find out how to fix it."

"I'm never going to kiss Shade's ass for any reason."

"You'll be surprised at what you'll be willing to do for your kids. I didn't truly appreciate that fact until I had one of my own."

"I'd sacrifice my life for any child I have. I don't need Shade's help, nor anyone else's. I've got this; you'll see." Moon walked off before Viper could say anything else.

The problem with Viper was he considered him just a soldier. Where the club was concerned, Viper was right. He preferred letting Viper and Wizard bear the bulk of the responsibilities while he could take the easy route when he wasn't needed. Becoming king of the mountain within the club had never held any appeal to him; his forte had always been women. There wasn't a woman he couldn't have when he put his mind to it, he told himself confidently. Once he put his mind to having Larissa, she would be putty in his hand. Then, when he had her exactly where he wanted her, he would get custody of his child and throw her ass back to the Destructors.

He was midway up the steps when his cell phone vibrated. He checked it and saw Larissa had texted him her address and the time of her doctor's appointment five days from now. Pocketing his cell phone, he continued climbing the steps, whistling.

Hell, he didn't need any advice from Shade. The brother should be the one coming to him for advice. Shade might be an expert marksman, but in a face-to-face battle, no one escaped from the dark side of the Moon.

# CHAPTER THIRTY-TWO

L arissa had to swallow back the lump of fear at the back of throat as she watched Moon drive away.

"Are you all right?" Fat Louise asked sympathetically.

"Yes. This is all my fault. I shouldn't have stopped to have lunch. If I hadn't, I would have been at The Last Riders', and he would have at least known I was going to tell him," she said numbly.

Sex Piston scowled. "It wouldn't have made a difference to that dick," she said heatedly. "He would just find something else to hassle you about."

"I should have come outside to talk to him alone."

"Why? So he really could lay into you without anyone hearing? Girl, do you know how many women end up dead when they've been knocked up? He might be a Last Rider, but I don't know shit about him personally, do you?"

Sex Piston was piling on more to worry on about.

"No, I don't, other than when I've seen him in town and at The Last Riders'."

"He doesn't have a record," Killyama told them, easing the fear she had made a baby with a career felon. "Moon served in the Navy for fifteen years. When he got out, he went to work for The Last Riders."

The longer Killyama talked, the more she felt the fear coming back. Nothing she was revealing would give her a justifiable reason not to let Moon be involved in her child's life, other than him living in a motorcycle club. If he did buy a house, like he said he would, that would be yet another point in his favor.

Why hadn't she listened to her instincts and continued on to Treepoint from Bowling Green instead of stopping for lunch with Killyama and Sex Piston? Beth walked out of the restaurant while placing her wallet back in her purse. Should she ask her about Moon? Maybe she knew something Killyama didn't. Trepidation held her back; she was a hairs-breadth away from driving back to Bowling Green.

Larissa felt Stud's eyes on her.

"Where are you staying?"

"I was on my way back to Treepoint to live with my sisters again. I was staying with a friend of mine in Bowling Green until I decided what to do. To be honest, Moon's anger toward me is understandable, but I witnessed it at The Last Riders as well. It terrified me. I'm concerned about my child being exposed to that type of behavior. I left Treepoint when he said he never wanted to see me again, and I didn't look for another job because I had every intention of returning to Treepoint and telling him I was pregnant before the baby came despite my family's concerns and my own misgivings. I even got in an argument with my mother about it. She wanted us to move to Aruba. We argued, and that's why when my friend asked me to stay with her, I agreed; her place is across the street from my mom's."

Her voice grew frustrated. "I was in Blowing Green, trying to come to a decision about wanting to give Moon the benefit of the doubt that he's not obnoxious, rude, and overbearing when my friend Taya wakes me up to call the police because she saw a man hiding in her next-door neighbor's yard. I called the police while she showed me where he was hiding from the window. You know who it was?"

"Moon?" Stud hazarded the guess with an embarrassed expression.

"Yes!" Larissa practically yelled in irritation. "I should have let the police come and arrest him. Instead, I told them it was a mistake. The big idiot sat there for days. And you know what he did?" Her shrill voice made the listening men flinch.

Larissa could see from Stud's expression that even wild horses wouldn't make him ask.

"What?" Killyama asked with strangled laughter.

"He broke into my mother's house!"

"I would have called the police on his ass!" Sex Piston vented.

Larissa's shoulders slumped in defeat. "I didn't want to get him in trouble. I decided to come back to Treepoint and ask to meet him so we could talk. I wanted to talk to my sisters first and try to ease their concerns. Killyama had been calling me, wanting me to come back, so I texted and told her, and she wanted me to stop for lunch on the way to Treepoint, that I would be able to see Sex Piston and the rest of them, so I thought, *what's a couple of hours?*" She made a self-deprecating face at herself. "I can't seem to do anything right where he is concerned."

Stud gestured toward the other men. Bikes started then drove out of the parking lot. Turning his gaze back to her, he said, "You could have explained this to him here."

Larissa shifted on her feet awkwardly. "He freaks me out when he talks to me. I'm scared of him. When he came to my office to talk to me, he punched a hole in the wall," she explained.

Stud's hardened expression relaxed. "I wouldn't head back to Treepoint just yet. Wait until you and Moon can talk. When you're feeling more comfortable, go live with your sisters. The brothers and I can keep an eye on you in case he decides to throw any more punches at walls."

Larissa shook her head. "I don't have a place to live here. I don't have a job here—"

"Don't worry about a place to stay," Sex Piston interrupted. "My parents have a spare room; you can stay with them for as long as you want."

"I couldn't impose—"

"Girl." Sex Piston waved away her protest. "Sizzle will love the company. So will Pop. You could still work with your sisters. Women in Jamestown have babies, too."

"I still want you to be my midwife." Killyama used her pregnant belly to move Sex Piston out of the way. "We got you, girl. That motherfucker comes here to throw his weight around, I'll kick his ass."

Larissa gave a shaky laugh. "I'm not normally a wimp … or at least I don't think I am. I'm just not a very confrontational person."

"*Pfft*," Killyama sounded. "Don't worry about it. None of us have that problem."

Stud gave her a wry smile. "I can vouch for that."

Larissa watched as he got off his bike and took out his cell phone. Curious, she turned to Sex Piston.

"Knowing my husband, he's giving Viper a heads-up that you're under the Destructors' protection."

"That's only going to make Moon angrier." Worriedly, she started to move toward him.

Beth, who had remained silent until then, placed a hand on her arm. "Let Stud talk to him. Viper is reasonable, and he's used to dealing with Moon."

"I don't want to make the situation worse. I've already

messed it up bad enough."

"You made some bad decisions," Beth told her frankly. "But so did we. We snuck everyone into the club when we shouldn't have. None of us were exactly eager to confess, either, because we didn't want them to know we broke the rules. I'm not great at confrontations, either," she admitted, giving her a comforting squeeze on the arm. "And my sister is even worse. The Last Riders are overwhelming at first, but once you get to know them, you'll find none of them would actually physically hurt a woman. I do believe Moon hitting Ginny was an accident.

"Stay with Sex Piston's parents for a few days. Viper will talk to him. I can, too. Give him the information he wants and show him you're willing to meet him halfway where the baby is concerned. He is the baby's father; you're going to have to learn to get along with him, whether you want to or not."

Beth's sensible advice was what she had desperately needed.

"I can do that." Larissa felt herself grow more confident. How on earth was she capable of being calm and collected when a mother and child's life depended on her capabilities, yet she became a complete basket case when it had something to do with Moon?

"Good." Beth gave her an encouraging grin. "Their bark is really worse than their bite."

Stud, who had moved from behind Beth, heard what she said. His expression was comical as he resumed his seat on his motorcycle.

"I talked to Viper. He's going to do what he can to slow Moon's roll down, but he doesn't have high hopes. I made the Destructors' positions clear—you're under our protection." He started his bike. "I told him to keep Moon on a short leash, or I will."

Sex Piston glided toward him in her high-spiked boots. "That's my man."

Looking away at the passionate kiss Sex Piston gave Stud, Larissa caught Jet staring at her. She started talking to Killyama until Sex Piston came back.

"Let's get you set up at your new place."

"Are you sure your parents won't mind?"

Sex Piston swung an arm around her shoulders. "Trust me; this is going to make their day."

She followed Sex Piston's car in hers; the drive took only ten minutes before she was pulling into a driveway in front of a modest home.

Before she got out of the car, she typed out the address of Sex Piston's parents' home, the date and time of her appointment, and the information he would need for his insurance. Her finger hovered over the *send* button. She was about to take the first step into allowing Moon into their baby's life, and trepidation filled her. However, she was going to override the fear she was feeling and give him the chance to prove that he wasn't the short-tempered, volatile, and obnoxious man he had shown himself to be. Just as importantly, she promised herself to be more open in regards to the baby and stop being so afraid of him. That was easier said than done.

Holding her breath, she pushed *send*. Why did she feel as if she had just placed her life under Moon's thumb? He would either flick her away like a bug, squash her, or let her move around freely. She didn't have high hopes for the latter and just wanted to survive the other options.

A fluttering of movements made her hand go to where her child was tossing and kicking.

"You're a boy, aren't you?" she speculated. "Sit tight. Something tells me this is going to be a rocky journey."

# CHAPTER THIRTY-THREE

S he had never felt so nervous in her life. Watching the clock for Moon to arrive was nerve-racking.

The crinkling of a magazine made her glance toward the office, where Jet was sitting, flipping through the magazine; he seemed unbothered about having to come to Treepoint with her.

Sex Piston had texted her this morning that Jet would be driving and staying with her during the appointment. She had protested that the appointment was with her sister, so she would be fine going alone, but Sex Piston had argued until she gave in.

"Gosh ... he makes me want to join the Destructors," Priss whispered, staring appreciatively at Jet.

Larissa gave her a dirty look. "Don't you even think about him. From now on, if they belong to a motorcycle club, they're off limits."

Priss made a face at her. "You were never the fun one of the three of us."

Unable to argue the truth, Larissa settled for watching the clock.

Priss saw where her attention had turned. "Lana texted that she's on her way."

The opening of the door had three sets of eyes move toward it as Lana came rushing in.

"Okay, let's get this started. I have thirty minutes before I have to be back from lunch."

Larissa frowned. "Moon isn't here yet."

"He will be," Lana told her as she headed to the examination room. "He was parking his motorcycle as I was coming in the door."

"Yippee," Priss mumbled under her breath.

Giving Priss a quelling glance, she warned both of her sisters, "We are going to be professional and polite, aren't we?"

Her sisters both raised their hands.

"I promise," Lana said.

"Me, too," Priss agreed.

Larissa looked toward Jet, who was watching them.

"Why are you looking at me?"

"I want you to promise, too."

"Then you're going to be disappointed." Indifferently. he turned a page in his magazine. "Moon will get as he gives."

"I can tell this is going to go so well." Larissa rubbed her temples. The headache she had been battling since the drive from Jamestown was gradually becoming worse the closer she came to seeing Moon.

The sound of the door opening made her lower her hand. Forcing a polite smile, she motioned toward the examining room. "We're ready."

She didn't miss the way Moon's poker face turned foreboding at finding Jet in the lobby.

"Why is he here?"

"Jet drove me here. He's waiting to drive me back to Jamestown."

"I'll drive you back."

"On your motorcycle? I don't feel comfortable riding on a motorcycle. I'm fine driving back with Jet. We need to get started. Lana has to get back to the hospital."

Larissa walked into the examination room and sat on the exam table as Lana took a stethoscope out of the cart she had set up for her sister to save time.

Moon took a position against the wall as Priss shut the door.

"You can take the chair, Moon." Priss moved around Lana to ready the equipment for the ultrasound.

Larissa sat self-consciously as Lana did a routine check of her vital signs.

"I see Priss has taken your weight. You've gained a pound. How are you feeling?"

"Good."

Her sister gave her a concerned frown as the blood pressure gave a beep. "Your blood pressure is slightly elevated. That's new."

Larissa felt blood rushing to her cheeks when she saw Lana and Priss glance toward Moon. who was still standing against the wall, observing them in silence.

"I want you to take the blood pressure kit home with you. Text me the readings. I want to keep an eye on it."

"Okay," Larissa agreed.

"Lie back."

As she lay down on the exam table, she felt Moon's eyes on her. So far, she had managed to look in his direction only sparingly. His cold expression showed he'd rather be anywhere than in a room with them.

Staring at the ceiling, she blinked back tears. This was all her fault. She could practically read the feelings come off him in waves. Her carrying his child was Moon's worst nightmare.

When she felt a tap on her arm, she glanced back down to meet Lana's concerned eyes. Silently, she gave her a thumbs-up that she was okay.

"Everything is looking good," Lana told her. "Moon, do you want to see?" Lana pushed a button so they could listen to the baby's heartbeat as Moon came to stand next to the machine.

Watching him from under her lashes, Larissa didn't notice one change in his countenance, so she turned her head and stared at the blank wall.

"Do you have any questions, Moon?" Lana asked politely as she turned the machine off and began wiping the gel off Larissa's abdomen.

"He's healthy?"

Larissa sucked in her breath as Moon spilled she was having a boy.

"What?" Moon stared at them while Lana and Priss glared at him, aghast at what he had done.

Priss' hands went to her hips. Larissa thought it was to prevent herself from hitting him with the metal tray, which was on the table next to her.

"When I texted you the information that you were having a boy, I specifically reminded you that Larissa wanted the baby's gender to be a surprise!"

Larissa turned her face away.

Rather than be apologetic, Moon doubled down. "Was it a surprise when I told you?"

Larissa turned back to Moon. "We're done here." She made sure to keep her tone even so he couldn't hear how badly he had hurt her. "I haven't had lunch yet. If you wouldn't mind, could you get us a table at King's? I'd like to talk with you before I go back to Jamestown."

Without a word, Moon left the room.

Her sisters stared at the closed door, their expressions mirroring the same disgust.

Larissa sat up. "Moon is angry I've put him in this position." She made the excuse for Moon, not wanting her sisters to hate him for the way he had behaved. "He's angry, and he has a right to be. I should have told him I was pregnant instead of taking off like a coward. We have to get along, whether we like it or not, for the baby," she pleaded with her sisters. "Gradually, we might be able to become friends."

Priss looked at her as if she had taken leave of her senses. "We've been looking forward to one of us having a baby one day, and he's going to ruin it for us."

Larissa slid over the exam table. "I'm sure he'd say the same thing about me being the mother of his child."

Lana rolled the ultrasound back in place. "I agree with Larissa, Priss. We have to be understanding if we expect the same in return." She moved to stand back in front of her. "But I do want to say one thing." Her voice became firm. "You didn't make this baby on your own. It took two. I'm not going to watch him behave this way when he comes in for the appointments, or he can wait out in the lobby. Either you can say something, or I will."

"I will."

"Good. Then I need to get back to the hospital."

"Thanks, Lana."

"Anytime, sis."

"You really going eat lunch with that jerk?" Priss asked after Lana had left.

"Yes. We need to find a middle ground, not for us to be able to get along, but for the baby's welfare. I want him to have a healthy relationship with our child, and it's going to start today," she said with determination.

"You want me to come with you?"

"No, I think Moon and I need to have this talk alone. Sooner or later, I have to be able to talk with him and come to a mutual agreement to be more cordial toward each other."

Priss gave her a conspiring nod. "Fake it until you can make it sort of thing?"

Larissa shook her head seriously. "No, more like work on it until it comes true."

# CHAPTER THIRTY-FOUR

Moon asked Evie to seat him in a corner booth in a back room. He ordered iced tea, then waited for Larissa when Evie returned to the front of the restaurant after seating him.

As he stared unseeingly at the bread basket the waitress had brought, he castigated himself for the way he had acted. Why did she get to him so badly? All he had to do was look at her, and every nerve ending in his body went on high alert. He had never experienced this reaction before with the numerous women he had been with. The more he kept an emotional distance from her, the more out of whack he felt because of the baby. How could he dislike the mother so much while the burgeoning emotions he was beginning to feel for his child were both in the same package currently? Sure, the upheaval would end once his son was born, yet he determined not to let what he was feeling for the baby entwine with Larissa and keep them separate.

She didn't keep him waiting for long before she was sliding into the booth across from him.

When the waitress approached, she ordered herself a tea.

Once the waitress left, they sat in silence, just looking at each other.

"Moon …"

———

L arissa managed to put her trepidation aside and talk as if they were at least on speaking terms. "I know you dislike me. I apologize for not telling you I was pregnant when I found out. I kept putting it off because I kept imagining if I were you, how I would react if a complete stranger came up to me and told me they were pregnant. I hesitated too long. Then, when I truly was going to tell you, you came to the office and said you didn't want to see me again. I just … I didn't know what to do at that point. I left to stay with my mom and give you time to get over your anger toward me. I had every intention of coming back, but my friend asked me to stay with her. She ne—"

Moon's face remained passive while he took a slice of bread from the basket and started eating.

As she talked, he listened with half an ear while his eye roved over the other customers sitting in the room.

She was still talking when he finished the bread then rubbed his hands together to get rid of the crumbs.

"You know, what I'm hearing is nothing but excuses. Save yourself the trouble. The waitress is coming back; do you want something to eat?"

Larissa smothered down her hurt feelings, hoping that once he had the chance to air his grievances, they could move forward.

"No, thank you. I'm not hungry."

The thought of eating any food in front of him sent her stomach rolling. His appetite didn't seem to be affected as he ordered a ribeye dinner and asked the waitress to bring more bread.

"I've been looking at several houses for sale. I've narrowed it down to four. I've set appointments for Friday at twelve with a realtor to show them to you."

"For now, I'm going to stay in Jamestown."

"For now"—Moon narrowed his eyes on her—"that works until you decide which home you want."

"When I'm ready to move back, I'll find my own place."

"Exactly when will that be?"

"The question is: why is it so important that I do?" She gave him a questioning glance. "You plainly told me you never wanted to see me in town before I was pregnant. You don't make any effort to hide how much you dislike me … The way gossip is carried around town, everyone knows how I became pregnant. The baby won't be coming for several more months, and I really don't want to go through those months with all of them watching every move I make. No, thanks."

"I don't give a rat's fuck what anyone in this town thinks. I want you near, in town, so if anything happens, I'll be there."

"Nothing is going to happen," she assured him. "Even if something does, I have friends in Jamestown who I can turn to in a moment's notice until my sisters, or you, can get there."

Clenching his jaw, Moon nodded his head toward the side without taking his eyes off her. "Plane one of those friends?"

Larissa's face became pinched. "His name is Jet."

Moon gave a huff of air through his teeth. "I was being generous calling him Plane. Did Luggage give him his nickname?"

"I don't know. I didn't ask. Who nicknamed you—Cow?"

Moon didn't appreciate the sarcasm coming back at him. "That's another thing; I don't want to see his face at your appointments."

"You don't have the right to—"

———

**M**oon leaned forward in his seat then stopped cold at her reaction. From the flash of fear, it looked as if she thought he was going to hit her. Before he could assure her all he was going to do was keep the glass of tea near her shaky hand from spilling, Jet was there. pulling her out of the booth.

"Go sit at my table." Jet pointed at a table not far from where they were seated. "I ordered you soup and a sandwich. I need to have a word with Moon."

Moon watched Larissa walk away while Jet took her seat.

"You want to talk to me the way you were talking to Larissa?"

"Fuck off!" Moon snarled at him.

"I will, gladly, once Stud gives me the word. Until then, you might as well get used to my face."

"Then get used to having a new one when I rearrange it for you."

Jet gave a hollow laugh. "You can try ... but you'll get more than you bargained for. Unlike you, I was given my nickname for dropping a bomb on a motherfucker who didn't know better not to fuck with me. While, from what I hear, you supposedly earned yours by how easy it is for you to lay women. Although, I'm sure I heard incorrectly. From the way you're treating Larissa, I can't believe you can find a woman willing to give you the time of day. Pretty low class of you to reveal the gender when she didn't want to know."

Moon's temper soared at the put-down from the Destructor. "Larissa told you?"

"No, Larissa didn't say a word. I heard her and Priss talking after you left."

"Stud's got a real treasure in you hearing all kinds of shit. Shame you couldn't be in the room with us; you'd have seen she couldn't bring herself to look at the ultrasound machine. Pissed me off."

Jet's astounded expression made Moon wish he hadn't shared the information.

"So, you told her the baby's gender because she didn't look at the ultrasound and didn't ask for a picture?"

"What mother doesn't want to look or ask for a picture of the ultrasound?"

Jet's eyebrows lifted so high they met in the middle of his forehead. "I might be wrong on this, but I would assume," he said scathingly, "a mother who understands how to read an ultrasound and wants to keep the gender a surprise."

The thought should have occurred to him, yet it hadn't. He had been so busy endeavoring to harness his rioting cock at seeing Larissa's swollen abdomen that it had taken everything he could not to toss her sisters out the room and bury his cock inside the warm depths that had been haunting his nights?

He wasn't proud of his behavior—regret had immediately kicked in—but instead of apologizing, he did what he always did and doubled down.

"I don't get it. What's with you? If I can figure that shit out, you should have, too. Either that, or you don't want to." Jet tilted his head curiously. "What's wrong? You fired up she's knocked up? You planted that seed, and it sprouted. Man up and tend the fucking garden."

"What if you thought you planted it in someone else's garden?" Moon asked snidely.

"From where I'm sitting"—Jet sent a coveted glance in Larissa's direction—"there's not a damn thing wrong with that garden. I wouldn't mind tending it if you don't."

Moon surged out of his seat, about to lunge over the table. Freezing cold struck him as Jet's laughter reverberated through his skull. The dark side of him was prepared to strike when Evie walked into the room to refill Larissa's drink.

Jet saw he had been given a reprieve by the other woman's arrival. "Relax … I'm not going to steal Larissa from you." He got out of the booth. "I won't have to. You're practically giving her away. You've been in a club so long that you've forgotten how to treat a woman who isn't. Your loss, my gain." Jet gave him a dismissive glance. "Enjoy the bread."

Moon pulled out his wallet and took out some cash. Trailing Evie out of the room, he caught up with her, paid for his uneaten meal, then took off.

As he got on his bike, his mind played back the way Larissa had flinched when he righted her tea glass, and when he had walked by her table to leave.

He drove back to the clubhouse and was parking when he luckily spotted Viper and Train coming down the steps. Moon got off his bike to intercept Viper before he could get on his motorcycle.

"Where you two heading?"

Viper gave him a suspicious glance. "Train and I are meeting up with Reaper at his place."

Moon nodded his head at Viper's SUV. "Can I borrow your ride?"

Viper's eyebrow rose. "You want to borrow my car?"

"Yes. Can I or not? I'm in a rush."

"Sure." Viper reached into his pocket to take out his keys, pulling one of the keys off the ring before he handed it to him.

Moon took the key from him.

"You do have a current license, don't you?" Train joked.

If he didn't want to get back to the restaurant before Larissa left, he would shove the license up Train's ass.

He was already moving toward the SUV, but he took the time to let Train know he didn't appreciate his humor.

"Remind me to show you when I get back."

# CHAPTER THIRTY-FIVE

When she walked out of the restaurant, Larissa came to a stop upon seeing Moon leaning against an SUV. "I'll drive you back to Jamestown."

Struck speechless, she was trying to form a polite refusal when she felt Jet walking up behind her.

"She's driving with me."

Larissa was tired and cranky enough that she wasn't going to listen to the two men trading barbs with each other. She could be back in Jamestown before the argument ended, so it would be quicker to go along with Moon, forestalling the budding argument before it could start.

"I'll ride with Moon," she acquiesced, not missing the goading smile Moon gave Jet as he opened the car door.

Giving her a sheepish glance, he turned back to Jet. "Sorry, I'm an ass. I'm going to work on it."

She didn't quite trust Moon's apology but got in the SUV.

As she buckled the seat belt, she was relieved when Moon got in the vehicle without further words being spoken between them.

Worried, she looked in the side mirror as they pulled out of the parking lot. What would she do if he didn't take her back to Jamestown like he said he would?

"I have no intention of kidnapping you."

Some of the tension began to ease out of her, allowing her to somewhat relax.

"I want to apologize for the way I acted today, and yesterday."

Suspicious, Larissa turned her gaze from the window as he talked.

"When I imagined myself becoming a father, this isn't how I thought it would go."

She could hear the truth in his words.

"Me neither," she said softly.

"I've been taking it out on you, which I shouldn't have done. I'm sorry."

Larissa stared down at her hands. "I'm sorry, too. We wouldn't have been in this position if I had been honest."

Moon flicked on the blinker then turned onto the long stretch of road that would take them to Jamestown.

When she checked the side mirror again, Larissa saw Jet was following behind them.

"I don't know about that." Moon took his eyes off the road, giving her an amused glance. "We would still have had sex. The only difference would have been is that I would have known the correct name to call you."

The drastic change in the way he was speaking to her raised her guard up. What had brought the sudden change?

"Do you mind me asking: why did you decide to apologize in less than thirty minutes?"

"You can ask me anything," he offered. "To answer your question, you can thank Jet."

"Jet?"

"He let me have it for spoiling the surprise we're having a boy."

"Like you said, none of this is how we imagined."

Regret filled his eyes. "I was a damn jackass. I'm really sorry. When you didn't look at the ultrasound and didn't want a picture, I assumed you didn't care enough because I was the father."

Larissa sucked in a surprised breath at the revelation.

"Jet was a hell of a lot smarter than me. He said it was because you would have been able to see the baby was a boy or a girl."

His apology relieved some of the sting he had inflicted by his action.

"I would have."

"I'm an idiot. I also don't want you looking at me like you did at lunch. I was fixing your glass so it wouldn't spill over."

"I realized that. I overreacted. I'm sorry."

"Whew …" Moon gave her a quick amused glance before switching his gaze back to the road. "It's a good thing for me that it takes nine months for a baby to be born; it's taken me this long to get my head on straight. Until the time he gets here, I'm going to work on us becoming friends … with your help, of course."

Uncertainly flooded her. She wanted to believe he was being honest with her, yet her inner voice was shouting it was just for show.

"Moon, you don't have to put on a pretense for me. I know you won't believe this, but I truly have no desire to keep you away from your child. You don't have to put on a front for me," Larissa told him sincerely. "I might not have shown it, but I'm truly a sensible person. The craziest thing I've ever done in my life was open your bedroom door. Since then, I've made one mistake after another. I really don't want to make any more. I would like for us to become friends, if the offer is genuine."

"That goes both ways. I have to chance you're being just as front up as I'm being."

"There's where you have the advantage."

Moon gave her a curious look. "What do you mean?"

Her lips curled in laughter. "You know yourself. I suck at pretending to be someone else."

Moon's laughter filled the car. "Yes, you do."

For the rest of the car ride, they both attempted to learn more about each other. At first, Larissa responded to Moon's questions warily, afraid he could somehow use the information as ammunition. On the other hand, Moon didn't seem to have the same reservations, easily answering her questions, sometimes even poking fun at his answers.

"Are you from Kentucky?" she asked.

"No. I was born in Hawaii. You?"

"I've lived in Kentucky my whole life. How did you end up here?"

"I joined The Last Riders when I got out of the service. The club originated in Ohio then expanded into Kentucky."

"You go back and forth between the two?"

"Yes," he answered casually. "Where do you prefer living, Treepoint or Bowling Green?"

"Bowling Green. I'm close to my mother. Pris and Lana are, too, but they want to start a birthing center where there is a need. There are several options in Bowling Green, which Treepoint doesn't have. Anyway, that's why I moved here."

"Your mother doesn't want to move here?"

"I wish." She sighed. "Mom is attached to her home. She's also close to a friend of mine. Mom considers Taya another daughter. The only thing that would drag her away from Bowling Green is a beach. She travels a couple times a year, and one of the four of us usually goes with her. She's saving for Aruba now. What job did you do in the service?"

"A little of this, a little of that …" When he steered the SUV into slow lane to let a truck pass, Larissa saw his eyes move to the rearview mirror, checking if Jet was still following. "Mostly reconnaissance."

"Reconnaissance?" She had to stare out her side window to keep a straight face. "You get many assignments?" She gave a small cough to hide her strangled laughter; it took everything she could do not to tell him she had witnessed his expertise.

"A few. Mainly boring stuff. How about you? Do you like being a midwife?"

Larissa turned from the window. "I love it," she replied simply. "I love everything about it. I get to develop a close relationship with my clients and help them bring the most important person into the world. Most women couldn't tell you the name of the doctor who delivered their baby years later, but they remember me. I become a part of their family."

"You could do the same if you worked exclusively in a hospital."

"I want to offer my clients a choice between traditional medicine and holistic. They can go to the hospital to have their baby or stay home if there aren't any expected complications. The hospitals are more 'what I say goes.' It's impersonal. What's more personal than having to spread your legs and being examined by numerous staff members and physicians? Yet, they … whew … I'm sorry. When I start talking about being a midwife, I can go on."

"Sounds like you take it more seriously than it being just a job."

"I do. All my family does. My mom was a neonatal nurse before she retired. What do you do, since you're no longer in the military?"

"A little of this, a little of that," he responded obliquely. "Work at the factory for The Last Riders, do security when they need me, assist the brothers on their jobs—stuff like that."

"Sounds time consuming."

"It is," he agreed. "But I've never been afraid of hard work, and it does come with rewards."

"So I heard."

Moon cocked a mischievous brow at her. "You mean the women?" He gave her a slow grin. "I can't say I had a problem getting them, even before I joined The Last Riders."

That Moon was an insensitive jerk was one of the few things she did know about him.

Wishing she were clever enough to give a tart comeback, she changed the subject. She was the one who had started it with the innuendo about the rewards of being a Last Rider. "How about your mother? Does she live in Kentucky?"

"No. I talk to her occasionally. We aren't close, like you are with your mother."

"Do you have any brothers or sisters?"

"No."

When she saw the bridge coming up ahead, Larissa was almost sorry they had reached Jamestown.

"Do you need me to give directions?"

"No, I looked it up when you texted me the address. How do you like staying with Sex Piston's parents?"

"They are very sweet."

Larissa didn't miss his cross expression at her answer.

"They really are!"

"I'm not doubting they are *to you*."

"They aren't to you?"

"I can't say."

Confused, she stared at him. "Then why did you make that face when I said they are sweet?"

"I'd rather you had told me you hate them and don't want to stay there," he admitted.

She couldn't help giving an appreciative laugh. "I like your honesty."

Moon brought the car to a stop in front of Sex Piston's parents' home to study her intently. Did he think she was joking?

"I'm serious."

His lips twisted wryly. "At least I can chalk one thing you like about me on the scoreboard."

Unbuckling the seat belt, she reached for the door handle in preparation to get out. "Thank you for the ride. I'm glad we were finally able to have a conservation without arguing."

"Technically, it's our second one we got through without arguing."

The way Moon was looking at her made her feel heated and needy. Her throat went as dry as a desert, meaning she was unable to get a word out, even if she could form one in her mind.

Jet's sudden appearance as he opened the door made her exit the car.

She was closing the door when Moon got out.

"I'll text you when I set up another appointment with Lana."

"Yeah … I …" He broke off with a glare at Jet. "You mind?"

Jet glared back, unperturbed. "Not at all. Go ahead. I'll wait."

Was she going to have to witness this pissing contest every time she went out?

"I'm fine, Jet. Thank you. Moon and I have come to an understanding."

"Wow. What a shocker."

Larissa frowned. "We're all three going to get along, aren't we?"

She stared at the men until Jet stepped away and moved back to sit on his motorcycle, then breathed of sigh relief that the budding argument between the two men had been averted.

"What were you about to say before you were interrupted?"

"I was just about to suggest we meet tomorrow to discuss which house …"

Had the conservation they had on the drive just been a ruse to get what he wanted?

"… I'm considering buying for myself. I get you're not ready to move back to Treepoint yet. When you're ready, at least you'll be more informed on what's available on the housing market. I would just like your input."

Indecision filled her.

"I'd like to find out before I sign on the dotted line that it's a home you wouldn't be worried about our child staying in when he comes for a visit."

Larissa set her hesitation aside. What if he bought a home with a swimming pool, or on a busy road? She'd rather give Moon her help than be sorry later.

"What time?"

"How's two?"

"I'll see you tomorrow."

"Thank you, Larissa."

She was confident she had made the right decision, based on the earnest way Moon had looked at her before he got in the car.

"See you tomorrow," he called out the window as he pulled away.

As she turned to walk inside, Jet's pitying expression stopped her.

"You fell for that, hook, line, and sinker."

As Moon's car turned the curve and disappeared out of sight, her composure slipped.

"No, I didn't," she argued, clearing her clogged throat.

"Then why go?"

"You can't fight a tidal wave; you have to swim for your life or get swept away."

"Ahh … so you're going to swim." Jet nodded approvingly.

"No," she said wryly. "I've never been much of a swimmer. I'm more likely to sink than be swept away."

"Then …I don't understand?"

"There is a third option." Protectively, she laid a hand on the swell of her abdomen.

"Which is …?"

"Prevent the tidal wave before it happens."

# CHAPTER THIRTY-SIX

"What do you think about this one?"

"Uh ... it's a lot of house." Larissa could only stare at the huge living room. Who in the world would need a living room this big?

"I want plenty of space. I've never really had any space to call my own. Only had bedrooms, not even with an ensuite."

"I've shared bedrooms my whole life, too. I still wouldn't buy a house this size."

Moon opened the fridge then moved around, investigating the other appliances. "Then it's a good thing you're not the one who's interested in buying the house."

"True." Nervously, she thrust her hands into the pockets of her maternity dress. She would never be able to afford any of the homes Moon had taken her to look at today. With each they were shown, the more inadequate she felt.

"I like this one the most so far." Moon stepped out of the pantry to stand in the living room. "What do you think?"

"It's a beautiful home," she said flatly.

Moon frowned. "Is there something wrong with it?"

"No." Other than if Moon took her to court to get custody

of their child, if it came down to how better he could financially provide than she could, there wasn't a thing wrong that she could find.

"I can take the largest bedroom and make the one next to it a nursey for the times I have the baby."

"That would work." She nodded. Walking to the window, she looked outside. "The construction going on in the neighborhood shouldn't disturb him there."

The home Moon was considering had been built in a new subdivision in Treepoint. Spacious lots had been sectioned out into one-acre lots where the larger homes had been built. Another section of the subdivision had been sectioned off to build smaller homes, and construction had just started.

"This area is very pretty. When I was looking for a house, I considered buying one of the three-bedroom ones, but it's going to take at least a year before any of them will be finished."

"You toured the model home?"

"I did."

Moon moved to the window with her. "We had a mild winter; some of them could be completed ahead of schedule. Might be worth a shot to ask your realtor to check it out for you," he suggested. "You met Drake Hall when we went by his office. Talk to him; he's the best realtor in town."

"Before I went to Bowling Green, I was looking on my own and was getting nowhere. I'll talk to him when you take the keys back."

He gave her a boyish grin. "I'm glad you're at least considering moving back to Treepoint."

Had her heart just double-tapped the walls of her chest? Moon had a lethal charm; she would have been easily taken in if her survival instincts weren't constantly on the alert. She couldn't explain the strange tingle of danger that ran down her spine when Moon spoke or moved in a certain way. Only that it happened.

At first, she had blamed it on their terse interactions during their initial meetings. Then she blamed it on finding out she was pregnant and the fear of his interactions. The more she discovered, the more familiar she became with the knowledge that the tingle wasn't easing—it was becoming stronger.

She turned from the window to give the room another once-over. "You'll have to buy a lot of furniture to fill all this space."

Moon shrugged. "One of the women in the club is a designer. I'll have her take care of it for me. I'll save the nursery for me to do, with your help, if you wouldn't mind?"

"I'd like that."

Moon nodded his head toward the window. "Jet going to be coming along?"

"I'll talk to Stud."

Despite the strange tingle urging caution, Larissa didn't want to backtrack the ground they had gained. Moon was no longer regarding her with hostility and seemed to be making an honest effort of overcoming the uncomfortable situation they had found themselves trying to navigate though. Whether it was a good faith effort or contrived, there was only one way for her to find out, and that involved him gaining her trust.

"Do what you think is best for you. I don't need Sex Piston breaking my neck if you're just doing it because I said something. I can get used to having him around. I'd rather not have to look over my shoulder while we're choosing what to buy for the baby. This is my first child—I want to enjoy the experience."

Larissa felt a lump in her throat at hearing the sincerity in his voice.

"Same." She gave him a misty smile.

After they turned off the lights and locked all the doors, they drove to Drake Hall's real estate office. Once there, she waited in the outer office while they discussed making an offer on the last house they had seen.

She was in the midst of making a list of baby items for Moon when the receptionist told her she could go into Drake's office.

Drake rose from the desk as she entered, motioning her to the chair in front of his desk. "Moon told me you might be interested in one of the new builds in Contessa Court?" he said, returning to his chair.

"Yes, if I can get it for the right price. When I toured the model home, the developer said it would be the end of the year before any of the builds would be completed. I wouldn't want to wait that long, so if you could check and see if they're on the same timetable, I was hoping I would luck out and they will be available sooner."

"I'll certainly check it out for you." Taking a form out of his desk, he reached for a pen. "How many bedrooms?"

"Three, and at least two baths."

"I'm friends with the developer. I'll see what I can do."

"I'd appreciate your help."

After they left the office, she felt as if a huge weight had been taken off her back. She had come to a decision while inside the office to buy a house in Treepoint. It didn't matter if it was in the same subdivision or not, she would buy one where Moon would have access to his child.

"Would you like to grab a bite to eat?"

Larissa gave him a disappointed sigh. "I would if I could. I've already made plans with Priss and Lana to have dinner and go to a movie."

"Oh. Okay, then, another time." His downcast expression tugged at her conscience.

"You're welcome to join us, if you'd like?"

"I wouldn't want to ruin your sisters' night."

Larissa burst into laughter. "I'm sure they won't mind."

"If you're sure, then; I haven't been to a movie in a while."

Opening the car door, she saw him looking around. "Is something wrong?"

"I was looking for Jet. Is he going to the movie with us?"

"No, I texted him that he could go on back to Jamestown. Lana and Priss said they would take me back."

"I'm surprised Jet went ahead and left without Stud's say-so."

"I texted him also."

"You were busy while I was selling my soul."

Larissa got in the car, and Moon closed the door then rounded the hood to get in the driver's seat.

"Did you try to bargain the price down?" Larissa asked, buckling the seatbelt.

"No, I don't bargain when there's something I want."

The evening started off shaky when Moon and she showed up at the Silver Spoon for dinner. She had texted her sisters on the way to the restaurant; both made an attempt to be friendly. However, the effort fell short, as mistrust shone in their eyes for most of the meal. It was only when Moon mentioned that she had talked to Drake about purchasing a house at Contessa Court that their frosty attitude began to thaw.

"You're definitely going to move back to Treepoint?" Priss asked excitedly.

"If I can find a house I want." Placing the slice of cake she had ordered for dessert in the middle of the table to share, she acknowledged speaking with Drake. "Most of the homes for sale in Treepoint need repairs. I want something ready to go." Larissa gave her baby bump a gentle pat. "I'm going to have my hands full with the baby. I don't want to do any renovations. I struggle enough just changing an air filter or a lightbulb."

"I can vouch for that," Priss teased her. "You nearly electrocuted yourself when you tried to fix the toaster."

"I'm not very mechanically gifted." Larissa flushed at her sister tattling on her.

Swiping the cherry off the top of the cake before anyone else could, Lana ate it then used the spoon to point at her. "Larissa has more lives than a cat. When she was two, she turned the stove over on herself. We lost count of the number of times she has nearly electrocuted herself. The toaster was just the tip of the iceberg," she confided to Moon. "Mom said she had to start dyeing her hair in her thirties because of Larissa.

"She woke up early in the middle of the night one time and decided she was going to surprise us all with breakfast. That was when she was three. At four, she talked me into letting her curl my hair. I had unplugged the hair curler and told her she could. She caught me not paying attention and plugged it back it." Lana butted her spoon against her to steal the last bite of the cake. "I still haven't forgiven her for ruining my fourth-grade pictures."

Piqued at her sisters ratting on her, she gave Moon an innocent face. "They're exaggerating."

Skeptical, Moon narrowed his gaze on her. "So, what your sisters are saying is you're accident prone?"

She wished she could form a quick comeback to put Moon in his place, but she could only sit there with her mouth open like a fish out of water. How could she come up with a comeback when she kind of was?

One thing her family enjoyed was a sense of humor, especially when it was directed at her.

Laying her spoon on the table, she tugged the sleeve of her dress down to her wrist. "What my sisters are failing to tell you is each of those accidents were a direct result of one of them doing something to instigate my behavior into having said accidents."

The laughter at the table was abruptly cut short. Priss started motioning the waitress for the check. Lana started choking on the cake she had stolen from her, placing the napkin over her face.

"How are they …?" Moon's gaze dropped from her eyes to the swell of her belly.

Larissa helped him out when he seemed lost for words. "Put it this way," she said silkily, "if you hadn't gone upstairs the night I went into your room, you still might be sitting at this table."

Moon's eyes shifted in concern to Lana. "Is she okay?"

Larissa looked toward her sister. "She's fine. She's just eating crow."

# CHAPTER THIRTY-SEVEN

"Your sisters may never speak to you again."

Larissa stared out the dark window as Moon drove her back to Jamestown. "Pfft." She released a puff of air sardonically. "Yes, they will. My sisters tend to forget the situations they put me in, so every now and then, I have to remind them."

"How were they responsible for you turning the stove over on yourself?"

"Mom had given Lana and me each a cookie. Lana had taken mine and told me she had hidden it in the stove."

"Was the cookie there?"

"No. I'm sure she ate it."

"Without a doubt." His amused voice had her rolling the window down. Damn. Maybe accepting Moon's offer of a ride to Jamestown wasn't the smartest move she had ever made.

"How about falling down the steps?"

"Either I was pushed or tripped."

"What about the toaster?"

"Payback for me burning Lana's hair."

"And I thought boys were the troublemakers."

"Nope. We're lucky we're having a boy. Girls are sneakier."

Larissa felt Moon's surprised glance at her.

"I would have thought you'd prefer having a girl."

"I just want a healthy baby, I'm more shocked than anything else. There haven't been many boys in our family. We haven't had one born in two generations."

"That long?"

"Yes. My mom isn't going to be thrilled. She was so sure I was going to have a girl that she's been buying everything pink."

"Your sisters have, too," he told her.

Larissa turned to look at him. "How do you know?"

"That's how I found out you're pregnant. I was helping emptying the office above yours when I came out of the elevator and saw them holding a sleeper. It was pink."

"Really?"

"Yes, that's how I figured out you were pregnant."

Larissa started laughing.

"What's so funny?"

She had to wipe her tears away from her eyes. "You don't get it?" she asked, gurgling on her laughter.

"No ... Should I ...? Damn."

She could tell by the tone in his voice that he must have figured out Priss' deception.

"Your sister texted me the wrong gender."

"I think so."

"We're having a girl?"

"Surprise!"

"That's not cool."

"Well, to be fair, you telling me in the first place wasn't fair."

"No, it wasn't," he admitted. "It also means I've done it twice."

"Don't worry about it. With my family's track record, it was a foregone conclusion I was going to have a girl. Are you disappointed about not having a boy?"

"Not really. I'm like you—the most important part is I want them healthy. Though, I will be on the outlook for any sneaky behavior her aunts might teach her."

The rest of the way back to Jamestown, they talked about the movie they had seen.

When they arrived back at where she was staying, Larissa was sorry to see the evening end. He had been considerate and attentive the whole evening. Having a man like Moon wanting to spend time with her was as heady as wine.

"Thank you for bringing me back."

"No problem. The least I could do for letting me tag along. When do you want to go shopping?"

"Does Saturday work for you?"

"Yes, it does. I'll know by then if my offer was accepted."

"Are you going to miss living in the clubhouse?"

"No, not all the brothers live in the club."

"Will you still be going back and forth between Treepoint and Ohio?"

"No. I only seesawed between the two because I didn't have anything holding me in place."

"Now you do?"

"Of course. I don't plan on being an absent father."

Larissa let out a small gasp.

"What's wrong?"

His concerned voice brought an inexplicable reassuring warmth to the dubious part of her mind, which was still doubting the change in his behavior.

"The baby kicked. I guess she liked your answer."

"May I?" Moon extended his hand toward her abdomen.

Taking him by the wrist, she placed it over where the baby had kicked.

The silence stretched out as they waited for the baby to kick again. A streetlight in front of the car exposed Moon's face. When the baby kicked, his tough features broke into a tender expression that most men wouldn't feel comfortable revealing.

"Are you sure Priss was trying to pull one over me? He kicks like a boy."

"I guess we'll have to wait and find out."

Her heart did the double-tap thump in her chest when Moon leaned forward to kiss her cheek.

"Thanks for letting me feel him kick."

"You're welcome."

"I've been worried I'd miss out on some of the small stuff." He straightened back in his seat.

"The baby is yours, too. I might not be the mother you envisioned having your child, but I don't want to steal the joy of becoming a father, too."

"Jet told you what I said?"

"About me not being the garden you wanted? Yes."

"Asshole."

"Why? You said it."

"Not within your hearing."

"At the time you said it, would it have mattered if I had?"

"No, it probably wouldn't have," he confessed.

"I can handle what you say about me, even if it is behind my back. I'd rather you talk honestly than be deceptive about your feelings."

"I get that," he agreed.

"I suppose you do." Unconsciously, she gave a heartfelt sigh of regret.

Moon had straightened in his seat, but his palm still rested on her abdomen as they talked. She could feel his

273

thumb gently stroking back and forth through the material of her dress.

"I should have said something the moment you spoke to me that night. I—"

"Let's not discuss that night," he cut her off. "How about we pretend I saw you downstairs and persuaded you to come upstairs to my room?"

Larissa shook her head. "I'm not good at pretending at something I would never do."

"You don't think I would have been able to convince you into having sex with me?"

"No, you wouldn't have."

"Wow. Even if you didn't know then I was an ass?"

"No, not even if you had been smooth as butter."

"Any particular reason why not? I'm not your type? My hair color—"

"None of those. I simply have never had a casual … hook-up."

"Never?"

"Never," she confirmed, thankful he wasn't able to see the red flush she was sure was staining her cheeks.

"You weren't a virgin."

"No, I wasn't. I had a boyfriend in college. We broke up after we graduated."

"Because you wanted to live in different places?"

"Bryer ended our relationship when the woman he was cheating on me with threatened to tell me."

"That had to hurt."

"Broke my heart at the time," she admitted.

"Are you over him?"

Larissa didn't have to think long for the answer. "Yes, I have been for some time," she replied instantly.

"Hmm … in that case, I might have been able to coax you upstairs. I can be very persuasive when I want to be."

"Of that, I have no doubt." Moving his hand away, she reached for the door handle. "I'll see you Saturday. I'll drive myself to Treepoint. Text me where to meet you."

"Larissa ..."

The strange tingling sensation ran down her spine at the sensual way he spoke her name.

"You can't tell me you didn't play pretend when you were a child."

"I did. Ask Lana and Priss how much I sucked at it."

"Sweetness ... you weren't playing the right games." Moon swept the collar of her shirt to the side of her neck to pull her toward him.

Had he turned the heat on? She was becoming overwhelmed, and he was only lightly touching her.

"I should go inside ..." she murmured.

"Why?" Moon shifted in his seat to bend over the console, bringing him closer to her. "Aren't you curious what a kiss between us would be like now that I know who you are?"

That could be a double-edged sword. What if the encounter they had shared was only because he'd thought she was the other women? Did she really want to know if the desire that had culminated in them conceiving a child was only because she had deceived him?

She twisted her hands in her lap, waiting for his lips to descend on hers.

When she remained silent, Moon must have taken it for acquiesce and brought his lips down on hers.

Her fears dissolved instantly. The heat suffusing her body couldn't be one-sided. Moon kissed her as if she were a priceless artifact that needed to be explored. His tongue traced the contours of her lips before delicately prying her lips apart.

A storm of emotions caused her to struggle with herself to end the kiss before she was too far gone, but another part pleaded with her not to. Dazedly, she didn't know which inner voice to listen to.

Clutching the front of his shirt, she opened her mouth wider at his silent urging, giving him what he wanted.

Moon's hand slid to the back of her neck, caressing the skin there, making her wish his hand were touching a more intimate spot.

Something about their chemistry was like throwing nitroglycerin on a forest fire. The ensuing blaze couldn't be put out. Only the thought of the scorched earth that would be left behind if she continued to let it flourish made her break the kiss.

"I guess we answered that question." Clearing her throat, she fumbled with the door handle before managing to open the door. "See you Saturday." She got out and shut the door,

Moon met her at the front of the car. Before she could say anything, he lifted the purse she had forgotten in the car. Blushing, she took it from him.

"Thanks," she mumbled.

"Anytime." Bending down, he placed a chaste kiss on the corner of her mouth.

As she walked up the driveway, she refused to look back, telling herself she should have shut him down when he had made the move to kiss her. She should have known better than to let Moon talk her into kissing him. How many times had Lana and Priss joked about her having nine lives?

*Stupid, stupid woman*, she blasted herself.

Curiosity killed the cat.

# CHAPTER THIRTY-EIGHT

W alking through the garage at the back of The Last Riders' factory, Moon waited for Shade to buzz him inside.

Hearing the clink of the steel door being unlocked, he opened the heavy door and went inside, finding Shade sitting at the desk, surrounded by monitors covering every inch of The Last Riders' property.

"Brah, you look like you need to get some sleep." Walking closer to the long desk, he saw Shade had spread numerous pictures out. "Still no luck?"

Pinching the bridge of his nose, Shade didn't bother to look up at him. "None."

Moon sat down in the other computer chair, rolling it closer to the desk to study the pictures. "I don't get what we're missing."

Shade dropped his hands to the armrests, leaning his head back. "I don't, either. There has to be two working together. One on our end and one in the factory in Ohio. If that's the case, then how are we not at least catching one of them in the act?"

"Damn." Moon continued study the pictures, his hand going to his chin to rub his jaw line. "The only suggestion I have is the same one I've been advising—shut it down to outside workers and only let the members do the work."

"Viper doesn't want to put the workers out of a job. Most of them have families to support."

"What do you think?"

"What I think doesn't count. Viper is the decision maker. I agree with you, but I won't be the one handing out termination notices."

From the pictures and the videos he had watched repeatedly, there was nothing that stood out which could lead to who was responsible for the thefts in the factory.

"We've tried it all, except terminating the employees. They stopped for a couple of months when the brothers started escorting the trucks, and then it started again."

"Because they found another way to combat that difficulty," Moon mused out loud.

"Yes, we haven't figured how they did it in the first place, and now we're stumped in whatever new method they're using." Shade lifted his head. "You haven't had your head in this for the last couple of months, what's the sudden turnaround?"

"No turnaround. I never lost my focus, just had to deal with my personal shit first."

Shade raised an inquiring brow. "How's that working out for you?"

"Coming along. Could be better, could be worse."

"You talked to Stud?"

"Had to. I wasn't going to cause a rift between Viper and Stud unless I had to. It was easier talking to him than starting a war. Besides, I want that fucking bike I ordered from him."

"He drive a hard bargain?"

"Not too bad."

Shade's lips twisted in a sardonic smile. "Could be worse, could be better?"

"Pretty much. I have to be reasonable—don't argue with Larissa and cut out any show of temper around her. If he hears one word of me not playing by his rules, my ass will be on the line, not the club's, and hell will freeze over before I get the bike I ordered."

"That's a tall order for you to fulfill."

"Not too bad." He shrugged. "I expected worse. He's already pulled Jet back."

"What about Sex Piston?"

"He said, all I have to do to keep Sex Piston from giving her two-cents worth in Larissa's ear is to make her bitch happy. We all know Sex Piston is a rottweiler where her bitches are concerned. Larissa has formed a bond with Killyama, and Sex Piston knows that. Plus, she likes Larissa. They call her an honorary bitch."

"Jesus."

"Yeah, believe me, brother, I feel Razer, yours, and Train's pain."

Shade stood. "Just don't make the same mistake Razer did. He'll never live that down."

"I have no intention of stepping in that litterbox. If I feel the need, Ohio is only a few hours away."

Shade started to pick up the pictures.

"Leave them. I'll look over them again."

"Good luck. Between Rider, Reaper, you, and me, we've looked through those pictures a thousand times, and that includes all the videos. Going to bed. Don't call me unless it's an emergency. I have to be at the factory by seven."

"Ouch. Razer still won't take over managing the factory full-time?"

"He can't. He's working on a project. I'm lucky he's still working two days a week."

"Might as well face it and take the job back full-time."

"Nope. Lily's expecting again. I'm not going to leave her to handle the kids alone."

"Congrats."

"Thanks."

"Lily going to use Larissa or Priss?"

"No." Shade picked up his Glock, placing it in the small of his back, then shrugged into his jacket. "She said she liked them too much to make them deal with me."

"You can't be that bad in a delivery room." Moon laughed.

Shade gave him the cold glance he was familiar with. "I won't tolerate any mistakes where Lily's care is concerned. The doctors know that, and it makes them nervous."

"It would make me nervous, too," he said wryly.

"Whatever it takes," Shade said with deadly calm.

"Whatever it takes," Moon agreed, just as serious.

Moon resumed analyzing the pictures after Shade left. Monitoring the cameras as the members came and left distracted him intermittently.

An hour after Shade had left, Moon saw Viper leave his home, walking toward the back of the factory. Raising the garage door at Viper's approach to save him the trouble of getting his finger scanned, he then lowered the door when Viper walked through and waited until he saw Viper outside his door before buzzing him through. Then Moon turned in the chair to face Viper.

"What's got you out so late?"

"Shade called. He said you were looking over the pictures."

"Went through some of the tapes again, too."

Viper reached into his pocket to pull out a pack of cigarettes. "I thought this would help." Tossing him the pack of cigarettes, Viper waited for his reaction.

"You even remember my favorite brand."

"Brother, I remember anything that makes you tick."

"You going to stay for a while?"

"As long as I need to. Have at it."

Moon nodded. Then he got up to let Viper have the chair. Taking his gun, he left the security room. Viper was already raising the garage door as the door of the security office closed behind him.

Striding across the parking lot, he went up the path behind the clubhouse. Going to the picnic table, he lifted himself to sit on the top, his feet going to bench where people normally sat.

Staring out into the dark night toward the mountains, he opened the cigarettes and took one out to light. Setting the pack down on the table within easy reach, Moon cleared his mind. Concentrating on the thefts in the factory like a never-ending reel, over and over the reel played. Intermittently, he would put out a cigarette and light another.

He'd gone through half a pack and dawn was beginning to light the night sky when he put out a cigarette half-smoked and rose from the table.

Returning back to the security room, Viper looked at him expectantly. "Well?"

"We've been going off the idea that it's an employee taking advantage of one of our weaknesses that we don't know about. It's more organized than that."

"How organized?"

"When I talked to Shade, I thought two. It's more than that. There's more going on here than we assumed. They're using the trucks."

Viper shook his head. "We've been monitoring them too closely."

"I don't know how, but they're stealing what they want during the shipping."

"Solution?"

"We have to bring in a plant."

# CHAPTER THIRTY-NINE

"I s there anything I forgot to buy?"

"Let me think ..." Larissa pretended to give Moon's question a deep thought as she looked at the salesclerk who was ringing up the colossal amount of purchases Moon was making. "Do you sell prom dresses?"

"No, but we get new merchandise every week." Humorously, the clerk continued ringing the purchases.

Her breath hitched in her throat when Moon gave the clerk a captivating wink.

"I'll leave my number, so you call me."

Reaching into his back pocket, Moon took out his wallet to take out his credit card. She realized he wasn't joking when he asked for a pen and paper to write his number down. The salesclerk's features turned a bright shade of pink as she gave Moon his receipt and card back.

"I'll make sure to give you a call," she gushed, "when the new inventory comes in."

Wanting to get away from the flirtation going on right in front of her face, Larissa reached for a couple of the bags within reach.

Moon moved the bags away. "Go ahead to the car. I'll come back for these after I carry the boxes out," he directed her.

"Okay." She stepped around Moon as he easily lifted a box containing the crib they had chosen and walked through the sliding glass door.

Outside, she waited next to the SUV while Moon lowered the box to the ground to press the *unlock* button.

"I could have carried a few of the bags," she snapped, angry at herself more than at Moon. Why did she care he had flirted with the clerk? What he did was none of her business. She had to keep her head on straight and not let the responsibility Moon felt for the baby she was carrying get tangled into believing he felt the same way toward her. Nor let her emotions overrule her common sense.

"I wanted your hands free as a precaution. The sidewalk has a big step down. With me carrying the box, I wouldn't have been able to catch you in time if you had any difficulty."

"I didn't think of that." Ashamed at herself, she glanced away from Moon. "I'm not usually such a Negative Nancy."

"It's cool." As he opened the car door for her, the smile he gave her reminded her of the one he had given the salesclerk.

She got in the SUV and waited as Moon went back inside the children's boutique. Scrolling on her phone to keep herself from imagining Moon talking to the clerk without her presence made the wait drag by.

After fifteen minutes, she wanted nothing more than to call Lana or Priss to pick her up. Not willing to make a fool of herself twice in the same day, she remained sitting in the car, promising herself it would be the last outing with Moon. Other than the baby appointments, there was no need for them to spend time together.

Once she came to the stark conclusion, Larissa found it easier to wait patiently and was even able to give Moon a nonchalant smile when he got in the car after loading the purchases in the back.

"Sorry it took so long. The clerk wasn't able to find the key to the storeroom where the dolly was kept. She had to call the manager."

"No problem. I was able to take care of a few emails." Brushing off his apology made her feel more in control than she had in a long time.

Larissa didn't understand the strange look Moon gave her.

Glancing back at the huge mound of purchases he had crammed into the SUV, Larissa shook her head at him. "You're spoiling her before she's even been born."

"Start as you mean to go on."

"I hope you're joking."

"I am."

Ignoring the boyish appealing way he was teasing her, she steeled herself to withstand the insidious way he managed to slip under the barriers she was attempting to barricade herself behind.

"Mind if I drop this load off before I drive you back to Jamestown?"

"Go ahead."

"Any news from Drake about the possibility of getting a home in the subdivision you wanted?"

"Yes. He called yesterday. Seems the developer has run into financing problems and is offering to sell me one of the model homes."

"Is it the size you want?"

"Slightly larger. Three bedrooms, three baths, and office space I can use as a bedroom. Luckily, I pre-qualified when I started looking for a home when I first moved to Treepoint. I made an offer, and they accepted."

"Congratulations."

"Thank you. The house will be big enough for my sisters and me to live in without us tripping over each other."

"I'm glad you'll be so close to my home. It'll make it so much easier for us."

Unable to help herself, she laid a hand on his arm. "Thank you, Moon," she said simply.

He darted her a quick glance. "For what?"

"For making this easier for me. My greatest fear was raising our baby while we're in a tug of war between us. I didn't want that for the baby, or us either," she confessed. "It's a war neither of us could win."

"No, it wouldn't be," he agreed with a grim edge to his voice.

She nervously running her hand down her jean clad thigh as she peered out the window, realizing they weren't going to The Last Riders' clubhouse.

"I thought you were dropping the baby items off?"

"We are. I closed on my new house yesterday."

Her head snapped toward him. "That was quick."

"Helped that it was a cash offer."

"I imagine."

Moon turned onto the street of the home he had bought, and as the house came into view, all she could think about was how in the world he had been able to come up with the cash to pay for the expensive home.

As if sensing what she was thinking, Moon glanced in her direction. "Don't worry; I didn't get the money from doing anything illegal."

"I wasn't—"

"You were … but that's okay. I've worked long hours for most of my life. Never really been into buying expensive toys or wasting money. I work too hard for my money to spend it on something that would just end up in a garbage dump or a scrapyard."

"Not a lot of people think that way."

"Maybe not." Moon brought the car to a stop. "But most people haven't been as poor as I was."

"You had a rough childhood?"

"Could have been better, could have been worse." Moon's hand went to the door handle. "You want to make us something to drink while I unload the boxes?"

"Okay."

Moon unlocked the front door before going back to the SUV.

When she walked into the house, she came to a stop when she saw the front room was already filled with furniture.

"Excuse me."

She moved out of the doorway and managed to play off her shocked surprise. "Wow. This is stunning. Did you have a furniture store on speed dial?" she joked while inwardly fighting the panic filling her at Moon being able to accomplish so much in such a small window of time.

Clearly, she had underestimated him, believing he was equal to her on what she could offer their child. There was no way she would be able to afford a home this size, much less afford the sleek furniture filling the massive living room.

"I wish." Moon started up the stairs, carrying the box containing the crib. "Sasha took care of it for me. She's a friend of mine. She loves decorating. If she likes a piece, she'll buy it then store it to use for when she gets a design job."

"That's smart." Larissa laid her hand on the back of the taupe sofa, appreciating the feel of the material. "She did a good job."

"I'm happy with how it turned out," he said, going back outside.

She left the living room and went into the kitchen to

make their drinks. After pouring herself a glass of orange juice, she fixed Moon a glass of iced tea.

She stood in the kitchen while she sipped on the orange juice, listening as Moon made several trips to the car. When she heard the sound of the door closing, she expected Moon to come into the kitchen. Instead, she heard his steps going up the stairs.

Placing her empty glass in the sink after rinsing it out, she carried the iced tea into the living room, expecting Moon to come back downstairs. When he didn't, she went upstairs and found Moon was measuring the room he had mentioned would be the baby's room.

"What are you doing?"

"Sorry, I got distracted trying to decide which side of the room to place the crib. I didn't mean to hold you up. It took me longer to find the measuring tape than I thought it would. Sasha borrowed it and didn't put it back where it belongs."

"No worries. I'm not in a rush," she assured him.

Larissa didn't miss the yearning way he looked at the cardboard box.

"You're dying to put it together, aren't you?" Handing him the iced tea, she laughed at the abashed look he gave her.

"I wouldn't exactly say *dying*, but pretty close," he admitted.

"Have at it. Like I said, I'm in no rush."

"Are you sure?"

"I'm sure. I didn't really have any other plans for the rest of the afternoon," she admitted.

"Cool. Let me get a chair, and you can keep me company. I'll be right back."

Larissa stared at the unfurnished bedroom, already regretting the decision not to ask Moon to drive her back to

Jamestown. His boyish enthusiasm had snuck under her guard.

Her hand moved to lovingly stroke her distended abdomen at the fluttery kicks she felt from within. "*Shh*, little one, Mama's okay," she softly murmured, sensing the baby was feeling the tumultuous emotions going on within her body.

She would text Priss and check when her last appointment was and get her to drive her back to Jamestown. Moon might or might not be putting on a charade for her, but until she knew for sure, it was safer not risk the chance of another kiss. She would keep her distance and keep their conversation light until Priss was able to come and get her.

She texted Priss and was relieved when her sister texted her back that she could pick her up in a couple of hours.

*Just two hours. I can do this*, she told herself. All she had to do was ignore the way her heart skipped a beat every time he smiled at her, and the warmth flooding when he moved his muscular body in a particular way. *God, did you have to make him so damn sexy?* she ranted inwardly. And lastly, whatever she did, she wasn't going within one inch of his mouth, despite how badly she wanted to kiss him again.

*I've got this.* She gave her baby bump another reassuring pat.

Startled, she glanced down at her stomach, at the strong kick she had received. Was she being ridiculous, or was the baby trying to warn her to leave?

Feeling silly, she brushed it off. Her confused emotions over Moon made her create mountains out of molehills.

Neither of them had mentioned the kiss they had shared, leaving her confused on how he really felt about her. She had never really been good at deciphering a man's behavior. At this stage of her life, she had never imagined herself to be as nervous as a teenager over whether a man was attracted to her or not. Unfortunately, she didn't have the experience to pick up subtle clues other women could easily read to lessen her anxiety. Coming to the only conclusion she could, only time would tell.

# CHAPTER FORTY

Larissa felt a spurt of satisfaction when she reached out to jiggle the crib and it remained steady.

"I think it's good now."

Moon wadded the paper directions into a ball before shoving it into the empty box. "Good thing I was able to convince you to stay and help me rather than going out to eat with your sister, or I'd still be working on that death trap." Giving her a peeved look, he continued picking up the protective packing for the crib.

Amused at the way he was acting, she handed him a piece of foam he had missed. "It wasn't a death trap."

"The way I put it together was an accident waiting to happen. Those were the worst instructions I've ever read, and I still say they had the illustrations mislabeled."

They weren't, but she didn't argue. His pride had taken enough of hit for the night.

"Since I made you lose out having dinner at King's, I'll make you something to eat."

"No, you don't have to. I'll grab something when I get back in Jamestown."

"I'm hungry, too. Besides"—walking to the doorway, he gave her a sheepish glance—"I ordered pizza. It should be here in a few minutes."

A slight rumbling sound came from her stomach at the mention of pizza.

"How can I argue?" She laughed. "I guess the baby is hungry, too."

"Great. I'll just take out the box to the garage."

She headed downstairs with Moon, then went into the kitchen to make them drinks while he carried out the box. She had just set the glasses on the counter when she heard the doorbell ring.

"I'll get it," Moon said, coming back from the garage.

She opened a cabinet, took out a couple of plates, and set them next to the glasses.

"Dinner is served," Moon joked as he walked into the kitchen.

The aroma caused her stomach to growl again. "I didn't realize how hungry I was."

She started debating the easiest way to maneuver herself onto the tall chair at the counter, when Moon bypassed the counter and carried the pizza to the dining room table.

"This might be easier to manage." Setting the pizza down onto the table, he pulled out a chair for her.

Larissa made a face at him. "Every day is a new adventure with this baby," she told him, sitting down. "Yesterday, I couldn't fit in my favorite sweats. Today, I can't seem to judge how to maneuver my belly enough to sit down."

Picking up the drinks, she brought them to the table to take the chair he had pulled out for her.

"Go ahead and help yourself." Moon nodded toward the pizza. "I just want to wash my hands."

She opened the box but waited until Moon came back and sat down next to her before taking a slice.

They ate in comfortable silence, and Larissa was glad she had changed her mind about leaving. When Priss had texted her that she was off work, she had told her that she had changed her mind due to the mess Moon had been making at putting the crib together.

"I appreciate you staying to finish the crib."

"No problem. Other than having dinner with Priss, I had nothing else to do."

"Sounds like you're getting bored?"

"A little. Sizzle won't even let me do the dishes."

"It's hard to be comfortable in someone else's home," he commiserated.

"Don't get me wrong; they're very nice."

"Still, it's not like having your own place."

"Yes," she agreed, taking another slice of pizza. "I'll be glad when I can move into my house. The closing date isn't until next month."

"That's a bummer." Moon set his pizza down on his plate. "Why don't you move back in with your sisters? I promise not to make an ass out of myself again."

"I believe you." She grinned at him. "You need my help to put together that dresser you bought?"

Moon grimaced at her. "I wasn't going to ask, but I'm not going to turn your help down if you offer."

"I would love to help. I love building furniture. Lana and Priss hate it, so I've always had to be the designated builder."

"So, then, if we're cool now, why not move back in with your sisters?"

"I would, but Lana's lease is up, and since she's going to be moving in with me, she can't sign another lease. She asked her landlord to extend her current lease for a month, and he wouldn't agree."

"That sucks."

"Yes, it does. Lana and Priss are going to rent a hotel

room for a month, so it just makes sense for me to stay in Jamestown rather than renting another hotel room."

"There is another option."

Larissa looked at Moon curiously as he got up to go to the fridge, coming back with the pitcher of tea to refill their glasses.

"You all could move in here. There are plenty of empty rooms."

She almost choked on a mouthful of pizza. "We couldn't impose on you like that," she managed to say in a hoarse voice.

"I don't know why not." He shrugged. "I planned to live at the club until the baby is born, anyway."

Larissa stared at him in shock. "You had the house decorated just to let it sit empty?"

"I have to be at work at six. Most nights, I don't get off until six or seven. It's just easier to stay there to gain the extra sleep. When you have the baby, it'll be worth the effort. Right now, I would just be coming back here to an empty house."

Sadness filled her at his thinking. He looked so lonely as he glanced toward the living room.

"You should all live here until the house closes," he offered again. "I promise not to turn into a dick again and won't make excuses to constantly come over."

Despite being tempted, she shook her head. "We couldn't—"

"I don't see why not. Give me one good excuse."

She took a bite of pizza to give herself time to think.

Moon laughed. "You can't think of one, can you?"

"Give me a minute."

"There's no downside. Your sisters can use my garage to store their furniture."

"You're making it hard to refuse."

"Then don't. You'll be even closer to Killyama," he cajoled. "When's she due?"

"Next week." She let out a sigh of defeat. "All right, I'll talk to Priss and Lana. *If* they agree, we'll take you up on your offer."

"Good." He smiled, closing the pizza box and taking their plates to the sink.

"But only if you accept what we would have paid at the apartment."

Moon started rinsing off the dishes. "I never refuse money."

Feeling better at accepting Moon's offer at his acceptance of the money, she called Lana and talked to both her sisters while Moon showed no conjunction about listening in on their conversation.

At Lana and Priss' enthusiasm, her last doubt vanished, and she told her sisters she would talk to them tomorrow before hanging up.

"You've made their night."

"What did it?" he asked, moving from behind the kitchen counter. "The large screen television or separate bedrooms?"

She cringed, realizing Moon had heard Priss' squeal of delight.

"The bedrooms. She's always shared a room with either me or Lana. All the bathrooms didn't hurt, either. Thank you, Moon. I promise to take good care of your home until we move out. If you change your mind—"

"I won't. While you're here, go ahead and decorate the nursery if you get bored. I'm sure you'll be a better hand at doing it than me."

"I couldn't."

"I don't see why not. That way, you can make sure it's baby proof."

"I don't expect you to totally give away the access to your home. Feel free to come by to work on the nursery."

"How about when you want to work on it, just give me a call, and I'll come over?"

"That works for me."

Moon glanced at the clock. "I didn't realize how late it was."

Larissa looked at the wall clock, stunned at the time. "It's after twelve."

"Thanks for confirming I can still read a clock," he teased.

Larissa made a face at him. "I'm just shocked. I thought it was like seven or eight."

"Me, too. I guess putting the crib together took longer than we thought." Moon frowned at the clock.

"Do you have to work in the morning?"

"I do."

She felt bad Moon was going to have to drive her to Jamestown then drive back.

"Sex Piston's parents go to bed early. I don't want to wake them. You could drive me to the hotel, and I can sleep with one of my sisters. That will save you the drive."

"Or you could take one of the bedrooms upstairs. I have a few clothes here. I could lend you a shirt to sleep in."

"I can go to the hotel."

"Why? You'll just wake them up. It makes more sense to stay here. My motorcycle is in the garage. I'll leave my car keys so you can drive to Jamestown tomorrow to get your things."

What Moon was suggesting sounded sensible, but she still hesitated to accept his offer. "I don't know …"

Moon arched a brow at her. "Worried I'll sneak into your room?"

Larissa lowered her lashes half-mast. "Jerk."

He chuckled. "Come on. Don't overthink it and just accept. You know it's the better option."

"Okay, I'll spend the night," she reluctantly agreed.

"Don't sound so excited," he remarked drily.

"I'm sorry to sound unappreciative. It's just … this takes a little getting used to."

Moon gave her a confused frown. "What does?"

"You being so nice and thoughtful."

"I can be nice and thoughtful, especially when it involves me not having to drive to Jamestown again. You're actually doing me another favor. I was dreading the drive."

"Then I'm glad to help."

"All right, then I guess the next step is you picking out the room you want to sleep in while I lock the doors and grab you a shirt."

Leaving Moon downstairs, she went upstairs. She opened the spare bedrooms and chose the one with the ensuite bathroom. She checked the bathroom to see if there were towels before closing the door. She wanted to take a shower before going to sleep.

"Larissa?"

Larissa went to the doorway of the bathroom and found Moon walking through the bedroom door.

"I was just checking to see if you had towels. I see you already beat me to asking for them." She moved further into the room to take the stack of towels and the T-shirt from him.

"I figured you would want to take a shower either tonight or in the morning."

"Thank you. I thought I would take one before going to bed."

"Is there anything else I can get for you?"

"No, this should be everything."

"All right, then I'll see you tomorrow. I'll come by

tomorrow after I get off work for the car. If you need anything, just text me."

"I will. Thank you."

"You're welcome. Good night."

"Good night, Moon."

She went back to the bathroom, where she took a warm shower, luxuriating in the warmth of the water and feeling the awkward tension drain off her now that she was away from Moon's alluring body.

The whole time they had been building the crib, she had forced herself to keep her gaze away from him. Every movement he made drew her eyes like a magnet, making her want to try every dirty sexual act she could think of with him. Her shocking thoughts made her work on the crib harder just to get the thing done and her out of the close confines of being near him.

Turning the water off, she towel-dried before slipping on the gray T-shirt. Then she rinsed out her underwear with plain soap and hung them over the towel rack before going to bed.

She lay down and closed her eyes, exhausted. Yawning, she was about to fall asleep when she felt a tightening in her lower calf.

The familiar feeling made her prepare herself for the coming pain. Even though she tried to keep from crying out, the excruciating pain made it impossible. She sat up in bed, then shifted to raise one leg to start massaging her calf.

A knock on the door and Moon calling her name had her gasping out for him to come in.

Moon took one glance and immediately hurried to her side. "Muscle spasm?"

"Yes," she gasped out.

Taking over massaging her leg, Moon sat down on the bed next to her. He rested her leg on his lap, then pressed down on the tight muscle with his thumb, massaging the bunched-up muscle.

"That feels so good." The muscle relaxing had her head falling to his shoulder. "I hate charley horses."

"Me, too. Sometimes I get them when I work out too hard."

"I had a couple last week. I'll get Lana do some blood-work tomorrow to make sure there isn't a reason."

"I'll call in tomorrow."

"There's no need. I only get them at night when I'm in bed."

"I don't care. I won't have you driving until we make sure there isn't something going on," he said curtly. "I'm not going to take a chance anything will happen to you."

Larissa lifted her head. "Don't you mean the baby?" she said jokingly, trying to ignore the fire running up her leg and him being just inches away from where she really wanted his fingers to go.

Moon frowned at her. "I meant you."

Her amusement faded. "I was just teasing."

His eyes bore into hers. "I don't consider your health something to joke about."

"I won't tease you again," she promised solemnly.

His hand curved around the underpart of her knee, the seductive sensation making her bunch the blanket under her hands to keep from touching him.

"I'm not opposed to you teasing me ... just don't expect me not to take the bait."

# CHAPTER FORTY-ONE

The hand on her calf tightened as Moon leaned forward, closing the small distance separating them. She knew he was going to kiss her from the sultry way he was looking at her.

Larissa's mind screamed at her to move away, yet her body seemed unable to follow the command.

When Moon's lips touched hers, she knew it was too late. Like his namesake, Moon had pulled her into his orbit, and there was no escape.

When his tongue parted her lips, her hands gripped his shoulders with the clear intention of making him stop, but her good intentions went out the door at the liquid fire consuming any rational thought that tried to make her realize what a terrible mistake she was about to make.

Her hands moved from his shoulder to his hair, tugging him closer.

*You've lost your mind*, she told herself as she willingly let him use her leg to slide her further down on the bed and found herself being pushed back onto the mattress. There was no doubt in her mind how Moon had gotten his nickname—she was seriously seeing stars behind her closed lids.

As he molded his mouth to hers, erotic need consumed her. The hand which had been massaging her calf slid between her thighs to stroke the cleft of her vagina. If Moon's kiss had her seeing stars, his touch caused a shimmering need to course through the flesh he was exploring with featherlight movements. Wanting him to touch her harder, she arched under his teasing hand.

She tore her mouth from Moon's and gasped for air, her hand wrapping around his wrist. "We should go to sleep."

Moon's hand stopped in place, except for the thumb, which was swirling over her clitoris. "Do you want me to leave?"

"Us having sex would be a complication we don't need." Biting down on her lip, she valiantly fought to keep from pulling his mouth back to hers. His kiss had the capacity to nuke any hesitations about how difficult it would be if they developed a sexual relationship. Their tenuous friendship could be destroyed before it had really begun, making it uncomfortable for her to be around him.

His eyes bore down into hers. "Are you attracted to me?"

"I think it's obvious I am."

His free hand took hers, pressing it against the hard length of his cock under the sweatpants he was wearing. "Every relationship is complicated." Moon bent down to trace his lips along the line of her jaw to her mouth. "We can take it as slow or fast as you want to go. Don't we owe it to our baby to see if there is something there?"

"I don't know," she whimpered.

A finger slid intimately inside of her sheath, making it nearly impossible to weigh the negative consequences if having an intimate relationship with Moon turned sour.

"I want you." He licked the back of her earlobe before

tugging the small lobe into his mouth as his finger stroked higher. "I want to fuck you with the lights on, without the dark hiding you from me."

Her neck arched back, pressing her head into the pillow as Moon released her earlobe to return to her mouth. His finger stopped moving inside of her as he devoured her mouth in a carnal kiss that silenced any thoughts of leaving the room until each and every one of the insatiable cravings he was igniting had been satisfied.

"I don't understand," she managed to say when he lifted his mouth to trail down to her neck.

"What don't you understand?" he asked when she wasn't able to complete her sentence.

"How you manage to make me forget my resolutions not to have sex with you. I've never had this problem before."

"That's easy to answer." Cool air bathed her heated flesh when Moon tugged her T-shirt down to expose her naked breasts. "You didn't want to fuck them."

The crude way he worded it made her inwardly cringe while, at the same, she had to admit it was the truth. She had never desired a man the way she did Moon. He was the complete opposite of the type of men she usually dated. Her ex-boyfriend had been fun to hang out with, to study with, but when it came to sex, it never had the passion needed to survive from either side. She would rather walk over hot coals than admit that fact to Moon, though.

"I did," she lied.

"Couldn't have been too exciting if you never had this problem before."

How could she argue with the truth?

His lips brushed over a hardened nipple before he used his tongue to wet the taut peak. His warm mouth surrounded the areola, dissolving any thought of making him stop. Her body was aching with an unsatisfied need that he was building until she wanted to claw at him to satisfy it.

Thrusting her hips upward to make his finger start moving again, she whimpered, desperate for him to end the agony.

"Moon … please …"

"You don't want me to leave?"

"No."

He switched to torment her other nipple. "Then tell me what you want."

His voice took on a tone that sent cold shivers of warning down her spine. At the same time, the heat stroked to life in the rest of her body was burning out of control.

Shifting his body more fully on top of her, Moon was careful not put any weight on the mound of her stomach as he released her nipple to slide downward.

She hadn't been aware that the T-shirt he had given her was bunched around her waist until Moon took her wrists and pulled them behind her back. Distracted by him pressing a kiss on her baby bump, she didn't pay attention to the movements she was making until he pulled his hands out from behind her back and started maneuvering his body downward until his mouth was on her pussy.

Surprised, Larissa tried to pull her hands out from behind her back to push him away, only to find them tangled in the shirt.

"Untie me, Moon …" she moaned.

"Let's play a pretend game." He swiped his tongue over her bud, sending goose bumps across her skin.

Raising her thighs, she tried to move his head away with her knee. He used his shoulder to block her, then gave a sultry laugh.

"It won't hurt you to have a little of fun. You act like a stick in the mud."

"I'm not. I can be a lot of fun."

"Around your sisters, you do loosen up, but they don't count. Around everyone else, you come across as someone very serious. I don't mean to hurt your feelings, just making you aware of how others could perceive you."

Larissa found it hard to take offense to his criticism when his mouth was buried between her thighs.

"You have fun with your boyfriend?"

"Ex," she corrected him. "Bryer and I dated when I was in college. We spent most of our time studying."

His hands slid under her bottom to lift her against his mouth. "No sexual games you've ever wanted to play?"

"No … I'm not into BDSM, if that's what you're getting at —" She moaned when his tongue slid inside of her, only to come out to flick at her clitoris.

"How do you know what you're into or not without trying it first?"

"I don't have to eat sauerkraut to know I won't like it."

Moon gave a husky laugh. "I don't want you to do anything you're uncomfortable doing. I have several games up my sleeve."

"I bet you do," she moaned huskily.

"We can take turns playing this game. Then, when you're more comfortable, we can move on to harder games. I'll go first." He parted her cleft to slide his tongue on the underside of her clit.

If her hands weren't tied, she would have used them to hit him to end the torment he was putting her through.

"Why do you get to go first?"

"You don't know how to play the game … yet. So, do you want to play?"

# CHAPTER FORTY-TWO

"**D**epends on how it's played."

Moon raised his head from between her thighs. "The first thing I'll do is give you a word to use when you want me to stop."

"This is sounding a lot like BDSM."

When he arched a brow at her, he made her feel like she had somehow disappointed him.

"I thought you said you weren't a Negative Nancy?"

She gave a sigh of concession. "Fine. My word is—"

"The word is *stop*." He didn't allow her to choose. "I don't want any confusion about what you want or don't want."

His attitude made her feel somewhat better about the game they were about to play.

"Okay."

"Since you have trouble playing pretend, I'll teach you how." Moon scooted himself back down so his face was once again resting between her thighs. "We're going to pretend that I've taken you captive. You want to marry me, but your father has hidden you away. I found you and have begged you to run away with me. You refused. I have taken matters into my own hands and have kidnapped you. I've locked you in a tower and been having my wicked ways with you."

"Wow." Larissa couldn't help but laugh. "You really have a good imagination."

He lowered his eyelids to half-mast. "Are you laughing at me?" he asked dangerously.

Her laughter died in her throat, realizing the game had begun for Moon.

The expression on his face had undergone a drastic change. Shivering in fear, she told herself that he was just playacting. Except … it felt very real to her.

"Not anymore."

His expression didn't ease at the quiver in her voice. "When I send you back to your father, heavy with my child, he'll beg me to marry you."

"Okaaay."

Moon's eyes went back to half-mast as his hand hovered threateningly over her patch of curly hair. "Are you mocking me?"

"Not anymore."

"Good. I don't want to punish you."

"I don't want you to either," she said truthfully.

His hand lowered to comb through the curls to part her cleft. Then his tongue started flicking her clit. Stinging sensations had her squirming on the bed until a hand came down on her curls.

She immediately stopped squirming. Trying to decide to be affronted or ask for more, she waited breathlessly to see what he would do next.

"Stay still." He went back to playing with her like a cat would a mouse. "Don't make me punish you."

No, she definitely didn't want to be punished … or did she?

Regardless of being indecisive, she wasn't able to prevent

herself from moving under Moon's experienced touch. He stimulated every nerve ending in her body, sending her withering under a skillful tongue that had already stroked two small orgasms out of her. She lost count of the hard smacks coming down on her mound. Her thighs came up to try to move him away from the exquisite way he was licking and savoring her as if he couldn't get enough.

Breyer had been the only man she'd had sex with, and he had only done this to her twice. Both times, she had been embarrassed at the newness of having oral sex. It hadn't made it easier that she could tell Breyer was doing it just to please her, which had made it impossible for her to experience any pleasure.

With Moon, it was the exact opposite. There was no room for embarrassment, nor did it look like a chore for him. Watching him was almost as sexually arousing as the act.

Her eyes jerked to the ceiling when he plunged his tongue inside of her over and over. At least this time, she was able to control her movement and lie still. The effort made a fine sheen of sweat cover her body. Bunching the sheet in her hands was the outlet that didn't earn her another smack.

Another orgasm racked her body.

"I can't do any more," she pleaded.

Moon lifted himself into a sitting position. Leaning down, he licked the sweat away from between her breasts. "Are you asking me to stop?"

"God, no ..." she moaned out. "I need to come."

"Do you want me to take you back to your father?"

She had forgotten they were playing his game.

"No ... I want to stay here with you."

She felt silly for playing along until Moon filled her head with graphic images of what he was going to do to her.

"I'm never going to let you out of this tower. You will be

waiting for me on bended knees, never knowing when I will come to bed you. I will come so often that you will dread hearing my boots on the stone steps outside the door. You won't remember what it feels like not to have my cock inside of you."

Larissa wasn't able to help the small scream that escaped when Moon plunged his cock inside of her. She was so ready for him, yet his cock easily filled her to the point where she became concerned she couldn't accommodate his size.

Biting her bottom lip, she wiggled, trying to ease the tightness.

Moon gave her a second to adjust then slowly began moving inside of her. His mouth covered her nipple to bite down. The small bites of pain from different parts of her body heightened the desire she was already feeling.

Gasping at the sensations, she tried to tell herself it was make believe, but the arrogant expression on his face and muscled body could have easily been a replica from the past without clothes to show what time period he had been born into.

Each stroke of his cock had her thighs tightening on his hips. She was almost there ... she could feel the tension rising. The small orgasms he had given her had only been a small relief, only to bring the desire to come achingly back stronger than before.

Moon didn't even appear affected, whereas she felt as if she would explode any second. The only sign he was human was a lone bead of sweat on his temple.

She was caught off guard when he suddenly raised his head and saw she was studying him.

"Stop."

Moon immediately stopped moving inside of her. "What's wrong?"

"Untie my hands."

His hands went under her to untangle her hands.

Once she felt her hands loosened, she pulled them free and shimmied her hips until Moon's cock slipped out.

With a grunt, he moved to the side to stare at her open-mouthed. From his expression, Larissa assumed it was the first time a woman had stopped him when they were in the middle of having sex.

"What did I do that you didn't like?"

Twisting the T-shirt until her breasts were once again covered, she jumped out of bed to face him. She didn't trust herself enough to stay in the bed with him. She had proven herself weak twice where he was concerned.

"You didn't do anything wrong," she told him.

"Then I don't understand? Were you worried about the baby?" he asked, clearly confused.

"No." Running a hand through her tangled hair, she tried to explain why she had stopped him in a way that would make sense.

"You were into it."

Larissa nodded. "That was the problem—I was the only one enjoying it. I thought you were enjoying it, too ... but you weren't, were you?"

She could see the conflicting emotions on his face, and hurt filled her. She was just another lay to him.

Closing her eyes tightly, Larissa blamed herself. What had she been thinking? He had just been making the best of a bad situation.

"I'm going to get dressed. You can drive me to the hotel."

Naked, Moon got of the bed to stalk toward her until her back was pressed against the wall behind her. Placing a hand on either side of her head, he pinned her in place. "There were parts I enjoyed." He ran the tip of his tongue over his bottom lip suggestively.

Outraged, she tried to shove his barring arm away. "So, there were parts you didn't?"

His eyes became mischievous. "It was a different type of enjoyment. I'm not really a fan of the missionary position."

Staring at him speechlessly, she didn't know what to say.

"I also prefer a more vigorous way of fucking."

"When we had sex at the clubhouse, it wasn't really vigorous."

"I was tired. I had walked from the bar to the club."

"Oh …" she mumbled embarrassedly. "Anyway, it doesn't matter. Take me to the hotel—"

Moon clicked his tongue at her. "I see how you are. Instead of satisfying me, you'd rather cut and run."

Indignation overrode her embarrassment. "You just practically said I wasn't pleasing you. I don't know what you expect me to do!"

He pressed his body closer to hers. "Let me show you." Burying his mouth in the side of her neck, he slid his hands to her waist to lift her against the wall until her breasts were at eye level. Leaving her neck, his mouth went to her breast to tug the T-shirt over the nipple. His chest held her in place against the wall as he hooked her legs over his hips one at a time. She felt the tip of his cock nudging the opening between her thighs.

"You're wet for me," he groaned out. His still hard cock found her opening and slid inside. "Am I hurting you?"

"No." She gripped his shoulders, unsure of what to do to make it more pleasurable for him. She thought back to minutes before, when they were having sex on the bed, and it finally clicked what Moon had been trying to tell her.

She had been letting him do all the work.

"My father will kill you for dishonoring me."

He raised his head to stare at her. It only took a second

before Moon resumed his role. His sinister smile made her second-guess the wisdom of playing his game.

"Then make it worth it."

Burrowing her hands in Moon's hair, she roughly pulled his head back. Then she kissed him passionately. Gripping his hips tightly with her thighs when his cock found her opening, she broke off the kiss to nuzzle his neck. She pulled her hands from his hair to run them over his shoulders to explore the muscular back, where she could feel the firm flesh as his cock started thrusting harder. His thrusts turned harder, his hand rougher as he lifted her thighs higher.

Unable to help herself, she bit down when she felt the tide of an approaching climax.

Moon's hand went to her hair to jerk her mouth away to cover it with his.

A climax hit her with the suddenness of a nuclear bomb, and Moon's body tensed against her when she began frantically meeting his thrusts with her own.

Letting her head fall to his shoulder when they finally stopped moving, she didn't have the energy to lift an eyelash as he carried her to the bed then lay down next to her.

His slick skin under her cheek reassured her that he had found some of the pleasure he had given her.

She snuggled closer to him when he pulled a sheet over them and promptly fell asleep, too drained of energy to get any words out. Her last thought was, *Please don't let him say anything to ruin what we shared.*

# CHAPTER FORTY-THREE

"You've lost your mind."

Unable to disagree with Priss, Larissa could only nod. They had come to pick her up at Moon's house before going to work and were sitting in his living room, where she had asked them if they were still willing to move in until her house was built or if they were reconsidering after they had talked to her the night before. Their reaction was exactly what she had expected, making her doubt the wisdom of the move.

"It was just a suggestion. If you don't want to, we won't." Priss's overexuberant response from the night before had undergone a change in the bright light of the day, either that or Lana's much more tentative approval had changed her mind.

Larissa stood up from the couch. "We should be going. I don't want to make you late for your shift at the hospital."

Both of her sisters remained seated.

Lana glanced at Priss before turning back to her. "We aren't saying no. It's kinda a big step for us to take. You go from having Sex Piston keep Moon away to asking us to move into his house. What's with the sudden turnaround?"

"We've agreed to get along for the baby."

"I'm glad to hear that." Lana smiled encouragingly.

"I'm not," Priss snorted. "The dude is a prick."

Larissa couldn't argue. Moon was a prick.

"He won't be living here with us," Larissa reminded them. "And it's only for a month."

Her sisters still didn't seem convinced.

"Aren't you worried about becoming more emotionally involved with Moon the more you see him?" Lana asked.

"Yes," Larissa agreed. "But I might as well get used to him before the baby is born."

"True. Moon is the father, so he's going to be in our lives a long while." Lana rose from the couch. "I'm not crazy about moving in here, but the hotel sucks worse."

"Priss?" Larissa asked.

"We always stick together." Priss gave a reluctant sigh. "I'm not going to break our sisters' code when you need me the most. Please be careful, Larissa. I love you, and I really don't want to have to watch another sister suffer through a broken heart this year. My fat ass can't handle helping you eat your way through a heartbreak. I still have to lose the fifteen pounds I gained when Lana was getting over Bennet."

Lana made a face at her. "Don't blame me for gaining weight. I didn't force-feed you to eat with me."

Priss made a face back. "No, just cooked all my favorites. You did it deliberately, wanting me to go to the gym with you."

"You're being ridiculous," Lana snapped at her.

"I am not. You keep baking those cinnamon rolls despite me telling you to stop."

"All you had to do was not eat them," Lana snapped back.

"Yeah, right." Pris rolled her eyes. "Who the hell can resist freshly baked cinnamon rolls? The only good part about staying in that hotel was you didn't have an oven."

Lana's hands went to her hips. "See if I make them for you again!"

"Oh, I'm *so* scared."

Larissa put a pause on her sisters' sparring, reminding them that they were going to be late for work.

Locking the door behind them, she felt buoyed that they hadn't put up a harder fight about moving into Moon's home. In a month, they would be able to move into their new home and get settled in well before the baby was born.

Undeterred by her shyness of how they had spent the night, Moon had kissed her before leaving, promising to call her later that afternoon. When she came downstairs, she found he had set out a muffin and a small bottle of orange juice for her to take. His house key was balanced on top of the orange juice lid. She had felt special and taken care of. She was used to such consideration from one of her sisters, but it was a novel feeling coming from a man.

For the first time in a long time, she didn't fear what the future held.

---

The women turned at the sound of the loud roar of a motorcycle.

Larissa picked up the small box out of the trunk as Moon parked his motorcycle beside Priss' car.

"Need some help?" he offered, getting off his bike.

"No, thanks, I can manage." Giving Moon a cold shoulder, Priss walked inside the house through the garage.

"She hates me." Moon didn't seem upset at the fact.

"She doesn't know you." Embarrassed at Priss' cold attitude, Larissa closed the trunk.

Moon's eyes twinkled at her. "I don't think that will help."

Larissa laughed at his droll humor. "Maybe not."

"It was the kiss that did me in, wasn't it?"

"Nah, I don't think that was it."

Moon took the box away from her with a wry smile. "I don't know whether I should take that as a compliment or not."

"Afraid of outing yourself as a good kisser? I already knew that."

Moon gave her an appreciative look as they walked through the four-car garage. "Most women can get catty when it comes to their men's past experiences."

Larissa gave an offhand shrug. "I have no reason to be upset. It's not like you're my man."

He stopped. "I'm not? Not even after last night?"

Larissa frowned, stopping next to him. "Why are you looking so mad at me? I would have thought you would be relieved I'm not blowing last night out of proportion."

His eyes turned stormy. "I thought I made it clear I want to build a relationship with you."

Startled, she stared at him. "I must have missed that part."

"Then what did you think? Another one-night stand?"

"Technically, we didn't have a one-night stand the first time. It didn't last that long," she argued back.

"Technically?" He took a step toward her. "I'll show you—"

Larissa jumped forward, reaching for the garage door's doorknob. Feeling safer with the metal knob in her hand, she turned back to him. "You're being plain silly. If I started calling you *my man* after one night of hot sex, you would put me in my place too quickly to talk about it."

Moon strode toward her dangerously. "Try me."

"I may have lived in Kentucky my whole life, but you're

never going to hear me refer to any man as *my man*. Just saying it makes my skin crawl."

"Really?"

Larissa felt a chill sweep down her spine. "Really." Giving him the same stone-faced glare that Moon gave her, she turned the doorknob. "Pfft," she muttered under her breath as she walked through the door. "He should go back to the 1950s and stay. I'll send him a flipping postcard."

"What did you say?" he asked, following behind her.

"None of your business ... Fred," she replied sharply.

Confusion marred Moon's expression as he set the box down on the kitchen table. "Fred?"

"As in *The Flintstones*." Jerking the box into her arms, she headed for the stairway.

"I would have carried it upstairs for you."

"I can carry my own box," she grumbled.

Coming down the steps, Priss took one glance at their warring expressions and moved to the side to let them pass. "Something wrong?"

"No," they snapped in unison.

"All righty, then." Her sister continued down the steps. "I'm going to throw a pizza in the oven and make a salad. You staying for dinner, Moon?"

"Yes, thank you."

"No," Larissa called out over her shoulder as she reached the top of the stairs.

She heard Moon say something to Priss but was too far away to understand the words. She walked into the bedroom that she and Moon had slept in last night and set the box on the dresser. She was turning around when Moon followed her inside and shut the door.

Leaning his back against the door, he crossed his arms over his chest. "I am not a caveman."

Larissa mimicked his stance. "I didn't say you were. I just inferred you had the attitude of one."

Moon frowned so hard that his eyebrows looked like one big caterpillar. "Woman ..."

"Here we go," she told him snidely.

"You're right."

Her jaw dropped at the admission.

"My pride was injured. I made assumptions that you are as attracted to me as I am to you. You didn't want to overstep any boundary you think I may have." He uncrossed his arms to place a hand over his heart. "I'm sorry I wasn't more forthright with you." Moon dropped his hand, then walked toward her and slid his arms around her waist. "So there isn't a misunderstanding this time, I like you, Larissa. I want to see where this attraction for you goes."

Larissa melted inside at his humble apology and honesty to show where he would like to move forward with her.

"I don't know what to say." Relaxing into his arms, she searched his eyes. "I would like that, too."

Moon's hand came up to tuck a loose strand of hair behind her ear. His touch was so gentle that barrier after barrier she had been hiding behind dropped, leaving her heart wide open.

"Say, I'll give it a whirl," he teased.

"I'll give it a whirl."

His hand slid to the back of her neck. "I'll have to tell the brothers that I have an old lady when I go back to the club."

"I'm not that old."

"It means you belong to me."

"Oh."

"Yeah, oh." He laughed then grew serious. "Of course, that means I belong to you."

"Okay." Unaccustomed to talking so candidly with a man

about their relationship, she shyly was unable to hold his heated gaze for long.

Her eyes went to the door when she heard Priss yelling the pizza was done. "We should go eat," she suggested.

"I would rather feed another appetite, but I guess it would be safer to go eat. I don't want Priss interrupting."

"Me neither."

Moon released her from his arms to open the door for her. Jokingly, he bowed, giving a gallant downward wave, indicating for her to go first. "My lady."

Larissa couldn't help the silly giggle that escaped as she passed him. "Thank you, kind sir." Feeling as if she was walking on cloud nine, she walked down the stairs.

The day had just gotten better and better as it progressed. Just when she had thought Moon would make sure she hadn't taken last night seriously, he made her feel as if she were the one who didn't want a commitment. Wow. Her mind was blown away with how gentlemanly he was treating her. He appeared shaken at being called Fred Flintstone. Bless his heart. She bet he had been raised by a single mother and was conscious of the trials and tribulations women deal with every day.

Still, as she came off the bottom step, a worrying thought trailed her into the kitchen.

What if she had played right into his hands?

# CHAPTER FORTY-FOUR

Moon drove away from his house after finishing dinner. He didn't want to be hanging around when Lana got off, not wanting to give them any reason not to move into the house.

When he stopped at a red light, he felt his cell phone vibrate in his back pocket. He took it out, read the message, then responded. The reply came back before he could repocket the cell phone. He read the text and memorized the address.

Once the light turned green, Moon headed toward the address. When he pulled into the driveway, he saw the front door light was on.

Parking his bike, he ambled over to the door to knock on it with his knuckles.

The door swung open as if she had been watching for him.

"Hi." The clerk from the baby store brazenly stood in the doorway with black satin shorts and a matching mesh top.

His eyes dropped to the two nipples peeking out of the mesh. "Hi." He grinned. "Nice outfit."

"I thought you would appreciate it."

His hands went to her waist. Lifting her up, he stepped inside the house, slamming the door shut with his foot.

Seductively rubbing her breasts against his chest, she buried her long nails in his hair. Moon kissed her parted mouth, thrusting his tongue inside. When she would have tried to slide hers inside of his, he pulled back.

"Shouldn't we introduce ourselves?"

"Uh … sure." The woman gave a fake embarrassed laugh.

Moon almost rolled his eyes at her. Did she honestly think he would believe she was new to inviting men over after a casual meeting?

"Chasity Collins."

"Moon."

"Hey, Moon." Chasity rubbed her breasts against him again. Then, licking the side of his neck, she sucked his earlobe into her mouth. "You want to fuck?" she whispered.

"Not standing up." He carried her to the sofa to plunk her down. "Got any liquor?"

Straightening herself on the couch, she motioned toward a cabinet in the kitchen. "Second cabinet, next to the stove, right side."

"Mind if I pour myself one?"

Curling her legs under her bottom, she gave him a sulky pout. "Help yourself."

He strode to the kitchen, where he found the liquor and the glasses. Pouring himself a glass of bourbon, he carried it back to the couch, then sat down next to her and took a drink. "Want a taste?"

When she would have taken the glass from him, Moon reached out to grab her by neck, pulling her to him. When he kissed her, Moon felt her irritation drain away as he tongue-fucked her.

"I'll never drink whiskey out of a glass again."

His lips curled sensuously as he pulled back to take another drink. "Didn't expect to hear from you so soon. You get new merchandise in?"

Her hands went to his shoulders to balance herself as she straddled him. Her pussy was knocking on the door of his zipper. "Not yet. We won't get anything new in until next Wednesday." Leaning forward, she licked his bottom lip. "You going to bring your girlfriend the next time you come in?"

"Yes."

Surprised, Chasity leaned away from him. "You're joking, right?"

He studied her seriously. "Why wouldn't I?"

Her eyes widened in horror. "Don't you think it would be a mistake to bring her there after we fuck?"

He shrugged. "I don't see why not? It didn't bother you to flirt with me in front of her."

"That's different."

"How? You were pretty damn obvious that you wanted me to fuck you."

"Because … I hadn't fucked you yet. But if we did, it would be different."

Moon drained the last of the bourbon. "Usually, women wait until after I fuck them before covering their bases. Let me see if I'm hearing this right. As long you can actually deny fucking me, it's okay for her to be in the store, but if there is any truth to us fucking, you don't want her in there. Is that it?"

"Pretty much. My boss is a bitch. If she finds out I'm coming on to any of the men who come in the stores with the mothers, she'll fire me."

"In other words, your boss has morals. Which you don't have. I would fire you, too. Luckily, I'm not your boss."

"You're just teasing me, aren't you? You wouldn't bring her back in there, would you?"

"No, I wouldn't." Setting the glass on a side table, he started playing with her nipples as she ground herself down on his cock.

"How often does your store get new merchandise?"

"Meredith goes to shows in California and buys what she likes then has it transported here."

"Interesting. You learn something every day. Are the orders very large?"

"Not very. Her store in Treepoint isn't very profitable. The one in Lexington is, though. They make a drop in Lexington before coming to Treepoint."

"Doesn't she worry about it getting stolen in transit?"

Chasity bit her lip as she ground herself down on his lap. "I don't think so. I check everything in when the truck arrives. Everything's there. If Meredith comes up short, believe me, that bitch would never let me hear the end of it."

Moon felt moisture build on her upper lip in her excitement. He wasn't even touching her, and she was bringing herself to a climax.

She was lowering her mouth back to his when the sound of his phone made her jump.

"Pardon me." He reached for his phone and accepted the call.

"You're late." Shade's cold voice would have poured ice water on his lust if the bitch straddling his lap hadn't left him cold already.

Disconnecting the call, he lifted Chasity off his lap. "Sorry, going to have to postpone this. I got called into work."

"Damn ... I'm almost ... Can't you wait for a couple of minutes? It won't take long."

"No can do." He stared down at her in sympathy. "You don't get much action here, do you?"

She made a face at him. "Are you kidding? This place is Dullsville."

"You should come hang out at The Last Riders' clubhouse on Friday nights. Tell them Moon said you could come."

"Are you kidding? I couldn't be seen dead in there. Only sluts go in there."

"Forget the invitation." Scorn dripped off his voice as he went to the door, leaving her seated there as if she couldn't believe he was leaving.

"You're seriously going to leave me hanging?"

"Yep, I sure am." Letting his eyes sweep over her scathingly, Moon didn't sugarcoat his next words. "You're a waste of my time. I only fuck sluts."

Shutting the door after him, Moon walked to his motorcycle to the sounds of glass being smashed against a wall.

He rode back to the club without making any more stops along the way.

Once there, taking the steps two at a time, he greeted Puck, who was on guard duty. "When did you get here?"

Puck yawned as he opened the door. "About an hour ago."

"How'd you end up with guard duty?"

"New recruit had to take a dump. He caught me as I was heading upstairs."

Instead of going inside, Moon gestured for him to go ahead.

"Get some sleep. I'll tag you out until he comes back."

Puck nodded. "Thanks, brah."

"If you see Shade, tell him I'm out here."

"Sure thing." Puck closed the door behind him.

He had just lit a cigarette when Shade walked out.

"Where's Pace?"

Moon took a hit off his cigarette. "Taking a dump."

"What'd you find out?" Shade leaned a hip against the banister.

323

"They haven't had any thefts."

"So, the only business in town who's had any thefts has been The Last Riders' and the convenient store."

"Yeah."

He pulled a thumb drive from his pocket and tossed it to Shade. "That contains all the surveillance videos at the convenient store for the last two months."

Shade slid the drive into his pocket. "Thanks."

"No problem." Moon slanted him a half smile as he took another puff. "I told you to call in ten minutes. You were late."

Shade gave him a smile which didn't reach his eyes.

"Thought I'd make you sweat it out for a minute."

Taking it in stride, Shade had called late to irritate him, Moon gave him a half salute at achieving his goal. They had been trying to get the better of each other since the moment they had met. It had been going on so long Moon no longer knew who was ahead.

"You miss the good old days of getting info?"

Shaking his head, Shade leaned further back on the banister and crossed his ankles. "No. There are certain priorities which come first with the club, and then there are those that come with Lily. I keep them separate."

"What happens when the day comes, and you can't?"

Shade gave him a level stare. "Then that's the day I give my cut to Viper."

Moon knew Shade meant it without a doubt.

"The new kid's taking a long time to take a dump, isn't he?"

Moon frowned. "Now that you mention it, he is."

"I'll go check on him."

Moon wasn't surprised Shade had ended the brief discussion. The brother had never much been into sharing the inner workings of his mind.

He was stubbing his cigarette out when Shade returned.

"Pace isn't in the club."

"Where'd he go?"

"Beats me. But stay here. I'll send a text to Viper." He took out his cell phone. "I'm shutting the club down until we find him. He shows up after the door's locked, he better have a damn good explanation."

As Shade went inside, Moon heard the steel lock click in place. Taking his gun out of his jeans, he kept it in his hand, on the ready.

Over an hour passed before he heard the lock slide open and Shade and Viper both came outside.

"You find Pace?" he asked, seeing their expressions.

Viper gave a grim nod. "He's dead."

"Dead?"

"Shade found him in the sauna."

Moon swore. "What happened?"

"A bullet to the back of the head. He was executed."

## CHAPTER FORTY-FIVE

Larissa took another bite of cake. If she hadn't been watching Killyama open her last baby shower present, she would have missed the brief flash of pain on her face. As the party progressed, Larissa timed the subtle hints that Killyama was in labor.

She was serving Beth a glass of punch when Killyama abruptly stopped Fat Louise mid-sentence to make her way to the table she was standing at.

Instead of giving Killyama a glass of punch, she filled a taller one with chips of ice and water.

Killyama stared at the plain water as if she were debating taking her head off. "Bitch, I asked for punch."

Larissa gave her an apologetic glance. "Sorry. Your pains are too close together to give you the punch. I made you a pitcher of fruit juice. Would you like me to pour a glass?"

Killyama's glare intensified. "I'm not in labor."

"You are." Larissa locked her shaking knees. Killyama was pretty scary when she didn't get her way. "Unfortunately, this isn't going to be something you can control. Babies come on their timetable, not yours. You're going to have to hand the reins over to me."

Killyama gripped the edge of the table, hunching over as she gasped in pain.

"Are you ready for me to ask everyone to leave, except for those who you want to be with you during the delivery?"

"Let me do it."

"Go ahead, or I will," she warned. "I texted Train already. He's taking Ela to stay with Viper to play with Aisha. He should be here any minute."

"I was going to do it."

"When? After the baby was born?"

"Yes."

"I promised Train I would text him when you went into labor. That was the only reason you were able to convince him of a home birth. Priss is preparing your bed, and Lana called another doctor to relieve her, so she should be here any minute."

"What's going on?" Sex Piston came up to the table.

"Killyama's in labor," Larissa answered for her.

Sex Piston took one look at her friend's face and turned to the group of women behind her. "Party's over."

The women who were from The Last Riders' clubhouse left. Those who remained consisted of her closest friends.

Train walked in the door as she was helping Killyama to her bedroom.

Killyama was directing Fat Louise and T.A. every step along the way. "Fat Louise, put the ice cream back in the freezer and punch in the refrigerator. T.A.—" Killyama cried out in pain. "Son of a bitch!"

Train stopped dead in his tracks.

"She didn't mean you personally," Larissa tried to assure him.

Killyama gave her a wild-eyed look. "Yes, I did." Her gaze

went Train's. "What took you so long? Can't you see I'm in pain?" she snarled. "I need you to massage my back."

Train took Killyama's other arm as they entered her bedroom. "I bet you're regretting not going to the hospitals to get the good drugs."

"Do you want to die?" Killyama practically snatched Train's soul out of his body at his question.

Priscilla moved to take Train's place. "The water is ready. Train, I placed a chair for you next to the birthing pool."

Briskly, Larissa started helping Killyama remove her clothes with Priss' help.

"Lie down on the bed. I want to assess how far you are dilated. Priss is going to take your blood pressure and start monitoring the baby."

She spread a warm bath towel over Killyama and started examining her. Step by step, Larissa explained what she was doing and seeing.

"You're in active labor."

"I could have told you that!" Killyama yelled.

Calmly, Larissa helped her to sit up. "Everything looks good. Do you want to sit in the pool, or would you prefer—"

"I want to sit in the pool."

"Very well. Use the bathroom before we'll get you situated."

After helping Killyama put on a toweling robe, Larissa waited in the bathroom while she went into the closed toilet area. She had already been instructed on how to clean herself before getting into the sanitized pool, which Priss had prepared.

When she came out, all three of them helped Killyama into the pool, making sure she was comfortable with the floating pillow as Train rubbed her back before letting her friends in.

"Damn, bitch. Where's the baby? I was beginning to think

you had her without us," Sex Piston wisecracked as she entered the room, followed by their troop of friends. Her expression softened as she handed her a bottle of water infused with electrolytes. "How are you doing?"

Killyama raised her head. "It's not as easy as you make it seem."

"I told you to take the drugs. I wasn't getting suckered into going natural. The more drugs, the better. Any regrets yet?"

"No."

Sex Piston gave a sarcastic snort. "Wait until that big head starts popping out. We'll see if you say the same thing."

"Did you get all the items you wanted at the baby shower?" Larissa directed the conversation to divert Killyama's attention away from the pain instead of focusing on it.

"Most of them," Killyama answered.

"What didn't you get?"

Lana arrived and had Killyama get out the pool to check her and the baby. Then Killyama decided she wanted to walk for a while and use the restroom again.

The afternoon dragged on as Killyama's labor intensified.

The water delivery was nearly textbook perfect. Killyama's little bundle of joy arrived to the cheers of the women anxiously waiting.

Blinking back emotional tears as Train greeted his beautiful daughter reinforced why she had become a midwife.

Priss took Train away to let him help with the baby while she and Lana helped Killyama deliver the afterbirth.

Once baby and mother were settled in bed, Lana and Priss started draining and dismantling the birthing pool.

Larissa kept an eye on the parents as she cleaned and packed the equipment they had used. When she was finished, she told Train and Killyama that she and Lana would be leaving, but Priss would be staying until morning, and she would be back then.

Train looked up from staring at the baby with gratitude on his face. "Thank you."

"You're welcome."

Before leaving, she shooed all of Killyama's friends out so the new parents could enjoy some bonding time alone.

After saying goodbye to Priss, Lana and Larissa left Train's house. There were two men standing guard outside.

Neither of them said anything until they were in Lana's car, where they stared at each other curiously.

"I wonder what that's about," Lana asked as she buckled her seat belt.

"I have no clue." Starting the car, she looked up at the front of the club. There were several men standing on the porch. "Look." Larissa directed her attention to where she was staring. "You think something is going on?"

"I don't know, but it sure looks that way."

She backed out of the parking spot and pulled onto the main road.

"You notice Beth? She kept her phone in her hand the whole time."

"Yes," Larissa answered without taking her eyes off the road. "I think she had 911 on speed dial. She was terrified for Killyama, but that wasn't anything new today. She wanted her to have the baby in the hospital. I tried to ease her worry, but nothing I said changed her mind."

"People always have—"

Larissa shook her head. "Beth's fear was different than what we usually hear."

"How so?"

Larissa debated on the wisdom of what Beth had said when she had pressed her on her fears.

"Larissa?"

She had never been good at keeping secrets from her sisters. Besides, Lana might be curious to ask Beth herself.

"She said The Last Rider women don't have easy births."

Lana frowned. "What did she mean by that?"

"I don't know." When she glanced at her sister, she read the worried look on Lana's face.

"Then I'll damn sure be finding out."

# CHAPTER FORTY-SIX

Moon sat patiently on his bike, waiting for Larissa to arrive. She had told him last night when he had talked to her that she would be coming to stay with Killyama this morning. He hadn't informed her when they'd talked the previous night that one of the brothers had been killed.

Knox had been able to keep the news of Pace's death a secret, but it hadn't been easy. He was going to release the information after they watched the security footage. The Last Riders had used all their contacts to keep the details quiet until they had a better grasp on what the fuck had gone down.

Straightening off the bike at seeing Larissa's car pulling into the parking lot, he waited for her to get out.

"Hey," he called out when she got within earshot.

Larissa gave him a heartwarming smile as she walked toward him. "Hey back at you."

Moon pulled her into his arms when she would have stopped. "I missed you." He hid his smile when she looked around to check if anyone was watching.

"I missed you, too."

Touching the bright spot of color on her cheekbone, he couldn't resist teasing her. "Why are you so embarrassed?"

"I'm not."

"You could have fooled me." Placing a casual arm over her shoulders, he started walking her toward Killyama's house.

"I guess I'm not used to public displays of affection."

It was everything he could do not to burst out in laughter. If she thought that brief kiss was a public display of affection, she would have a fucking heart attack if she ever attended one of The Last Riders' parties.

"I wouldn't call that much of a display."

Moon felt her studying him as they walked up the path.

"Are you laughing at me?"

"No." He hazarded a glance in her direction. She wasn't buying it. "Maybe a little," he admitted.

Bristling under his touch, she pulled away from him to put her hands on her hips. "Excuse me if I become embarrassed when you kiss me where anyone could see!"

His eyes widened at her anger. "There's no one around."

"There are men standing on the porch," she argued back.

"They weren't paying attention."

"They seemed to be."

"Why does it matter if they did? Jesus, Larissa, we're grown adults. You need to loosen up."

"*I* should loosen up?"

Wincing, he wished he had just let it drop and placated her. That was how Train managed to survive, from his viewpoint.

Poking him in the chest, she continued screeching at him. "I'm sorry I'm not as sophisticated as most women you've been with. I prefer not to engage in sex with more than one person, and I certainly wouldn't in the middle of a den."

Moon crossed his arms over his chest to protect the spot

she was drilling a hole into with her finger. "I bet Priss couldn't wait to run home to tell you and Lana that tidbit."

Larissa gave him a warning glare. "You're a smartass, you know that, right?"

"That fact has been brought to my attention several times."

"I bet it has," she snapped. "We need to get one thing straight ... I'm never, *ever* going to have sex with you while another woman is present."

Yeah, like that idea would ever occur to him. The woman could barely handle a twosome, much less a threesome.

"I wouldn't ask you to."

She must have heard the undertone in his statement and drawn the correct assumption.

Dammit, he had never been good at dealing with other people's feelings, which explained why he had never achieved his marriage goal.

Moon tried to circle her shoulders again. "I didn't mean that the way it sounded."

Shrugging away from him, she stared at him indignantly. "You meant it exactly the way you said it. I'm not an idiot." She turned her face away from his and seemed to lose her bravado. "The Last Riders' parties aren't a well-kept secret, despite how hard your club tries. Women talk. I would never try to fit into your lifestyle. The only one who is going to have to change is you. You're going to have to be the one who has to figure out if it will be worthwhile enough to give it up."

"Are you saying if we get serious, you expect me to give up being a member of The Last Riders?"

"Only the sexual part. I understand if that's non-negotiable."

"Depends on what is negotiable." Taking her by the forearms, he tugged her to him. "I'm willing to give up the parties."

She stood stiffly in his arms. "In return for what?"

"Let's see ..." He pretended to mull it over. "I'm a pretty sexual guy, so you promise to have sex with me at least five days a week?"

She gaped at him. "Are you serious?"

"Five too much?" Pretending to be serious, he settled his hands on her hips, letting her feel the burgeoning hardness pressing against her. "I was thinking six, but if you're happy with five, I will be, too."

They stared at each other for a long minute to see who would break first. Larissa did, breaking into laughter that had her wiping tears from the corners of her eyes.

"Five?" she hiccupped. "We had sex three times the other night. I guess that means I only have to have sex with you a couple of more times, and I'll be set for the week."

"Anything else you want to negotiate?" he asked, finally succeeding in tucking her under his arm as they continued walking toward Killyama's house.

"No, I think that's about it."

"I'm relieved to hear it."

"Can I ask you a question?"

He tensed at hearing the gravity in her voice. "Yes."

"Beth said something yesterday which has me curious."

"What did she say?" Had Razer told Beth about Pace?

"She said The Last Rider women don't have easy births; what did she mean by that?"

Moon stopped walking to turn her toward him. "You should ask her. I wasn't around when they went into labor."

"You weren't here, but you know what she meant, don't you?"

Moon stared at her, deciding to be honest. "Beth was attacked the night she went into labor. The attacker was one of the parties responsible for Reaper's kidnapping. She could have died, and one of her twins nearly did. Then Winter was attacked when she was pregnant by one of The Last Riders' enemies. She went into labor, and both her and the baby would have died if not for Killyama." Moon watched Larissa grow paler during each description.

"Anyone else?"

He nodded. "Lily. During her first pregnancy, she was kidnapped by her father. She had the baby and went into a coma."

"Jesus ..." Larissa whispered, her hand moving protectively to her abdomen.

"Look at me." Moon gripped her chin, forcing her eyes to meet his. "You have nothing to worry about. There is nothing more important to me than your and the baby's safety. Trust that I can take care of you both."

"I do."

"You don't sound so sure."

"I am." This time, she sounded more certain. "I'm pretty good at taking care of myself, too."

Moon let his mask drop for a second at her words. It was the only warning he was going to give her.

"That's good to know."

# CHAPTER FORTY-SEVEN

M oon rubbed his eyes tiredly, resting them from dissecting the security footage of the night Pace had been killed.

Damn, he needed a cigarette. If it weren't for the hassle of having to take a shower and change his clothes before going to see Larissa, he would take a break.

When he heard a beep, he looked at the security monitor showing Viper and Shade entering the garage from the factory. He waited three seconds before he pushed the button to let them into the security room.

They looked just as exhausted as he was.

"Any news?" Viper sat down in front of the computer next to him, staring bleakly at the security video Moon had been watching.

"No." His gaze returned to his. "You?"

"Nah. Sorry, brother."

Moon turned his chair to look at the footage. "Pace goes in and doesn't come out of the whirlpool room. I've checked the footage from a week before Pace was killed until two days after, even though we tore the fucking room apart to make sure no one was still hiding in there after we watched the security feed. I can't figure it out, and neither can Rider or Reaper." Moon looked away from the monitors and back at Viper.

Shade had taken the last chair at the end of the security desk and was squeezing a football stress ball.

"I'm too old for this shit." Viper turned in Shade's direction.

"Don't look at me. Take it up with Reaper and Rider. The club was their bright idea."

Moon's gaze went back and forth between the two men. "You're joking, right?"

Viper's silence made his chest constrict.

Viper was the only reason he was still in The Last Riders. Regardless of whoever took over as president after Viper, his ass would be out. And it wouldn't even fucking matter because, without Viper in the club, he wouldn't want to be here, anyway. He knew Viper was closer to the other brothers than him, whereas he felt Viper was the older brother that life had denied him.

"Not really. I don't know if I can go through another possible traitor, like Memphis."

Moon rested his elbows on his knees and leaned forward in his chair. "It's not your fault Pace got killed."

Viper didn't seem convinced. "I'm the one who asked Wizard to send me someone to take point on hiring someone to snoop around for us."

"You didn't know Pace was Wizard's nephew."

"It doesn't matter to me who he was related to. He was a kid, still wet behind the ears."

"Shit." Moon grew more vehement. "He was twenty-six and served two years in the Army before he was dishonorably discharged. Wizard sent Pace here because he was tired of his sister nagging at him to let him become a Last Rider.

He should have sent anyone but Pace. I warned both you and Shade that he was too gung-ho. That's why he got thrown out of the Army and lost every job he managed to get. He reacted without thinking of repercussions. Hell, remember when Wizard told us he saw an Uber driver being carjacked by a gang? Pace waded right in and nearly got his ass killed then. Spent two weeks in ICU, yet it still didn't make him think before his mom's house caught on fire and he ran back in for her fucking photo album.

"It sucks he's dead. I don't know who fucking killed him, but I do know for fuckin' sure that Pace told Puck he needed to take a dump to get back inside the club for a reason. That reason is what got him killed, not you. All he had to do was tell Puck what he was really up, which is why Wizard sent Puck, anyway."

"Unless it was Puck who killed him."

Shade's soft input made Moon's eyes jerk to his. "You don't seriously think it was Puck, do you? He was on the porch the whole time."

Shade nodded his head toward the monitors. "He could have done something to the security feed."

"Puck would have taken the bullet for Pace if he could have," Moon argued back.

"I agree."

Moon reared back in his chair aggressively. "Then why did you say it?"

"That's what I heard a couple of women saying. They aren't buying that the coroner ruled it as a suicide, either. They're grasping at straws, which is, if we're honest, all we have left."

"He didn't commit suicide." Viper's grim voice drew their eyes. "I don't give a fuck what the coroner ruled."

A snort of anger escaped Moon. "The old buzzard should have retired ten years ago. He can't tell the difference between a kneecap and a brain." Frustrated, he stood up to pace in the office.

"Pace's gun was there," Shade continued, squeezing the football.

"I don't care if it was in his hand," Moon argued. "He didn't off himself."

"He was also the one who hired the informer." Viper leaned back in his chair to hook his foot on his knee. "What in the fuck are we supposed to do now? We don't even know who in the fuck Pace hired."

"I was hoping they would have come forward by now to either you or hightailed it to Wizard," Moon admitted.

"Me, too." Viper studied the tip of his boot as if it held the answers for the universe.

"Wizard has no clue?"

"No. And the only people who knew Pace had hired someone were Wizard, Shade, Puck, you, and me."

None of them brought up the fact that Puck had the knowledge, which could have been the reason Pace was killed. All of them liked and trusted Puck, and despite Shade voicing what the women were saying, Moon didn't really believe Shade thought Puck had betrayed the club.

"Me telling Pace to keep it to himself who he'd hired is biting me on the butt, isn't it?"

"The idea was if we didn't know, we couldn't spill the beans to the person we're trying to catch," Moon objected heatedly.

Viper dropped his foot back to the floor. "Yeah, well, this has been a waste of time. We don't know anything more than when we came in here to begin with. I'm going home to fuck my wife. Feel like doing me a solid tonight and babysit Aisha for us?"

Shade nodded. "I'll go with you. Save you a trip to bring her to my house."

Instead of heading to the door with Shade, Viper remained standing next to his chair. "You going to get some sleep when you get off? You look like shit."

Moon shook his head. "Nope. Going to take Larissa to get the rest of her stuff from Sex Piston's parents' house."

Viper's mouth quirked into a smile. "I bet this is the most you've driven a car since you left the service."

"You would be right."

"I thought you swore never to ride in one again?"

"Put it this way, the end justifies the means."

Viper stared at him seriously. "Brother, I've said this before, but I hope you know what you're doing."

Moon stared up at him just as seriously. "Brother, I hope I do, too."

# CHAPTER FORTY-EIGHT

L arissa wiggled her toes in the warm water, wondering if there was any better feeling in the entire world. Her life would be perfect if she had a sack of burgers and fries from Marty's. She should have stopped and got herself one before coming home. She glumly contemplated why the owner had to be the meanest ass in the universe; she knew she wouldn't be getting a sack of the delicious burgers anytime soon.

For a brief couple of months, the town had enjoyed a delivery service until the driver fell in love and left. Several of the town locals had tried their hand at the delivery service and failed miserably. It wasn't worth taking the snide comments the owner handed out, never mind the fee for napkins or ketchup packets.

"One good thing, if our clinic fails, I could always start delivering hamburgers," she consoled herself out loud.

A knock at the front door had her reaching for her phone. She pulled up the Ring app and saw Moon at the front door.

"Come in!" she yelled, setting her phone back down on the end table.

Her smile of greeting was met with an annoyed frown plastered on Moon's face as he walked down the entrance hall toward her.

"What's wrong?"

"Did you forget to lock the front door?"

She thought about using "pregnancy brain" as a convenient excuse, but it would be a lie.

"I knew you were coming."

"I don't care if you knew I was two minutes away. You lock the fucking door," he snapped.

Her shoulders tensed at the tone he used with her until she read the worry evident in his eyes.

"I'm sorry. I didn't mean to upset you. I'll be more careful."

Moon looked as if she had just taken the wind out of his sails. "You are?"

Larissa nodded. "Yes."

"Why aren't you arguing with me?"

She shrugged. "Because you're right." Looking down at her feet, she started wiggling her toes again. "And ... I heard about Pace." She looked up through her lashes to catch his reaction.

Moon sighed loudly. "I was going to tell you."

"You've had several opportunities, so why haven't you?"

"To be honest ..." He sat down and picked up the towel beside her, placing it on his lap, then lifted her foot closest to him and rested it on the towel. He used the ends of towel to gently dry her foot before he started massaging her sole. "I wasn't ready to discuss it. Maybe in a couple of days."

Resting back on the arm of the couch, she luxuriated in being cared for, as if her comfort really mattered to him. She didn't want to spoil the moment by pressuring Moon before he was clearly ready. She decided to wait and give him more time to process losing his friend to suicide.

Being a midwife, she had witnessed fathers doing little things for the mothers many times. Propping them up on pillows, rubbing their backs, foot massages, getting them the food they're craving ...

Regarding him as his fingers moved to rub the side of her foot, she decided to go for it. Nothing was ever gained unless you did it yourself ... or asked someone else to do it for you.

"Um ... you hungry?" she ventured slowly.

"You?" Moon's fingers went to her toes.

Larissa nearly lost track of what she was about to say. Lord ... *oh my* ... his fingers were magical. She had to swallow hard before answering.

"Starved. I would offer you something, but I was too tired to make it to the grocery store. I planned to get take-out on the way home."

Sliding his hand down her foot, Moon cupped the heel in the palm of his hand then started rubbing the back, near her ankle.

Every drop of blood turned into molten silver at the speed of light.

"Why didn't you?"

"Huh?"

"Why didn't you stop and get take-out?"

"I wanted hamburgers."

Moon's eye narrowed on her. "I'll call and order a couple of burgers from King's."

"Those aren't the hamburgers I was craving." Pouting, she tried to keep a straight face.

"Is there something wrong with your lip?"

She sucked her bottom lip back in. "Papercut," she mumbled.

"That's painful," he commiserated.

She gave him sad eyes and took another shot. "Not as much as wanting the hamburgers from Marty's."

Moon ran his hand up the back of her calf to knead the taut muscles. How she kept her eyes from rolling back into her head, she'd never know.

"No."

"Please …"

"I'm not dealing with that asshole."

"He's not that bad."

Moon arched a brow at her. "Then why didn't you stop and pick them up?"

"My feet hurt too badly."

"Yeah, right," he snorted. "How about I run to the grocery store and buy some hamburgers and buns—"

She started crying. "Because I don't have his grill for you to cook them on. The pickles won't taste the same, either. He marinates them in something and won't tell anyone in what."

Moon seemed bewildered at her behavior.

Larissa was at the point she didn't care she was coming across as a loon. She wanted those freaking hamburgers.

"Have I asked you to do one thing for me since I've been pregnant?"

His hand on her calf stopped moving. "No …"

"The least you could do is get me those damn burgers!" she shouted at him. "I would go get them for you if you wanted them!" She wouldn't, but he didn't need to know that. "It's your fault I'm pregnant, anyway!"

"How is it *my* fault? You snuck into my room." Moon stared at her disbelievingly.

Larissa cried even harder when he raised his voice at her. "You're the one who doesn't know how to use a condom! Not me! Next time, buy a better quality! Did you buy the cheapest, thinnest ones you could?" she berated his choices.

From his expression, she could tell she had hit it on the nail.

"I didn't buy the condoms. Wizard buys them in bulk, and I—"

"Who is Wizard?" Larissa looked at Moon wildly.

"The president of The Last Riders in the Ohio branch—"

She grabbed one of the throw pillows within reach and started pounding him with it. "I'm pregnant because you used a condom bought in bulk!" she screeched at him. "Who does that?"

Moon jerked to his feet. "They're good condoms—"

She threw the pillow at him then flung her hand out toward him. "You got one on you now?"

She could tell from the big jerk's face that he did.

"Let me see it."

When he didn't move, it sent her off into another level of fury.

"Don't make me get up." She stopped crying to warn him in a deathly quiet voice, "Let. Me. See. Them. *Now.*"

Moon looked like a deer caught in a headlight, frozen in place.

Infuriated, she lifted her foot out of the water in preparation to get off the couch.

"Dammit." Moon reached into his back pocket for the condom and held it out to her.

Larissa stared at the packet, reading it through puffy eyes. "You son of a bitch!" she screeched. "You used an ultra-thin condom!" Throwing the condom at his face, she picked up the towel that Moon had used on his lap to cry into. "I hate men!" she sobbed. "I bet if you could get pregnant, you would have bought a name brand so thick it couldn't be cut without a pair of scissors."

"Larissa, calm down … let's go get the rest of your things. I'll stop and get—"

"Go back to the clubhouse. I'm not going anywhere with you!" She continued to sob into the towel.

"You're going to get sick if you keep crying that way."

"What do you care?" she hiccupped between sobs. "You want me to believe we're in a relationship—"

"We are," he tried to soothe her.

She lowered the towel to glare at him. "Then why are you still carrying around condoms?"

Moon stared at her speechlessly, his mouth hanging open like a damn fish.

She picked up the towel to continue crying. "Leave!"

He sighed loudly. "I'll go get you hamburgers from Marty's."

"You mean it?"

"Yes."

"Thank you." She lowered the towel to start fanning her face with her hand. "You don't know how much that means to me."

"I'm getting the idea. I do," he replied, turning toward the hallway.

"When you order the food, tell Marty it's is for me. He gives me extra pickles."

"Okay."

Putting her foot back in the water, she saw Moon was almost out the door. "Don't come back unless you get enough for my sisters and yourself. I'm not sharing mine!"

She grabbed the pillow from the floor and put it behind her back. Then she opened the drawer of the side table and took out a box of Girl Scout s'more cookies.

She heard the door close behind Moon.

She had learned one thing by being a midwife: the only time you have control over people to get them to do anything you want was when you were within a few months of giving birth. You had to use that power wisely ... and not take any prisoners.

347

# CHAPTER FORTY-NINE

Moon shot himself out of the house before Larissa could give him any further demands. He barreled into Priss when he turned from shutting the door but managed to prevent both of them from tumbling to the ground.

"What the ...?" Priss stared at him with wide eyes.

"Sorry, I'm in a hurry."

Her gaze went from his to the door behind him then came back to his. Understanding dawned on her expression. "What does she want?"

Moon swore he saw burgeoning fear on her face.

"A sack of burgers."

"Was she crying?"

"That's putting it lightly."

"Ugh!" Priss muttered quietly, as if Larissa could hear them from the living room with the closed door separating them. "You have to do whatever needs to be done so she doesn't get to the crying stage!" she whisper-screamed. "I found that out when she wanted a banana milkshake for lunch the other day. And she nearly took off Lana's head when she came home with Trefoils. She had to go back out and get the s'more cookies."

"I would rather have to deal with a Girl Scout than Marty."

Priss gave him a pitying look. "Clearly, you've never had to deal with the mother of one of them. Lana came back with two boxes of every flavor, just so she could buy two boxes of the s'mores. She made the mistake of telling them that her pregnant sister was craving them."

Moon was starting to appreciate what Train had to live with, having Killyama as a spouse. The brother deserved a silver star.

"A heads-up would have been nice."

"Why? And let you miss the joy of impending fatherhood?" she said snidely.

He debated hightailing it to Ohio as he tried staring her down.

His shoulders slumped. It seemed Priss was immune to his intimidation tactics.

"Do you want any burgers? Larissa told me she isn't sharing."

"I'll take a sack. And get one for Lana. Saves me from having to make dinner."

"Glad to help out," he said insincerely.

Moon started to move around her when he noticed Priss made no move to enter the house. Instead, she turned to head in the same direction as him.

"Aren't you going into the house?"

Priss backed further away from the door. "Nope. I'm going to wait in the car until you come back."

"I'll pay you fifty bucks to get the burgers."

She vigorously shook her head. "I'll pass. Marty is worse than Larissa."

There were already customers waiting outside Marty's when he approached the restaurant. Eyeing them, he evaluated the chances of getting them to go inside and place an order for him.

Lucky made a face at him. "Save your breath. None of us are going to help you out."

Not dissuaded, he made his pitch to the other people standing outside. "I'll give you three hundred dollars to order my food for me."

Beth, Nickel, and Evie all shook their heads.

"Sorry," Beth apologized. "I've already ordered. Marty will know I'm ordering for someone else."

Nickel wasn't apologetic. "No. I didn't even want to place my own order."

Moon gave Evie a pleading look.

"Forget it. He knows I'm married to King. If he makes one more sarcastic comment about me coming to get his food, I'm going to shove him in the freezer."

"Fuck," Moon groaned, giving up.

He opened the door and warily went inside to walk toward the counter. The whole restaurant was empty. What used to be a bustling, fun place to sit around and shoot the shit had become like entering a lion's den—you didn't know if you would walk back out with all your limbs still attached.

Stopping at the counter, he waited for Marty to come out from the back.

The first time he had come here after Marty had taken over, he made the mistake of calling out for service. When he had left then, he swore to never come back. It was a promise he'd had every intention of keeping until Larissa went off the wall on his ass.

He had to wait several minutes before the huge man came

lumbering out with his beef hands filled with sacks of food.

"What in the fuck do you want?"

Moon bit his tongue on what he wanted to say. "I want to place an order," he replied politely.

"No shit." Marty's beady eyes stared at him. "What do you want to order?" he snapped, setting the bags down on the counter.

"Four deluxe sacks. One of the sacks is for Larissa; she likes extra pickles."

"Go outside and wait. Takes about ten minutes. Tell the fuckers outside their food is ready."

Moon nodded then hurried outside.

Everyone outside looked at him expectantly.

Vengefully, he didn't mention their food was ready.

It was only when Beth asked fearfully if ten minutes had passed that he said something.

"He said all your orders are ready."

He shrugged off their angry glares but started to worry if he had pissed Marty off by making him wait for them to come inside and get their orders.

He again ignored the furious glares coming from Beth, Evie, Nickel, and Lucky as they walked back out.

"Don't bother asking me to switch shifts when you want me to," Nickel told him as he passed by.

"I'm going to tell Razer that you're the reason his hamburgers are cold," Beth threatened.

Lucky stopped in front of him. "You know I'm going to pay you back."

"Bring it on, brother." Unconcerned, Moon crossed his arms over his chest.

Evie came up to him. "You're not allowed in my restaurant anymore."

His arms dropped at seeing how mad she was. "You're kidding?"

"Try me," she snarled. "I hope Larissa twists your dick into knots."

"That's a little harsh."

Evie flipped him off before crossing the street.

Moon watched everyone leave, knowing he had earned a place on their shit list. Damn, maybe he should have given more thought about making them wait.

After exactly ten minutes, he walked inside and strode up to the counter. Waiting expectantly for Marty come out, he had to twiddle his thumbs until five minutes later.

From Marty's expression, he knew one of the people outside had tattled on him.

Yeah, he had made a mistake. He was finally willing to admit that.

He handed Marty his credit card and picked up an ink pen, ready to sign his name and get the fuck out of the restaurant.

Marty's gloating expression should have given him a clue when he handed him the receipt. Poising the ink pen over the signature line, he ran his eyes over the total. Then they flew upward at the amount billed.

"You charged me too much."

Marty's beady eyes narrowed on him. "The extra hundred is what it cost when you wasted my time."

"That's illegal," Moon blustered.

"Nobody's forcing you to sign it. I can donate the sacks to the police department. They won't go to waste."

His fingers shook as he swirled his name onto the receipt.

"You the one who knocked Larissa up?"

Moon started to ignore his question, but he didn't want to chance Larissa not getting another craving for his food.

"I'm the father of her baby, yes," he admitted through clenched teeth.

"You going to marry her?"

"That's none of your business."

"In other words, no." Marty maneuvered his huge belly around the counter to sit on a chair. "My daughter is supposed to come for a visit. When she does, I better not catch you sniffing around her."

Moon juggled the bags in his arms. "I can guarantee no man in town will go near your daughter." Keeping his face devoid of expression, Moon started for the door.

"Good." The son of bitch wasn't done. "And make sure none of your biker buddies come here, sniffing around her, either."

"I won't have to." He opened the door and managed to get out of there without shooting the rat bastard.

Packing the food into his saddlebags, he rode home. He had enough aggravation to last him for the day. As soon as he dropped the food off, he was going to head back to the club.

When he parked his bike in the driveway, he noticed Priss wasn't sitting her car. Leaving his food in the saddlebag while carrying the rest to the door, Moon used his elbow to ring the doorbell.

He again had to grit his teeth when he heard Priss call out to come in. He opened the door and walked down the hallway, from where he saw Larissa already sitting at the table. She had changed while he was gone.

Wearing a pretty pink robe, she looked so cute sitting there with an expectant look on her face. He felt his cock harden at how beautiful she looked with her hand resting on the baby bump, which kept her unable to pull the chair closer to the table.

He set the food down on the table before he turned to leave.

"Where are you going?" Larissa asked as she immediately started opening a bag.

Moon didn't bother to turn around. "To get my sack."

# CHAPTER FIFTY

"I appreciate you getting the food for me."

"You're welcome." Moon sank down next to Larissa on the couch. Placing an arm over her shoulders, he pulled her closer to him. He almost told her *anytime* but couldn't form the word to get it out.

Reaching around him, Larissa opened a drawer in the end table and pulled out a box of cookies.

"Would anyone like one?" she offered, taking the cookies out of the box.

"Tha—" Moon cut himself short when Lana and Priss glared at him from the dining room table, where they were still eating. "Thanks, anyway."

"We have other flavors in the kitchen cabinet, next to the glasses. Help yourself," Larissa told him as she took a cookie for herself.

Not wanting to dislodge her, he stayed where he was.

Lana got up from the table. Moon heard her opening a cabinet then saw her carrying two boxes of cookies toward him. "Here. Knock yourself out." She handed him one of the boxes. "I'm going to bed. It's been a long day."

"Night, sis." Larissa ate another cookie as she eyed the box Lana had given Moon. "I hate those. Are you sure you don't want one of mine?"

"I'm sure." Moon opened the plain tagalongs, wondering if Beth or Lily knew of anyone selling Girl Scout cookies in town.

Larissa turned on a movie as Priss cleared the table before she came out of the kitchen with a glass of milk and a box of cookies in hand, then set the milk on a coaster on the end table next to him.

"See you in the morning. Good night."

"Good night," Moon and Larissa replied as they ate their cookies.

"You don't like the lemon ones?"

Larissa turned her eyes from the television. "How'd you know?"

"Wild guess."

"I only like the s'mores. The others are only so-so."

"Since we didn't make it to Jamestown tonight, when do you want to go?"

"We don't have to. Sex Piston offered to bring them tomorrow when she comes to see Killyama's baby."

"How's the baby doing?"

"She's adorable." Larissa's eyes went all dewy at the mention of the baby. "I barely got her away from Train to weigh her."

"Really?"

Larissa happily nodded her head. "He didn't want me to wake Killyama up, and we had a chance to talk. I was able to watch him with Ela and Bina. He's a good father."

"I agree. He has the patience of a saint."

Larissa eyed him as she munched on yet another cookie. "Would you mind handing me my milk?"

Moon handed her the glass, and Larissa took a drink before handing it back to him, and the cookies.

"I'm sorry for how I acted earlier."

Placing the cookies back in the drawer, he started playing with one of the ribbons on her robe. "That's okay. I shouldn't have argued with you about going to get the burgers. You're eating for two." He quit playing with the ribbon to place his hand on where their baby lay sleeping.

"Sometimes, I think I'm eating for four," she joked.

Moon felt his heart stop. "You would tell me if we're expecting multiples, right?"

Larissa burst out laughing. "Of course. I promise we're only having one."

He was able to breathe again at her reassurance.

"Worried the boutique hasn't had time to restock?" she teased.

"I worried more about how I could hold two at the same time."

Moon noticed her fidgeting with the bow on her robe as she watched television.

"Is something wrong?"

"No."

He knew there was when Larissa didn't look at him.

"Larissa?"

"Are you going to go back to the boutique when she calls?"

"Not without you."

She continued fidgeting with her bow. "Are you going to go out with her?"

"No." Moon took her hand to link it with his. "I have no plans on seeing any other woman."

Larissa snuggled against him at his answer. "I love watching old movies." Yawning, she laid her head down on his shoulder.

He hadn't even paid attention to the movie she had turned on. He didn't know the name of it and couldn't care less. Surprisingly, he actually got caught up in the old movie.

"You know, I was thinking," he said quietly.

"About what?" she asked, her attention still on the movie.

"You're going to be able to move into your house at the end of the month, right?"

"If everything goes through, yes."

"What if, when the closing is final, Lana and Priss stay here, and we moved in there to enjoy some alone time before the baby is born?"

Larissa jerked her eyes to his. "That makes no sense. Why would you give up this house to come live in mine?"

"Because I know you'll want to make your own nest at your home. We can do it together. I also thought you might be able to talk your mother into a visit and stay until the baby is born. You all will be cramped. It makes more sense for us to move into your house. Unless you're not ready to move in with me?"

Her eyes went dewy soft again. "I think it's so sweet that you thought of my mother coming for a visit. I was waiting to move into my house before inviting her."

"After the baby is born, we can reevaluate our relationship. If it goes like I hope, we can switch houses with your sisters and mother. If it doesn't, you and the baby will be situated in your new home, and I'll move back once your sisters leave."

"Mom won't move to Treepoint. She'll never leave Bowling Green permanently."

"Your mother never had a grandchild before." He lowered his mouth to nuzzle her neck. "What do you think of my idea?"

"I'll have to talk to my sisters first."

"Talk it over with them, for sure. The ball is in your

court," he assured her. "Just keep in mind"—Moon started playing with her earlobe with the tip of his tongue—"I don't feel comfortable fucking you with your sisters in the bedrooms next to yours."

Her neck arched back, providing him with better access. "We should finish watching the movie," she suggested, placing a hand on his chest and pushing him back to put a little space between them.

Letting her resume snuggling against him, Moon had to concentrate on who had killed Pace to get his dick under control.

The movie was almost over when he looked down and saw Larissa had fallen asleep. Carefully standing, he lifted her into his arms then carried her upstairs, where he laid her down on the bed, covering her with an extra blanket from the bottom of the bed. He gazed down at her for several minutes before turning the light out and leaving the room.

Downstairs, he switched off the lights and checked the doors before leaving. Then, out in the cool night air, he took in a shaky breath.

She was getting under his skin. How in the fuck could she be a raving bitch whom he wanted to ditch one second, and the next, a kitten he wanted to stroke until she came apart in his arms?

As he stared up at the sky, he saw it was the first quarter moon. He missed Hawaii. There, he had been able to sit on the beach and stare out at the moon and the stars and dream of the family he would have in the future, not like the one waiting for him to come home. Shaking off thoughts of his childhood invariably brought back bitter memories. Memories which were better off left in the past.

# CHAPTER FIFTY-ONE

"I think that's all of it."

Larissa couldn't understand why Moon looked so pleased. The mountain of boxes he had transferred from the storage unit, plus her things she had taken to his house, was now sitting in the living room in her house, waiting to be put where they belong. She was so overwhelmed trying to figure out which job she should tackle first, she didn't notice Moon coming up behind her.

"It looks worse than it is."

Larissa waved a helpless hand at the stacks of boxes surrounding her. "Usually, Priss or Lana do the moving. How am I supposed to know where they want their things to go?"

Moon turned her to face him. "You look like you're ready to run for the door."

She was desperately trying not to burst into tears. "I'm not any good at this type of thing."

He frowned down at her. "What kind of thing?"

"Normal stuff, like moving."

The comforting hug he gave her lessened the panic threatening to overwhelm her.

"I know it seems a lot, but with both of us working together, we'll get it done. It doesn't have to be done in one day, does it?"

"No, I suppose not." She nodded against his chest.

"Are you regretting us moving in together?"

"No, moving always makes me nervous. I hate for things to be out of place."

"Technically, nothing's out of place if we haven't taken them out of the boxes. It's a brand-new house; you haven't found a place for the things to go."

"You're right." Taking a deep breath, she pulled herself out of his arms. "Okay, where should we start?"

The words were no sooner out of her mouth than she heard a knock on the front door. Opening her mouth to call out, "Come in!" she caught Moon's glower.

"I'll just get that."

He wasn't appeased. "If I catch you doing that again, there will be hell to pay."

"Oh … I'm *so* scared." Lighthearted, she went to answer the door.

Surprised to find Lana and Priss on the other side of the door, she started laughing when she saw what they were holding— a welcome doormat and a bottle of apple juice.

Lana walked inside with the juice while Priss laid the mat down before following her.

"I thought you had to work?"

"We lied." Lana gave her a hug. "We thought we would help you get a good start, and you can do the rest when you figure out where you want things."

Priss took a long look at the boxes then glanced toward her. "I forgot how much stuff we had in storage. I bet this is driving you nuts."

"If you had arrived a few minutes earlier, you would have seen me whining on Moon's shoulder," she confessed.

"Lucky for Moon,"—Lana rolled up the sleeves of her sweater—"we're here to save the day."

Priss was less enthusiastic. "I should have scheduled appointments, for real."

Lana wasn't having it. "Most of this is your stuff. Larissa, have you picked out which room you want the baby in?"

Larissa led her sisters to the bedrooms, showing them the master bedroom first. She raised the blinds. "I thought this room would be Moon and my room. The room next to it would be the baby's. The one at the end would be either yours or Priss'." Leading them to the small room off the front door, she turned on the light inside. "And one of you could take this one. It has a private bathroom."

Lana nodded at her then turned toward Priss. "Which one do you want?"

"I can take either. Which one do you want? The bedroom upstairs is bigger, but this one has a private bathroom."

"Then, if you don't mind, I'll take this one. With my hours, it'll be the quietest, and I won't wake the baby up when I get ready for work. We can evaluate who gets the master bedroom if Moon and Larissa decide to move into his house."

"That works for me," Priss agreed.

Both sisters looked at her.

"Works for me, too." Larissa nodded cheerfully.

"Good. Then let's get to work. I have to be back at the hospital in a couple of hours." Lana took command, which made Larissa ecstatic.

"Moon, your job is carrying the boxes to the rooms written on the boxes."

Moon seemed as relieved as she was.

"Priss, I would just stack your boxes to the side. There's no need opening them until we're ready to move in, unless you need to get something out. I'll do the same with mine.

"Larissa, you can empty your boxes, and when Priss and I get done, we can help. Moon, when you get to the boxes for the kitchen, you can start opening them. Just set them on the counters, and you and Larissa can decide together where things go. Any questions?"

They all said no.

"Then let's get cracking."

---

Two hours later, Moon and Larissa both appeared shellshocked at the amount of work they had been able to accomplish.

"I think you two are good to go now." Lana looked extremely satisfied as she glanced around the empty living room. "When does the new furniture arrive?"

"Tomorrow. Moon said he took off half a day."

"Good. Don't forget not to lift anything heavy."

"I won't," Larissa assured her sister. "Where's Priss?"

"Here." Walking into the room with an armful of clothes, she gave them a wry smile. "I couldn't resist. I'm tired of wearing the same clothes."

Moon went to the kitchen and came back with an empty box, which he handed to Priss. "Feel free to come and get anything you want."

"I pretty much took what I wanted. I should donate the rest to the church's store." Putting the clothes she was carrying into the box, Priss looked toward Lana. "Are you ready?"

"Yes."

After giving Larissa brief hugs and Moon a quick good-bye, they left in a rush so Lana wouldn't be late.

"Whew." Moon stared at the door after them. "If I hadn't

seen it, I wouldn't believe it. Lana is like a hurricane. She sweeps in, and you don't know which way you're going."

Larissa laughed at his assessment. "Lana takes after Mom. She's really smart. I wish I took after Lana. She doesn't let anything faze her, takes charge, always knows what to do …" She stopped when she saw Moon was staring at her curiously. "Anyway, I'm glad they came by."

"I am, too. You seem like you're in a better mood."

"I am." Brushing her hair back behind her ear, she felt for the first time like she could manage what work was left to be done.

"Are you hungry?"

Larissa patted her stomach. "We both are."

"Make that three."

Her face fell. "I was going to the grocery store but didn't make it there."

"That's fine. Let's get changed. We can eat out and head to the grocery store."

"Okay, I'll go change."

"I need to take a quick shower."

It was only when they were heading to their bedroom did it sink in that she would be sharing a room with Moon.

"I'll shower while you get changed."

Glad at the reprieve of undressing in front of Moon, she hurried to change before he could come out of the bathroom. She'd had three weeks to decide to move in with him, so she couldn't understand why she hadn't considered they would be living together not as roommates but as a couple.

As she brushed her hair, she tried not to let her nerves get the best of her.

"It's going to be okay," she told herself, unaware she had spoken out loud.

"Yes, it is," Moon concurred, coming out of the bathroom.

Larissa stared at him sheepishly. "I'm just a little nervous. I've never lived with a man before," she admitted.

"You didn't live with your boyfriend?"

"God, no. We were both so busy getting our degree that that was our only priority. At least, it was mine. He lived at his home. It just made more since so he could concentrate on his studies and wouldn't have to work. And when he was matched with a hospital after graduation, I found out he was cheating on me."

Larissa kept her eyes on her reflection in the mirror as Moon dropped the towel around his hips to pull on a pair of jeans.

Sitting on the bed, he tugged on black leather boots. "That must have been upsetting."

"It was, and it wasn't. A friend of mine had told me he was cheating on me, but I didn't believe her. Come to find out, she was telling me the truth." Larissa changed the subject before Moon could ask any further questions. "Are you ready to go?"

He stood up to pull on a dark gray shirt. "I am. Where do you want to eat?"

"I'm craving steak. How about King's?"

Larissa couldn't understand the pained look he gave her.

"I'll stay in the car until you get us a table. You can text me when you're seated."

"Why?"

"Put it this way … mistakes were made."

They ended up going to a casual dining restaurant that had steak on the menu. The Pink Slipper was the closest to an Applebee's that Treepoint was ever going to get.

Moon and she sat and talked as they ate. The more time she spent with him, the more comfortable she felt. He was a fun companion, attentive, and made her feel special in a way she had never felt before.

After finishing her meal, she watched as he ate the last of his cheesecake. She caught more than one woman's eyes straying to their table. He drew their eyes like a magnet, like he did hers. Like he had caught Lana's the night at the bar.

Larissa twirled the melted ice cubes in her drink, her mind on that night. What if she hadn't gone into his bedroom? Would Lana be the one sitting here tonight?

"You've gone quiet all of a sudden. What are you thinking about?"

She smiled at him. "Nothing."

"You're lying."

Larissa made a face at him. "Yes, I am."

"So, what were you thinking of?"

She leaned forward to cup her glass between her hands. "Do you ever wish you could do a do-over?"

Moon gave her a cautious glance. "Somehow, I don't think I'm going to come out ahead by answering that question."

"I already know the answer to that question."

Moon frowned at her. "There's no way you could know my answer to a question you haven't asked. Don't presume to—"

"Never mind," Larissa cut him off, waving to their busy waitress when she would have rushed past them. "I'll take the ticket."

Moon sighed. "Come down off your high horse, Larissa. The question you presume to know the answer to is: would I go back in time and not have sex with you, therefore we wouldn't be looking forward to having a baby in a couple of months? Is that not the question you think you know the answer to?"

"Yes."

"Then let me give my answer. No, I wouldn't do anything different, other than turn on the damn light."

She nodded, reaching into her purse for her credit card.

"Stop, Larissa. I'm paying for our meal."

"I want to."

"If you want to pay for something, you can buy half the groceries."

She put her card back in her purse.

"What was the question you wanted to ask?"

"Nev—"

"If you tell me never mind one more time, when we get home, we're going to play a new game—how many times can I spank that pert ass of yours until you tell me you're sorry."

She gaped at him. "You wouldn't dare."

"Try me."

"I'll pass."

"Good choice." He handed the waitress his credit card, then stared at Larissa until she started squirming in her seat. Her mom would look at her the same way until she would confess to doing something, knowing it would lead to punishment.

Inevitably, she caved and confessed. Avoiding his gaze, she stared back at her glass. "Do you ever think about fate?"

"I can't say I have."

"The night we had sex ... do you think, if you hadn't gone upstairs ... and had stopped and talked ... and Lana approached you, do you think you would have ...?" Larissa couldn't bring herself to finish the question.

When Moon remained silent and just continued to stare at her, she found herself trying to explain further.

"If Lana had made a play for you, would you have ... been receptive?"

He didn't answer, nor did he move his eyes away until the waitress came and set the receipt and card back on the table. Scrawling his signature, he handed the slip back. Only when she was out of hearing distance did Moon speak.

"The real question you should ask yourself is: would you rather Lana were sitting here with me, carrying my child?"

Larissa picked up the glass to take a drink to buy time. When she placed the glass down, she nearly dropped it. Moon reached out to right it, his demeanor so void of emotion that it was scary.

"I feel guilty," she admitted. "I feel as if I stole something from her."

Moon's expression showed his surprise. "For God's sake, what?"

"Her happiness. I feel guilty I'm so happy."

# CHAPTER FIFTY-TWO

Moon found himself gutted by what Larissa said. If she had reached across the table and taken a filet knife to his stomach, the feeling would be the same.

"Are you ready?" he asked hoarsely.

"Yes."

Rising, he took her arm to help her up from the chair before he placed his hand on the small of her back, then escorted her out of the restaurant.

"Are you angry at me?" she asked breathlessly.

Slowing down, he pushed the key fob, unlocking the SUV. "No, I'm not angry at you."

"You seem to be."

He clenched his jaw at hearing the hurt in her voice as he opened her car door. Leaning inside once she was seated, he guided the seat belt across her to click it in place. Then he raised his head and cupped her cheek, forcing her to meet his eyes. "You drive me insane. You know that, right?"

"I'm sorry."

"Don't you fucking cry."

He felt like dog shit when she started blinking rapidly, her eyes watery.

Moon released Larissa, jerking himself out of the SUV. After making sure she wasn't touching the door, he closed it.

"Motherfucking shit," he cursed heatedly as he walked around the front of the vehicle. "Fucking hell." Snapping his mouth closed, he got in the car.

"Moon, I ..."

He started the car, and despite his anger, he drove back to her house.

"I thought we were going to the grocery store?"

Ignoring her, he parked in the driveway, got out of the car and opened her door, then unclicked her seat belt to help her out of the car. Taking her by the arm, he then frog-marched her to the house. Once inside, he led her toward the bedroom.

"Moon ..."

Shutting the door behind them, he stared at her. They stood in the darkened bedroom with the moonlight filtering through the curtains.

"Do you want to know what I really think of fate?"

"No ... I don't think I do," she answered timidly.

"It doesn't fucking exist. I think when people are unhappy with their choices, they use it to explain the fallout they find themselves in when shit hits the fan. It's a fucking cop-out. Instead of admitting they made a fucking mistake, they say 'fate stepped in' or 'that's the way fate meant it to go.'"

"I truly didn't mean it that way."

Moon paced around the bedroom, raking a hand through his hair. "To be clear, if Lana had approached me, I don't know how I would have reacted. If you want me to say I wouldn't have accepted any invitation she threw out there, you're barking up the wrong tree." He continued pacing as he talked, not wanting to see the hurt on her face. "But we didn't talk, because it didn't happen that way. I went upstairs and went to bed.

"One thing I can guarantee is if we had ended up having sex, she wouldn't have been sitting at that table with me tonight. I like your sister, but she takes charge of everything. We would have been butting heads constantly. I don't say anything because she's your sister, and I stay out of it.

"You constantly put both of your sisters first, ahead of yourself. When you make dinner, you give yourself the burned piece, or the messed-up one. You give them the best portion. In the apartment you shared, Priss said you slept on the couch while they slept on the bed. When I was at your mother's house, there were pictures everywhere, yet I only saw a couple of you. Lana and Priss drive nice cars; your car is older."

"Because I prefer to save money, and I hate having pictures taken of me."

"That's my point. I don't waste money, either, and I don't like pictures. I have more in common with you than both of them combined." Moon strode to her in the darkness to pull her to him. "You can thank your lucky stars that I didn't hook up with Lana that night." Hovering his mouth over hers, he continued, "Because I would have fucked her and never given her another thought. If I had knocked her up instead of you, I would have worked out a similar custody agreement, but you can bet your bottom dollar that I wouldn't be getting her hamburgers from Marty's. I wouldn't be living with her. The only difference it would make is you would be trying to explain to Lana why you're fucking her kid's father."

Without giving her a chance to deny his assertion, he kissed Larissa with the intention of driving his point home, thrusting his tongue into her mouth as his hands went to her dress to hike it to her waist before walking forward, pressing her back against the wall. He continued the kiss, not being gentle or soft with her. No, he was determined to make her realize he wasn't a piece of meat to be given away just because her sister wanted it more than she did.

"You think I would give a fuck I knocked your sister up if I wanted you?"

"No …" she gasped. "You wouldn't."

Impatiently, he lifted her thighs to his hips to grind against her. He greedily took her mouth the way he wanted —no holds barred, tongue thrusting, mating, leaving no room for hesitation.

When she started timidly responding, it was everything he could do not to crush her against the wall.

His hand slid to her pussy to find his way blocked by her panties. "I hate dealing with panties. Ditch them when you're with me."

"Even when we're out?"

Moon laughed at how scandalized she sounded. "You've never gone out without wearing underwear?"

"No!"

"When we go to the store tomorrow, don't wear any."

"No … I couldn't."

He could barely make out her refusal as his fingers slipped under the silky fabric. Finding her clit, he pinched it, rubbing it between his thumb and forefinger.

"Why not? Is that too naughty for you?"

"I prefer wearing underwear."

"I prefer you don't. Don't you want to please me? I want to please you." Holding her in place using his hips, he pulled her dress off, leaving only her bra. Releasing the front clasp, he pulled an exposed hard nub into his mouth.

"Your breasts are getting bigger." Switching his mouth to her other breast, he palmed the underside, lifting it to his lips. He could feel her trembling in his arm.

Releasing her clit, he found her pussy damp and ready for him. It blew his mind that, despite how many women he had fucked, she felt as if she had been made for him.

Her breasts were the perfect C-cup, with cherry nipples begging to be played with. She was so sensitive that all he had to do was stare at her, and he could see them poking under her shirt. She would wear a thicker bra if she knew, so he had no intention of telling her.

The further along she got in pregnancy, the prettier she became. When they were at the restaurant, Moon had seen other women staring at her enviously and knew she thought it was him whom they were staring at, while Moon had read the envy in their eyes and knew what they had been really jealous of.

She glowed with happiness. Her high cheekbones had a rosy glow, and her luminous eyes had glittered in the soft lighting.

"You're so ready for me," he groaned as he slipped inside of her slick pussy. Licking her nipple, he grinned when he heard her escalated breathing.

"Don't come," he ordered, stroking his finger inside of her as she bucked against his hand. Moon didn't stop until he felt her come apart in his arms.

Only when she went limp in his arms, resting her head on his shoulder, did he carry her to the bathroom. Turning the water on, he only waited a couple of minutes before carrying her inside the shower stall.

"Uh ... the water is freezing."

Holding her safely, he let her touch the tile. "You didn't think I was going to let you off that easily, did you?" He clicked his tongue at her disapprovingly. "I've never been called altruistic where that is concerned."

Grinning back at her dirty glare, he reached for the body-wash, squeezing a good amount onto a washcloth that he had snagged on the way from the closet. He started washing her body, paying special attention to her breasts. He only moved on when they were pretty little cherry nubs.

Rubbing the cloth over the swollen contours of her belly, he then lowered it to wash between her legs, laughing when she tugged on his hair as he lingered too long. He then straightened and started washing himself.

Holding her eyes with his, Moon rubbed the wash cloth over his chest then lowered the soapy cloth to his groin. "Are you going to make me do this myself?"

She was stubborn, crossing her arms over her breasts while her eyes shot daggers at him. "Next time, wait until the water is warmer."

"Ah … next time, don't try to go to sleep when we're in the middle of having sex," he countered. He could still hear her say how she had deprived Lana of that happiness. It kept playing on repeat in his fucking brain.

"I thought we were done."

Dragged out of his guilty thoughts, he wanted to punish her.

From the fucking moment he had met her, sight unseen, she had turned his life upside down. Just when he thought he had developed a plan and it was coming to fruition, she was fucking it up again. So far, he had been playing the game her way; it was time she started playing it his way.

"You thought wrong."

# CHAPTER FIFTY-THREE

Larissa shivered as the warm water rained down on her. The sexual intent clearly visible on Moon's face both thrilled and frightened her. She felt her nipples tighten when he cupped a breast, pulling it upward to meet his mouth.

"First, I'm going to make you beg me to fuck you again. Second, I'm going to make sure you know which sister I want. Then, I might, just might, let you go to sleep."

The deep timber of his voice made her knees shake while a deep ache wanted her to respond in a wild and wanton way that she was sure Moon was used to—she still saw the same lack of true desire in his eyes.

He wanted to exert his dominance over her while holding himself back. From the way he carried himself with such confidence, strength, and power, when he was in a room, your eyes were drawn to him. She had seen it over and over when they had gone out. He had a tough visage, which caused men to stare at him enviously and draw women like a flame. There was never a hint of vulnerability that made her feel she was drawing closer to him emotionally.

Left with the choice, she could either take what he was

willing to give her, or she could fight him for the control he was determined to have over her. Locking her knees, she decided to step out into a brave new world.

She slid her hand down his chest, feeling the slick flesh under her palm as she ignored the qualms warning her not to underestimate Moon. She had the sexual skills of a novice, while he was at PhD level.

"Fuck me ..." Sultrily, she leaned forward to lick his bottom lip. "Pretty please." She moved her hand downward and closed her hand around his cock. "You're so hard ..." she whispered into his mouth. "You know, I saw you at the bar that night," she confessed, gripping Moon's cock in a firm grip then gliding up and down in smooth movements.

Going slow, each time she reached the tip, she would teasingly slip her tongue into his mouth then quickly dart back before he could deepen the kiss. Their tongues began dueling as her hand started moving faster. Then Moon buried his hand in her hair, dragging her mouth away.

"You're playing with fire."

His hoarse voice excited her more than touching him. He was finally showing the same reaction when she responded to his touch.

"If I were afraid of being burned, I wouldn't be with you." She met his eyes defiantly. "All I could think of when I saw you sitting at the bar was how hot you looked. I've never approached a man in my life, but that night, I was about to get out of my seat when I saw Lana looking at you. She wanted you." As she talked, Larissa continued to glide her hand over his cock, gradually continuing her speed. "We both wanted you. You have that problem a lot, don't you, Moon? You told me I'm your old lady, want me to consider you my man, yet ... you have no intention of belonging to any woman, do you?"

Larissa felt his body tense against hers, and it wasn't

because he was about to climax. She had hit a nerve; she could sense it. In fact, she could practically see the shock he was hiding behind his remote demeanor. His body might be responding to her touch, but his mind was free and clear. No matter how his body reacted, his mind refused to succumb to whatever the temptation.

Lowering her mouth to his shoulder, she licked the droplets of water off his tanned skin. "You're such a hardass. You have no intention of ever letting anyone have control over your life. That's why you switch back and forth between clubs. You can stay for as long as you want. And when too much is expected of you, you find a way to go back to the other club."

"Shut up," he growled, trying to shrug away from her mouth.

"Make me."

He groaned, tightened his hand in her hair, jerked her head away from his shoulder, and slammed his mouth down on hers. She felt the angry passion he kissed her with. She must have gotten too close to the truth, and Moon didn't like it, not one little bit.

"Why is it, when we have sex, you can't just shut the hell up and fuck?" Gripping her wrist, he moved her hand away from his cock. Then he turned the shower off and opened the shower door to grab a towel before turning back to her.

She bit her lip and didn't say anything else, discerning from his jerky movements that she had pushed him too far.

After roughly rubbing her dry, Moon pulled her toward the vanity, where he took out the blow dryer, plugged it into the wall socket, and started blow drying her hair. Larissa watched him through the mirror.

"If I weren't pregnant with your baby, you would never have given me the time of day," she stated flatly.

"You were sitting in the back corner, left side. I saw you

when you went to the bathroom two times. I kept waiting for Lana to come over to talk to me, and when she did, I was going to ask her who her friend was."

Larissa stared at him in the mirror, trying to discern the truth from his expression. "You could have come over."

Moon's lips curled in a smile. "And how do you think Sex Piston and Killyama would have reacted if I had?"

Wryly, she made a face at him.

"Exactly." Picking up the brush, Moon started brushing her hair. "I was interested but not enough to face that firing squad."

Larissa laughed. "I can't say I blame you."

He turned off the dryer to stare at her in the mirror. "Your breasts are getting bigger." He tweaked her nipple with his thumb. "You're sexy as fuck."

Standing behind her, Moon played with her breasts. His concentration renewed her nervousness.

"I've never really been a breast man. I prefer ..." His hand dipped much lower.

Embarrassed from where his hand had gone, she tried to turn her head away. His other in her hair held her head in place.

As he stared at her fixatedly, Moon used his thigh to part her stance wider. She could only stand there helplessly, waiting for his next movement.

This was payback. She inexplicitly sensed his mood. He wanted to see how far she would go before calling a halt to whatever game he had decided to play with her. Feeling like a tiny mouse caught between a furious lion's paws, Larissa was frightened whatever move she made would be the wrong choice. So much for stepping into a brave new world.

"Moon ..." Hearing the hitch in her own voice, Larissa wanted to bop him with the blow dryer he had laid aside at the satisfaction she could read in his eyes. Dominance oozed out of him, from the tight grip he held her hair in to the possessive hand blatantly playing with her. Larissa focused on the bright red color flooding her cheeks rather than the fingers rubbing her clitoris.

"The next time we shower together, I'm going to shave you. Why hide this beauty?"

"I can do it myself."

Moon clicked his tongue reprovingly at her. "And spoil my fun? Why would you steal that enjoyment from me?" He took a step back and took her with him. The movement provided a better view of what he was doing to her. "You're so wet. You want me, don't you?"

As Larissa felt the hard length of his penis pressing against her lower back, her head fell back on his chest. It was hard to concentrate on what he was saying when his fingers were propelling her toward another climax.

"I want you; is that what you want to hear? You already know that. It's obvious every time you touch me. I have no willpower where you're concerned. But you're used to that, aren't you?" She studied his expression and saw the truth he didn't try to hide. Here came the payback. She had slipped under his guard however briefly when she had tried to make him lose control; that was untenable to him.

"Jealous?"

She started struggling in his grasp. Using her movements to aid him, Moon sank a finger into her opening, sending an orgasmic spasm through her. She would have fallen to the floor if he hadn't held her in his grasp.

"I could hate you. I don't care how many women you've been with!" She finally managed to say when she was able to form a coherent thought.

"Would you like a number?"

"You jerk!"

When she finally succeeded from him, she went into the

bedroom to pull on a pair of pajamas as Moon stood in the bathroom doorway to watch her.

"I don't need a number. I'm not stupid; you've been playing in the major league, while I've only been up to a bat a couple times in the little league. I may lack your experience, but that doesn't make me totally inexperienced. This isn't the first relationship I've been in, in which I've been more invested than the man. I lied to myself the first time, pretended I was just imagining he didn't look at me the same way I looked at him … right up until my best friend told me they were sleeping together behind my back. All I ask is for you to be honest with me."

She sat down on the bed and stared at him earnestly. "I know you're in a hard position—a woman you had no relationship with is carrying your child. I ran off, and you want to make sure I don't do it again. I could totally understand if you thought it would be easier to make a life with me rather than having to deal with all the other crap of having to deal with a potential custody fight or arrangements which could possibly leave you with little or no control on how your child is raised. I get that."

Larissa dropped her guard and let Moon see how sincere she was being with him. "I don't want you to have to live a lie. Not when you don't have to. I'll stay in Treepoint until our child turns eighteen. We can share joint custody. I won't expect any money from you and will even carry the insurance. I'm even willing to let you be the one to decide how we split the time. I'm willing to do whatever it would take to make you happy, because I can't keep fighting a losing battle with myself."

Moon frowned at her. "What kind of battle?"

"To not fall in love with you." Vulnerable, her voice dropped to a whisper.

As he strode across the carpeted floor, she didn't have

time to react before she found herself lifted and placed in the middle of the bed, with Moon pressing her down into the soft mattress.

"I love a good fight."

"I'm serious, Moon. Sometimes, you frighten me."

His head jerked up. "Why?"

"I don't know why ... I can't explain it. I think you could be really cruel if you wanted to be."

Moon ran a gentle finger across her cheekbone. "There's no need to be frightened of me."

His voice had dropped to a low purr, which made her nipples tighten. The seductive way he was looking down at her also had her stomach muscles clenching. God, Moon could make her hot with one look.

"I could never be cruel to you when you're carrying my child."

He gave her no assurances of what would happen after the baby was born, she noticed.

Grazing her lips with his before pressing down to part them, Moon didn't give her the opportunity to say another word. Using all his skills, he reignited her desire until she was writhing beneath him.

"Please, Moon, I can't take any more."

"What do you want?" he growled into her ear as his fingers stroked her to a fever pitch.

"You ... I want you," she admitted.

"How?"

"Can I choose?"

"Oh yes, I'll fuck you any way you want."

The sexual promise in his voice nearly made her climax. Gritting her teeth, she tried to hold it back. She wanted his cock inside of her when she came.

"Can I ride you?"

Moon rolled off her then helped her straddle him. It was

everything she could do not to let her eyes roll to the back of her head when he filled her.

"Do you want me to move?"

"Not yet. I don't want to come yet," she admitted.

He gave her a wicked grin. "Afraid I won't be able to get it up again? There's no need to worry. I'm not a one-trick pony."

Biting her lip when he started teasing her nipples, she swatted his hand away. "You might have another round in you. I don't."

Any idea of controlling her climax went out the window as Moon started bucking underneath her. Boneless, her head dropped to his chest as her climax subsided, leaving her limp and angry at him.

"I wasn't ready to come," she told him peevishly.

"Saddle up; the night isn't over yet. You're going to ride again."

# CHAPTER FIFTY-FOUR

Tying his hair back, Moon stood over the bed, watching as Larissa slept. He glanced at his watch. He only had a few minutes to spare if he was going to be on time for work.

Sitting down on the side of the bed, he tried to gently nudge Larissa awake by removing the pillow she had placed over her face to block out the sun shining through the window. As he lightly kissed her, he couldn't help but smile when she raised a hand to push his face away.

"Go away," she mumbled, reaching for her pillow again to smash it down on her face.

Amused at how cute she looked, Moon tried to move the pillow away. "Isn't that dangerous for the baby?"

"If I can breathe, he can breathe." Raising her arms, she pinned the pillow over her face, but she did lift the pillow so it only cover her eyes. "Go away."

Moon laughed. "I'm going. I just wanted to know your plans for the day."

"You could have texted me when I was awake."

"I wanted to know before I left."

"So, I could get your permission before you leave?"

His grin widened. No, she wasn't a stupid little airhead.

"I don't expect you to ask my permission," he lied without losing a beat. "I just want to be kept informed in case I can meet up if I get off early. If Viper doesn't need me, he might cut me loose for the day."

"Oh ... now I feel bad." Larissa moved the pillow off her eyes. "I'm sorry. I misjudged you."

Pretending to take affront, he stood up from the bed to take his bike keys from the nightstand. "I have to go. Have a good day. I'll see you when I get home."

Larissa sat up in bed as he headed for the bedroom door. "Moon, I'm sorry." Pushing her tousled hair from her face, she stared at him beseechingly. "I'm going to go to the office for a couple of hours. Then neither Priss nor I have any appointments for the rest of the day. The church is having a family fun day. There's going to be a rummage sale, and a farmers' market. Killyama told us that Ginny is going to be selling some of her jellies. She said Ginny's jellies are to die for."

He had to cross his arms over his chest to keep from laughing when her hand went to her baby bump.

"I need at least one of those jellies."

Moon recognized that tone of voice. It was the same one when she had wanted her cookies or hamburgers. The woman could become a raving lunatic when deprived of a food source she craved.

"Why? Have you tasted one?"

"No, but I have to. I feel they're going to be even better than what Killyama told me."

"What makes you think that?"

"Because when I asked Sex Piston if they were good, she said they tasted like dish soap."

"How did you decide who to believe?"

"I helped Killyama have a baby," she told him, as if the

bond between Killyama and her trumped the relationship Sex Piston and Killyama had shared for years.

Larissa gave him a wondering look. "Have you tasted Ginny's jelly?"

He nodded. "Every now and then, she brings a few jars over to the clubhouse."

Her gaze turned piercing. "Is it as good as Killyama says it is?"

"What time does the farmers' market open?"

"Ten."

He gave her a cunning smile. "I would be there early if I were you. Everyone will be going for the blackberry, but don't snooze on the apple. That's my favorite. She makes it from crabapples."

She gave him a conspiratorial nod. "I got you. How does breakfast for dinner sound?"

Moon glanced at his watch again. "Sounds like you need to get your hiney out of bed and get a move on, or you will be buying store-bought jelly for our toast."

---

Moon drove down the main street on the way to the club, passing the church, where he saw several of the brothers' wives setting stalls up for the farmers' market. Ginny, Lily, Beth, and Rachel were already there, and Winter was getting out of her car.

He gave Lucky a casual wave as he drove past, then came to a stop at the red light. As he waited for the light to change, he glanced toward the lone motel, narrowing his eyes at seeing at least ten motorcycles parked at the back from his viewpoint. The actual building could be blocking his sight of more. So, when the light turned green, he took a right down the side street to get a better look.

As he drove down the side street, Moon saw he had been right. The back parking lot was filled with motorcycles.

He did a U-turn at the end of the street and traveled back up the street, taking a quick picture with his cell phone as he passed, which he then sent to Shade and Viper.

Returning to the main street, Moon took a right to head back toward the church instead of going to the club. Lucky was the only brother watching over the women, as far as he could see. If Shade wanted to rip him a new one for being late, so be it. He wanted to hear an all-clear from Viper or Shade before leaving Lucky alone to oversee the women's protection.

His gut instinct was having a field day. The motorcycles looked like they belonged in a junkyard rather than being on the road. Usually, motorcycle clubs took care of their bikes. Those who didn't were clubs who mainly spent time on the road, traveling from one state to another, dodging the law after creating chaos for the town they had descended upon.

He was parking his bike when his cell phone rang.

"Yo."

"Are you watching the motel?" Shade asked in a cold voice, giving no hint if he was worried about the picture he had sent or if he was late for work.

"No. I'm at the church. I didn't want Lucky here alone without backup."

"Nickel and Rider should be there," Shade told him sharply.

"If they are, I don't see them. Their bikes aren't here, either."

"Stay there. We're on our way."

Shade didn't bother saying goodbye, just disconnected the call. He wasn't surprised when his phone buzzed with a text message, sent out to all The Last Riders to show up at the clubhouse.

Pocketing his cell phone after texting Larissa to stay away from the church sale, he strode over to where the women were arranging their stalls.

"Hi, Moon," Willa greeted him as she placed quilts on a table. "We aren't open yet, but feel free to look around."

"Thanks."

Walking to the table where Ginny was setting up, he eyed the jars of jelly she was setting out.

"We don't open for another hour," she began.

Taking out his wallet, he looked at what had already been set on the table and saw two other boxes she had yet to unpack. "How much are you expecting to make today?"

Ginny smiled at him. "I'm hoping to raise two hundred for the church. I wanted it to be five hundred—Lily usually makes the most, but I'm hoping to win the prize this year—but Gavin and Silas took half of my inventory. They promised to give me the money I lost before I have to turn the money over to the pastor to be counted."

"What's the prize?" Trying to mask his interest, he looked toward the stall where Beth was setting up to sell cookies.

"Whoever wins gets their choice of which Sunday school class they want to teach. I want the nursery, and so do most the women."

"I could help you with that, and you won't even have to unpack those boxes next to you."

Ginny stared at him suspiciously. "How?"

"I'll buy everything you were going to sell today for five hundred."

She seemed undecided about accepting his offer.

"It wouldn't be fair to sell it to you before the sale starts."

"Then, technically, it wouldn't be fair to count the money from Reaper or Silas if they didn't buy it from the sale today, either." He counted out five hundred-dollar bills then took out another three. "I'll give you the extra three if you deliver them to Larissa's house. I'll text you her address. It's in the new housing development."

Ginny still stared at the money indecisively.

He placed another two hundred on the pile. "Will that do it?"

She grinned at him. "That'll do it. I'll box everything up and put in my car until after the sale. Then I'll deliver them before going home."

Shaking his head at her, he stared at her seriously. "Go ahead and pack what's on the table back in the boxes. I'll load them into Lucky's car. He can deliver them for you later today. That way, you can go ahead and leave for home."

Ginny stared at him curiously, but he was already walking toward Beth's stall. He didn't let her get a greeting out. "How much?"

He bought out Beth's stall then moved on to Lily's when Lucky finished setting up the tent he was working on and stopped him.

"Brother, save some for the customers."

Moon raised a brow at him. "You haven't seen the text messages?"

"No, my phone ran out of charge." Lucky frowned. "It's charging inside the church. Is something wrong—"

The loud sounds of motorcycles could be heard coming down the street. Both men turned to look in the direction they were coming from. Lucky, unaware of the bikers staying at the motel, showed no concern at the roaring motors coming closer, whereas Moon narrowed his eyes, hoping it was The Last Riders and not the nomad group.

When the first one came within sight, he took a quick glance around to place each of the women.

Lucky turned to look at him at the same time. "Who in the hell are they?"

The concern in Lucky's gaze only compounded that his

JAMIE BEGLEY

initial gut instinct had been right. Lucky was just as uneasy at the sight of the unknown bikers as he was.

"Fucking trouble. Where are Nickel and Rider?"

"Rider went to the bank for cash and change, and Nickel went to the gas station for ice. They should have been back by now."

"Be nice if they were here," Moon stated the obvious as the nomad bikers reached the point in the road where they could enter the church parking lot.

It was anti-climactic as they watched them continue to ride past.

"Damn." Lucky gave a loud sigh of relief. "I was worried for a second there."

Moon was as surprised as Lucky sounded until it became clear why the nomad bikers hadn't stopped. The Last Riders were giving them an escort out of town. His gut muscles didn't relax as his eyes met the last biker riding in front of The Last Riders.

His long, dirty blond hair hung to his shoulders as the biker's gaze took in the parking lot.

As the out-of-town bikers passed, Viper and Reaper swung their bikes into the parking lot, stopping next to Lucky and him.

"They don't seem too happy," Moon remarked, his gut still clenched despite the bikers being almost out of sight.

"They aren't." Viper turned his motor off. "We showed up just as they were about to ride. They said they had just stopped for the night to rest and get some sleep before moving on. They want to grab a bite to eat before leaving. I told them our restaurants suck and to move along."

Lucky looked at Viper skeptically. "They? Who was in charge?"

"None of them admitted to being their leader." Viper's scowl showed he didn't believe them.

"I'm willing to bet it was the one riding the black and silver vintage Vespas. Most of the others seemed to be riding secondhand crotch rockets."

"I agree." Reaper kept his eyes on his wife as she repacked the canning jars back into her boxes. "What is Ginny doing?"

The men all turned their head to look toward Ginny.

"Moon bought out her stall and told her to go home. He also bought out Beth's and was about to buy out Lily's," Lucky explained.

Reaper's gaze turned back to Moon's. "You were getting the women out of danger."

"I knew if they spotted your women, they would stop."

Reaper gave him a curt nod. "Thanks for having our back."

Moon returned his nod. "Anytime. I was just lucky I caught the red light and spotted their bikes behind the motel."

Lucky made a twisted face. "I shouldn't have let Nickel and Rider leave. I wanted to keep the women in one place."

Viper took his own share of the responsibility. "I fucked up. I should have sent more men. I've been so busy watching the club after Pace's death that I failed to take into account what the women could be stepping into in town."

Moon felt bad for Viper. The Last Riders' president never failed to hold himself responsible, even when shit was out of his control.

"You sent them with Nickel and Rider and knew Lucky was here."

"I'm not exactly chopped liver," Lucky joked, but there was no humor on his face.

"You warn Stud they're heading his way?" Moon asked.

Viper nodded. "The Destructors will meet them as they come off the bridge and let them know Jamestown's restaurants aren't any better."

Reaper was still facing the direction the bikers had gone. "What do you think they were really in town for? You think they were just passing through?"

Moon felt the vibration coming from his phone. "No, I don't. I think it was a scouting mission. I think they're part of a bigger group, testing the waters."

He reached for his phone and pulled up his text messages, seeing Larissa had sent him a message.

*Our morning appointment was canceled. Going to have lunch with Sex Piston in Jamestown since you don't want me to have any fun at the church.*

"Fuck," Moon snarled as he hurried toward his bike.

"What?" Viper called out after him.

"Larissa is heading for Jamestown."

# CHAPTER FIFTY-FIVE

S he was five minutes in the drive toward Jamestown when Larissa regretted overreacting to Moon not wanting her to go to the church's fundraiser. How had she forgotten there wasn't even a gas station between the two towns?

Mistakes had been made, she admitted to herself. If she hadn't already told Sex Piston that she was on her way, she would have turned around and gone back to Treepoint.

Drumming her fingers on the steering wheel, she stopped chiding herself. Crazy Bitch was going to join their lunch to bring the children she was fostering so when she wrote a letter to Eryn, she could tell her how they were doing. So far, the two younger children were thriving under Crazy Bitch's care, and Lennon had developed a bond with Ginny and taken to staying with her.

When she checked her rearview mirror, she saw a group of motorcycles quickly eating up the distance between them and her.

"Is he for real?" she said aloud to the empty car. Moon couldn't seriously be following her to Jamestown just because she had refused to answer his call after she texted him where she was headed. The dude had serious control issues. They were going to have a serious discussion once they arrived in Jamestown.

As the motorcycles drew closer, she was able to see some of the men's faces. None of them looked familiar to her, so she guessed Moon was riding farther behind. She wasn't concerned until two rode onto the oncoming lane to pass her.

The dangerous maneuver on the two-lane road made her grip her steering wheel when, instead of speeding up to pass her, they rode alongside her for a minute to stare into her car.

Not only did she not recognize them, but their expressions creeped her out.

Was there another motorcycle group other than The Last Riders in Treepoint? She didn't think they were from the Destructor's club, either; she had met several of them during her stay with Sex Piston's parents.

Her heart lurched at seeing an oncoming car as the two motorcycles were still next to hers.

Instinctively, she wanted to swerve off the road to keep herself from becoming involved in a collision if the motorcycle riders didn't move over in time. The gravel on the side of the road gave her pause, though. Then she thought it would be safer to start braking, praying the motorcycles would use the opportunity to get over.

"Are you insane?" she screamed, terrified.

Wildly, she glanced out her side window, seeing them laughing at her as they finally started passing her to get over. The truck they had been playing chicken with blared its horn as it passed the motorcycles.

With the truck disappearing out of sight around a curve, she was alone on the road once again with the bikers. She was even more certain she had never seen this group of bikers before, and fought down the fear that rose in her throat. She was safe in her car for now, and she planned to stay that way until she reached Jamestown.

Another two riders passed her, also blatantly staring into her car before moving in front of her.

"This is bad." She reached for her cell phone, about to call Moon, not knowing who else to call in the situation she had found herself in.

Before she could press his number, she saw one of the riders ahead of her raise his hand then hit his brakes.

She dropped the phone instinctively to grab the steering wheel but barely managed to stop the car before plowing into the back of the motorcycles.

Frightened, she watched as more motorcycles came up behind her, caging her in, except for the side of the road. She turned her steering wheel to ease off the road and onto the gravel. Giving the car gas, she tried to move around the motorcycles, only to find the riders maneuvering their bikes over, too.

She bit her bottom lip when she realized she was in a terrible predicament. She started to frantically look for her cell phone. When she found it, the only number she was going to call was 911. At this point, she didn't care if anyone thought she was overreacting—she was terrified. The cell phone, however, was nowhere to be found.

She unbuckled her seat belt and leaned forward as best as she could to run her hand under the passenger seat in search for her phone.

A tap on her window had her jerking upward again.

A face plastered to the glass made her gasp in fright.

"Whatcha doing?"

His silly grin didn't ease her tension; it merely heightened her concern.

"Don't be afraid. We just want to say hi."

Disgusted when he pressed his pelvis against her window, she wanted to gag at the suggestive way he slid his hips against the glass.

"Go away!" she shouted. "I called the police. They should be here any minute."

"Ooo, we're so scared. Aren't we, Octopus?"

Raucous, jeering male laughter could be heard coming from outside her vehicle. Then taps sounded on her other windows as her car started to be rocked back and forth.

She frantically started looking for her phone again. Her protruding belly prevented her from leaning forward to reach under the seat. She stretched her fingers out, then finally felt the plastic case just as she heard the sound of the back window breaking.

"Go away!" she yelled.

The men took no heed of her shouts.

"Damn, women in Kentucky have no sense of humor," she heard one man say.

She rose up when she heard a back door opening, and frantically pressed the door lock button again, but it was futile. One of the bikers had gotten into the back seat and was opening the other passenger door to let another man inside before leaning forward to open the front passenger door.

At this point, Larissa thought it would be safer to get out of the car rather than to remain inside, out of sight of other cars, which she hoped would pass by.

Planning to flag down any car, she tried to move between the men gathered outside, only to find herself pinned against her car door with a brutal face staring down at her.

"Going somewhere, little mama?"

Larissa tried to push the hulk of the man away from her. "Don't touch me! I called the police!" she lied.

"Does it seem like I give a fuck?"

No, she had to admit the ugly man did seem like he didn't.

"You should have stayed in your car. It's safer inside. You're slowing us down. Get in the back seat. Me and a couple of my friends want to show you our driving skills."

"I'll pass. I'll just stay here until you all get past—"

"Nah … that doesn't work for us. What's the fun in that?"

Averting her face so she wasn't forced to smell his rancid breath, she protectively laid a hand over her belly. "Please, just leave. I'm pregnant."

"Yeah, we can see that." His leering gaze revolted her so much that she had to hold back the instinctive gag reflex from throwing up.

He brought his face closer to hers. "If you care about that baby, you're going to get in the back seat and do what you're told, or I'm going to put you in there, and I won't give a fuck how big that belly is."

She was already scared, so the sound of more motorcycles approaching had her about to take off at a run, terrified more of their friends were arriving.

The lone motorcycle coming within sight didn't lessen the fear confronting her; it was only when the motorcycle passed them and the rider on the bike looked toward them that she recognized Shade.

Hysterical, she wanted to call out his name for help, but her scream died in her throat at his expression. Shade looked at her as if he had never seen her before, driving past without lowering his speed.

She helplessly looked after him as he went around another curve, then felt her knees give out. She was so scared, and if Shade was too afraid to stop, it spoke volumes about the danger she was in.

Knowing she was going to have to protect her baby, she started searching the ground for something to protect herself with. There wasn't a branch or large rock within sight.

Her only choice was to steal one of their bikes.

*You don't even know how to ride one*, she scolded herself right before she found herself being pulled away from the car door.

She fought the ugly bastard who was shoving her into the back seat of the car, only to find herself falling forward when he lurched to the side and dropped to the ground.

Astounded, she stared down at the man who no longer had the back of his head.

All the bikers surrounding her stood just as paralyzed as her.

"Shut up!" one of them yelled.

A heavy hand landed on her cheek, knocking her into the side of the car. She held on to the roof with one hand, while her other went to her stinging cheek. She hadn't even been aware she was screaming.

"Which one of you motherfuckers got trigger happy and shot Hyde?"

The bikers were eyeing each other mistrustfully when the sounds of more motorcycles could be heard coming closer.

"Get her in the fucking car!" the biker closest to her yelled.

Larissa gave a small scream of agony when someone used her hair to jerk her from the side of the car as a grungy biker opened the door.

Knowing it was going to be her last opportunity to escape, regardless of the pain, she took off running in the direction of the sounds of the motorcycles. She was only able to take a couple of running steps before one of the bikers stepped to the side and caught her.

"Fuck!"

Instead of carrying her back to the car, he turned with her in his arms when he heard the curse from one of his friends.

"Fuck, I knew we should have kept your ass behind, T-bone," the man holding her snarled.

"I'm not afraid of those motherfuckers," another biker scoffed as the motorcycles drew nearer.

"They'll go on past, like the other one did," the man holding her huffed out, trying to keep her from struggling out of his arms.

"They're stopping."

From the way they all started moving around her to block her from sight, Larissa supposed the other motorcyclists weren't part of their group.

As they came closer and stopped, Larissa was able to tilt her head and could see the bikers sitting a few feet away.

Her eyes were caught by Moon, who was sitting on his bike behind Viper's and Reaper's.

One of the bikers who was holding her hostage stepped forward. "We told you before we aren't looking for a fight!" he yelled toward Viper.

Viper's gaze made her shudder, not to mention the venom dripping off his cold words.

"Gave you one pass already today. You should have hauled ass to the state line. Your opportunity to leave Kentucky has gone. Welcome to your final resting place."

# CHAPTER FIFTY-SIX

F ear clogged her throat at Viper's promise. She wished he had waited to make the threat once she was in the free and clear instead of still standing in the middle of them.

The loud roar of motorcycles coming from behind them made the bikers holding her turn their heads.

Even though she easily recognized Stud, his brother, Calder, and their men following them, she still didn't heave a sigh of relief. This was not going to be pretty, and she was standing smackdab in the middle of this mess. She didn't have to be told these bikers were the reason Moon had told her not to come into town. From the way he was still looking at her, she was almost as afraid of him as of the bikers surrounding her.

At least he wouldn't kill her and leave her body to be found years later, she tried to calm herself.

"Let the woman go," Viper barked out his order.

"You'll let us go if we do?" the biker holding her yelled back.

"No, but we'll let you fight for your life instead of cutting you down where you're standing. Maybe a couple of you can still come out alive."

"Doesn't seem like much of a choice."

Viper shrugged. "Only one you're going to get. You fucked around and found out."

The biker holding her reached for something at his side. The next thing she knew, a knife was being pressed against her belly.

"I'm willing to bet this little mama is carrying one of your kids. Am I wrong?"

"You're not as stupid as I thought," Viper said snidely.

"Not stupid enough to let go of the only thing that could keep me alive."

Viper stared at him in disgust. "*Me*? Not *us*? Wow, they got a friend in you, don't they?"

The knife jabbed at her when the man holding her wildly looked around him. "I meant us," he corrected himself. "You know I meant us!" the goon shouted at his friends. "He's trying to get us to turn against each other!"

"Move the knife; you're hurting her." Moon remained casually sitting on his motorcycle.

The knife against her eased back.

"You've got five seconds to step away from her, or you're going to be lying on the ground next to your buddy," Moon stated in an impassive voice.

Larissa saw her life flash before her eyes at the look settling on her attacker's face. He wasn't going to let her go. He thought using her would keep him alive.

One second, she was held pressed against his side, and the next, chaos erupted as the man holding her fell forward onto the gravel.

The bikers started pulling out their weapons while they all scattered, trying to find a place to use as cover.

Finding herself free, she started running toward The Last

Riders when the one called T-bone caught her by the back of her shirt.

She had no more been forced to a stop than he was jolted backward by a bullet hole between his eyes.

She was pulled down on top of him, and started screaming at his sightless eyes so close to her face, unaware Moon's bike had shot forward and was right in front of her.

Hysterical, she didn't hear Moon's loud yell of, "Get on, Larissa!"

She couldn't make her body cooperate, frozen in fear that one of the bullets she could hear being shot would strike her.

"Dammit, Larissa!" Moon shouted.

A rough hand jerked her to her feet and practically carried her to Moon's bike. Then Ginny's husband roughly sat her down on the back of Moon's motorcycle.

"Hold on."

Gavin's warning was the only one she was given before Moon's bike took off, weaving through The Last Riders and the Destructors.

She belatedly realized The Last Riders had protectively surrounded them, providing them cover from the mayhem. She expected to be struck by a bullet at any second, until Moon went around a curve. As she held on to his waist with a death grip, they headed toward another curve. Instead of being frightened of the speed he was traveling, she felt safe and protected at the skillful way he handled his motorcycle.

When they turned another curve, Larissa saw the road had been blocked off by two cars with road flares spread across both lanes. Several cars were stopped, waiting for the cars to be moved. A third car had been parked off to the side, on the gravel. Sex Piston and Crazy Bitch were standing in front of it.

Decreasing his speed, Moon rode his motorcycle to where they were stopped.

"You know what to do," he ordered the women.

Sex Piston and Crazy Bitch nodded.

"Come on, Larissa. You're coming with us." Sex Piston reached for her arm to help her off the motorcycle.

Grateful, she let her help her off then lead her to the car where Crazy Bitch had opened the back door.

As she started to get inside, Larissa watched Moon take off back in the direction they had come from.

"Moon!"

He was going back into that craziness.

Wanting to stop him, she tried to get back out of the car, but Crazy Bitch slammed the door shut before she could.

Sex Piston, who had gotten in the driver's seat, turned around. "Keep your ass back there."

"He's going to get himself killed! They're shooting at each other!" Larissa yelled as Crazy Bitch got into the passenger seat, slamming her own door.

"Your man isn't the only one out there risking his life to get you safe," Sex Piston told her as she maneuvered her car onto the road in the direction of Jamestown. "Girl, you might as well learn this lesson now: our men belong to a brotherhood. When one man puts their life on the line, they all do. That means until the danger is over, they're all in. Then they ride away together or not at all."

The harsh reality of being with a man belonging to motorcycle club hit her full force. Was she willing to live with the fact that Moon would be regularly putting his life in danger every time one of the club members needed him?

Did she really have a choice? When those bikers had tried to shove her into the back seat of her car, she knew if they succeeded, her life would be over. Despite overwhelming concern for her unborn child, it had been Moon whom she'd fought to keep herself alive for. Deep down, she knew he would recover from her death with little or no damage, but he would be burdened with the grief of losing his child for the rest of his life. That, she couldn't bear for him. She loved him too much to ever let him experience that type of grief. She pressed her trembling lips together knowing the battle she had been fighting about loving Moon was over. She had lost. Somehow, she knew it wouldn't be the last victory he would claim in the future.

# CHAPTER FIFTY-SEVEN

Moon sped back to where The Last Riders had the out-of-town bikers surrounded and unarmed. Bodies littered the ground, forcing him to park in the middle of the road and walk to where Viper was questioning the men.

Seeing Moon approaching, Viper broke off talking with the brothers. "Larissa okay?"

"Sex Piston will take her to the hospital and stay with her until I can get there." Moon stared down grimly at the men sitting on the ground. "You find out which one is the leader?"

Viper shook his head. "I can't say I'm surprised. Who would want to admit to being in charge of this shitshow?" He turned his head at the sound of a police car coming to a stop behind where The Last Riders had parked their bikes. "Fuck, that's all we need," Viper muttered under his breath as the acting sheriff drew closer.

Greer Porter swaggered forward, the small limp resulting from a stroke barely noticeable as he eyed the men lying on the ground then glanced at the men sitting on the asphalt.

"The least you could have done was let me in on the fun." He snorted at Viper. "All you left me do to is the fuckin' paperwork. So far, filling in for Knox has been more of a pain in my ass than seeing any action."

"That's only because everyone is afraid of breaking the law with you in charge."

Moon's admiration for Viper grew at the brother being able to keep a straight face at the lie.

Greer narrowed his eyes on him. "You trying to bullshit me?"

Viper expression remained impassive. "I wouldn't do that."

Greer shrugged. "Why not? It don't bother me none." Staring at the men, he raised a cocky eyebrow. "I don't mind ass-kissing, especially when it's my ass being kissed."

He sauntered over to where a dead body lay on the road. Using his boot, he flipped the man over. Then he walked to where the bikers were grouped together and studied each of them before directing his gaze back to Viper. "Who in the fuck are they?"

"That's what we're trying to find out," Viper replied. "They tried to kidnap Larissa." Viper pointed toward Larissa's car, with all the windows busted out, surrounded by the motorcycles that had boxed her in.

Greer's expression grew harsh. "She the gal Moon knocked up?"

"Yes," Moon answered through clenched teeth.

Giving the men on the ground a dismissive glance before sauntering back to Viper, unfazed at the carnage around him, Greer said, "I can give you about ten minutes to finish this before I have to let my deputies, ambulance, and the coroner through." He pulled up his sagging gun belt as he shared a meaningful glance with Viper.

One of the bikers on the ground tried to heave himself up, only to be met with Reaper's elbow sending him sprawling back down to the ground.

"You can't leave us with them!"

Greer gave the man a disgusted snort, making no attempt to prevent Razer from shoving the biker back down. Then, unsympathetically, Greer stepped on the man's hand when it dropped close to his boot. "You came here, thinking it's Hickville, USA. We don't play around with scum trying to steal our women, especially when they're carrying our youngins. You can thank your lucky stars you didn't go after mine or any of my kin," he spat out contemptuously. "At least they'll give you a decent burial. You'd be dinner at a hog farm I buy from if you had messed with mine. I would've bought the fuckin' hog and had your ass for breakfast."

The biker started crying.

Content he had made his point, Greer's gaze swung back to Viper. "Hurry up. I ain't got all day. Wasted enough of my day already. Better have several jars of Ginny's and Lily's preserves sitting on my desk when I get done here." He reached into his pocket and took out a pack of gum, removing a stick before placing it back in his pocket. He unwrapped the gum, then placed it in his mouth. "By the way, you might be interested in knowing Missouri State Police shared information to be on the lookout for a stolen semi. Seems the trucker was found dead in the stall of a restroom at a rest area there. The truck is still missing. Want to hazard a guess as to what the truck was carrying?"

Moon stared at the pathetic motorcycles the rogue bikers had been riding. It wasn't much of a guess. "Motorcycles."

Greer nodded at him. "They were going to be sold at a swap meet. Would be nice to let the Missouri Police know where they can find the semi, *if it comes up in conversation.*"

Adjusting his sagging gun belt once again, Greer turned on his heel. "Don't forget about those preserves."

After he turned his squad car around and went around the curve, the brothers all stared at each other.

"Damn," Moon heard one of the new recruits mutter. "I'm not going to argue over Greer's prices of weed anymore. A few bucks aren't worth dying over if I piss him off."

"Me neither," another agreed, his expression worried. "I threatened to buy it from someone else when his went up the last time."

Moon's eyes met Reaper's. If the recruits were perturbed by what Greer had said, they were in for a rude awakening if they made the cut to become a Last Rider. No one could be more vicious than Reaper, Viper, or Shade when they deemed an enemy deserved to be eliminated.

"Anyone else still think they were passing through Treepoint?"

Viper's question drew his attention away from Reaper.

"No. No, I don't," Moon ground out, reaching down to pick up the biker who he had seen riding the Vespa. "You want to tell us why you were in Treepoint?"

"Go fuck yourselves! We're not going to tell you shit. You can't scare us. You're not going to kill us after the cop saw us alive," the biker scoffed at him. "You're just trying to scare us to get information out of us."

Moon gave him a twisted grin. "Greer wasn't playing at being bad cop just to get a confession out of you. He's as mean as a rattlesnake. He was actually playing nice. If we run out of bullets, all we have to do is call him for more. He might charge us a fortune for them, but he'd give them to us."

He moved closer to stand over the biker, letting him see the full force of his fury. Then, grabbing him by his shirt, he jerked him to his feet. "That was my woman in the car." His fist flashed out, hitting the biker in the ribs, knocking him back a step. Moon took another step forward, striking him in the gut. "*My child* …" When the guy doubled over, Moon's boot kicked out, smashing him in the face, sending the biker back to his knees.

Going to his haunches, Moon used the biker's hair to lift his face. "These motorcycles aren't worth the parts to fix them. The only bike worth a crap is the one you were riding. You rode them to Treepoint to ditch them somewhere in the mountains, didn't you? The semi wasn't stolen for the cargo, was it? The semi was the score, wasn't it?"

Moon could see he had hit upon the truth before the biker hastily lowered his eyelashes.

"Who did you hand the semi off to?"

The biker's defiant eyes spat at him.

In one quick move, Moon reached toward the sheath he kept strapped to his ankle, sliding his knife free.

"Moon …" Viper cautioned.

"Don't worry; I'm not going to kill him … yet. I'm just going to make him wish I did."

Adeptly, his hand darted out, stabbing the biker in the same place Larissa had been cut.

His defiant attitude changed.

Moon smelled the fear which began permeating the air from him and the other bikers as they watched.

"How were you and the others going to get out of Treepoint after you ditched the bikes?"

The biker's jaw clenched stubbornly. "Fuck you!" he screamed. "I'm not telling you shit!"

Moon gave him another grin before his hand darted out again to stab the biker on the opposite side. "Answer my question," he told him coldly. "I hope who you're protecting is worth dying for."

"You're going to kill me, anyway."

"Maybe … maybe not. Would you rather at least fight for your life than giving it away without a fight?"

"How do I know you're not lying to me just to get the information?"

"You don't. You're just going to have to take my word for it."

It took two more cuts before the man broke.

"We were going to use the woman to rent a couple of vans," the biker admitted.

Moon rested his hand on his thigh, keeping to his side of the bargain. "What were you going to do with her after you rented the vans?"

"We would have let her go," he whined.

"Bullshit." Moon chose the soft part of the biker's belly to demonstrate he didn't appreciate being lied to.

"Okay!" the biker sobbed. "We would have had some fun with her, and then I would have passed her along."

"That, I believe." Moon's hand holding the knife rested back on his thigh. "Who would you have passed her along to?"

"Whoever wanted a piece of ass and was willing for pay for it. She would have been a hot commodity with her being knocked up."

It was everything he could do not to sink his knife into the biker's throat. Biding his time instead, he resumed questioning the lowlife.

"Where's the semi?" He really didn't give a fuck about the semi, but Greer did. It would give him bragging rights, and Greer loved to brag. He deserved to get more out of the shit he was going to have to cover up than the preserves.

"I don't know …" Then the biker screamed when Moon started to raise his hand, "I really don't! We drove it to a truck stop in Sparta, Kentucky. Unloaded the bikes, and I drove it to a truck stop. A hauler was waiting for us. Last I saw it, it was being loaded onto a semi hauler."

"How much you get paid for the semi?"

"Ten grand."

"How were you given the money?" Moon asked one question after another.

"I was given the money on delivery."

"Who hired you?"

"It was friend of mine who just got of prison. He wouldn't tell me the name of the person who bought the semi. He said I didn't need to know."

"What's the name of your friend?"

"Rick Pine."

"Where can I find him?"

"I don't fucking know. When he wants a job done, he calls. Last time I saw him, he was living with some chick in San Diego."

"Where's your cell phone?" With his free hand, Moon reached out for the cell phone. After a small hesitation, it was reluctantly placed on his palm.

After giving the phone to Reaper, Moon turned back to the biker. "What's your password?"

The man snarled out the four digits as he stared at him, his face full of hatred. "You'd better leave it alone. Rick doesn't like anyone messing around in his business."

"I can't say there's much in life that scares me. The only thing that does is standing over there with your phone." Moon stood up. Then, glancing at Viper, he received the nod he'd been waiting for before looking back at the biker. "Get to your feet." Moon handed his knife to Viper as the biker stumbled to his feet.

Glaring at him, the biker pressed a hand to the wound on his stomach that was bleeding profusely. "You think you're so fucking bad." He sneered at him as he derided him, "You had to get me half dead before you could take me on. I hope you do go after Rick. You really *will be The Last Riders.*"

Loosening his neck muscles by tilting his head from side to side, Moon braced his feet apart as he let the fury he had been holding back take full reign. "Maybe so … but you won't be alive to see it."

# CHAPTER FIFTY-EIGHT

Fumbling to close the front clasp of her bra, Larissa nearly jumped out of her skin when the curtain was flung to the side.

She swung around so the front part of her body wouldn't be exposed, then hastily reached for the hospital gown she had removed when hard hands turned her around.

Being confronted with Moon's harsh visage made her wish she had begged the doctor, who had just left, to admit her into the hospital.

His inscrutable expression gave her no clue as to his mood, but his stormy eyes showed rage not as easily disguised.

Taking in what she was doing, Moon grasped the two parts of the bra and easily slid the front closer in place. His eyes moved down from her bra to the white bandage placed over the wound on the side of her abdomen.

"The baby is fine," she said huskily. "We both are. He barely broke my skin."

The only discernable reaction Moon showed was to place

his hand on the swell of her belly, as if to reassure himself that his child was safe.

"I shouldn't haven't gone to Jamestown before talking to you," she admitted. "Sex Piston told me that you had seen the bikers and alerted Viper, and he shared the information with Stud. You didn't want me at the sale in case the bikers were looking to cause trouble."

Removing his hand from her abdomen, Moon reached for her top lying on the hospital bed. He picked it up and lifted it over her head to help her put it on. Once she was wearing the soft coral top, he handed her over her pants.

His silence spoke volumes. She could tell he was furious at her.

Sitting down on a chair, she maneuvered herself into the pants then slid her feet into the sandals he dropped in front of her.

"Please don't be mad. All you had to do was tell me why you didn't want me to go to the rummage sale."

"Larissa." Moon's harsh expression tightened until the muscles in his jaw became visible. "We'll discuss this when we're home. Until then, I suggest you don't say anything."

Deciding to accept his advice, she remained seated, staring at the clock on the wall until the nurse knocked on the glass door before coming though the curtain.

"I have your discharge papers."

After listening to her discharge instructions, she rose from the chair. "Thank you for all your help."

"You're certainly welcome."

She left with Moon and stopped outside the door.

"Sex Piston left me her car," Moon told her, pointing to where it was parked.

Those were the last words he spoke to her until they arrived home.

Nervously, she walked through the front door, bracing herself for what he had been holding back.

"I'm going to take a shower." Hoping to delay the confrontation, she tried to slip away from his side.

"Later."

With shaking knees, she followed him into the living room. *Going for a good defense is a good offense*, she told herself before he could talk.

"I was going to turn around right after I was on the road, but I had already made the lunch date with Sex Piston."

Moon gave her a deadpan stare and crossed his arms over his chest. "Do you ever think before you act?"

"Sadly, no," she admitted. "It's a bad habit of mine."

"Are you seriously trying to make a joke?"

She shook her head, shamefaced. "I'm telling the truth."

Hearing the hurt in her voice didn't lesson his irritation.

"I overreacted. I admit it. Again. Like I said, it's a habit of mine. I should have called you back when you sent the text, but I didn't want to start an argument. I might have a bad habit of overreacting, but you have a habit of being bossy." Taking a seat on the sofa before her knees gave out, she continued, "I told you before I hate arguing … and instead of calling you after the text, I did something I knew would make you as mad as you made me."

"That makes no fucking sense."

"I know." Unconsciously twisting her hands together, she tried to explain. "To be fair, you could have told me why you didn't want me going to the church."

"You're going to be a mother," Moon snapped at her. "Don't you think it's time you start acting like you have a brain instead of striking out like a child?"

"Old habits die hard."

From the furious step he took toward the couch, she wished she had chosen a better choice of words.

"Do you have any fucking idea how scared I was when I turned that corner and saw you trying to get away from that biker?"

"No, but I know how scared I was." Her voice hitched as the gravity of the situation she had been in hit her again.

"Are you hungry?"

The abrupt question made her blink at him. "No."

"Go take your shower and get ready for bed. I'll be there in a few."

Nodding, she dejectedly got to her feet.

She went to her room, then into the bathroom to remove her clothes. Instead of placing them in the laundry basket, she shoved them into the trash can—she didn't want a visual reminder of today's events every time she opened her closet door.

Adjusting the showerhead to hit the wall of the shower, she kept her body turned to keep the bandage dry. Washing her hair was more difficult, but she managed to do it despite her sore scalp. She should have waited until she was less sore, but she could still smell their putrid scent on her.

After toweling dry, she chose a silky pajama set, craving the softness against her bruised skin.

She lay down on the bed and buried her face in a pillow when she heard Moon enter the room.

"Go away." She didn't even bother to remove the pillow after telling him to leave.

Curious, she heard him set something down on the nightstand. She'd thought he was placing his phone and keys, but a familiar odor made her lift the edge of the pillow. What she saw had her sitting up to push the pillow behind her back.

"Is that for me?"

"Of course."

"How did you get it so fast?"

"I had Nickel pick up the food for me. He brought it when he dropped my bike off."

Larissa eyed the bag of hamburgers. "Are you still mad at me?"

"Yes."

He sat down on the edge of the bed next to her thighs, and his hands went to her waist to tug her pajama up and over the waistband of her bottoms. He pressed his lips against the bandage where the knife had cut her, then lifted his eyes to meet hers. "You can't do shit like this anymore, Larissa. You can't just pick and choose which part of a relationship you want with me and go on your merry way when I say or do something you don't like just because you don't want to argue. I'm not going to walk around on eggshells because you can't fucking handle a fucking disagreement. You don't have a damn problem acting like a lunatic when you want hamburgers or cookies, but you get nearly kidnapped because I told you not to go to a fucking rummage sale?"

Feeling an embarrassed flush spread across her cheeks, she stared at the blank television screen rather than meet his eyes. "That's different," she mumbled.

"How?"

"Because then it's what the baby wants. He's very demanding. He takes after his father."

"Or his mother," he countered, his eyes falling to where his hand was resting over the bandage. "I don't need to go into detail about how fucking lucky you are that all you got was a few stiches and bruises."

"No," she replied huskily, her eyes meeting his.

He pulled his hands away. "We're going to have to come to an agreement here and now, and you're going to stick with it."

The seriousness in his tone made her quietly ask, "What

415

kind of agreement?"

Was this it, then? Hadn't her mother warned her numerous times that no man would be able to deal with her long term? The sharp pain in heart at the thought of losing him hurt much worse than when the knife had wounded her earlier today.

"I want you to promise me that when I do or say something to make you angry, you have to wait for at least thirty minutes before you do something stupid."

"I can do that." She nodded, relief rushing through her.

"Then you're in complete agreement?"

"Totally." She smiled at him as she reached for the bag of burgers, her smile widening when she saw he had brought up a pack of cookies, too.

Moon's hand forestalled her. "I'm serious, Larissa."

"Me, too. I promise."

He moved his hand away, letting her have the bag.

"I don't take it lightly when promises made to me are broken," he warned.

She gave him a grin, regaining a small bout of confidence. "I'm too big to be put over your knee," she joked, pulling out one of the burgers.

"You won't always be pregnant."

Something in his voice had her hand pausing midair with the burger. She felt a sexual shiver course through her body.

Before she could get her senses back under her control, Moon took her wrist, moving the burger to his mouth and taking a bite.

She gave him a baleful look when he moved his mouth away and she saw the big bite he had taken.

"Did I say I would share?" she teased, placing the remainder of the burger in her mouth.

A wicked glint flashed in his eyes. "You have no idea how pleasurable sharing can be."

# CHAPTER FIFTY-NINE

Moon forcibly swung the factory door open so hard that the workers were caught off guard. Hell, they should be grateful he didn't have the physical strength to rip it off the building.

"What the fuck?" Train glared at him, setting his coffee down on the worktable after spilling the contents down the front of his shirt.

"Sorry," Moon apologized, striding to the workboard. "That woman would make a man want to take a dive off a twelve-foot diving board into a pool of concrete."

He stormed to the postage weighing station, where he picked up the first package in the cart to set it down on the scale. Reading the weight, he clicked the numbers on the machine then pressed the button to print the postage.

"That sucks," Train commiserated with him, tearing a wad of paper towels off the roll sitting on the next table to mop at his shirt. "Killyama might drive me nuts sometimes, but I've never wanted to dive into concrete."

Moon looked at Train questioningly. "You think I'm talking about Larissa?"

Train frowned. "Who were you talking about, then?"

"Her fucking mom. I'm about to kick her ass back to Bowling Green."

"Larissa might have something to say about that." Moving to stand next to him, Train picked up the package he had just weighed to redo it.

"I'd be doing her a fucking favor." Moon snorted. "That bitch is so toxic that a warning sign should be tattooed onto her damn ass."

Train burst into laughter. "She can't be that bad."

"She's a fucking nightmare." Moon picked up another package, slamming it onto the scale. "From the moment Kendra hit town, she's made my life a living hell."

"How?"

"She was supposed to be staying with Lana and Priss, but somehow, that fucking bitch has managed to worm herself into Larissa's spare bedroom. She cleans from the moment she gets up until bedtime. Heaven forbid if I leave a glass on the counter; she'll put in the sink before I can even finish it. And if I have to eat one more vegetarian meal, I'm gonna lose my fucking mind."

Train took the postage stamp away before Moon could place it on the package. "I'm sure she just wants Larissa to be healthy."

Moon glared at him. "Bullshit. The bitch is constantly needling Larissa about how much weight she's gained. Even told her she should go to yoga five days a week instead of two. I found Larissa crying in the bathroom when I got off working yesterday. Kendra had found her cookie stash and threw them away."

Train winced. "The ones you just bought for her?"

"Yes," Moon snarled, picking up another package, but Train took it away from him.

Moon threw himself down on the chair at the workstation and watched as Train started doing the mail.

"And you want to know how my damn day started this morning?" Moon continued his rant.

"Sure." Train didn't seem sure, but Moon didn't care. The other brothers had returned to work.

"When I walked into the kitchen this morning, I nearly cracked my skull open. The battle ax had mopped the floor!" Moon slammed his fist down onto the worktable. "Who in the fuck mops the kitchen floor at six in the morning?" he snarled.

"Someone who wants to take your ass out." Razer's amused voice could be heard from the office to the side.

The workers around him broke into laughter, proving the motherfuckers had been listening.

"Bitch is lucky I didn't wrap that mop handle around her throat." Vindictively, he replayed this morning, except switching the ending of the encounter with a much more satisfying one.

"Sorry, if you're expecting any sympathy from me, you're not going to get it. I'd rather deal with Larissa's mother than Sex Piston and that band of bitches constantly in my grill."

Moon grimaced. The brother did kind of have a point.

He stood back up and took the package away from Train that he was about to weigh. He was calmer now that Train made him realize his situation could be worse, much worse.

After watching him for several minutes, Train must have decided it was safe to leave the equipment with him and went back to his own station.

As he worked, Moon didn't join in with the conversations going on around him, his mind elsewhere.

It was only when Train tapped him on the shoulder that he realized Train had been trying to get his attention.

"Sorry, what did you say?"

Train gave him a speculative glance. "I asked if you were

ready to get some lunch."

"I'm good. I'm going to finish this cart and take off for the rest of the day."

"Brother, I wouldn't do whatever you're planning."

Not bothering to deny he had any plans, Moon continued weighing the packages.

He heard Train's exasperated sigh as he walked out the factory door but didn't change his mind. The bitch had sealed her fate when he landed on his ass in front of her. Who mops the floor at six in the morning? The bitch *was* trying to take him out.

Kendra had been making his life miserable since she had contrived to stay in Larissa's house instead of with her other two daughters. He was smart enough to discern it wasn't because she shared a closer relationship with Larissa, nor that it was because of the baby. No, there was more to it than that. He had a strong suspicion exactly what the bitch was up to.

Working through the lunch hour, he finished the mail cart before wheeling it into the back of the factory. He keyed his ID code into the keypad, and the two doors swung open for him to wheel the cart through, then they automatically swung closed after him.

After he pushed the cart next to the loading area to place it next to the other carts with filled orders, he walked to the sign-in sheet to mark the corresponding number on the cart, writing his initials as being the one who had wheeled the cart into the bay area.

He hung the clipboard back onto the wall, then gave Nickel, who was sitting in the security room, a casual wave as he walked back to the metal door. As he neared, the doors automatically swung open. However, he came to an abrupt stop as he stared at the door.

"I'll be motherfucking ..."

Striding back inside the factory, he went to the office. Razer looked up when he walked through the open door.

"I know you're leaving." Watching him from over the computer monitor, Razer let his irritation show. "I heard you tell Train. You could have asked me first—"

"Forget that." Moon shut the door. "Call Viper and Shade."

---

M oon waited until Viper and Shade texted him that they were waiting in the security room before he started making his way there. He keyed in his ID number, walked through the metal doors, and then Viper buzzed him through as he neared the security door.

Nickel, Viper, and Shade eyed him expectantly as he came through the doorway. Then Viper gave him a searching look as Moon motioned Nickel to give him the seat at the control monitor.

"You son of a bitch." Viper grinned at him. "You figured it out, didn't you?"

Giving Viper a gloating smile, Moon sat down at the keyboard, his fingers quickly pressing down on the keys to pull up the footage he wanted. "Oh yeah."

Their gazes centered on the monitor as the video he wanted came up. He pressed *Play*, and the security footage started rolling. Two factory workers were loading the numbered mail carts into the freight truck.

"Watch and learn," Moon instructed them.

Nickel stared at him quizzically. "What are we looking for?"

Moon stared at the screen intently, watching the two workers push the carts up the loading ramp. "Not what —who."

# CHAPTER SIXTY

Tired, Moon let himself into the house. All he wanted to do was grab something to eat, shower, and go to bed. However, he saw Kendra sitting at the dining room table, scrolling on her cell phone, while Larissa worked through what seemed to be a godawful amount of paperwork. There were several stacks of papers and two towers of books.

He placed a caressing hand on Larissa's shoulder and started gently rubbing her bunched muscles. "Hey." Bending down, he kissed the corner of her mouth, despite Kendra watching. "You look busy."

When he caught the faint blush spreading across her cheeks, he figured it was because she felt uncomfortable with him kissing her in front of her mother.

"Hey." She shut her laptop and gave him a relieved smile. "You worked late tonight."

Puzzling at the tense atmosphere he detected emanating from the two women, he nodded. "Viper needed my help with a problem."

"Were you able to help him?"

"I think so. You move your office to the dining room table?"

She laid her hand on the closed laptop, and Moon felt the tension in the room increase.

"I don't want to get behind. Mom thought it would be less stressful for me to work from home."

"I see." He moved his gaze away from the laptop to slide it toward the end of the table.

"Kendra," he acknowledged her cooly.

"Moon."

When he first met Kendra in Bowling Green, he had sensed something was off between Larissa and her mother. Since she had come to Treepoint, he had become surer.

Larissa kept saying how close they were while he thought the mother and daughter were polar opposites. Kendra even acted differently with Larissa than she did with Lana and Priss.

The discrepancy was so obvious that he had asked Larissa if they all had the same fathers, or if she was adopted. She hadn't talked to him for two days.

He broke the stare-down, not because he was backing down, but because he was hungry as fuck.

"Any dinner left?" Releasing Larissa's shoulder, he started for the kitchen.

"We had eggplant parmesan." Kendra's lofty voice grated on his last nerve. "There's plenty left. Larissa wasn't very hungry, yet she managed to make some room for a bowl of cereal when I was talking on the phone with Lana."

Turning on his heel at Kendra's less than subtle recrimination, he didn't bother moving closer to the kitchen. He hated anything eggplant. He actually hated anything that grew in the ground, other than potatoes. Kendra cooking eggplant parmesan after she had just made soup the day before filled with nothing but eggplant, squash, and zucchini after he had explained his dislike of the fucking things sent his blood simmering.

"Despite my attempts to get her to eat more nutritious food for the baby's sake, Larissa still doesn't take my advice and eat healthier, like I do."

As he stared at the pinch-faced prune, it was everything he could do not to cut her down to size. The problem with that was he was worried the cunning bitch was somehow recording him, wanting to use it to make him look bad. He didn't put anything past her. It would be a dirty tactic he wouldn't be above using himself.

"Are there any left?"

Kendra looked at him like he was stupid. "I said there was plenty," she replied condescendingly.

"I meant cereal."

The prune-faced bitch's face tightened. "No, I threw them out. She can't be tempted if they aren't there."

*And there it is.*

Moon was a firmer believer in letting people sink themselves. No matter how close people watched their winning hands, inevitably, they would fuck themselves over by one slip of the tongue. He liked to call it *I'm smarter than you* syndrome.

"Maybe." Moon looked down into Larissa's clueless expression that told him she was unaware of the battle of wills going on between him and her mother, then studied Kendra's cunning one. "Or it might make her want them even more."

Throwing that bait over his shoulder, he walked back toward the kitchen.

"The soup is on the second shelf." Satisfaction was obvious in Kendra's voice.

"I'm making us breakfast for dinner."

"I already ate."

"Wasn't planning on making any for you." Uncaring of how rude he sounded, he placed strips of bacon in a frying pan before taking a bowl out of the cabinet. "I'm making it for Larissa and me. I've been at work since seven—I'm starving. I don't want soup. I agree that Larissa needs something more substantial besides cereal. I'm going to make her a healthy omelet. She taught me her recipe. How does that sound, Larissa?"

"Amazing." Using the edge of the table, Larissa lifted herself to her feet. "I'll help."

Kendra's expression drew so tight that Moon expected it to crack like a hardboiled egg.

"What about"—Kendra gave Larissa a secretive look—"that paperwork you needed to get done tonight?"

Pretending he hadn't seen the exchange, Moon started cracking the eggs. "What paperwork?"

Larissa sat back down to open the computer. "I was working on a report. It's due at twelve."

Moon raised an eyebrow in her direction. "A.M.?"

"Yes."

Flipping the bacon over, he walked to the table.

Larissa was looking at the screen so didn't see him approaching.

Kendra did.

"Moon, you should keep an eye on what you're cooking …"

Larissa's head jerked up, her hand immediately going to shut the laptop.

He moved her hand away and raised it again, staring at what Larissa had been working on. "Why are you writing a report on who's the most successful general in history?"

"Uh … I'm helping my mom's friend's son write a topic paper for his history class."

Larissa sucked at lying. She was so bad at it that all he

425

had to do was give her a certain look and she would spill her guts. The guiltier she felt, the easier it was to find out what she had done. He had found out that little trick when he caught her taking his cigarettes out of his jacket pocket. The first two packs that had gone missing, he had blamed himself for leaving them at the club. When the third pack had disappeared and he had reminded himself to double-check they were in his pocket the night before, it led him only to one culprit. She had sung like a canary when he called her out.

"Helping or doing?" He saw where the curser was in the middle of a new paragraph, so he had no doubt of the answer.

"Uh …" Larissa looked toward her mother then him.

Moon narrowed his eyes on her.

"Doing," she confessed.

He reached over her shoulder. With two quick strokes on the keyboard, he deleted the paper, then hit another button and deleted it to make sure she couldn't hit *Redo*.

He had the satisfaction of seeing Kendra's astonishment before returning to the kitchen to check on the bacon. Whistling, he started stirring the egg whites in the bowl.

"I can't believe you did that," Kendra hissed from across the room. "Do you have any idea how long it took Larissa to write that paper?"

"Too long, considering how many words it was," he said uncaringly.

"What am I supposed to tell Patrick when he calls?"

"You can tell him, from me, to write his own fucking papers." Pulling the bacon out of the frying pan, he poured the egg whites in. As the eggs cooked, he made toast, sliced an avocado, and poured two glasses of orange juice.

He slid Larissa's omelet on a plate and topped the plate with the sliced avocado, two slices of turkey bacon, and a slice of toast. Carrying it to the table, he placed it down before heading back to make his own plate.

His omelet was more substantial, with everything but the kitchen sink and regular bacon that he had fried after Larissa's was done.

He opened the fridge to search for the jelly he had bought off Ginny. When he didn't find it, he closed the fridge and went into the pantry to get another jar.

The whole shelf where he had carefully placed the box of jellies and preserves was empty.

He walked out of the pantry and went back to the fridge, this time searching for the store-bought jelly he only used for peanut butter sandwiches. Nada.

Carrying his plate with the bone-dry toast to the table, he sat down. "Where are the preserves?" He kept his voice even.

"I threw them out."

The self-satisfied declaration coming from Kendra was exactly what he had expected. From the wealth of satisfaction he could read on her face, Moon would bet his last dollar that the prune-faced bitch had just been waiting for him to ask.

Larissa stared at her mother as if she had grown two heads. "Mom, why on earth would you do that?"

"They were filled with sugar, of course." Kendra smoothed her styled hair as if unconsciously checking to make sure no loose tendril had escaped.

Moon had been around a lot of women in his life, and he had never seen a woman more concerned about her appearance, regardless of the time of the day or night.

"Don't look so upset. I bought a fruit spread, if you absolutely have to have something. If Moon weren't so concerned about those DNA killers, he would have seen the jar on the shelf in the pantry."

"The one that says *no sugar added*?" Biting off a piece of

427

omelet, he chewed as he debated whether to kick her ass out of the house tonight or in the morning.

"Yes. I prefer Larissa eat fresh fruit, but if she absolutely wants it, at least it doesn't have any sugar or preservatives."

"Or any taste," he said cuttingly.

"I find them very tasty, but then, my taste buds haven't been ruined by commercial junk put in my body."

He ate the rest of the bacon, then took a sip of the orange juice and nearly spat it out. He placed the glass back on the table and got to his feet. Going to the fridge, he took out the orange juice. It was the same brand he always bought.

Holding the container, he turned back to the table. "What's wrong with the orange juice?"

"I replaced it with an all-natural brand."

"Then why is it in the bottle I bought?"

"To prove you can't taste the difference."

His fingers tightened on the bottle. He had just bought the juice the day before.

When he pinned his gaze on Kendra's forehead, a sound coming from Larissa interrupted the pitch he had been about to make.

At her pleading glance, he set the juice back in the refrigerator.

He reassumed his seat at the table to finish his food as Larissa stared miserably between him and her mother.

"Mother, tomorrow, I think it would be better if you moved in with Priss and Lana."

Moon was surprised at Larissa finally taking a stand against her mother. So far, she hadn't said anything, regardless of how derogatory Kendra behaved toward them. He had been about to make the same suggestion, except using more profane language, after they ate.

"Don't be ridiculous, Larissa. With Moon working, I need to be here in case you go into labor." Giving a long-suffering sigh, Kendra put her hands in the air. "I promise I'll let you eat your food without interjecting my input from now on. I was just trying to do what I truly feel is better for your and the baby's health."

"Mom, I get that, but what you did was disrespectful. Moon spent a lot of money on those preserves from Ginny. Throwing food in the trash was a total waste."

"I wasn't about to destroy someone else's body by giving it away. Like I said, I'll keep my opinions to myself from now on."

"Mom"—Larissa stood, reaching for her empty plate—"I'll text Lana and Priss that you decided to move in with them tomorrow."

"You're throwing me out over something as silly as preserves?"

"It's not just the preserves. I don't get why you're acting this way. You have Moon thinking I was adopted. What's going on?"

"I'm just anxious with you being so close to your due date."

Moon's lips thinned in anger when he saw Kendra reach out and grab Larissa's hand.

"I apologize." Kendra's eyes moved in his direction. "I'll go to the grocery store in the morning and rebuy the orange juice and jelly. Darling, you know I only want what is best for you and the baby. I didn't mean to go overboard."

Moon's stomach sank at the relieved expression filling Larissa's face.

"I know you do, Mom. You always have."

He wanted to cry when Larissa bent down to hug her mother.

"I'm so happy we worked this out. I wanted to be able to spend this time with you alone before the baby arrives. After she comes, it won't be the same."

"No, it won't."

Moon's instincts kicked into high gear. He didn't think Kendra's words were meant at face value.

"I'll do the dishes and turn in for the night," Larissa said, moving toward the kitchen.

"I'll take care of the dishes. You go to bed." Moon stood with his plate, took Larissa's from her, and went into the kitchen.

"Are you sure?"

"I'm sure. This won't take me long."

"All right. Good night, Mom."

"Good night, Larissa," Kendra replied before resuming scrolling on her phone.

Putting the dishes in the sink, Moon started cleaning up the mess he had made. Once the dishes were in the dishwasher, he walked to the table and sat down.

Kendra didn't bother acknowledging he was there.

"I think we need to talk."

Setting her phone on the table, she gave him an inquiring look. "What would you like to discuss?"

"For starters"—he was done pussyfooting around with the bitch—"I want to know what game you're playing."

"I don't know what you mean."

He narrowed his gaze on her. "Why have you really been treating Larissa like shit?"

# CHAPTER SIXTY-ONE

"Tell me, Moon, how am I treating my daughter badly?"

"You put her down at every opportunity in front of me," he snapped.

Kendra tilted her head. "If you felt that way, why haven't you said anything before now?"

"I didn't want to upset Larissa."

"Really?" Kendra gave him a direct stare. "Or have I finally angered you enough over your precious jelly to say something?"

If any of the brothers were there, they would be amazed at the rigid self-control he was exerting to keep himself from tossing her out the front door.

"Unlike you, I haven't wanted to upset Larissa," he repeated.

Kendra gave him a smile that didn't reach her eyes as she rose from the table. "I think I'll have a glass of wine. Would you like to join me?"

"No, thanks."

Moon half-turned in his chair to watch her as she went to the fridge.

Taking out a bottle, she poured herself a generous glass before putting the bottle back inside. Before closing the door, she pulled out a bottle of beer, then brought the wine and beer back to the table and set the bottle of beer in front of him.

"Maybe this is more to your taste. Alexa," she called out to the speaker sitting on the kitchen counter, "play some soft music."

The strains of "Killing Me Softly" started filling the air.

"I don't think Larissa needs to hear our conservation," she explained as she sat at the table. Kendra took a sip of the wine before setting the glass down then folding her hands on the table. "Moon, may I be frank with you?"

Twisting the beer cap off, he took a drink. "Please do. Just be aware that I plan to be just as blunt."

"Please do. That is my intention for us—to be honest with one another."

Moon waved his hand at her. "Go for it."

"Thank you. I will. Moon, I have raised my daughters to have a brain where men are concerned. Unfortunately, their emotions get the better of them, and I've had to sit back and watch two of my daughters get their hearts broken. Lana, I'm hoping after her disastrous failed engagement, will be somewhat more discerning before becoming involved in another relationship. Larissa"—Kendra's expression turned sorrowful—"on the other hand, is my most trusting child, trying to find the best in everyone. Especially when she loves them."

Straightening his relaxed posture at hearing that Larissa loved him, he instantly went on high alert. Kendra's piercing stare made him want to fidget under her regard. In an effort to guard his reaction, he lifted the beer to his lips.

"You don't have anything to say about what I just said?"

"I refuse to get in an argument with you over Larissa and my relationship."

"Yet you had no problem showing me your anger when I threw away the preserves and juice. Can you understand my concern?"

"You could have made the point without throwing good food away."

Kendra's expression became fiercer, her upper body leaning toward the table. "You were so far up on your high horse that I thought you were going to beam me with the juice bottle, but for several days, you've let me criticize Larissa repeatedly without saying one word."

"I was going to say something tonight."

"Yet it took you less than two minutes to say something about what you cared about."

"I didn't feel comfortable getting between you and Larissa's relationship, just as I don't want you to interfere in our relationship."

Kendra leaned back in her chair, her hand going to the wine glass. "Moon, may I cut to the chase?"

"I wish you would," he said drily.

"Don't patronize me." She looked at him as if he were a bug under a microscope. "I may be sixty-one years old, but I see you. Larissa does, too. You aren't fooling either of us."

"Exactly how am I trying to deceive either of you?"

Kendra's lips curled disdainfully. "Please ..." Snideness dripped from her voice. "Don't patronize me. A blind man would have seen you hiding across the street from my house. Both Larissa and I saw you. Your intent was to scare Larissa into coming back to Treepoint. When she called to tell me what happened in Jamestown, I told her to come home. She refused, wanted her child to have a father in their life. Even when you started playing nice, she took your efforts at face value and allowed you to talk her into moving back to Treepoint. As far as I can tell, she has made a good faith effort with everything you have suggested for her to do. Even to the point that Lana and Priss are living separately while you play house with Larissa."

"I don't like what you're implying."

"I'm not implying; I'm coming right out and saying I think you're full of bullshit."

Moon was surprised Kendra had let the profanity slip out of her mouth.

She read his surprise. "You have me all wrong, Moon. Don't underestimate me like you have Larissa. I'll go for your balls where my daughter is concerned." Kendra sniffed the air as if she were smelling something disgusting. "You might be pretending you shit flower petals whenever Larissa is around, but I can smell bullshit a mile away. I'm going to disillusion you about something else, too. Larissa might love you, but she doesn't have blinders on."

"What does that mean?" Moon took another sip of his beer. He was going to let the bitch get out what she had been storing up, and then he was going to rip her into shreds.

"It means, when you do show your true colors to Larissa, and I believe you will, you're going to be dealing with far more than you expected."

Kendra leaned forward, her hand going to one of the stacks of books on the table, toppling them over. "Take a look at these books. I bet you think I'm the one who convinced Larissa to write that paper for my friend's son. I didn't. He called and asked her. Larissa gave in when Kyle told her that he would flunk the class and wouldn't be able to graduate this semester. Larissa is too kindhearted for her own good.

"This other stack of books is for one of her previous mothers, who is trying to get through college with three children at home." Kendra laid a hand on the stack of paperwork next to the computer. "This is all the work she has been working on to prove Treepoint needs a birthing center. She's already put in hundreds of hours, and they keep asking for more. Lana and Priss have tried to help, but Larissa has put in the majority of the work. She puts her whole heart into everything she does to benefit others. She's a gentle soul in a world that only values strength. Are you aware how many scholarships she was offered before she was even out of middle school? She refused all of them. Instead, she worked part-time to help me pay to send Lana to medical school. She had her choice of Ivy League schools, but she went to a local college to save money so Lana and Priss could chase their dreams."

Kendra picked up her wine glass to take a drink then stared down into the burgundy depths as she continued to talk. "When she moved in with a Bryer, I was so happy for her. I thought she finally found someone who saw how special she was. Other than a girl who she grew up with, Larissa didn't have friends." The slight trembling of her lips revealed the inner emotions Kendra was containing. "Finally, I thought she would be able to live a normal life. However, it didn't take long before I found out she was doing the majority of his schoolwork, and as soon as that degree was in his hands, it came out that he had been having an affair. He didn't even have the balls to break it off with her; he let his side piece do the dirty work for him."

Setting the glass down, she pinned him with her gaze again. "Do you know why she doesn't work in a hospital?"

Moon had to clear his throat. "She told me it's because she prefers being more personally involved with her patients."

"That's true." She nodded. "But it isn't the only reason. Larissa couldn't take her patients dying. She could never reach the level of detachment needed to work in a hospital. When she worked with patients who were dying and they reached the point where nothing could be done for them and the patients were ready to give up, she couldn't. My daughter is a fighter, and she couldn't handle failing her patients. With each death, I saw a part of her die inside as well."

Kendra picked up her glass to finish her wine. Standing, she then looked at him across the table. "Enjoy whatever game *you're* playing with my daughter. Larissa is the daughter who is most like me." Her face filled with amused mockery. "You don't believe me? It's the truth. I was just like Larissa. Oh, I don't have her intelligence, but I was too empathic to a fault. You want to know what changed me?" She didn't wait for him to answer her question. "My children. Where they are concerned, they became my priority. Don't underestimate me, and certainly don't Larissa. I might not have the physical strength to take you on in a fight, but don't think I can't take you down another way."

"Are you threatening to destroy my relationship with Larissa?"

"No, I won't have to. I think you're going to sink your own battleship."

Kendra walked to the kitchen, where she washed the wine glass then placed it to the side.

"Kendra …" Moon rose to his feet when he saw Kendra start around the counter, about to leave. "I know how to protect my young, too. *You* would be wise not to underestimate *me*." Moon saluted her with the beer bottle then lifted it to his lips.

Kendra halted in place, giving him a small nod. "Don't worry; I won't."

# CHAPTER SIXTY-TWO

Unable to take watching another episode of *Love on the Rocks*, Larissa turned the television off. As she stared around the clean living room she had dusted and mopped that morning, she was at a loss as to what to do next. After going on a cleaning spurt for the last couple of days, there was nothing left to do.

Drumming her fingers on the arm of the couch, she debated working on the mound of paperwork on the table. Nah ... she preferred to work on that in the early evenings.

She got up and wandered through the house, trying to find something to do. *You could have gone to lunch and movie with Mom, Lana, and Priss*, she reminded herself. But she'd turned down the invitation, because she had looked forward to some me time. Moon would be at work during the day, and her mother would be out of the house, giving her free reign to do whatever she wanted to do.

When she found herself back in the living room without anything to do, she went into the garage. Disappointed, she was about to give up when her eyes settled on the car. Both Moon's car and hers could use a washing.

Happy, she gathered everything she would need then opened the garage door, Backed both cars out, then got busy.

After cleaning the inside of Moon's car first, she switched to hers. Of the two, hers needed cleaning the most. She didn't know why he owned a car, anyway. Unless they went somewhere to together, his main mode of transportation was his motorcycle.

A couple of times, she had asked if they could take his motorcycle when they went out, to which he had used the excuse of her being pregnant but promised to take her for a ride once the baby was born. It was one of the things she was looking forward to the most, ranking higher than the baby no longer being wrapped around her bladder.

Humming, she crawled out of the back seat of her car. She brushed her sweat-dampened bangs away from her eyes and pressed a hand to the middle of her back. Thank goodness she was wearing a pair of blue jean shorts and a tank top which Killyama had given her that read "*Mama Knows Best.*"

She went to the spigot at the side of the garage to turned on the water hose. After wetting each car, she turned the water off, dipped her mitt into the soapy water she had prepared, and then started scrubbing Moon's car.

As she sang along with the music coming from the radio in the garage, it didn't take long before she moved on to her car. With her back to the road, she heard a motorcycle coming down the street. She must have been outside longer than she supposed for Moon to be coming home.

She leaned over the trunk to reach a couple of twigs that must have blown down, then turned to greet Moon when his bike pulled up next to the car.

As he turned his motorcycle off, she said, "Hi, I didn't realize it was getting so late—"

"What in the fuck do you think you're doing?" He didn't let her finish her sentence.

Larissa frowned at him. "I'm washing the cars."

"Your mother and sisters have been calling you. I called. Why didn't you answer the fucking phone?"

"I must have left my cell phone inside."

Moon was too angry to care about her excuse. "They're worried sick."

Larissa straightened off the car as Moon took out his cell phone.

"She's fine. She was outside. There's no need for you to come. I'm here. I took off the rest of the day."

Feeling bad that Moon had left early. she started to apologize when he ended the call. "I'm sor—"

"If you wanted your car washed so damn badly, why didn't you just ask me? Or did you just need an excuse to show your ass to everyone in the neighborhood?"

Disconcerted, it took a couple of minutes for her to gather her scattered wits.

Jutting her chin angrily, she raised herself to her full height. "Don't you ever dare to speak to me in that tone again." She was unaware that her plain features had taken on a rosy glow, turning her eyes into a magnificent shade of golden brown that gave her a beauty normally not witnessed by others around her. "I didn't ask you to wash them because you work constantly, and I didn't want you to have to spend your only day off washing the cars."

"You didn't have to wear shorts showing your ass!"

"Look around you!" she shouted back at him. "Who's here to see?" Larissa waved her hand at the block filled with half-built homes. "No one is here other than us." She pulled off the scrubbing mitt and threw it into the soapy water bucket, not caring that the water splashed onto Moon. Then, turning on her heel, she stomped to the spigot to turn on the water hose.

"What are you doing?"

"Guess." She sarcastically gave him a harassed glance as she squeezed the handle on the end of the hose to start squirting the soap suds off the car.

"Give it to me. I'll do it."

"You want it?" she asked with make-believe sweetness. "You can have it." Switching the nozzle to full blast, she pretended to hand it to him. Instead, when the nozzle was within a couple of inches of his face, she let him have it full force.

"What the fuck!" he yelled.

"I told you not to use that tone with me." She danced backward when he tried to take the hose from her while keeping the hose trained on him. "*Ooo* …you aren't such a big man now, are you?" she goaded him.

When he nearly managed to tear the hose out of her hand, she ran to the side of the car. Positioning herself, she aimed the nozzle so that all she had to do was use her wrist to send the spray across the roof of the car in whichever direction Moon tried to escape.

"Tsk, tsk." She clicked her tongue at him, drenched hair clinging to his face. "You look all wet." She chuckled, her free hand slapping the roof of the car. "You don't look so sexy now, do ya? You look like a drowned rat!"

Her merriment was short lived when Moon suddenly sank out of sight. That was when the reality of what she had done made her sprint toward the garage. Throwing the hose at him when he tried to catch her, she was smart enough to become frightened when she saw the metal nozzle hitting him on the side of his face.

"Sorry, that was an accident!" she screamed, reaching the door into the house. She slammed it door, locked it, then took off running toward their bedroom.

"Oh God. Oh God! He's going to kill me!" Gasping, she

had almost made it to the hallway leading to their room when she saw the door opening.

Darn it, why hadn't she locked the door? *Oh Lord, he's going to catch me.*

The frantic thought had her rushing into the bedroom. Turning to slam the door after her, she barreled into Moon.

"Have you lost your mind?" Grabbing her by the forearms, he pulled her to his wet chest. "Are you trying to put yourself in labor?"

"No, you just scared me with the way you were looking at me!"

Walking her backward, he shut the door using his boot. "How am I looking at you?" he asked her silkily.

The sexual intent in his eyes sent a sensual shudder coursing through her body.

"Like you want to have—"

"Like I want to fuck you?" he finished for her, bending his head toward hers.

Larissa turned her face away, dodging his kiss. "I think we should wait until you aren't so angry."

"I'm not mad anymore. I'm horny."

She studied him doubtfully. "You still look mad." Feeling the mattress behind her knees, she pushed at his chest. Then she froze when she felt his teeth graze the side of her neck. Tensing, she trembled in his arms.

"You have a hell of a temper when you let loose."

"You provoked me."

"*I* provoked you?" Moon gave a throaty laugh. "Hell, I was the one provoked. You're lucky I didn't fuck you on the trunk of the car."

"You wouldn't dare." Arching her neck back to look at his face, she was stunned at the look there.

"Oh yes, I would."

The big jerk used the opportunity of her pushing away from him to tug her clinging top off.

"You would have tried to have sex with me out in the open for anyone to see?" Wincing at the scandalized shriek in her voice, she attempted to bat his hands away from unbuttoning her jean shorts but failed miserably and found herself tumbling backward on the bed.

Kicking out at him, she thought she had won the battle of wills when Moon backed away. She raised herself on her elbows and realized he was merely using the opportunity to remove his own clothes.

"Do I look shy to you?"

Larissa had to swallow the lump in her throat. No, Moon was not shy. His bronze body gleamed under the ceiling light, highlighting every nook and crevice of his muscular body. God, his body was fit and toned to the point there wasn't a spare inch of extra flesh. He was all hard angles and planes, leading to the turgid length of his cock under a nest of curly hair.

Unable to look at him any longer, she had to blink back tears she felt gathering in the back of her eyes.

A calloused hand turned her face back to him.

"You're beautiful," she said reverently.

A frown crossed his forehead. "What's wrong with that?"

"I'm not." Old wounds returned to haunt of her. How many times had she been made fun of as a child for not being as pretty as other girls? That she was such a geek no boy would ever want her? Were those insecurities what had led her to letting her ex-boyfriend take advantage of her for so long?

Moon planted his hands on each side of her head. "You're sexy as fuck."

When he licked his tongue over her lips before thrusting it inside her mouth, her mind was transported

442

into Never Never Land, where Moon was kissing her like she was the most beautiful woman on earth. As if she was one of those women who made men turn their heads when they walked into a room. The type of woman men would die for.

Her legs came up to circle his hips, pulling him down. "I want you ... so bad ... even though I know I shouldn't," she managed to get out.

Moon sensuously slid his cock inside her warm, aching center. Arching her neck, she gave a low moan.

"Why shouldn't you?" he murmured, licking a taut nipple.

"You're going to break my heart, just like everyone else."

"You could break mine just as easily," he countered.

Her hands grabbed his hair, forcing him to end the torment on her breasts as his body thrust inside of her over and over.

"I don't think your heart has ever been broken by a woman." She slid her hands over the slick muscles of his back as she held on. "No woman would willingly give you up."

She could tell from his expression that he didn't want to admit she was right.

Sliding her hands down to his buttocks to pull him tighter against her, she gloried in the erotic feel of the muscles moving underneath the firm flesh. "I can't blame them either. I don't want this to ever end."

Biting his shoulder, she fought the climax that was building inside of her as his body forced her higher and higher, leaving her no choice but to take the dive that she had tried to prolong. His groan told her he had found his release as well.

She read the male satisfaction on his face as he rolled off her to get out the bed, though it only fed the hollow emptiness that was gradually increasing each time they had sex. While she wanted the physical intimacy to last longer—

forever—Moon plainly did not. Using his sexual experience, he called all the shots.

"I'm going to take a shower. You coming?"

Rolling over, she pretending to yawn. "I'll take one when I get up."

Bending down, he brushed a kiss over her mouth. "Enjoy your nap."

She waited until she saw the bathroom door close after him before she buried her head in the pillow. Like the satellite he was nicknamed after, Moon preferred his solitude. He carried an air about him that even when he was with his friends, a part of him remained detached. If his friends, who had known him for years, couldn't breach that air of isolation surrounding him, how did she think to have any hope? It was becoming more obvious that she wouldn't. Did she love him enough to be content to take only what he was willing to give her? Like she had with her ex?

*No*, she answered her internal question. There was no comparison between the two. God help her, but she would take whatever Moon was willing to give her. She also loved him enough that she would let him go when he wanted to. There wouldn't be a lasso strong enough to hold Moon when he didn't want to be held.

Her hand went to the swollen belly. "Don't worry; you won't have the same problem," she softly murmured.

Fluttering movements within her brought a tender smile to her lips.

"He's going to love you."

# CHAPTER SIXTY-THREE

"Any plans for the day?" Moon asked, humor evident in his expression.

She removed her gaze from him and the stack of pancakes to the unappetizing glob of oatmeal her mother had given her instead of the pancake tower she had prepared for Moon. "Nothing much. Priss is coming over this morning to bring the birthing pool and the equipment we will need."

Moon's eyes grew anxious. "Are you having a contraction? I'll call in—"

Larissa raised her hand. "I'm not having any contractions. We're just getting prepared. Relax. There's no need not to go to work."

"You sure?"

"Positive," she assured him.

"I want to be there when you go into labor," he told her inflexibly for the millionth time.

"Moon, you're not going to convince me to go to the hospital. I'm having the baby in my home. Didn't Train tell you it was the most beautiful experience of his life?" she reminded him.

"You forget the part where he said he'd rather cut both his nuts off than go through that again?"

"I did." Making a face at him, she snuck a bite of pancake when her mother wasn't looking. "He was exaggerating."

Watching her mother out of the corner of her eye, she tried to steal another bite, only to have Moon take her spoon away with a wicked grin.

"Meanie."

He laughed at her and slid the pancakes across the table to her, taking the oatmeal for himself.

She gave him a grateful smile and she dug into the pancakes before her mother noticed the switch.

"Thank you."

"You're welcome." Rising from the table, he gave her a mischievous glance. "Of course, you're going to have to explain how you ended up with the pancakes. I'm out of here."

"Coward."

"You ready to throw her ass out the door?"

"Shh … she can hear you. You know I'm not."

"Then you're on your own." With a brief peck on her cheek, he was gone.

She was lifting her fork speared with a generous bite of pancakes, when she looked toward her mother to see she was being observed.

Under her perusal, she ate the bite. She didn't feel bad enough to stop eating them, but she did feel bad that she had been caught.

"You're terrible."

"I'll eat oatmeal tomorrow," she promised, carrying the empty plate to the sink. "I couldn't resist. You could have given the oatmeal to him."

"It was meant to be a peace offering."

"Aw, that was sweet. I'm glad you're liking him better."

Her mother gave her a sage look as she took a tiny sleeper out of the laundry basket. "He's a prick."

Larissa gaped at her mother. "You really have to quit calling him names."

Her mother gave a sarcastic snort. "I'd love to hear what he calls me when you're not around. It's pretty obvious we can't stand each other."

"Mom, you promised to behave around him."

"I am. Didn't I make the Easy Rider wannabe pancakes?"

"Lord, Mom, make sure you don't say that to his face."

"I wouldn't. No more than I would call him a son of a bitch."

"Why do you dislike like him so much?"

She could hear her mom's sigh from across the room.

"That young man sets off my last nerve."

Larissa's hand went to her lower back, feeling a nagging pain. "I can tell." Crossing the room, she sat down on the couch next to her mother and began folding the baby clothes in the basket. "I really want you two to get along."

"Darling, Moon and I will never get along."

"Why?" Larissa looked up from the laundry basket to find a morose expression on her mother's face, as if she was about to say something she didn't want to say. Warily, she dreaded her mother's next words.

She loved her mother and knew she only wanted her to be happy. If she really disliked Moon for good reason, she didn't know if she could keep lying to herself that they had a future.

After a brief pause, her mother's expression lightened, easing her worry. "Because he's a prick."

---

Bending down, she opened the bottom drawer of the baby's bureau to set a stack of clothes inside. When she rose, she felt a gush of wetness running down her legs.

"Mom!" she yelled.

A moment later, her mother came running into the baby's nursery. Mother and daughter just stared at each other.

"My water broke."

"I see that." Her mother sounded as if she had swallowed a frog. "Are you in any pain?"

"No!" she wailed.

Her mother frowned. "Then why are you yelling?"

"Because I don't have the pool set up! None of our equipment is here. Priss—"

"Calm down." Her mother stepped around the pool of water on the floor to take her arm. "I'll call Priss while you get changed."

In her room, she washed off and changed into a gown, managing to gather her composure enough to fight the anxiety over finding herself in labor.

Hearing the front door slam open and Priss calling her name provided yet another level of calm. She would be in good hands with Priss here. She wouldn't have to depend only on herself to monitor the baby if any difficulties arose.

Her mother had just finished putting padding on the bed when Priss came rushing into the bedroom. Setting her medical bag on the dresser, she gave her a steadying look. "We got this."

Larissa nodded. "I know."

"Lana is on her way. Let's get you in bed so I can check how the baby is doing." Taking her by the arm, Priss helped her get situated on the bed before moving to her bag.

Larissa raised her gown for Priss, then looked at her mother, catching the fear she didn't have time to hide.

"Have you timed your contractions?" Priss asked when she returned to her side.

Larissa used a scrunchie to tie up her hair. "I've only had a few mild ones. I thought they were Braxton hicks. Mom, did Moon say he was on his way?"

Her mother shook her head. "I thought we would wait until we know how far apart the contractions are."

Giving her an exasperated look, she pointed at her cell phone. "Call him."

"Do I have to? Can't it wait until the baby graduates high school?"

"Mom!"

"All right, all right. I'm just teasing you to lighten the situation. I'll call the son of a bitch."

# CHAPTER SIXTY-FOUR

"How much longer we going to sit back and watch this crap and not do anything?" Moon complained to Shade and Viper as they all watched the live security monitor.

"Until we know who killed Pace." Viper gestured toward the monitor. "The camera at the club shows he wasn't there. They've been lying low. Shade and Reaper haven't seen any evidence of him meeting any of The Last Riders away from the factory. So, how are they passing off what's stolen?"

"I vote we ask the motherfucker." Moon was pacing back and forth in the small booth. He wanted to quit wasting time and beat the information out of the thief.

Viper swiveled in the computer chair. "Whoever's behind this is the ringleader. I don't want the little peon. I want the head."

"Between Cash and me, we can get—"

Moon broke off to mute his phone, but when he saw it was Kendra, he accepted the call. That bitch of a mother of hers wouldn't call him if her life depended on him answering.

"Yes?"

"Larissa is in labor."

A rush of fear bombarded at him. Staring at Viper and Shade, he blanked out for a moment, his mind going to all the terrible things that could happen if anything went wrong during the delivery.

"Moon?" Kendra's voice came over the phone.

"Moon?" Viper asked, seeing his reaction.

"I'm on my way." Feeling as if he had swallowed a frog, Moon disconnected the call.

"I need to leave. Larissa is in labor."

Both men stared at him inquiringly when he made no move to leave.

Viper's lips quirked into a smile. "Shade, perhaps you should drive him."

Shade stood up to take one of the vehicle keys off the pegboard on the wall. "Let's go. She already at the hospital?"

"No, she's having the baby at home," he croaked out. The event he had been looking forward to had taken on a nightmare quality.

"Brother, it's going to be all right," Viper sympathetically assured him.

Moon nodded, steely determination settling into his mind, clearing the fear that had struck him unexpectedly. "She will be … right after I drag her ass to the hospital."

---

M oon rushed into the bedroom, only to find himself sprawled out face-first on a sheet of plastic. Stunned, he just lay there, trying to gather his scattered wits and pondering when his life had gotten so out of control.

When he raised his head, he was faced with a variety of expressions on the faces staring down at him.

Lana was standing by the end of the bed, looking at him in concern. "Are you all right?"

Apologies were written all over Priss' face as she bent down, trying to help him up. "I was laying out the birthing pool. I was going to move it the side once I was able to find an electrical socket the cord could reach."

While the other two were filled with concern over his fall, the wicked bitch from Bowling Green was making no effort to hide her amusement.

"You wouldn't fall so much if you looked where you were walking," she advised him with a smirk.

Ignoring Priss' outstretched hand, Moon got to his feet. He shook his hair out of his face, then opened his mouth to give the bitch a piece of what was left of his mind when a low moan came from the bed. Feeling the color wash out of his face, he stumbled over a cord, barely managing to save himself. He sat down on the bed before he hurt himself further and kicked the cord away.

"Are you okay?"

She grinned at him. "I was going to ask you that question."

Moon gave Kendra a thunderous expression. "Your family is trying to take me out, aren't they?"

Larissa rolled her eyes at him. "You're being ridiculous."

Deciding not to argue the obvious, he took her hand. "How far apart are the contractions?"

"They're are about ten minutes apart," Lana answered from next to him. "She hasn't gone into active labor yet."

"Good." Moon bent down to slide an arm underneath her shoulders, the other under her knees.

Larissa gave a startled scream when he started lifting her. "What are you doing?"

"We're going to the hospital. My baby is going to be born there, like ninety-nine percent of the population."

"Moon, put me down!" she shrieked at him. "I'm having the baby here."

"Nope, you're having the baby in the hospital," he argued, fighting off the sudden dizziness assailing him.

Afraid he would drop her with how dizzy he felt, he laid her back on the bed.

"I'll be back in a second." Reaching out to hold on to the headboard, he waited until the room quit spinning.

"Where are you going?" Larissa looked at him strangely.

"To get Shade. He's waiting downstairs. I'm going to get him to carry you to the car."

Larissa gave him a long, drawn-out sigh. "Moon, you are not bringing Shade in here. We've talked about this. I'm having the baby here. Go have a seat." She gestured to a chair on the opposite of the bed. "Priss and Lana are going to set up the birthing pool."

Determining he was useless until the dizziness passed, he went to sit down. He just needed a couple of minutes. The contractions were ten minutes apart. He still had time to get her to the hospital.

Putting his head in his hand, he tried to think himself better.

"Darn it."

Moon lifted his head at hearing Priss' mutter.

"What's wrong?" Larissa asked.

"The air pump isn't working. This setup is brand new. It should be working."

Lana went to the air pump and unplugged it then moved it to another outlet. "It's not working."

Priss gave her sister a wry look. "No joke. I'll drive to the office, get the air pump from the extra birthing pool, and bring it back. I won't be five minutes."

"Hurry!" Larissa yelled after her.

Priss didn't answer; she was already gone.

Moon raised his brows at her when he caught her eyes. "You ready to go to the hospital?"

"No, I'm not," she snapped.

His heart stopped when he saw her face twist in pain. "You're having a contraction."

Larissa's eyes shot sparks at him. "How do you know?"

"I can tell."

"Can you tell what I'm thinking, too?"

Moon glanced away from her glare. "Yeah."

"Good. Then sit there and shut up."

Moon snapped his mouth shut when Kendra gave him a threatening glare.

Taking out his phone out, he started texting.

"The contractions are coming eight minutes apart, Larissa." Reaching down, Lana pulled out Larissa ponytail to gather the loose tendrils then tied a tighter ponytail.

As he witnessed the affectionate gesture, he caught Kendra staring at him. Bitch was probably planning how to kill him in his sleep.

Priss was back before the next contraction hit.

"Here we go," she said, plugging it in.

Nothing happened.

"What in the world? It worked perfectly when I check it out last week."

"Are you ready to go to the hospital now?" he asked eagerly.

Four sets of female eyes turned on him.

"I'm not going to the hospital." Larissa's pearly whites snarled at him. "You've been on board with us having the baby here. It's too late to change your mind."

"How's it too late?" Moon looked at Lana. "How far apart are the contractions?"

"Eight minutes."

"Shade can have you at the hospital in three minutes."

"Moon …" Larissa grabbed Lana's arm when she made a movement toward him. "Fix the air pump."

"I don't know anything about air pump motors. Train and Rider are the ones who work on the bikes. You want me to—"

He gripped the arm of the chair when Larissa gave a low moan.

A wave of nausea hit him, forcing him to swallow the stomach acid rising into his throat.

Kendra's critical eyes latched on to his face. "Are you okay?"

"I'm fine, Mom. The contractions aren't as bad as I expected."

"They're going to get worse," she told Larissa matter-of-factly before steering her grave look back toward him. "And I was asking Moon. He looks as if he's going to hurl."

"I haven't had lunch." Moon started fanning his face. Why was it so fucking hot in this room?

"None of us have. It's going to be a while. Why don't you take a break and make yourself a bowl of soup?"

The mention of food turned his stomach. "I'm not hungry."

Larissa extended her hand to Lana. "I want to move around."

Moon wanted to get up and help her, but he was afraid if he moved from the chair, he would vomit. His head was still swimming, and there was no way he was going to do another faceplant on the floor.

Off the bed, Larissa went to the air pump. "Priss, go to the garage. There is a tub with a yellow lid. That's where I store the air mattress for when Mom would come and visit us. Bring that air pump; it might work on the pool."

"Good call," Pris replied, already heading for the door.

"Mom, could you quit glaring at Moon? I don't think he's feeling well."

His misery was making the old bitch's day. He could tell from the amusement plain on her prune face.

"He's going to pass out."

Moon glared at Kendra. "I'm not going to pass out. I hit my head when I fell. I think I have a concussion." Shifting to his other ass cheek when the women all gave him penetrating stares, he lifted his hand to the back of his head. "I feel a lump."

"You fell face forward," Kendra informed him drily.

"Let me check." Lana made a move toward him.

"I should go to the hospital and get an MRI. Larissa and I can go together. That way, I won't miss the baby being born."

"On the other hand, Shade could drive you, and we'll call you when the baby is born," Kendra countered.

"If I die from a concussion, it's going to be your fault."

Larissa came to his side to peer at his head. "Where does it hurt?"

Kendra crossed her arms over her chest. "He isn't hurt; he's faking it."

Lana came to his other side. "I don't think he's faking it. I think he's having Couvade syndrome."

Growing worried at the way Larissa and Lana were looking at him, he leaned back in the chair to lay his head back. "We need to go to the hospital," he begged.

"Don't worry." Lana patted his arm. "You'll better as soon as the baby's born."

"I'll be dead by then," he groaned. "That syndrome sounds bad. What is it?"

"It's fake sympathy pains, moron," Kendra huffed out in exasperation.

"What's wrong with Moon?" Priss asked when she walked back into the room.

"What isn't?" Kendra answered mockingly.

If Priss weren't blocking his sight, he would have given the bitch a gesture her old ass would have been able to recognize.

"Behave, Mom." Larissa nodded toward the pump in Priss' hands. "See if that will work on the pool."

Priss plugged the air mattress' air pump in, and after several adjustments, the low hum of the motor filled the room.

"It's working!" Priss yelled.

"Yay." Slumping back further into the chair, Moon wanted to cry.

"Ow." Larissa pressed a hand to her abdomen, bending over.

"Oh God!" Moon shouted.

"Oh my God." Kendra gave him a disgusted face. "Larissa, I have several reservations about your taste in men."

Larissa patted him on the shoulder. "I think it's cute. Do you need anything, Moon?"

"Something cold to drink would be nice." His throat was as dry as the desert.

"Mom, would you get Moon a glass of orange juice? I think it would help him feel better."

Kendra's brows furrowed. "Are you serious?"

Larissa nodded. "Please. I wouldn't mind some lemon water, too."

*There's no way I'm drinking anything she gives me*, he thought.

"Am I the only one hot?" Frantically, Moon started fanning his face harder. "Lana, you're standing next to the control. Turn it down."

"Moon, is Shade still here?"

Moon nodded at Larissa eagerly. "Yes. You finally ready to go to the hospital?"

"No. I want you to go downstairs and sit with him for a while. The baby won't be here for hours. Take a break."

"I'm not leaving your side …" Moon hunched over and grabbed his stomach. He felt as if he had been hit in the gut with a bowling ball. He broke out in a cold sweat. "Turn the air conditioner off. It's freezing in here," he complained.

Lana and Larissa simultaneously yelled, "Shade!"

The sneaky bastard must have been listening in the hallway because it didn't take him but a hot second before he stepped into the room.

"You need some assistance?"

"Yeah," Moon started before the women could. "Convince her to go to the hospital before I die."

Larissa gave Shade a pleading look. "Could you please help Priss fill the pool then convince Moon to go to the living room until I need him?"

"Be glad to."

The whole time Shade filled the pool, Moon was determined to keep his ass exactly where it was … right until Shade finished and he was dealing with more excruciating pain in his stomach than he had experienced in his whole life. He didn't have any strength left to fight the brother when Shade took his arm and lifted him from the chair.

"How have you gone through this three times?" Forced to lean the majority of his weight on him or risk falling, he let Shade usher him out of the room.

"I better be the one who cuts the umbilical cord!" Moon shouted over his shoulder. "Or there's going to be hell to pay."

"Brother, you don't have the strength to cut a fart, much less the umbilical cord."

"Watch me. I just need to get some fresh air. Take me to the dining room and open the sliding doors."

Shade settled him at the table before opening the sliding door, allowing a small breeze inside. "Better?"

Moon nodded. "I think I have a concussion."

Shade's lips twisted wryly. "So I heard. Why are you holding your stomach?"

"I think Larissa's mother poisoned my breakfast."

"Brother, you need to get a grip."

"I will once the baby is here, safe and sound."

"I've got bad news for you. It only gets worse after they're here."

"God …" Moon moaned in pain, clutching his stomach. "Don't tell me that. I won't survive."

Shade went to the kitchen to get the juice Kendra had set there before going back in with Larissa.

Seeing Shade was about to bring it to him, Moon shook his head. "I don't trust she didn't put anything in it."

Shade took a drink, making a face when he put the glass back down. "Poison might make it taste better."

Moon threw an angry glance toward the bedroom. "Bitch knows I hate that no-sugar shit."

"Can't blame you there." Shade went to the fridge to take out the regular juice.

"Don't bother. There's no sugar in it, either."

Shade raised his eyebrows. "It says—"

"Trust me; it's the same."

"How about I just make us some coffee?"

"I'd appreciate it."

Moon lost track of time as they sat in the dining room. And as the afternoon progressed, he grew sicker.

"As soon as the baby is born, I need you to drive me to the hospital." Holding his cup with a shaking hand, he confessed to Shade how much pain he was in. "I think my appendix has ruptured."

Shade's deadpan stare didn't expose what he was thinking. "I'll take you whenever you're ready."

"Thank you, brother. I can always count on you." Fighting back unmanly tears, he was about to ask Shade for some paper towels when Priss came running to the end of the hallway.

"Moon, come on. It's time."

Using all of his strength, he ran into the bedroom and found Larissa on the bed with her legs opened wide. As he stepped further into the room, he was able to witness the head coming out.

Looking up from the sight, he met Larissa's eyes.

"Can you see?" she asked him excitably.

Moon opened his mouth to answer, only to find himself falling into a bottomless void.

# CHAPTER SIXTY-FIVE

"I see you're feeling better." It was everything she could do to keep the amusement out of her voice as she watched Moon hold their baby to his bare chest.

"Please don't remind me of how much of a jackass I made of myself. I'm never going to live it down."

Larissa smiled at him tenderly, lowering her guard with Moon's full attention centered on the baby. "No one will know. Mom, Lana, and Priss all have promised not to say a word."

"Shade promise?"

"Not exactly." Ruefully, she patted the arm close to her. "But I'm hoping he won't."

"Even if he doesn't, it'll get out. I already got two texts asking if everything was okay. They saw the ambulance I called parked outside."

Larissa couldn't help it; she gurgled with laughter, remembering when her mother had looked out the window when Moon was delegated to the living room to see the ambulance outside.

When her mother had gone outside to tell the drivers

461

they weren't needed, they told her Moon had called the ambulance to take Larissa to the hospital and they were only waiting for the go-ahead from Moon before coming inside. She had sent them inside to check on Moon instead before returning to the bedroom to tell her about his shenanigans.

"Did you really think you'd be able to convince me to go to the hospital?"

"If you were feeling half the pain I was, I don't know how you didn't want to. At one point, I think I cried out for my makuwahine."

Larissa had to wipe away her tears of laughter. It took several minutes to get herself back under control. The memory of Moon passing out at the foot of the bed when she was giving birth wasn't something she would forget anytime soon.

"Have you called your mother to tell her she's a grandmother?"

"No, I'll call her later."

Larissa frowned. She had broached the subject of his mother several times, and each time, he had given her guarded responses, which left her in the dark as to what their relationship was like.

She was about to question him again when Priss returned to the room, taking the baby from Moon to give to her.

Climbing in the bed with her, Moon watched as she attempted to feed the baby for the first time.

She was beginning to become anxious when the little mouth didn't latch on, but when he did, she gave a startled jump. Moon's low laughter at her reaction overflowed her heart with contentment.

*God, please let this feeling last.*

"Smile."

Priss' request made them both raise their heads to smile as she took a picture of them.

She set the phone down and finished taking down the birthing pool, which after all the hiccups it had put them through hadn't been used.

As far as births went, she couldn't complain. Moon had definitely been the one who took that bullet where that was concerned. She had expected much worse. Overall, she found it a beautiful experience. The best part was, with Moon by her side, she felt like they were truly a family. "Are you still okay naming him Jace?"

Moon nodded, watching as the baby curled tiny little fingers around his forefinger.

"Jace Eric. Sounds like a winner to me."

"Me, too," she agreed softly, meeting Moon's gaze.

Priss interrupted the special moment by clearing her throat. "I'm going to take off, unless you need anything else?"

"No, thanks. I really appreciate your help today."

"Anytime, sis. Mom is taking a nap. If you need anything, just let me know. Lana gets off at seven, so if you need anything from the store, just text her, and she can pick it up on the way home."

"We're good. Thanks again, Priss. I owe you a week vacation when I come back to work."

"Going to hold you to that." With a quick kiss on her cheek, her sister left them alone.

"When are you planning on going back to work?"

Moon's neutral expression didn't give any hint away of what he was thinking. They hadn't talked about her going back to work once the baby was born.

"I haven't taken on any new clients. I thought I would take six or seven weeks off."

"Who's going to be watching the baby?"

Larissa knew this part was going to be sticky, which was why she hadn't brought it up before.

"Mom."

His expression didn't change, his focus still on Jace.

"She'll go home the day after tomorrow and get everything packed up and begin the process of selling her house. When she comes back, she'll move in with Priss and Lana. During the day, she can come over here to babysit while I work. She'll be gone before you get off work unless a client goes into labor. You won't have to see her often. What do you think?"

"Sounds like you have it all organized."

"Only if it's okay with you." She searched Moon's features but still had no idea what he was thinking.

"It's a sensible solution I can go with."

"Thank you."

He finally raised his eyes. "You didn't think I would agree?"

"I know you haven't exactly been getting along with my mother."

"She's not my favorite person in the world, I admit. But the baby will be safe with her, and if she is as protective over Jace as she is over you, he will be in good hands."

Relieved Moon was being so amiable, despite the bickering that had been going on between the two of them, his agreement took a huge weight off her chest.

"He's asleep," she murmured.

"Looks like you're ready for a nap, too."

"I am," she admitted tiredly.

Moon got out of bed and took Jace, placing him in the bassinet Priss had placed next to the bed.

She was about to lie down when she saw Moon take something out of the nightstand.

"I have something I want to give you."

Her heart lurched at seeing the small box he held out to her. Taking the distinctive Cartier box, she flipped the lid up. The sight of an exquisite pair of diamond earrings instead of the ring she thought he was gifting her with made her camouflage her disappointment.

"They're beautiful, Moon. Thank you."

"You're welcome. Thank you for my son."

"You're welcome."

"Get some rest. I'll be in the living room."

When Moon would have turned away from the bed, she grabbed him by the hand.

"Stay."

He searched her eyes before nodding. "I could use a nap, too."

She rolled over when Moon climbed back in bed, then laid her head on his chest. Listening to his steady heartbeat under her ear reassured he was there. But for how long?

Each night she had gone to sleep in his arms, she dreaded the new day ahead. Would it be the day he would decide he no longer wanted to be with her? She wanted to open up to him about her fear, but what if he didn't give her the reassurance she needed?

Snuggling against him, she linked her fingers with his, then closed her eyes and felt herself doze off, only coming aware when she felt him withdraw his hands from hers. Pretending to still be asleep, she rolled over, giving Moon his space. The day was coming when he would leave; she could feel it in every bone of her body.

Partway lifting her lashes, she gazed down at the angelic baby lying just inches away. She only hoped when Moon did decide to leave, he didn't take her whole world with him.

# CHAPTER SIXTY-SIX

"How's your first day back going?" Priss asked, waving her hand in front of her monitor.

Larissa made a face at her sister. She had been so intent on updating files that she hadn't heard her sister enter her office.

"Good."

"You don't miss the baby too bad?"

"How?" She grinned. "Mom's brought him by three times to be fed."

"The benefit of working ten minutes from home."

Perching herself on the side of her desk, Priss slanted her a curious glance. "I've missed having alone time with you so we can talk without anyone hearing."

"Me, too," she admitted. Between Mom or Moon being around, they hadn't been able to share any confidence since Jace's birth.

"How's it going with Moon?"

Larissa bit her lip. How much did she want to confide in her sister? Priss always kept their chats private, but with Mom living in the same house, would she let something slip?

Priss must have read her hesitation.

"Come on; I won't tell Mom or Lana."

"It's going well. He's fantastic with Jace. I don't have to ask him to help out. I think Jace prefers him to me unless he's hungry."

Priss stared at her doubtfully. "You're exaggerating."

Larissa gave her a sad smile. "A little."

Priss frowned. "What's wrong?"

Picking up the ink pen on her desk, she put it in the revolving pen caddy. "I'm probably being oversensitive," she admitted glumly.

"Are you experiencing some postpartum depression?"

"No." Larissa started fiddling with her caddy.

"Larissa … what aren't you telling me?"

Larissa moved her hand away from the caddy to lay it flat on the desk. "We haven't had sex since Jace was born. It's been three months. I told him there's no reason we can't. I even put my birth control pills on the vanity in our bathroom to show him I'm taking them." Larissa felt her cheeks flush. She had never really confided in either of her sisters about her sex life before, but she was tired of holding it inside.

Priss seemed unsure as to what to say. "Uh … have you come out and told him you want to have sex?"

"I've done everything but say it out loud. I tried to take a shower with him last night …" Staring at a picture hanging on the wall rather than looking at her sister, she felt herself turn redder. "He got out and said he didn't want us both out of earshot of Jace. Then I told him I would bring the monitor into the bathroom."

Priss' frown deepened. "What did he say?"

"That by the time I did that, he would be done showering."

Priss grimaced. "Ouch."

"Yeah." Glumly, Larissa started turning the caddy again.

"Maybe he just wants to make sure you're healed. He could be worried about losing control and hurting you."

"Maybe." She was skeptical. She didn't buy that reason at all. Something was going on with Moon since Jace's birth.

"You don't believe that's the case."

"Not really. Moon has never lost control during sex." Larissa worried her bottom lip. "I don't think he wants me. Why should he? He has a clubhouse full of sexy women, waiting to give him anything he wants."

"You really think he's cheating, don't you?"

"No."

Priss' gaze sharpened on her. "You don't sound too sure."

"Is any women a hundred perfect sure her boyfriend isn't cheating?"

"I don't know. I haven't ever been in a serious relationship to judge."

"I'm probably just overthinking what's going on. We just had a baby; he is most likely adjusting to being a father. Like I said, I'm probably overthinking it." Bolstered by her talk with Priss, she grinned at her. "I could go home tonight, and he could be ready to rock my world."

Priss gave her a thumbs-up. "There you go. There's the sister I know and love. I'm not used to you being so down." Breezily walking across the office, she gave her a mischievous look. "By the way, it couldn't hurt if you're wearing something to knock his socks off when he gets home."

"You know, I might stop and pick up something up on the way home."

Larissa finished up the chart she was working on, then told Priss she was leaving a little early. Feeling in a much better mood, she drove to the clothing store on Main Street, next to King's restaurant. When she was unable to find a parking spot on the street in front of the store, she parked in King's parking lot at the side of the restaurant.

Once she was inside the clothing store, she wandered around the different departments, unsure of what she was looking for. About to give up and make another shopping trip with one of her sisters, she sighted a pale blue maxi dress. She carried it to the dressing room to try it on.

It made her feel like a million bucks. It accentuated her newfound bust before it fell loosely around her waist, hiding her baby belly. Spinning, she saw the back was bare except for on lone tie in the middle. She had never known her back could look sexy. Would Moon think so? There was only one way to find out.

Excited about getting home and changing into her new dress before Moon came home, she checked out then rushed to her car.

She opened the rear car door and had just laid the dress over the back seat when she heard motorcycles passing on the street.

Recognizing Viper at the front of the massive group of motorcyclists following after him, instead of getting into the car, she waited to see Moon so she could wave to him.

Smiling, she waited for him to pass by, and she was beginning to think he wasn't riding with the group when she spotted him.

Her smile faltered and died. A woman she didn't recognize was riding on the back of his motorcycle. The woman had her whole body pressed against Moon, with her arms wound tightly around his waist. Resting her chin on Moon's shoulder, she was cheek to cheek with him.

Larissa waited until the last motorcycle passed by before she got into the car. Automatically, she drove home.

She carried the dress inside and hung it in the hall closet before heading toward the living room. Finding her mom in the kitchen, she managed a smile as she came around the kitchen counter.

"How's Jace doing?"

"Still sleeping." Closing the oven, her mother gave her a perceptive glance. "He's due to wake any moment. I made some lasagna, and I just put in a baguette. I set the oven to warm so you can eat dinner when Moon gets here."

"Thanks, Mom." Moving to the fridge, she poured herself a glass of lemonade. "Why don't you stay and eat dinner with us?"

Her mother had made a point of disappearing before Moon arrived home since she had started babysitting. By the time she had been ready to return to work, they were lucky her mom's house had sold and she had already moved in with Priss and Lana.

"I would, but Lana, Priss, and I were invited to Sex Piston's house. They're having a small get-together. I think they're trying to set me up."

"I forgot that was tonight."

She went to the cabinets and took out dinner plates, then brought them to the dining room, where she started setting the table. "It'll be good for you to meet new people," she said absently, her mind still picturing the woman riding on Moon's motorcycle.

"Is everything all right, sweetie?"

Larissa came back to the kitchen for glasses. "Just a little tired. After dinner, I think I'll have an early night."

Her mother didn't seem convinced. "You know, if you need to talk, I don't have to go."

"Go. Meet my future stepfather," she teased. "I'm fine."

"I'm worried about you." Her mother stopped beside her. "You never smile anymore, unless you're holding Jace. Are you and Moon having problems?"

Jace's cry coming over the monitor gave her the excuse to escape.

"Everything is fine. Moon is a wonderful father. I'll see you in the morning. Text me if you meet anyone interesting."

"You know I won't." Her mother gave a mock shudder. "Why is it when people try to set me up, it's with men who have one foot in the grave or have dementia?"

"I don't know, possibly because they aren't aware you're a cougar?"

"How many times have I told you I dislike that term?"

"How many men your own age have you dated since Dad died?"

The look her mother gave her had her deciding to make good on her escape.

She picked up Jace from his crib and carried him to the rocking chair. Sitting down, she unbuttoned her top and unsnapped her maternity bra. She used a cleansing cloth to clean her nipple then settled him against her chest as she started rocking the chair.

She had switched Jace to her other breast when she heard Moon walk in the door. Usually, she called out to him when he came in. Tonight, she remained silent, gently rocking the chair.

Staring at her son, she thought how much he looked like his father. He was a little carbon copy of the man standing in the doorway, watching them.

"Is Jace asleep?" Moon whispered.

"No, he's wide awake." Using her knuckles, she rubbed the soft skin of his cheek. "He finished. Would you mind burping him so I can take a shower?"

Moon came forward to take the baby from her arms. She was aware of his eyes dropping to her uncovered breasts. Raising her hands, she pulled the two sides of her top closed over her breasts as she got up from the chair.

"Dinner is in the oven, if you're hungry. You don't have to wait for me."

As she passed Moon, she kept her face averted from him.

"How was your day?" he asked as she was about to walk into the bedroom.

"Good." Usually, she would ask how his day had been. Today, she went into the bedroom and shut the door behind her.

She took her time showering and only dried off when couldn't postpone getting out any longer. No longer having the desire to wear the new dress she had bought, she pulled out a pair of buttery soft jeans and slipped on a wine-colored crisscross top that tied at the waist. Then she padded barefoot down the hall to the living room. Moon was sitting on the couch with his feet propped on the coffee table, Jace wiggling on his lap.

"He's getting bigger every day."

Moon might not love her, but it was obvious he loved his son.

"Yes, he is," she agreed on her way to the kitchen to take the lasagna out of the oven.

When he saw she was setting the food on the table, Moon placed Jace down in the small portable crib they kept in the living room, then wheeled the crib to the table and sat down.

Placing the bread on the table, she took the chair opposite of his. She served him a generous mound of lasagna before she gave herself a smaller portion. She did the same with the bread.

"You're not hungry?" he questioned.

"Not very."

Lasagna was her favorite, but tonight, her stomach was too twisted in knots to have much of an appetite.

After taking a small bite of the gooey pasta, she lifted her head. "You have a good day at the factory?"

Moon's head swiveled from the baby to her. "It was slow."

"Hmm," she said, taking another bite of the lasagna. "The day must have dragged on for you, then."

"It was pretty boring." Tearing his bread into a small chunks, he placed a piece in his mouth.

"Really?" Reaching for her glass, she took a drink of water. "You didn't seem bored to me when I saw you riding by with a woman on your motorcycle."

# CHAPTER SIXTY-SEVEN

A myriad of expressions crossed Moon's face. Larissa could tell he was trying to explain why he hadn't been at the factory.

"Several new members from the Ohio chapter came in last night. We took them around town to show them Treepoint."

Tearing a small bite off her bread, she popped into her mouth, watching as he continued eating. "Who rode with you?"

"I believe her name was Saffron."

"Lovely name."

Moon gave her a quick glance. "Are you angry?"

"Should I be?"

He set his fork on the table. "We went for a ride around town then came back. That's all there was to it."

Larissa nodded and took another bite, continuing to eat.

Assuming she was done talking, Moon picked his fork back up. She waited until he had a mouthful of food before asking her next question.

"I didn't see Shade, Rider, Viper, Reaper, or Train with women on their motorcycles."

Moon set his fork back down. Placing his elbows on the table, he linked his fingers together. "I see you do have an issue with me letting Saffron ride on my bike."

"I'm just curious why she didn't ride with someone else." She shrugged. "Was it because Lily, Jo, Winter, Ginny, or Killyama would have been upset, or the men didn't want her to?"

"I don't know. I didn't ask. It was no big deal."

Gathering her courage, she met his gaze directly. "It is to me. I've asked you numerous times to take me for a ride, and you always make an excuse. Yet you don't have a problem letting Saffron plaster herself against you. She was practically kissing you."

"You're exaggerating."

She didn't argue back, merely holding his gaze.

"If you want to go on a ride that damn bad, call your mother to come over to babysit. I'll take you wherever you want to go," he snapped.

Lowering her gaze to the table, she bit the underside of her bottom lip to keep from crying. She didn't want him to know how badly his words had hurt her.

"I don't want to ride with you anymore. I'll never ask you again."

"It wasn't a big deal."

Larissa heard him take a breath, as if to calm himself from arguing with her further, she supposed.

*It's a big deal to me.*

"From now on, I won't let any of the women ride on my bike unless there aren't any bikes available. Satisfied?"

Larissa stared at him cooly, taking in what he said. What he wasn't saying was that his motorcycle was off limits.

When he looked back at her, it was as if he was giving her

a gift by conceding what practically counted as nothing. The hurt in her heart deepened.

"Let's change the subject."

"Thank God."

It was everything she could do not to run from the table, go to her room, and have a good cry. Her backbone kicked in, however, preventing her from that humiliation. There was no way she was going to spend the rest of the night crying, shut away. Nor, on the other hand, did she want to spend the rest of the night in his company, pretending she wasn't hurt.

"Sex Piston's parents asked me over tonight with Mom, Priss, and Lana. They're having a game night. Would you mind if I go?"

If he looked more relieved, she would bash him over the head with the pitcher of lemonade.

"No, I think it would good for you to get out of the house and have some fun. Jace and I have this, don't we?"

Any other time, she would have been charmed by Moon pretending to high-five the baby. Instead, seeing the love Moon felt for his son plain on his face gave her an aching feeling.

When he turned back to her, she couldn't even find a trace of affection for her.

"Then I'll go get changed, if you're sure?"

Moon helped himself to another serving of lasagna. "Why bother? You look fine."

"It'll be nice to get out of a mommy top for a couple of hours." She slid out of her chair and carried her dishes to the sink.

After quickly checking on Jace, she left the living room. Then, taking the new dress from the hall closet, she went to the bedroom to change.

She texted her mother that she would be coming along,

then hurried to pump. After changing into the dress, she brushed her hair out, realizing it had gotten longer without her notice. Left loose, it fell in soft waves past her shoulders. Quickly, she put on a minimum of makeup then dabbed perfume on her neck.

About to turn from the vanity, the earrings Moon had given her caught her eye. Shrugging, she put them on. Why not? It wasn't like Moon had taken her any place special to wear them. To finish off, she grabbed a thin sweater and the milk, then left the bedroom.

Moon was sitting back on the couch. He had placed a blanket on the cushion next to him and was reading to Jace.

Unaware of his eyes watching her as she crossed the room to the kitchen, she placed the milk in the fridge.

"You look nice."

She turned around at the compliment and walked to the couch. "Thank you." Hunching down next to Jace, she lifted his shirt to blow bubbles on his stomach. Jace reacted the way he always did, with his tiny legs kicking and his face scrunching up into a happy smile.

"Mama loves her baby boy," she crooned to him, nuzzling his neck. Then she placed a kiss on his cheek and rose when she heard her cell phone ringing.

"I put a fresh bottle in the fridge. If you need anything, just call. Good night."

Moon caught her by the wrist. "Don't I get a kiss?"

Leaning down, she brushed a kiss over his lips. When he tried to deepen the kiss, she pulled away.

"They're waiting."

"Have fun," he called out after her.

"I will," she called back, shutting the door. She was going to have some stinking fun, even if it killed her.

Her mom had been right; Sex Piston's parents were trying to set her up. They had invited a smorgasbord of men in their acquaintance to a cookout at their house. From the different range of men, she also thought her mother wasn't the only one they were trying to matchmake.

She was standing by herself, watching the men vie for her mother's and sister's attention. Sipping on a glass of iced tea, she watched in amusement as Lana became more and more flustered at the men gathered around her.

They had only been there about thirty minutes before Lana broke away and came to her side.

"Whoa!" she breathed out, grabbing the glass of tea from her hand.

"Too much?" She laughed.

"I thought two of them were going to start fighting for a minute there."

"You said you wanted to get out more," she reminded her. "They're bikers, too. A couple of them are almost as good-looking as Moon."

Larissa made a sarcastic sound with her lips. "There are several who are better looking."

As they talked, she noticed Killyama shift in her seat at the patio table near them to blatantly listen.

"Just remember, my man is taken." Killyama might have sounded like she was joking, but the threatening look in her eyes left the unmistakable impression that she wasn't playing when it came to Train.

The subtle threat must have gone completely over Lana's head.

"I'll keep that in mind." Lana's smile was friendly.

"I would—"

"Who's the man with the long brown hair?" Larissa

decided to save her sister in case she slipped up and said the wrong thing.

"That's Jesus. Train invited him."

"Who's the man talking to Mom?" Lana asked, her prolonged gaze centered toward their mother, who was making her interest obvious.

"That's Keller. That dude is out of both of your mother's and your league," Killyama answered.

"Why?"

"Just take my word for it. He's from the Ohio branch of The Last Riders, or he used to be. He just got out of the service. Train said he's trying to decide if he wants to join again or go his own way."

"I can see that," Larissa mused out loud. "He seems to be the type of man who wants to do his own thing."

Killyama regarded her as if dissecting if she was interested in Keller or not.

"Moon decided not to come?" Killyama asked.

"No, he's watching the baby."

"He didn't care you came?"

Larissa took her tea back from Lana. "No," she admitted huskily, still hurt at the picture of the woman riding on his bike.

"He know how many people would be here?" Killyama perceptively stared her down.

"I told him that Sex Piston's parents were having a game night, so he knew more people would be here other than my family."

Killyama turned more fully toward her. "I bet he didn't know so many bikers would be here."

"He wouldn't care," she told her glumly, watching the ice in her glass melt. "We got into an argument before I left. That's why I called and asked if I could come."

Surprise filled Lana's expression. "You didn't say anything on the way over here."

Larissa shrugged. "Moon said I was making a big deal of nothing."

"He did?" Killyama's eyes narrowed on her when she nodded. One of Killyama's long legs came out to push the chair next to her out. "Sit," she ordered. "Tell me about what Moon doesn't consider a big deal."

# CHAPTER SIXTY-EIGHT

**M**oon made a silly face at his son.

"Your old man just messed up. Big time," he confessed.

He had become so used to Larissa staying in the house for the last three months that he had forgotten to take into account she had been out and about for work today.

She was hurt; he could see it in her eyes and every line in her tensed body. Remembering how close the woman, Saffron, had clung to him as if she had never ridden a motorcycle made him feel worse.

When he saw that Jace had dozed off, Moon carefully held the sleeping baby in his arms as he carried him into Larissa's bedroom, where he tenderly placed the baby in the bedside crib. Sliding the sock monitor onto Jace's foot, he then double-checked the baby monitor on the nightstand before Moon left his son sleeping.

He skipped through the channels on the television while he continued to castigate himself for fucking himself over. Had he really tried to gaslight her that it wasn't a big deal?

Seeing *Warlord's from Hell* was on, he clicked the select button.

If he were a smart man, he would have apologized and told her the fucking truth. Hell, when had he ever done the smart thing? It was his own fault Larissa wasn't sitting here, watching *Warlords* with him.

The best part of his night was watching the series with her. She had a thing for the main warlord who wore a black uniform and a head covering that hid his whole head. He had noticed several times that her nipples would poke through her top when the warlord chose one of the captives to share his bed.

Moon snorted sarcastically. He bet the fucker who played the warlord needed a respirator to recover from getting so much pussy.

Larissa had once rudely told him to shut up and leave her alone to watch her show in peace when he asked her a simple question after coming back from the bathroom. Her show? He made another rude sound. She wouldn't be watching the fucking show if not for him.

Drumming his fingers on the arm of the couch, he looked at his cell phone, wondering how long she would be gone. At least three hours, he guessed. She was really hurt. She would want to make him pay for not apologizing. The good thing, at least, was that she was at Sex Piston's parents' house. The only ones who would be there were a bunch of old goats who hadn't been laid since the turn of the century.

He thought about going to his knees to pray that bitch of a mom of hers found at least one of them to interest her. If she did, he would owe Stud the motorcycle Viper had given him that had belonged to the out-of-town biker. Stud had been trying to buy it off him, but he had refused. When Stud asked what it would take for him to sell it to him, Moon named his price—set Larissa's mom up with one of his elderly acquaintances and get the old witch off his back.

He had been ecstatic when Stud called to tell him he had arranged for his in-laws to host a game night with their friends, and they would invite Larissa's mother. He didn't know they invited the whole family, but he supposed they did it to make Larissa's mother feel more comfortable.

After the show ended, he checked on Jace, who was sleeping soundly. To pass the time until Jace woke for his next feeding, he showered. Then he found a pair of loose gray sweats but didn't bother with a T-shirt.

Feeling in the mood for popcorn, he put a bag in the microwave while he loaded the dishwasher. He had already put the leftovers in the fridge, so all he had to do was wipe off the counters and table. He had just finished when the popcorn was done.

Grabbing a beer and the popcorn, he went back to the couch to search for something else to watch. He put his feet on the coffee table and reached for his cell phone that sat on the end table. Picking it up, he saw he had received a text while was in the shower. It was from Train.

He clicked on the message; it was a stack of pictures. Pressing on the first one, he grinned. Kendra was surrounded by men. About to scroll to the next picture, he stopped to look at the picture again. The men Sex Piston's parents had invited to their game night were different ages. There were a couple of older men, but the ones who made his eyebrows lift were the bikers his own age or younger. He thought there would only be a few geriatric bikers there. Then he sat up from his relaxed position, when he realized that "game night" seemed more like a fucking backyard cookout rather than them playing a few hands of cards.

Using his finger, he flipped to the next picture, and found Larissa sitting at a patio table with Killyama, Jesus, and

Keller. Both men were staring at Larissa as she was talking to Killyama.

His jaw grew tighter with each picture he flipped through.

Jesus was notorious for not giving a fuck if a woman wanted to make a move on him, regardless of if they belonged to another brother. He would flippantly joke, "You snooze, you lose." Moon planned to beat him to a bloody pulp if he made a move on Larissa.

The real problem was the other man sitting at the table. Jesus, he could take; Keller, he was smart enough to know he couldn't. Keller was unbeatable. He was the only Last Rider who had gone through the gauntlet and fought seven of the original Last Riders on the same day and walked away alive to have the bragging rights. The craziest thing about it was he didn't. Keller never bragged about it to the other brothers, and when any of them tried to get him to talk about it, he would walk away. All of the brothers had tried to surmise why he had done it then refused to speak about it anytime it was mentioned.

Hearing Jace's low cry, Moon got up, taking his cell phone with him. He changed Jace's diaper, then carried him to the other room to heat his bottle up, describing what he was doing as Moon talked to Jace the whole time. He had developed the habit after listening to how Larissa interacted with their son. Rarely did she use baby talk with him. Instead, she used a soft tone, talking to him as if he were an adult interested in what she was doing. Moon had noticed Jace's eyes cling to his mother as if he could understand everything she said.

Cradling Jace, he gave him the bottle after checking the temperature.

"You want to watch a movie with me?"

Picking up the remote, he turned it to the Discovery

Channel, to a program Larissa would approve of. Watching jungle animals habitats bored him to death, but he wouldn't be yelled at if Larissa walked in the door with *Warlords From Hell* on.

After watching a lion take down a helpless crocodile, he thought she might not appreciate this show, either.

He switched the channel to *The Andy Griffth Show*; at least he wouldn't want to blow his brains out from boredom.

Glancing at his cell phone, he frowned. She sure was taking her sweet time coming home. Was she still talking to Keller and Jesus? If she was, he was going to follow his first instinct and take Jace to Shade's to babysit before surprising Larissa's ass by showing up.

"She wouldn't do anything." Snuggling Jace closer, he nuzzled his neck, smelling the faint aroma of Larissa's perfume.

God, how much he loved his son. Shade had been right; he worried constantly something would happen to him. Some inner paternal instinct constantly nagged at him to be wary. He didn't understand why, but a scared, sinking feeling struck him every time he left the house. That was why he had bought the monitoring sock. He had an ever-present fear that something would happen to his child. The fear grew each day until Larissa had started chiding him about being too cautious where Jace was concerned. It had gotten to the point he had come up with excuse after excuse as to why he didn't want to go out, preferring to stay put in the house. Since Larissa had gone back to work, and over the last couple of days leading up to that, he was constantly on his cell phone, watching the cameras he had installed inside his house.

Watching how well Kendra treated Jace hadn't eased his anxiety, either. His sense of dread was so palpable that several of the brothers had noticed the change in him.

Shade and Viper had tried to tell him that it was just him being a new father, and that the trauma of losing his stepbrother and stepsister had traumatized him at such a young age that the fear had been transferred to losing Jace. Despite their talk, he couldn't be swayed by his decision. He had told them once they caught Pace's killer, he wouldn't work at the factory anymore. What work The Last Riders needed him to do, he could do over the Internet or once Larissa got home from work.

He had expected them to argue that he was being excessively protective over Jace, so he was surprised when they agreed with him that if he felt that strongly about Jace, they would do anything to ensure his safety. Shade had even installed state-of-art security around and within both Larissa's home and the one her family was living in, in case they decided to let Jace spend time there. Viper had also made an appointment with another pediatrician to check on Jace in case Larissa or Lana had missed something. Moon had sent Larissa and Kendra out on a Mother's Day outing for that appointment. Jace had been given a clean bill of health from the doctor, and Moon was told he had a growing, healthy baby.

Taking Jace's plump hand in his, Moon stared at the tiny hand that held his heart in such a small grasp. "I'll never let anything happen to you. I promise."

Jace blew bubbles up at him, wiggling his hand away to shove it in his toothless mouth.

Moon laughed. "If I switch the channel to *Karate Kid*, you going to tell Mama on me?" Taking his chance Jace wouldn't, he changed the channel. Then he picked up his phone and called Train.

"You finally decided to call?"

Why was Train breathing so heavily?

"Have they left yet?"

The music in the background was cranked up so loud that Moon took the call off speaker phone, not wanting to keep Jace from falling asleep.

"Who?"

"Who in the fuc ... do you think I'm talking about? Have Larissa and her family left yet?"

"I can barely hear you!" Train shouted. "You could have been asking if Jesus or Keller had left."

"Have Larissa and her family left?" he repeated irritably.

"Brother"—Train sounded as if he was moving away from the music—"Larissa left about fifteen minutes ago. She should be home in twenty."

"Thanks. Talk to you lat—"

"Brother." Train's voice stopped him from disconnecting the call.

"Yeah?" Moon adjusted Jace's head so it rested more comfortably on his arm.

"Larissa left, but her family is still here."

His grip tightened on the phone. "How's she getting home?"

"Jesus offered her a ride."

"Why didn't"—he started to yell, but Jace's eyes popped up. Giving him a gentle smile, he watched as Jace's eyes gradually closed again—"you call me?" he said in a softer voice.

"I'm not going to lie. Killyama caught me sending pictures to you, hid my phone, and threatened she'd whip their ass if anyone gave me theirs. I just found it when you called."

As angry as he was, Moon still had to ask, "Where did she hide it?"

"She was sitting on it."

# CHAPTER SIXTY-NINE

Holding on to Jesus' waist, she saw the lights of her house ahead. Finally, she was almost home.

The ride home on Jesus' motorcycle had been as much fun as going to church on a pretty Sunday—you wanted to go, but you knew you'd rather be doing something else. Or be with someone else, she clarified. Any joy of exhalation of riding that she had imagined experiencing with Moon had fallen short with Jesus.

He drove as if every bump in the road would send her flying off the motorcycle. She could have jogged faster than he drove.

As Jesus pulled into the driveway, Keller's motorcycle pulled in next to him. Both men turned their bikes off as she climbed off.

"Thank you, Jesus. I appreciate you both cutting short your evening to bring me home."

As she thanked Jesus, she saw his eyes move from hers to over her shoulder.

"No problem. Moon, how's it going?"

Turning, she found herself chest-to-chest with Moon.

The look of rage on his face made her take a step back. However, Jesus' hand on her back kept her from toppling over onto his lap.

When he saw that Jesus was touching her, Moon pulled her into his arms.

"What's wrong?" Larissa asked.

"You want to tell me how you left with your family yet ended up coming home with Jesus?"

Stunned that he was showing her a high and mighty attitude after she had caught him riding with Saffron today sent her blood simmering.

"They weren't ready to leave, and when Killyama saw Jesus and Keller were leaving, she asked them if they would bring me home so Mom and my sisters could stay."

"You should have called me, and I would have come and got you."

Her hands went to her hips. "Why on earth would I have you take the baby out to pick me up"—Larissa pointed at the baby monitor in his hand—"rather than me accepting a ride from Jesus?"

"Because he has the morals of a fucking alley cat, and he knows you're my old lady. Your ass has no business being on any motorcycle except mine."

She gaped at him. "You big hypocrite!" She angrily whacked him on his arrogant chest with her purse. "You're making a big deal of me riding with Jesus, yet you were all kissy face with Saffron!" she screeched at him.

"Yeah, I am!" he snarled. "And I was not all kissy face with Saffron!"

Her anger reached a boiling point. Normally, she would run a mile to keep from having an argument, but Moon being so blatantly unreasonable was more than her pacifist soul could take.

Spinning around, she faced Jesus. "Does this look kissy

face to you?" Before Jesus could jerk his face away, she pressed her cheek to his.

"What the fuck!"

Feeling Moon's hand on her forearm, she whacked him with her purse again as she stepped away from Jesus.

"Ouch! That fucking hurts," Moon complained, moving out of her reach.

"Good." Giving him a look of pure satisfaction, she turned back to the two men on their motorcycles. "Well?" she snapped.

Confusion filled their faces.

"Well what?"

"Did that look kissy-kissy to you?"

Jesus seemed unsure about the best way to reply, while Keller burst into laughter.

"Totally kissy-kissy," he agreed.

"See! I told you!" Turning, she went to walk past Moon, only to stop mid-stride to whack him again.

"Give me that." Snatching the small purse out of her hand, he raised it over his head, out of reach.

She refused to give him the pleasure of jumping for it, so she kicked him instead. "Keep it." Relishing the way he warily moved to the side when she continued on past him was the best part of her stinking day. "Why don't you shove it where the sun doesn't shine, you"—there were several names she could have used to describe what she thought of Moon, but she settled on the most appropriate one—"prick."

She stormed inside the house but caught herself before she slammed the door shut, not wanting to wake Jace.

Leaving the door ajar, she flounced angrily into her bedroom, coming to a stop when she saw Jace's crib was empty. Was he in the crib in the living room?

She was about to head to the living room when a thought entered her mind as she passed the nursey. Opening the door to Jace's room, she saw the small lamp on his bureau was on. The room was dim, but she could easily see Jace sleeping in his crib.

Crossing the room, she smiled lovingly at her son. As he slept with a crunched-up face, he looked so much like Moon that she felt tears swimming in her eyes. She wanted to pick him up for a cuddle but restrained herself, turning instead to tiptoe quietly from the room, only to come to a stop at seeing Moon in the doorway.

Brushing past him, she went into their room and pulled a nightgown out of her dresser.

"Are you planning to ignore me for the rest of the night?"

He was standing in the middle of the room with his arms crossed over his chest as if waiting for an apology. It blew her mind.

Imitating him, she stood like him. "If you're waiting for an apology, you're not going to get it." She kept her voice low even though Moon had closed their door. She was done letting him see how much she cared about him riding with Saffron. "I'm the one who deserves an apology."

Conflicting emotions crossed his face. "You had no business being on Jesus' bike, or any motorcycle for that matter," he stated calmly.

"Why not?" She raised her hands in defeat at what he'd said. "You certainly weren't going to take me."

Moon nodded. "No, I wasn't."

"Why?" Hurt that he refused to let her ride with him while he let another do so sliced through her. It showed he was never going to share the more important parts of his life with her. "You don't want people in town seeing us together?"

"Don't be ridiculous. People see us together when we go out," he argued back.

"We haven't gone out together since Jace was born. Are

you with Saffron and you don't want to tell me because of Jace?"

Moon raked a hand through his hair. "Larissa, there are parts of the club I can't discuss with you. Saffron being on my bike today is one of them."

"What in the heck does that mean?"

"Club business is kept private."

"So, you're not allowed to tell me?"

"No."

"Does it go for all of the women or just me?"

"The rest of the women belong to the club."

"And I don't?"

"No."

"I see." Her crossed arms dropped to her waist. Turning, she stared down at the nightgown dangling from her hand.

"I don't think you do."

Hearing his frustrated sigh only heightened her awareness that Moon would never let her into his world, that he only wanted to allow her into a small part of his life, and she wouldn't have been allowed in at all if she hadn't gotten pregnant with Jace.

"All the women are Last Riders. They attend church meetings, are willing to accept the rules of the club, and when they break the rules, they accept the punishment."

Listening, Larissa turned back to face him.

"They accept that Viper has the final say-so over our lives as long as we belong to the club," Moon continued. "They keep their mouths shut with whatever goes down because they know if one falls, we all fall." Moon paused.

Letting him talk without interrupting to ask questions was hard, but he was filling her in on some of the blanks she'd been wondering about. When he paused, she could tell he was debating leaving out something, but when his eyes met hers, she mentally prepared herself. Something told her that she wasn't going to like what he was about to tell her.

"To become a Last Rider, there are certain requirements. The men have to fight six of the original members."

Thank goodness she wasn't a man, was all she could think. She had seen most of The Last Riders; she could imagine the damage having to fight so many would cause.

"There are also requirements for the women to become members."

Was she willing to fight six women for the right to become a Last Rider? Maybe, she mused, if one of those women was kissy face Saffron.

She straightened to her full height to show him that she wasn't scared, which she was, but she didn't want him to know. Would they give her time to take fighting lessons?

"How many women would I have to fight?" she asked with more confidence than she felt.

"You don't have to fight any women. Actually, fighting between the women is prohibited. They could get thrown out."

Whew, thank God. They would have stomped her ass.

Larissa tried to look disappointed, but she didn't think Moon bought it.

"That's a shame. I can think of at least one woman I wouldn't mind fighting."

Moon's lips curled in amusement. "You wouldn't be allowed to use a purse."

She made a face at him. "Then what do the women have to do? Do a bake-off? Clean the clubhouse? I'm warning you now that I would rather fight six of the men than clean a clubhouse, or the men's clothes, or clean their bathrooms."

"I can't guarantee you wouldn't have to do any of the cleaning, laundry, or cooking. We all get a weekly chore list, the women and the brothers."

Larissa narrowed her eyes at him. "So, what else do the women have to do to become members?"

"They have to fuck or give a climax to six of the eight brothers who are allowed to give votes."

She felt her jaw drop open. "You're kidding."

Moon didn't say anything. He didn't have to—his expression said it all.

Clearing her suddenly dry throat, she slung her nightgown over her shoulder. "You know what, Moon?" She cleared her throat again. "It occurs to me that I don't need to know The Last Riders' club business. I have to maintain patient confidentiality as a healthcare provider; I would resent you if you asked me to break that confidence. How about we just forget I asked and move on?"

Taking baby steps to the side, she tried to be as inconspicuous as possible, wanting to make it into the bathroom and end this embarrassing conversation.

Had Lily fulfilled the requirements? She must have ... Damn, those still waters ran deep ... Winter, too? Ginny? Her mind raced as the women who belonged to The Last Riders came to mind.

Her eyes flew to Moon's as another thought clicked into place. Her hand fisted the bottom of her gown, and her voice went dangerously low. "How many of the women members have you given your vote to?"

Moon took a step back. "I haven't counted."

"Don't you dare lie to me." She started pacing back and forth around the bedroom. "Oh, God. Oh, God." Coming to a stop in front of him, she tilted her head back to glare at him. "How many?" she whisper-screamed.

"I ... didn't ..." He held his hands up in the air, pretending to push down. "Calm down."

"Don't tell me to calm down." She spoke too quietly. Moon had to lower his head to hear her. "Not only did you give them your vote, you had sex with them more than one time, didn't you?"

"Larissa, go take your sh—"

"In fact"—her fist went to rest on her hip as she took a step closer until they were chest-to-chest—"you can have sex with them any ole time you want, can't you?"

"I can." Moon put a hand up again, trying to calm her down. "But I haven't since you—"

"Since I came to Treepoint from Bowling Green?" she finished for him.

"I haven't. I swear." At least he'd managed to keep his dick …

Another thought occurred to her.

"Have you kissed a woman?"

She knew he had before he opened his mouth.

Fury hit her like a tornado. One second, she was standing there, and the next, she was whaling on any part of his body she could reach.

"You son of a bitch," she hissed. "I'm never going to kiss you again."

At first, Moon just stood there, as if stunned. His hesitation nearly cost him the ability to father more children in the future. At the last second, he must have read the vindictive gleam in her eyes and moved, narrowly being nailed in the groin.

"Whoa. That's playing dirty."

"Isn't that right up your alley?" Moving a few steps back, she tugged the nightgown off her shoulder to fold it in half. Then she started twirling it in her hands.

Moon's eyes widened. "What are you going to do with that?"

"Guess."

Before he could react, she snapped the gown out, hitting him on the hip. Too late, she came to her senses at what she had done.

Instead of being angry like she'd expected, Moon seemed overjoyed. His reaction scared the bejesus out of her.

She spun to run into the bathroom, but a whimper coming from the baby monitor had her jerking to a stop.

Moon was standing right in front of the bedroom door, blocking her path. From the unholy grin on Moon's face, he knew the cards had turned in his favor.

"Go take your shower." When she would have argued, his eyes dipped to her breasts. "I'll change Jace and bring him in so you can feed him."

Looking down, she hastily raised her hands to her breasts. The damp spots on the front of her sundress made her rush into the bathroom.

She quickly took her dress off and stepped into the shower. What had gotten into her? She had been fighting her jealousy ever since she had seen Moon with Saffron on his motorcycle, and when he appeared outside when she arrived home as if he was some avenging angel, it had struck her last nerve.

It wasn't a big deal when a woman rode on his motorcycle, yet when the tables were turned …? Then finding how the women became members put the icing on the cake. Was he one of the members who could give a vote? If so, how many women had he voted for? She had been aware the women there were available to the men but had assumed he hadn't been with them *all*.

Why should he be content with her when he could have the whole candy store anytime he wanted?

Raising her face to the water, she let the first tears of the night escape.

Because she didn't want to let Jace become impatient and Moon warm him a bottle, she turned off the shower to dry off.

Sliding on a mid-length cream, pink flower robe, she knotted it at her waist. Facing Moon again after her outburst wasn't going to be easy. Bolstering herself that maybe by the time she was finished nursing Jace, the big lug would be asleep, she opened the bathroom door. If not, she promised herself to be the calm, reasonable, sweet-tempered woman she normally was, even if it killed her.

# CHAPTER SEVENTY

As they lay side by side on the bed, Moon was reading a story to his son when he heard Larissa slowly open the bathroom door. He watched from the corner of his eyes as she hesitated walking to the bed, and there was no doubt in his mind what lured her toward the bed was Jace, her mother's love overriding having to come anywhere near him. She was a smart cookie who realized the argument they had engaged in was far from over.

Oh no, it wasn't.

It was everything he could do not to give a satisfied grin when she hesitantly climbed into the opposite side of the bed.

Before tonight, he had no idea Larissa could be such a termagant when she became angry enough. He liked it a lot. She was damn lucky Jace had woken up when he had. If he hadn't, she would have found herself on the bed with her legs over his shoulders.

Damn, she was a spitfire when she was roused and allowed herself to escape from whatever intellectual head-space she was more comfortable staying in.

Kendra had actually done him a big favor when she revealed how smart Larissa was. He had delved deeper into Larissa's background and looked further past the degrees she had accomplished. In the file he had hastily compiled on Larissa, he had discovered she was extremely intelligent. After what Kendra had said, he dug deeper and found a mind-blowing eye-opener.

There was average intelligence, which, from his first reports, he had known she had taken several gifted classes through her school years. Hell, he had taken several gifted classes himself.

Rolling to his side, he watched as Larissa parted her robe and unsnapped the front of her gown, exposing the engorged nipple to the seeking mouth. Larrissa had raised Jace to a sitting position on a pillow while she lay on her side with pillows behind her back. Lovingly cupping the back of Jace's head, she ran her fingers over his scalp as he fed.

Curious, Moon wondered if Larissa was aware just how smart she was, or had Kendra held back the information? It couldn't have been easy for the widowed mother of three to find out all three of her daughters had more than their fair share of intelligence.

Lana being classified as moderately gifted must have been her first clue that Larissa was following in that direction. How had she reacted when she found out Larissa was more than moderately gifted and had tested profoundly gifted? When people said a person was one in a million, Larissa literally was.

Schools and academic think tanks had scrambled to vie for Larissa's capabilities. Something must have happened when Larissa had turned ten, though, because Kendra stopped letting her participate in any gifted programs other than those offered by their school district.

He wasn't sure, but if he had to guess, it was because

Kendra hadn't wanted Larissa's childhood stolen from her. Either that or, with her spending so much time on academics, had Larissa shown delays in other areas of her life? Was that why there weren't as many pictures of Larissa as there were of Lana and Priss? Kendra could have recognized Larissa was spending most of her time on academics and couldn't experience the same normal situations her sisters were going through. If she did, Moon had to give her credit for making that hard choice. It couldn't have been an easy decision to make.

If she had let Larissa continue on the path she had been on, would Larissa be here in Treepoint, or would she be working at some prestigious university, or more than likely a branch of the government determined to use her capabilities for their own purposes?

When he looked at the natural way Larissa switched Jace to her other breast, his gut clenched. Not only had Kendra changed the course of Larissa's life, she had changed his.

"You have to be tired." Larissa's soft voice dragged him out of his thoughts. "You can turn the light off and leave the lamp on. I won't disturb you when I put Jace back to bed."

"I'm not tired."

"If you're not tired—"

Moon almost burst into laughter when Larissa covered her mouth as she yawned.

"—you can take care of Jace while I go to sleep."

"I would be happy to. Of course, that means I'll have to wake you up after I put him to bed."

Her eyes widened. "I'm tired."

"You tire yourself out trying to kick my ass?" he asked ironically.

"I have to work in the morning."

"As do I."

"That's why I suggested you should go to sleep."

Moon quirked an eyebrow at her. "Not because you're afraid after you swatted me with a nightgown and hit me with your purse?"

"I apologize. I shouldn't have, but you provoked me."

"*I* provoked you? I think it was the other way around."

"You had no right to be upset I rode home with Jesus."

"I had every right." Raising his hand, he brushed his knuckles over Jace's cheek. His son was suckling, as if he hadn't just emptied the spare.

"Killyama said you don't. You broke the rule first."

"Technically, I didn't. You're not a Last Rider."

"Nor do I want to be."

Moon saw the hurt look in her eyes before she lowered her lashes. "I don't get how it's okay for me to have sex with six of The Last Riders, but heaven forbid I ride home with one of them. That makes no sense to me."

"It doesn't matter if it makes sense to you; it makes perfect sense to me, and that's what counts."

"Fine." Her eyes turned into a tempest of emotions. Damn, she made his dick hard as granite when she lost her temper. "Pick the six I should have sex with, and I will. Or better yet, how about I just follow the example you set with the women and do all of the men?"

Moon could tell from her strained voice that if Jace weren't in the room, her voice would have had his ears ringing.

Giving a low laugh, Moon spurred her on even more. "You'd give up after two."

Larissa rose to lift Jace off the bed and into her arms, glaring at him as she burped him. Moon kept his face impassive, knowing it was pissing her the hell off.

"I may surprise you." The look she gave him over Jace's head was definitely threatening.

"I love surprises."

Turning Jace around, she picked up the book he had laid down on the bed and started reading it to the baby.

"If you're *really* interested in getting votes, the club has parties every Friday night. Anyone can go to the parties to scope out if they want to join."

Larissa broke off reading. "Do they do more than *scoping it out?*"

"Occasionally." He could practically see the wheels turning in her head. "Before you start accusing me, remember where my ass has been every Friday night since you came back to Treepoint."

She started reading again.

"So," he drawled out, "you want to go, or are you all talk?"

"Wild horses wouldn't keep me away," she snapped. "Now, will you let me finishing reading to Jace?"

"Of course," he replied magnanimously. "In a sec. I have to work late on Friday—we have a truck we have to load—but you can meet me there. You're going to have a fun time this weekend. We're having a masquerade party."

"Where do we get the clothes?"

Shrugging, he started massaging Jace's little foot. "No clue. I wasn't planning on going. I'll probably figure something out."

"What should I wear—"

He shook his head at her. "How about we surprise each other? You know how much I love surprises. Besides, I don't imagine anyone puts a big effort into what their wearing. It's more how great you look wearing as little as possible." He threw in a salacious wink to really piss her off.

Seeing her hand tighten on the book she was holding, Moon prepared himself to be bopped with the picture book.

He held back his grin when she started reading again, then took out his cell phone and started scrolling through the news. Occasionally, he would glance over and see Jace was still wide awake. It was almost midnight before he noticed Jace's eyelids begin to droop.

"You should put him to bed. He's almost out," Moon suggested in a firm voice.

"There's only one page left of the story."

"Put him to bed, Larissa. We both have to work in the morning."

Throwing him a dirty look, she got out of the bed.

He waited until she was in front of the bed before he set her off again by saying, "Put Jace to bed in the nursey, Larissa."

She stopped in her tracks. "Since when?" she argued. "You're the one who wants him to sleep in here at night."

"Tonight, I think we have a little business to settle. Take him to the nursey."

"Okay, I will."

The firecracker had agreed too quickly to fool him. She might be smarter, but he was wiser.

"Oh, and Larissa," he softly called out before she could get through the door. "Don't be too long. You don't want me to come looking for you."

# CHAPTER SEVENTY-ONE

"Seriously?"

Coming to an abrupt stop in the bedroom doorway after putting Jace down, Larissa gaped at Moon. The big doofus had removed his sweatpants and was sitting naked in the middle of the bed.

She shut the bedroom door and tried to think of disgusting creatures, like snails, snakes, and spiders, to keep from gawking at Moon.

*Why?* she mentally cried out. *Why does he have the power to melt my body into molten lava?*

*It's just not fair!* she whined.

"Come to Papa." He grinned wickedly.

Balefully, she pretended uninterest while her reproductive parts were yelling at her to get her some.

She walked to the side of the bed, then flipped the blanket over to cover his hardened cock. "Mama not in the mood." Reaching for a pillow, she shoved it under her arm. "I can't believe you think I'm going to sleep with you tonight. From what you said, I already have your vote. I need to save my strength for Friday. I'm going to be very busy ... Why don't you go see if Ms. Kissy Face has room for you in her bed?" Proud of herself for keeping her voice low and even, she gave him a dismissive glance.

"But I don't want to fuck Saffron; I want to fuck you."

Unable to help herself, she turned around to give him an obscene gesture. "Just in case you don't read sign language"— she disdainfully turned back to the door—"allow me to translate for you—go fuck yourself."

She would sleep on the floor before she would sleep with that big—

"Don't you want to know who I kissed, since I'm being so honest tonight?"

She spun around, snapping her fingers at him. "I don't give a fig who you kissed. Kiss her a thousand times and see if I care—"

"It was Chastity."

Drawing a blank, she frowned at him. Did she know anyone named Chastity? She didn't think so ...

"The saleswomen at the baby boutique."

"You didn't!" Her hand clenched the pillow.

"I did."

Outrage filled her. The woman's seductive demeanor came back to her in a rush. Unconsciously, she took a step back toward the bed.

"At the store?"

"Nope." Moon's eyes moved to her feet. "I went to her apartment."

Larissa was surprised she didn't feel hurt. No, she was too furious to be hurt.

"Did. You. Have. Sex." With each word, she took a step closer to the bed. "With. Her?"

"No." His grin widened. "But I did get to first base."

One second, she was standing beside the bed, and the next, she was hitting him with the pillow.

"I'm never going to be able to go to that store again! I'll have to drive to Lexington!"

She was whaling on him with the pillow when she heard his laughter.

"You're laughing at me?"

"Yes." He started laughing harder. "You do know that pillow is ultra soft, right?"

Losing what sanity she was hanging on to, she clenched the pillow with both hands and flew at him. Squeezing her eyes closed, she tried to smother the cheating prick.

"What are you trying to do?"

Her eyes popped open. "Smothering you!"

Moon snatched the pillow away and threw it across the room.

She didn't let it deter her from getting even. But when she swung her fist at his mouth, she found it grasped in Moon's hand. Failing at the first attempt, she swung her other fist, only to have it caught, too.

"I hope your lips rot off," she spat out vindictively.

Since both her hands were trapped, she was left with no recourse. She lowered her head and bit him on the shoulder.

His laughter strangled in his throat.

*"Damn,* woman, you get vicious when you're roused. *I like it."*

Stricken at what she had done, she raised her mouth and tried to jump off Moon and run from the room.

"Nuh-uh." Clicking his tongue at her, Moon rolled over and pulled her underneath him. "You've been a naughty girl all night. That's twice you've bitten me." He pinned her hands to the mattress, then started scrunching down her body.

"I only bit you once." Struggling against him, she tried to throw him off her. Apprehensively, she watched as he shouldered his way between her thighs.

"Did you forget the first time we fucked?"

She had.

"I'm sorry," she apologized around the lump in her throat.

"Don't. I don't mind you getting a little rough." Moon nuzzled her bunched-up robe and nightgown aside to slide his mouth over her smooth, shaven pelvic area.

She tensed when his tongue parted her cleft. Then he ran his tongue down each side before turning his mouth in a new direction. When Moon laved his way to her inner thigh, she tried to wiggle her hands out of his grip.

"Now, now ..." he said in a crooning voice, "fair is fair."

Despite the warning, she jumped when he bit down. The biting nip barely hurt in comparison to the passion that hit her with the force of a hurricane.

"That's one," he purred against her skin. Then, when he turned his head to reach her other thigh, she braced herself for his next bite.

She was unaware he had released one of wrists until he started rubbing her clitoris. Instead of using her free hand to stop him, she stifled her passionate cries, not wanting to wake Jace.

When the next bite came, she was helpless to stop the climax that erupted, sending her into an ecstasy she didn't want to come back from.

When she regained her senses, she found herself fully impaled by Moon's cock. She threw her back into the maelstrom she had just escaped from, clinging to Moon as he carried her away on another frenzied, storm-ridden journey into oblivion.

"Kiss me ..."

Moon's raspy command dragged her back to reality.

"No. I'm never going—" A low moan escaped her at a fervent thrust.

"I only kissed Chastity for some information I needed."

Her eyes searched his. "What kind of information?"

"That's on a need-to-know basis." His hands went to her hips, setting a pace that had her wanting to return to the beckoning oblivion. "I would have rather kissed a fucking garden snake than her. Now kiss me."

She arched her neck to keep her lips out of reach of his descending mouth.

Not deterred, his lips seared the flesh on her neck.

"I didn't have to tell you."

"Why did you?" she gasped out.

Moon gave a throaty chuckle. "Two reasons. One, to light your fuse—you're a firecracker when you get mad."

Furious he was admitting to deliberately creating an argument, she started pummeling his shoulders. "I can't stand you sometimes."

Moon retaliated by biting down on her shoulder.

Her core turned into a pool of aching need. Striving to keep herself from losing all rational thought, she fought to keep track of what he had said.

Her hands went to his hair, making him raise his face so she could search his eyes. "You said there were two reasons."

"I'd rather be the one to tell you, in case she ever decides to."

"You're covering your ass."

"I'm covering yours." His expression became harsh. "If you did find out, I'd rather you take it all out on me than let her see you hurt."

She stopped hitting him, trying to think through what he had said. It wasn't easy to do with Moon's body moving erotically inside of her.

"I'm never going to forgive you."

"Did I ask you to?"

She frowned up at him. No, he hadn't.

"Good, because I won't. I'm never going to kiss you again, either."

"Not even"—his lips smoothed over the bite on her shoulder—"if I promise to save all my kisses for you from now on?"

She swallowed hard at the promise. As heartbreaking as it was to find out he had kissed another woman, he hadn't had sex with her in months. He'd said there was a reason, he just wouldn't tell her what it was.

Killyama had been mum about certain things about the club when she had gone to her house during her pregnancy. Was that why all the women joined the club—to keep tabs on their men?

She had no intention of going to that party or joining the club, but Moon didn't know that. But what if she did go, just to find out if he had engaged in more than a lone salesclerk? With it being a masquerade party, it could be illuminating what she could find out. And if she found out he had been spreading more than his kisses around? Then kisses wouldn't be all he wouldn't be getting from her anymore.

"I'll think about it."

While denying herself his passionate kiss, she wasn't able to withstand the driving force of his cock pushing over and over inside of her. Unable to continue to resist his raw passion, she succumbed to the dark bliss waiting in Moon's arms …

# CHAPTER SEVENTY-TWO

"I'm not wearing that."

Larissa picked up one of the delicate sleeves of the costume Moon had spread out on the bed then let it fall back down.

Moon reached out to snag Jace's hand before he could grab the slinky material.

"I am not wearing lime green." She shuddered at the thought of the bright color against her skin tone; it wasn't her only complaint about the mini dress. "I don't know what you were thinking. The top is a halter—one of my boobs wouldn't fit in the whole top."

"You're exaggerating," Moon scoffed at her, giving Jace one of his toys to play with. "It's not like you have much to choose from. The party is tomorrow night."

"Have you decided what you're going to wear?"

"No clue. You have any ideas?"

"Several," she answered snidely.

"Your mama is being mean to me again." Woefully, Moon made a sad face for Jace's benefit.

"Cut it out." She picked up the creepy green mask with

feathers before Jace could drool on it, then put it in the nightstand drawer.

"Sorry, your mother is being callous to me again. Better?"

She moved to the foot of the bed, and her hands went to her hips. "You think you're being so cute, don't you?"

Moon gave her an offended look. "You don't think I'm cute?"

"Several four-letter words comes to mind where you're concerned, and *cute* isn't one of them."

"Ouch." Moon turned his face back to Jace. "You hear that, son? That's called being facetious."

Larissa raised her hands in defeat. "Spare me. I'm going to fix dinner."

In the kitchen, she took out roasted chicken cutlets and started fixing lemon chicken. As she prepared the meal, she mulled over what costumes she could wear. Even if she found one on the Internet, it wouldn't get here in time. That left her with two choices—clothing she already had, or she could borrow one from Mom, Priss, or Lana. The only other option was to sew one together. Mom had taught her at an early age, and she had made a couple of tops and dresses, so if she found a pattern she liked, that would be her best bet.

After dinner, she found the website she was searching for. Moon kept Jace occupied as she searched, but when she failed to find anything she was brave enough to wear, she took a break to feed Jace and put him to bed.

When she walked out of the bedroom, she saw Moon set the monitor aside before he resumed watching an episode of their favorite series.

"Did I do it to your expectations?" She lifted a lone finger then started counting off. "I put on his sock, checked to make sure it was on, made sure nothing was in the crib with him, and double-checked to make sure the window was locked."

Moon's eyes didn't stray from the television screen. "I'm just being cautious."

Larissa dropped onto the sofa, pulling the laptop onto her lap. "You're being a nut. I thought you would quit being so overprotective after a couple of months. Instead, you're getting worse."

"I am not," Moon denied.

Unconsciously, she nibbled on her bottom lip. Why were women's costumes made to show more body parts than they covered?

"I'm waiting to come home from work one day and find you've put him a plastic bubble."

"They sell those?"

Sending him a harassed look, she went back to searching for a pattern. It was hard to concentrate with the show on. Moon had introduced her to it. At first, she had been disgusted with the extreme violence and would read while the show played in the background. Until she got an eyeful of the main character when his costume had come off. The actor, and his body, was ooh la la.

She had even secretly googled the actor, which she had never done before. From what she could find out, he was a new actor and was taking the world by storm. The show's producer had sighted the then unknown actor at a bar with his friends and had approached him. Now fans were lining up for his appearances.

The craziest thing about it was that no one knew what the actor's face looked like. On screen, it was always covered, even during the sex scenes, while his body was bare.

"You hear my question?"

Dragging her eyes away from the visually stunning man on the television screen to the big doofus sitting on the couch had her yet again questioning her life choices.

"I heard. I was just trying to ignore you. You are not going to put Jace in a bubble."

"I was joking."

Larissa lowered her eyelids to half-mast.

"Never mind." Moon rose from the couch. "I'm going to make some popcorn; do you want some?"

"No, thanks." If she was going to fit in any of the costumes she was looking at, she was going to have to starve until the party.

"You sure? If you do, I'll make an extra bag."

"I'm sure."

She went back to watching the show, the aroma of popcorn tempting her.

"Make me a bag," she called out.

Ignoring Moon rolling his eyes at her, she became engrossed in the show.

The main warlord had just picked a woman from his harem to spend the night with him. Poor thing didn't know one of the other women was killing off anyone unlucky enough to please the warlord.

Absentmindedly taking the popcorn from Moon, she continued watching.

"Please," Moon snorted from her side. "That is so fake. You can tell the actress isn't into the scene."

"She seems pretty into it from my viewpoint," Larissa said around a mouthful of popcorn.

"Nah," he criticized. "The dude must have bad breath."

"I can guarantee you she doesn't care." Opening her can of sparkling water, she took a sip. "I'd kiss him."

Moon gave her a dirty look. "He's not into it, either. His dick is as limp as a dead shrimp."

Her hand paused in the popcorn bag. "Shrimp? That's a mackerel."

"My bad. I wasn't staring a hole through the television. I can't believe you'd kiss him."

"Why not? He hasn't been French kissing Chastity."

"You're never going to let me live that down, are you?"

"Nope."

"It was a just a kiss that may have lasted a couple of minutes. She wasn't even that good."

"Hmm. I'm curious, does Jesus have the right to vote?"

Moon opened his can of beer. "No."

She would have to ask Killyama. Something told her that Moon was lying through his cheating teeth.

"Who do you think is better at riding a motorcycle—Jesus or you?"

"Me. Why?"

Shoving another handful of popcorn in her mouth to keep from laughing at Moon's jealous expression, she continued to bait him. "Just curious."

"Well, you can stop. You won't be riding with the brother again."

"You can't stop me. If he offers, I will."

"He won't be offering."

Larissa frowned at him. "Why not?"

Moon gave her a satisfied grin. "Because when I went into work this morning, I told him it would be hazardous to his health."

"You didn't."

"I did."

The smug look on his face made her clench her can.

"I wouldn't," Moon warned, "unless you want me find out how many times I have to paddle your ass before you beg me to stop, then I would fuck you until you had to crawl out of bed."

"You wouldn't dare."

"Try me."

Larissa set the can down on the table. "You wish."

"You were much easier to deal with when you were scared of me."

Deciding it would be more prudent to ignore Moon, she watched the show without baiting him further. Damn, she was going to have to take a cold shower. A slight movement from Moon reminded her that he was still there. Why should she have to take a shower?

As the credits rolled, she eyed Moon. Her desire took a nosedive, however, when she saw him using a toothpick to dig the kernels out of his teeth.

Moon stopped what he was doing to stare at her curiously. "You need something?"

"No. I'm good."

He stretched his arms, yawning. Rising, he rubbed his abdomen as if he had eaten too much. "I'm going to hit the shower and have an early night. I didn't get much sleep last night," he wisecracked.

"Good night."

"Good luck finding your costume."

She balefully watched him leave when he didn't attempt to kiss her good night, only his threat keeping her from beaning him with the empty can.

Disappointed, she started scrolling through the costumes again. She was at the point of just calling it a night and go as a nun. Her lips twitched as she imagined The Last Riders' reaction if she did. There wouldn't be any votes going on. The only thing stopping her from deciding that was the costume was that it was much too Halloween-y.

When she found another site, she sat up straight. *Persistence pays off*, she crowed to herself. Crossing her fingers, she pulled the pattern up. It didn't seem too complicated. The problem was: could she finish it in time? The closest fabric store was in Jamestown. If she could talk her mother into coming in early in the morning, she could be back in Treep-oint by her first appointment. She could then work the pattern when at work.

Cheerful, she got off the couch, disposing of the two empty popcorn bags and cans. She felt much better about going to the party now since none of The Last Riders would know it was her under the costume.

She quietly walked into their bedroom to check on Jace. From the hall light, she could see Moon lying sprawled out on the bed, wearing a pair of black underwear that hugged his gorgeous ass.

*Damn.*

She pursed her lips in disappointment at seeing the underwear, which he had started wearing after Jace's birth; she had hoped they would be back in his drawer after last night.

That wasn't the only disappointment she was dealing with. He was sound asleep. Here she was, all wired up from watching the scrumptious warlord, while he was out like a light.

Tempted to slam the door shut, she had to settle for making a face at him to keep from waking Jace.

Walking through the dark, she went to the bathroom. After showering, she changed into her nightgown before climbing in next to Moon. Shoving him over to make more room for herself, she glared at the dark ceiling when he didn't wake.

Feeling vindictive, she wondered if he would wake up if she rolled him off the bed. She then gave herself a stern lecture.

What happened to the kind, sweet woman she used to be? She had been the least temperamental woman in her family. What had happened to change her?

Moon had.

Mr. Hot Lips had run over her feelings with his stupid motorcycle, playing kissy face with Saffron.

*You've got to get a grip, Larissa,* she told herself.

*I will, after I find out for sure he hasn't been cheating at the club.*

*What if he has?*

Then Moon would be the first Last Rider to actually make it to the actual moon, courtesy of a one-way rocket, and she was just smart enough to do it.

# CHAPTER SEVENTY-THREE

"You look fantastic." Priss gave a complimentary whistle. "All the women will be jealous."

Mesmerized by her reflection, she was amazed at not only finishing the costume but that it had come out nearly as good as the picture on the website.

"You think so?" How would it feel to be the one envied this time? She could count on one hand how many parties she had attended in her life and still have two fingers left over. One, she had left in tears when she was ten, and the other two, she had left after a couple of hours.

"Oh, yes!" Priss assured her. "Doesn't she, Lana?"

When Lana didn't answer, Larissa looked at her sitting on the bed, texting on her phone.

"Lana?" Larissa tried to draw her sister's attention. "Is there a problem with one of your patients?"

"Sorry," she apologized. "I was checking on a patient's status."

Larissa could tell Lana was concerned. "Anything I can do?"

Lana's gaze shied away from hers. "I'll let you know."

Her sister had been acting weird ever since she had come over with Priss. Larissa had never seen her so distracted where a patient was concerned. Working in the emergency room, Lana was much better at remaining emotionally detached from patients than she was. If patients needed aftercare or to be hospitalized, they were handed over to other physicians. Lana must have taken an interest in the patient for her to be checking on their progress so often.

Either that or she didn't agree with Priss.

Would she be making a fool of herself?

"I like the outfit. I just don't know if it would be considered a masquerade costume. I think it looks more Halloween-y."

Untying the red scarf at her neck, she unfurled it to expose the two holes she had sewn into the material. She situated it over her eyes and tied it at the back of her head. "Better? I didn't want to scare Jace in case Mom brought him in here."

"Sure."

Lana's tactful comment had Larissa regretting her choice of costume for the umpteenth time.

"Maybe I shouldn't go. I only said I would go because I lost my temper with Moon."

"That'd be a good idea—"

"Don't be ridiculous. You look great." Priss walked to the bed to snatch Lana's cell phone away. "It's a masquerade party at a motorcycle club. I bet most of them will be wearing Halloween costumes. You're making a big deal over a party where their main goal is to get laid."

"That's not *my* goal," Larissa said hollowly.

"Of course not," Priss assured her. "Yours is to make sure Moon isn't buttering anyone's roll."

Her lips parted. "You think he is?"

"Oh my God! No!" Priss gave her and Lana irritated glowers as she fought to keep Lana from snatching her cell phone back.

"Quit worrying about the hospital, Lana. You're not on duty. In case you're not paying attention, we're having an emergency here." Giving Lana her phone back, Priss then gave her a threatening glance when she tried to open it again.

Lana shoved the phone into her purse. Her silent perusal made her wish she were still reading her messages. But then Lana gave her a thumbs-up.

"I love it! You wearing the scarf as a mask totally works."

As far as reassurances went, it sucked, but she was out of time. Killyama had promised to meet her at the clubhouse so she wouldn't have to go in alone.

Turning back to the mirror, she wanted to pat herself on the back for getting the costume finished in time. She ran her hand over the silky material of the sleeve. She could hardly wait to see what Moon had to say about her costume. Untying the scarf at the back of her head, she re-tied it at her throat.

Priss came up behind her to fluff up the back of her hair where she had messed it up before giving it an extra coating of hairspray.

Lana crossed one leg over the other as she watched. "Did Moon tell you what he's wearing?"

Larissa swatted the can away. "No. He wants to keep it a surprise."

Turning from the mirror, she saw Lana staring at Priss and her suspiciously.

She flushed when Lana didn't buy the bill of goods she was selling, which earned a shove from Priss.

"All right," she started to admit, moving away from Priss

before she could be shoved again. "I called Killyama, and she finagled it out of Train for me. He's going as some guy who all the women on the Internet are crazy about. His costume consists of a pair of sweatpants, with his underwear band showing, a cap, and a hula hoop."

Both of them stared at her as if they thought she was joking.

"Huh?" Priss asked.

"You're joking?" Lana seemed just as confused. "How is that a masquerade costume?"

She had been just as clueless when Killyama had told her.

"I'm not joking." Lifting her cell phone off the nightstand, she pulled up Moon's inspiration. Pressing *Play* on the screen, she turned the phone toward Priss and Lana.

Priss sat down next to Lana on the bed.

"Wow." Lana raised her eyes to meet hers. "Is Moon that limber?"

Larissa rolled her eyes. "If he is, he damn sure hasn't shown me."

The man on the video jumped up to grab the branch of a tree. Then, holding the limb with one hand, he raised his legs until he made an L shape. Sliding the hoop over his feet, the man then settled the hoop around his waist before dropping his legs again. When he put his now free hand back on the tree limb, the hoop started twirling at the jerking movements of his hips.

"The guy does resemble Moon," Lana observed. "I wish the front of his hat didn't shield his face."

Priss gave a slow smile. "Me and you both, sister. You sure you're not holding out on us, sis?"

"Moon's tattoos are different than this guy's. Besides, Moon might be good-looking, but coordinated, he isn't."

All three women watched the video for several minutes.

Finally, Larissa was able to tear her gaze away from the gyrating hips.

"Moon would get a concussion trying to do that trick," she told her sisters sarcastically. "He nearly broke his neck climbing a ladder to change a light bulb in the hallway."

Priss kept her gaze centered on the phone. "What time are you two leaving for the party? I might hang around for a while."

Larissa turned the phone around to see the influencer had dropped from the limb to use the hoop as a jump rope. The guy was a physical specimen that, as a doctor, she wouldn't mind researching to find his genetic code … to replicate it for the good of women worldwide.

Closing her phone, she put it in the pocket of her jacket. "Save yourself the trouble. He's working late, and he doesn't even know when he'll get off. Killyama promised to stick with me until he shows." She fiddled with her scarf again. "I wanted to go late, but he told me that he's going to beg Shade to let them get off early if they don't take a break."

"Hmm." Priss gave her a sympathetic look, which she didn't believe for a second. "I could throw a costume together and go, too."

She didn't believe for a second Priss' motive was selfless, but Larissa didn't discount the idea. She would feel more comfortable with Priss there.

"What would you wear?"

"A hula hoop."

Lana started laughing so hard she fell back on the bed.

"Har, har." Glowering at Priss, Larissa went to her vanity to pick up the lipstick she would be wearing. She would put it on before walking into the clubhouse. "You're just a barrel of laughs."

Lana rose up, wiping her tears of laughter away. "She

wasn't joking. I can see her wrapped around Moon all night. Be careful, Larissa. Priss might steal your Last Rider."

"*Hmph*," she snorted. "She'll give him back when she realizes how much popcorn he goes through. And I certainly don't see her putting up with his weird habits."

"Like what?" Priss asked dubiously.

"At night, he's constantly checking on Jace. He's only let him sleep in the nursery one night since he's been born. He's got cameras all over the place, except for the bathrooms and our bedroom, and thinks I don't know."

From Priss' expression, nothing she was saying was a big enough turnoff to change her mind about wanting to see if Moon would exhibit his skills using the hula hoop at the party. It was time to pull out the big guns.

"And he never puts the toilet seat down."

"Never mind." Priss wrinkled her nose. "I'd rather stay home and read a good book. Killyama will be there. You can talk to her until Moon gets there."

"Are you sure?" Larissa guiltily adjusted her scarf. "I wouldn't mind if you went."

"I would stop while you're ahead."

Deciding to take Lana's advice, she headed for the bedroom door with her purse and cell phone.

In the living room, she gave Jace numerous kisses before giving him back to her mother.

"Thanks again. I appreciate you keeping him tonight. We shouldn't be too late."

Holding Jace in the crook of her arm, her mom started rocking him, her face filled with confusion. "Moon said you wouldn't be back until morning."

"No, I just want him to think that's the case."

"Okay. Then I guess I'll see you later tonight."

After saying good night to her sisters, Larissa grabbed her keys off the hall table.

"Larissa …" her mother called out, "text me a picture of Jesus in his costume for me."

Larissa paused. "Why?"

"So I know which one he is. Since you won't be staying, I thought I would check the party out when you get home."

Her mouth dropped open, appalled at the thought of her mother going to a Last Rider party. Killyama had filled her in on how wild the parties could get.

"You can't go," she said firmly.

The disciplinarian in her mother came out. "And may I ask why not?"

Larissa told her the truth. "Mom, there is no way. Dad would turn over in his grave."

"*Pfft*. Then your dad shouldn't have up and died on me."

"He had a heart attack after you convinced him to join the Mile-High Club on the way back from Hawaii."

"Are you going to throw that at me again?" Her mom bristled. "The man was in perfect health. How was I supposed to know he had a bad ticker? Am I supposed to never have sex again?"

Larissa was dumbfounded at her mother's memory.

"You started having sex with younger men six months after Dad died. You could at least stick to men your own age."

"No way. I won't put myself through that again. Younger guys have longer—"

"Lives," Lana hurriedly finished for her.

"O … kay …" her mom drawled out. "I was going to say dicks, but we can go with that if you're too embarrassed with me discussing sex with you."

"We are." Nodding fervently, Larissa left before her mother started talking other merits of being with younger men.

Poor Jesus. She should really warn him that her mother

had set her sights on him. He had given her ride home. The least she could do was drop the hint for him to get a physical and to increase his health and life insurance coverage.

He wouldn't be the first kill for her cougar mother. She'd hate for Jesus to be her fourth.

# CHAPTER SEVENTY-FOUR

How in the world had she talked herself into coming to this party? And where was Killyama? She should have been here by now. If she weren't such a wimp, she would use the back door of the club instead of waiting for Killyama as they had planned.

She was about to head back home when she saw Killyama coming up the path. The closer she walked toward her, the more Lana's words played in her mind. Killyama's appearance showed how vastly different they had dressed for the party.

Her outfit was Halloween-y, just as Lana had warned. She hadn't been terribly worried because Killyama had told her she was coming as a bounty hunter. On which planet did bounty hunters dress the way Killyama was? Wearing long, black stiletto boots with black leather-clad legs tucked inside, she wore a black tube top, which left her midriff bare, exposing the swells of her breasts. Over the outfit, she wore a black leather coat, which billowed out from her lithe body to her feet. On her head, she wore a black hoodie, which seemed to cowl around her neck. At least Killyama wasn't wearing a mask.

She came to a stop a few steps from her. "What in the fuck are you wearing?"

"I told you I was being a bad Sandy."

"Bitch, there's bad, and then there's *bad*. What you're wearing is pathetic."

It only took Killyama one stride to take her by the arm and lead her down the path she had come from.

"I knew better than coming." Struggling to keep up with Killyama's quick strides, she nearly tripped when she would have turned in the direction of the parking lot, only to be jerked back in the direction of Killyama's house.

"Why are we going to your house? You don't have to keep me company. I'll—"

"I'm not going to miss shit. You're going to get out of this crap. I've got something you can wear. Something told me your idea of bad wouldn't be the same as mine."

When they reached her house, Killyama flung open the door and ushered her toward the bedroom. Releasing her arm, she went to the closet and returned with a confection of black tulle.

"Get your ass in gear. Change your clothes."

Larissa didn't have the courage to fight her. She unzipped the satin jacket and took it off, feeling self-conscious when she saw Killyama's eyes flicker over the modest tank top underneath.

"You weren't going for the wow factor, were you?"

"Moon's only wearing sweatpants."

Killyama didn't ask permission before shoving a dress over her head once the top was removed.

"Bitch." She tugged the dress down as soon her hands cleared the sleeves. "You're lucky I borrowed this dress off

T.A. when we had lunch today. Something told me that asshole didn't warn you."

Larissa's hands went to her hips, stopping the slide of the dress. "I'll never fit in T.A.'s dress!"

"It'll fit. T.A. wore it when she was pregnant. You'll have room to spare."

Frightened that she was going to ruin the dress by tearing the inner lining, she carefully lowered the fabric over her hips. The dress easily glided down to fall just below her knees.

Killyama moved behind her to zip the back.

Before she could look at herself in the dresser mirror, Killyama grabbed her arm to steer her into the bathroom.

When she entered the room, her jaw dropped at her reflection.

Killyama stared back at her in the mirror. "Now"—her hands went to her hips—"what in the fuck am I going to do with your hair?"

Still dazed at how she looked in the dress, she didn't pay attention to Killyama turning on the water in the sink until she nearly knocked her out by pushing her head under the water.

"What are you doing?" she sputtered.

Killyama didn't waste time with words.

No longer did she feel a heavy weight of a towel land on her shoulders than her head was being raised out of the water.

Reaching for a brush, Killyama brushed the tangles out of her hair then squirted a glob of something on her hands, smoothing it through the damp stands. She ran the brush though her hair again, then stepped back to survey the slicked-down hairdo she had created.

Slinging open a drawer, she rummaged through the contents until she took out a square case. She pressed a tiny gold button, opened it, then dumped a pair of earrings onto the bathroom counter. "Put them on," she ordered. "What size shoes do you wear?"

"Uh … eight."

"First luck I had tonight." She disappeared into the bedroom.

After getting the second earring on, Larissa went into the bedroom to see Killyama had made a pile of items on the bed.

"Get them on," she ordered from her closet. "If Train beats me to the clubhouse, I'm going to beat your ass."

Hurrying to the bed, Larissa opened a package of black stockings and sat down on the bed to put them on. Then, sliding on a pair of heels, she gingerly stood. Thank goodness they were a more reasonable height than the ones Killyama was wearing.

Gingerly, she stood up to pick up the last item on the bed —a pair of sheer black gloves that reached her forearms.

"Turn around."

Following Killyama's snapped command, she turned to check sight of herself in the dresser mirror.

Behind her, Killyama reached over her head to place a mask on the bridge of her nose. Tying the mask, she then took a quick perfunctory glance before pushing her toward the door.

"Let's go."

They barely made it through the front door before Killyama slammed it behind them. Larissa tried to keep up without falling.

"Thank you, Killyama. The dress is beautifu—"

"Don't thank me; it's T.A. That rich husband of hers bought it for her for some party they went to for his son. Make sure you give it back. The fucker notices when something is missing and won't let us hang out there until we give

JAMIE BEGLEY

it back. She has a pool in the backyard, so don't fuck it up for us, or Sex Piston will kick your ass."

"I'll get it dry cleaned tomorrow and give it right back. Afterward, I'll stop by your house to visit the baby and pick up my clothes."

"The kids are staying the weekend with T.A. I'll bag up your clothes and send them with Moon."

"Oh … okay."

As they neared the back door, her footsteps lagged behind.

"What in the fuck is the holdup?"

"I'm nervous," she admitted.

Killyama recached for the doorknob. "Bitch." She gave a long-suffering sigh. "Haven't I had your back so far?"

"Yes …" She did look pretty amazing from the brief look she had caught of herself in the mirror.

"Didn't I have your back when you told me Moon let another bitch ride on his bike?"

"Yes," she admitted again.

"I'm not going to let anyone fuck with the woman who had my back when I brought my kid into the world. I got you. You good now?"

"Yes." Larissa gave her a shaky nod.

"Then get your ass through the fucking door before I throw it inside," Killyama snapped.

Not wanting to find out the hard way if she was bluffing, she went inside.

Two women behind the counter, making trays of food, watched them enter from behind their masks.

"Hey, Killyama." Picking up a tray, one of the women, dressed in a tight red dress that had a gold zipper running down the length of it, skirted the counter to pass in front of them. "Forget your mask?"

"No." Killyama reached out to pluck a grape off the tray,

popping it into her mouth. "Just wanted to make sure you knew who's kicking your ass if that zipper gets lowered around Train." Pulling up the cowl at the bottom of her hoodie, she covered the bottom half of her face, leaving only her eyes and forehead exposed.

The other woman behind the counter laughed. "Watch it, Margarita. Killyama isn't playing around."

Margarita must have been irritated at being called out by the way she flounced out of the kitchen.

Easily recognizing Winter's voice, Larissa took the opportunity to admire her costume. While the other woman was dressed completely in red, Winter was dressed in black and white. Her top was a frilly blouse that fell off her shoulders, and as Winter came around the counter, carrying the other tray, Larissa realized the bottom wasn't a skirt but puffy pants. The hat she was wearing was flat, as well as the brim.

Taking in her appearance, along with the mask she was wearing, Larissa gave her an appreciative smile. "*Zorro.*"

Winter smiled back. "You're the first one tonight to get it, unless Viper is standing next to me, Larissa."

Larissa unconsciously raised her hand to touch her mask at Winter guessing her identity.

Winter laughed. "Don't worry; no one else will be able to recognize you so fast. I saw you walking past my house with Killyama as I was leaving."

After they walked out of the kitchen together, Killyama nudged her to the side, toward the bar area, as Winter was swallowed up in a crowd much larger than she had expected.

"I need a drink."

Remaining on the other side as Killyama made herself a drink, she scanned the room to check if Moon was there, taking in the party-goers with consternation.

Killyama had saved her from humiliation. She was going

to kill Moon. The Last Riders were going to have to carry him out on a stretcher, she promised herself.

A few of them were wearing costumes that were Halloween-y, like Winter and Viper's by choosing famous masked characters, but wow, they hadn't done homemade. Their costumes were a different caliber than what she had devised. Several, she guessed, had spent a bundle to stand out.

Any plans she had made to find out if Moon had been cheating on her flew out the window before she could ask.

He was cheating. There was no way he wasn't. The women were gorgeous, and if they were decked out in revealing clothes like they were tonight, it would take a saint to resist them.

Moon was no saint. Hell, he didn't have the willpower to go a night without making popcorn. No wonder he had no interest in having sex with her. He probably didn't have the energy.

Spotting Saffron wasn't difficult. The leggy blonde was hard to miss. Dressed as one of the women from *Warlord from Hell*, she looked sexy and alluring. Everything she was not.

Women belonging to the warlord were only permitted to wear certain colors, according to how often the warlord would call for them. The favorites were allowed to wear black and gold, the ones called occasionally were allowed to wear red, women who were rarely called wore green, and those who had yet to make it to the warlord's bed wore blue. Only the favorites wore an intricately designed head chain, which circled the women's faces, like *The Lone Ranger's* mask but made of gold. From the bottom of the mask hung thin tassels, studded with black pearls.

Saffron had almost all the accessory down to the gold slippers, except for the one item that one of the favorites from *Warlord from Hell* was killing everyone for—a gold choker that had dangling stones. Each time the main favorite was called to the warlord's bed, she would be gifted a precious stone the next morning, if they had pleased the warlord. So far, the main favorite on the show had been given a ruby, an emerald, and a sapphire. The favorite wanted a diamond and was literally killing the others to reach her goal—to become the warlord's woman.

"Here you go."

Dragging her gaze away from Saffron, she saw Killyama had placed a tall glass within her reach. "I can't."

Killyama raised another glass that looked like the one she had given her. "Bitch, you aren't the only one with a hungry mouth to feed. It's ginger ale."

Taking a sip of her soda, she continued looking around, her confidence evaporating at watching the provocative women throughout the room. Returning her gaze back to Killyama, she found herself being observed.

Larissa slightly lifted her shoulders, silently admitting she had been comparing herself to the other women.

"How do you survive?"

Vindictive humor filled Killyama's expression. "I put the fear of my boot in them. Makes my days a little brighter."

When she didn't laugh, Killyama grew serious. "I trust Train."

"Have you heard if Moon is cheating on me?"

"No, but if he was, Train wouldn't tell me."

Larissa worried her bottom lip as a woman came up to the bar, dressed in a mesh sapphire dress and mask. Little designs were spotted throughout, leaving most of her skin bare, the design becoming more intricate over her private areas.

She waited until the woman stepped away from the bar before asking, "Is she a Last Rider?"

"Not yet." Killyama dragged a whiskey bottle closer.

"Nuh-uh. Remember, we have babies to feed."

"I wasn't going to drink it. I was going to throw it at that bitch."

Larissa couldn't blame her. The back was more indecent than the front. There was no design on the back, allowing a clear view of the woman's thong.

"I don't know many of the rules, but Moon did tell me women aren't allowed to fight each other."

"Fuck off."

Larissa laughed. "You don't mean that."

"No. You're too nice for us to be best buds, but I don't mind hanging around you in small doses. I'll help you work on becoming more like me. Moon won't be able to not fall in love with you."

"Your help would be greatly appreciated." Ruefully, she smiled sadly at Killyama. "I love him so much it hurts."

Three men came up to the bar, dressed identically, excepted for the difference in color uniforms and masks.

"*The Three Musketeers*, Puck?" Killyama slid a beer to the one closest to her.

"Yeah. I wasn't happy with it, but Jesus talked me and Nickel into going along with it."

Killyama gave the other two beers. "How?"

"One lucky lady is going to get three votes."

"Or several lucky ladies," Jesus butted in. "Depending on Nickel's stamina."

After that, Killyama and her tuned them out when they started teasing each other.

"By the way, before I forget, where did you get the jacket you were wearing?"

"I made it."

"You see something like it in a store?" Killyama refilled her glass with more ginger ale.

"No. I just thought it would be cute to be dressed like one of the Pink Ladies."

"Huh?"

"From *Grease*." Larissa nodded her head, waiting for the Pink Ladies to click at the mention of *Grease*.

"Oh …"

Clearly, she didn't get it, the confusion evident on Killyama's face.

"Didn't the girls in *Grease* wear black jackets, not red satin? They sure as fuck didn't have *Last Riders* written on the back. Didn't they show some tits, too? The way you had that jacket zipped up, with that scarf, you could have gotten a G rating. I saved your ass there."

"Yes, you did," she agreed thankfully. "I forgot to mention, I love your outfit. I wouldn't run if I were a felon and you came for me dressed like that."

"That's right, because you know I'd catch your ass."

Larissa started to laugh then stopped when she realized Killyama wasn't joking. She changed the subject. Something about Killyama scared her. The woman was actually acting as if she were a real bounty hunter.

"You think Train and Moon will be much longer?"

"If he's not here in five more minutes, I'll …" Killyama broke off, her eyes widening and a gleam entering her eyes that Larissa had never seen before.

Larissa turned to see who she was staring at.

"Holy shhhiitt," Killyama purred.

She wanted to purr herself. One of The Last Riders had just walked in, wearing the costume of the main character from *Warlord from Hell*.

"Who's is *that*?"

Larissa began to explain, "He's a character from *Warlord f—*"

"I know who he's supposed to be." Killyama eyed the

warlord as if she were about to rip his costume off. "I meant, who is in the fucking costume?"

"Oh … I have no idea. You'd have a better clue than I would." Larissa couldn't take her eyes off the warlord. "He must have spent a fortune on that costume."

"Worth every fucking cent, however much it was."

She had to agree. Whoever it was seemed to have all the accessories. He even had a choker grasped in his gloved hand.

"Is Train coming as anyone?"

Killyama shrugged. "I forget."

The warlord strode across the room to where Viper and Winter were standing in their *Zorro* costumes.

Was it her, or did the man in the costume move the same way the actor did in the show?

Larissa tilted her head to get a better view when a man dressed as the *Phantom of the Opera* blocked it.

"Do you think he's a recruit or a Last Rider?"

Killyama braced her elbows on the bar to continue to gawk at the warlord. "From how long Viper is talking to him, he's a Last Rider. He doesn't give new recruits the time of day at parties."

"*Warlord from Hell* is really popular. Moon got all the brothers watching—"

Killyama shot her a speculative glance. "Could he be Moon?"

# CHAPTER SEVENTY-FIVE

Could the man dressed as the warlord from *Warlord from Hell* be Moon? Larissa gave Killyama's question a fleeting thought before having to admit that, as much as she wanted the fake warlord to be Moon, it wasn't.

"I wish." Disappointed, she tore her gaze away from the warlord and looked back to Killyama. "Moon wouldn't go to the effort. When I pressured him about what he was wearing, he finally decided on sweatpants and a hula hoop. He didn't think anyone would go to any trouble over their outfits. That's why I was coming as a bad Sandy."

Killyama became piercingly direct. "Dump his dumb ass."

"Maybe he didn't know," she hazarded to guess. "He isn't living with The Last Riders anymore and wasn't aware how all-out everyone was going to be."

"Either that or the conniving motherfucker didn't want any of the other brothers sniffing after you while he was working."

"Moon trusts me. He knows I wouldn't cheat on him."

"That's your second mistake."

Larissa kept her face straight as she saw Train come up behind Killyama to listen.

"What was my first?"

"Falling in love with him right off the bat just because you had sex. No one is that go—"

Train took a step forward, sliding an arm around her waist.

Larissa would have burst out laughing, but she was afraid Killyama would kill her right after she took her husband out.

Surprised at being grabbed from behind, as she turned around, Killyama reacted by throwing her arm in an attempt to smash Train in the face with her elbow. Luckily, Train must have expected the reaction, catching her arm mid-air and using her momentum to propel Killyama behind the bar counter. Pinned on three sides with the bar counter on one side, and the liquor wall on the other, she was maneuvered to the wall at the end of the bar.

Seeing Train going down for a kiss and Killyama not stopping him was like discovering your idol had feet of clay. Damn, if a mighty warrior like Killyama could be brought down with a kiss, what chance did she have to bring Moon to his knees? Secretly aspiring to have the confidence and assertiveness which Killyama had an overabundance of, she hoped some of it would rub off on her.

Eh ... even the strongest warriors needed a night off.

When the kissing started getting touchy-feely, Larissa moved slightly away from the bar to give them some privacy.

Glancing toward the front door, she wondered what was taking Moon so long. He'd been working with Train; wouldn't they have gotten off at the same time?

Unless ...

Larissa worried at her bottom lip, skimming her eyes over the crowd to a covered head in the middle of the room.

Could the warlord be Moon? She had thought his gray

sweatpants influencer idea was crazy. Was it to throw her off?

But why keep his identify a secret?

Navigating her way through the crowd, she saw the warlord was talking to the *Phantom of the Opera*. If she could get close enough to hear, she would recognize Moon's voice.

"Hi, Larissa?"

"Hi, Lily."

Dressed in all white, Lily was easily recognizable, despite the mask. Long black hair fell to the middle of her back. She carried herself with the grace of a model and had the height and beauty which made Lily stand out, regardless of how many beautiful women were around.

"You look lovely tonight," Larissa complimented her.

"Thank you. I wouldn't have recognized you if Winter hadn't told me. You look beautiful."

"Thanks to Killyama. She hooked me up."

Drawn into conversation with Lily about going on a shopping trip and lunch with Killyama and her sister, Beth, when they were available, Larissa agreed, letting Lily continue to talk while she tried to listen to the warlord and the phantom. So far, the only one talking was the phantom ...

"All right, it's settled then."

Realizing too late that Lily was walking off and she had inadvertently agreed to a girls' day out without paying attention to the date, she figured she would have to call Lily tomorrow to find out when.

She twisted to the side and moved around a woman who was dressed like Cat Woman without the ears and another in a sequin gown that reflected the lights from the ceiling. Lowering her gaze at the glare coming off the shimmering gown, she accidentally plowed into a hard body coming from the other direction.

"Excuse"—she instantly became tongue-tied at seeing she had bumped into the warlord—"me."

She hoped to hear his voice but was disappointed when he only nodded his head.

The warlord's hands had come to her forearms in reflex when she stumbled into him. Expecting him to release her, she frowned as she tried to look through the mesh of his mask to at least determine his eye color. It was a useless endeavor.

Biting her lip, she took a chance. "Is that you, Moon?"

The gloved hands on her arms tightened.

Was that a yes or a no? Couldn't he talk in that getup?

Before she could ask again, someone dressed like a pirate came up to the warlord, hitting him on the shoulder.

"Cool costume, Moon. You seen Wizard? He blocked my car, and Willa's ready to go."

Stunned that the town's preacher was dressed as a pirate at The Last Riders' clubhouse, and his wife was there, too, she reexamined everyone she had met in town since she had moved here. Was everyone in town a Last Rider or joining?

The warlord shook his head yet pointed off in the distance.

"Thanks, anyway."

The town's preacher took off in the direction Moon had pointed.

"What happened to the gray sweatpants?" she hissed, trying to keep her voice low. "If you didn't want to come with me, you just should have said so." Hurt, she jerked herself free of Moon's arms. Spinning around, she then found herself caged in by the massive amount of partygoers who were still coming through the door. She squeezed past one masked man, who nearly took her out with his long, pointed nose, and found herself hemmed in at the bar.

Killyama studied her face then looked behind her. "You find out who he is?"

"Moon."

Killyama's face filled with disappointment. "Damn. I was hoping it was someone I didn't know."

"Where's Train?"

"I sent him on a beer run. Listen ..."

Warily, Larissa didn't trust the way Killyama was staring at her.

"One good deed deserves another, right?"

"Depends on what it is," she cautiously agreed.

"Hook me up with that warlord costume tomorrow, and we're even. Cool?"

"You'll have to ask Moon. I'm not talking to him."

"Why not?" Killyama put her hand up when she started to explain. "Never mind. I don't care. I want to borrow that outfit for Train. There's no need to be selfish. It's not like I'm asking for Moon to come with it."

"You can have both of them," she offered angrily.

A hand came around her arm, pulling her away from the bar. Unable to break away from the hard grip, she found herself in the kitchen.

The room was less packed, but the door was blocked with people standing around.

"Let go, Moon." Furious at him, she was about to kick him when Puck walked through the swinging door.

"Keller?"

Everyone's attention swerved to Puck.

"He's not in here," someone called out. "I saw him going upstairs an hour ago."

Using the opportunity to jerk free of Moon's hold and seeing a door to the side open, she took her chance that it was another way back into living room with Moon blocking the kitchen door and the rest blocking the backyard door.

Thankfully, she had slowed enough that she didn't break her neck when there were steps and not another room like she had expected.

When she reached the bottom step, she recognized where she was immediately. The Last Riders used this basement area as a workout room. Killyama had opened the door one day when during a prenatal visit to show where she worked out. She hadn't gone inside, which was why she hadn't recognized the stairs.

The basement was pitch dark.

"What in the ever-loving hell?" Lamenting to the empty basement, she turned around, preparing to go back upstairs, but froze upon hearing footsteps coming down.

She would be damned if she was going to let him talk himself out of this one.

Frantically, she gingerly moved around the area, trying to find a place to hide. If she was lucky, she would find another door.

Walking with her hands held out, she came to some kind of metal pole. Skirting it, she started moving faster, hearing Moon's footsteps hit the tiled floor of the basement. When she moved forward, her knee bumped into something.

Leaning down, she rubbed her knee. Then, putting out her hand again, she realized she must have bumped into a low table.

She used her hand to guide her as she moved around it. Then, straightening herself, she took another wary step forward, only to go flying.

"*Oof!*" she muttered out loud. Expecting to find herself sprawled out on the floor, it was a relief to find herself sprawled out on what felt like a couch.

She quickly bounded up, determined not to talk to him. However, her quick movement sent her crashing into Moon and sending them both falling back onto the couch.

To be fair, from Moon's startled grunt, he was just as surprised as her.

"Get off, you big goon." Her hand flew up, about to pound him on his shoulder.

Had she lost her mind? What was she doing? If she left, was she ready to hand him over to those women upstairs without a fight? Her mama hadn't raised no fool. Nor was she going to look a gift horse in the mouth. She had secretly been lusting over the warlord from the first episode she had watched.

Circling his shoulders, she pulled him back down, as he had been attempting to lift himself off her.

Moon must have had enough, because he tried again to get up.

Clinging to him, she tried to think of something to get him to stay other than having to come right out and apologize.

"How do you want me to please you tonight?" she purred, sliding her hand over his chest and finding the top button. "I can give you any pleasure you desire, Warlord."

Moon stiffened over her. Then, when he rose up to a sitting position, she felt the thigh next to her tense as if he were getting ready to rise from the couch.

Swiftly, she beat him to it, sliding off the couch and maneuvering between his legs, her hands going to his thighs to stop him.

As she lightly massaged the firm muscles under his costume, her breath hitched in her throat. If she had known throwing herself at Moon's feet had this effect, she would have done it long before.

"I seek to give you the ecstasy only I can." Sliding her massaging hands upward, she brushed over the hardness of Moon's cock. Leaving one hand rubbing over his hardness, she used the other to unbutton his pants.

On her knees, she leaned forward, her mouth finding the flesh she had uncovered. An unintentional soft moan escaped her at the heady excitement she was experiencing at having Moon under her control.

Caressing her way to his cock using her tongue, she inhaled his male scent. She had never wanted Moon more. If he was cheating on her, she was going to make sure no one would be able to live up to the ecstasy only she could give him. Wasn't that how the warlord's women felt?

She sucked the head of Moon's cock into her mouth, and the soft texture over the hard steel underneath fueled her desire. At his sudden grunt, she strove to make him lose complete control.

Running her tongue down the length of his cock, she lowered her head further, taking as much of him as she could. She raised her head, then went down again, over and over, taking more of him each time.

Her body was on fire, but when Moon's hand went to her breast, she pulled it away. She wanted it to be all about him. What only she could do for him.

Under her tongue, she felt his cock begin to strain. She removed her mouth at his groan, and her hand went to his cock to stroke him into a release. Dipping her head to his thigh, she ran her tongue down the sensitive area until she came to the fleshly part. Nipping the skin between her teeth, she felt him jump. She pressed him down so he couldn't jump off the couch, and soothed the small bite.

Losing herself in wanting to give Moon sexual pleasure that would make any warlord envious, she felt a rush of satisfaction at hearing the sounds of his breathing deepen then become harsher as his excitement increased. She had never really been into it before when Moon had initiated role playing, but his costume had taken her to another realm.

From the way he was thrusting his hips into her mouth,

Moon had lost his own sense of reality. His thrusts became more urgent, driving his cock further in her mouth. Passionately, she accepted him, fully immersed in the role of pleasing the warlord.

"Come, my warlord," she crooned, running her tongue up the underside of his cock.

She would have sworn Moon stopped breathing as his cock swelled longer and harder before he lost whatever control he had been holding on to with her. She held him in her mouth until his climax played out and ragged groans tore from his throat.

She released Moon's cock, then placed her hands on his thighs to lift herself up. "Did I please you, Warlord?" she whispered seductively.

In response, she felt cold metal slide around her neck.

A rush of heat filled her when she heard the snap of the lock clicking in place.

With a giggle, she leaned forward to whisper in his ear, "I'm going to use the restroom and tell Killyama good night. I'll meet you at the bar."

She got to her feet and turned in the darkness. Barely remembering the table in time, she went sideways, her foot hitting a hard object. Instinctively, she jerked her foot back then gingerly toed the area, finding nothing in the way.

She headed in the direction where she could see a stray beam of light toward the ceiling until she finally found the steps. Practically bouncing up them, she entered the kitchen, seeing it was full.

She walked through the swinging door that led into the living room and almost let the door hit her in the face at the orgy displayed before her very eyes. In fact, the only ones not having sex were Killyama and Train, who were sitting at the bar, talking.

Killyama met her stunned gaze with a shrug. "You get used to it."

*Not in a million years*, she thought.

The urgent need hitting her bladder had her lowering her eyes to make her way across the room instead of running out the back door.

About to die of embarrassment, she had to tap The Last Rider wearing the beak nose mask to move to the left so she could access the restroom.

Whoever he was didn't complain about her interrupting, merely sliding the woman he was having sex with against the wall and continuing to thrust inside of her.

With the noises going on, on the other side of the wall, it took a couple of minutes before she managed to relieve herself.

She washed her hands, all the while admiring the warlord's necklace, and wished wholeheartedly that she had told Moon she would meet him at home instead of having to navigate her way back through that orgy fest again.

She took a deep breath to steady her nerves then left the restroom.

Larissa was sure her face was bright red before she made it back to the bar. At least she could stand with her back to the room and pretend Jesus wasn't having sex with Saffron just a few feet away.

"It's become rowdy since I left." She liked to think she had an open mind, but darn, she wished the door were a little less open until she left.

Killyama's lips twitched. "You could say that. It was only tame when you were here earlier because Lily was here. Winter and Willa usually aren't far behind her."

She was relieved she wouldn't accidentally see them having sex and be unable to look them in the eyes again. She didn't want to imagine how hard it would have been to have lunch with Lily, and then go shopping.

"Where's Moon?" Train asked, turning in his seat to face her.

"He should be here any second."

Killyama pointedly stared at her neck. "Cool necklace."

"There he is." Train saved her from having to say anything.

She looked toward the kitchen doorway, which she had expected Moon to come from, but found it empty. Twisting her neck back toward Train and Killyama, she saw them staring at the front door instead.

Grabbing the counter of the bar to keep herself from falling off the bar stool, she felt a dizzying sensation when she saw what Moon was wearing—exactly what he'd said he was going to wear—gray sweats and a cap. About to pass out, she then saw the hula hoop in his hand.

Horrified, she looked away when Moon waved at her, making his way toward her, Larissa unintentionally locked eyes with Killyama's.

"Someone has some explaining to do."

# CHAPTER SEVENTY-SIX

"You were the one who thought *he* was Moon," Larissa said in a stricken whisper.

"*Me?*" Killyama waved at the necklace on her neck. "I'm not the one who earned that chunk of gold."

Train's head went back and forth between the two. "Did I miss something?"

"Oh yeah," Killyama told Train with a know-it-all look.

Beseechingly, Larissa silently begged her not to tell.

Killyama gave her conspiratorial wink. "I got you."

Braving another look in Moon's direction, she saw one of *The Three Musketeers* had asked him what the hoop was for. Then everyone moved out the way so he could give them a demonstration.

Moon twisted his hips, sending the hoop spinning around his waist. Of course, none of the women were looking at the hoop; their attention focused solely on Moon's body.

God had to be a sculptor, because when He created Moon, He brought His finest achievement to life. The physical perfection wasn't marred by the few tattoos he had chosen. Instead, they made him human. The angels in heaven had to have shed tears when Moon had been sent to Earth.

It was why she was so afraid of losing him. She knew how bad it was going to hurt when he left.

Killyama, resting her arms on the bar, watched Moon's exhibition as she swiped Train's beer away from him. "Damn, bitch. Now I understand. It'd be hard not to love a man who can move his hips like that."

The cords in Train's neck bulged out as he snatched his beer back before Killyama could take a drink.

Killyama nodded toward the hoop Moon was using as a jump rope. "I'm buying you one of those motherfuckers."

"I'm not going …"

Oblivious to the arguing couple, Larissa slid off the bar stool, attempting to sneak out of the kitchen door before Moon could reach her.

She only made it as far as pushing the door open before Moon's arm circled her waist.

"Where are you going? The party is just getting started."

Did he know it was her, or was he hitting on another woman?

*Like you have the right to criticize after what you just did*, she thought hysterically.

Maybe if she could slip away without talking to him, he would never know she'd been there. She irrationally forgot that several Last Riders knew she was there and what costume she was wearing. It didn't matter, anyway. Moon kiboshed the hastily formed plan before it could even be enacted.

"I just got here. Papa needs some me time with Mama before heading home. What's the rush? Sexy-as-fuck costume, by the way. Lily came by the factory to meet Shade. She told me how fantastic you looked, but damn … fantastic doesn't do you justice. I have a few better adjectives I would have used."

"I don't want to keep Mom out so late," she lied huskily. Fearful that her expression would reveal more than she wanted it to, she kept her back to him.

"I just talked to Kendra; they're good. Jace is already asleep, and she's going to bed. We'll be home before Jace wakes up for his next feeding."

She wanted nothing more than to turn in his arms and confess what she had done, but she couldn't bring herself to admit that she had made another colossal mistake while at the clubhouse.

She promised herself that if she didn't break down in tears, she would lock herself in and never leave her house again. Well, other than to go to work. She wouldn't even go grocery shopping. And she would confess to Moon ... once she got a few beers in him.

With his chest plastered to her back, her stomach quivered in longing. How could she want to drag him upstairs into his bedroom after the stupid mistake she had just made? She didn't know; only that she did. The big ass had the ability to turn her insides into a big marshmallow. All she could focus on was burning the warlord's image from her mind.

*Cut it out, Larissa. You're losing it*, she thought hysterically. At least she wouldn't have to worry about Moon being upset about what had happened. He would just rub it in that she had only gotten one vote while she was here.

Dismally, she pleaded with him, "I'm not in the mood anymore. I want to go home."

"I can't put you in the mood?"

How was she supposed to resist his seductive murmur in her ear?

Moon's muscled arm holding her around the waist tightened, pulling her back until she could feel his hard sex against her bottom.

In the background, she heard the song "Human" by Rag'n'Bone Man.

"Come on; dance with me."

*Oh, sweet Lord, give me the strength to resist the dark promise I can hear in his voice.*

Her prayer went unheard as she bonelessly allowed herself to be turned in his arms and propelled to where the furniture had been moved aside and everyone was dancing.

Maintaining his firm hold on her, she nearly slipped away from the trance Moon's body had lulled her into when he turned her around in his arms.

The music switched from "Human" to "Sex on Fire" by Kings of Leon, which snapped her back to reality for a split-second until Moon drew her back close to him. The sensual movements he had exhibited with the hula hoop were nothing compared to how his body moved against hers as they danced.

Like a drowning victim, she gasped for air when one of his hands cupped her bottom, making her uncoordinated movements flow in unison with his.

Making one last-ditch effort to save herself, she wedged her arms between them. "I think we should go."

"If you're thinking, then I'm doing something wrong." With one of his hands, he gripped the back of her hair, tilting her face up, and then Moon tucked her head into the crook of his shoulder.

"There's something I need to tell you."

"Larissa"—Moon dipped his mouth to hers—"shut up."

The erotic pull of his voice engulfed her again. This time, she wasn't strong enough to fight. Instead, she willingly gave in to his erotic kiss.

One song blended into another as they swayed together.

She was so oblivious to what was going on in the room, it wasn't until Moon stopped dancing, sliding an arm over her shoulders and steering her to the staircase, that she came back down to earth.

"Where are—"

She forgot what she was about to say at Moon's throaty growl as he nuzzled the curve of her neck.

This amorous Moon, she had never dealt with before. He had aroused her to the point that if he led her off a cliff, she would willingly jump. Having all Moon's attention focused directly on her, as if his only goal was to get her in bed, was a heady emotion for a girl who had become used to being called a freak before she was six. As she grew older, the taunts and name-calling had gotten even worse. Boys her own age didn't tend to be kind when their developing masculinity was threatened by a girl who was taking college level courses while they were just learning the basics of algebra. Lana and Priss, who had similar issues, had been her only friends. If not for them, she truly didn't think she would have been able to bear the isolation she had gone through.

They had been there to let her cry on their shoulders when those she trusted betrayed her, and they were still constantly watching over her. Their sisterly bond had only strengthened with time.

"You owe me big time."

"How?" Confused, she lifted her eyes to him. The carnal way he was looking at her made her reinstate going off the cliff with him.

"It was everything I could do not to fuck you with everyone watching." Pausing only long enough to unlock his bedroom door, he then pulled her inside the darkened room. Not bothering to turn the light on, Moon shut the door with his foot, already turning her fully in his arms. "I deserve a big reward."

"What do you want?" she whispered softly, willing to give him anything he asked for.

"You."

Her head fell back weakly as his mouth covered hers. As she clutched his shoulders, all she could do was hold on when she was lifted off her feet. Reality slipped away as he pressed her onto the soft bed, covering her body with his.

"This time is going to be for you." Parting her thighs, Moon slightly shifted his body weight until his mouth was blowing warm air on the crotch of her panties. "I'm going to be so good to you."

Arching into his mouth when his tongue slid under her satin panties, she tried to smother the erotic cries that he was inciting by biting down on her hand.

His tongue transported her into another realm of desire, one she didn't think she'd survive when she came back to earth.

"What is the big reward you wanted?" she managed to get out between shallow gasps, trying not to be distracted by what he was doing.

"I'm going to fuck you in ways you didn't know you could be fucked, and you're going to let me."

---

S hifting out from under Moon's arm, she scooted to the side of the mattress to slide out.

"Where are you going?"

She thought he was sleeping, so she nearly jumped out of her skin when he spoke.

"I'm trying to go to the bathroom," she explained, waving her hand to the side, hoping to touch the lamp to turn a light on.

"What's the hold-up?"

"I can't find the lamp—"

Light filled the room before she could finish her sentence.

Looking in his direction, she saw he had turned the lamp on that was on the other nightstand.

"You good now?"

"Yes." Glancing around, she spotted what she was looking for, almost obscured under a blanket that Moon must have thrown to the floor.

She gathered the dress and put it on before moving toward the door.

"Don't leave the door open." Moon's mumble came from under the pillow he had put over his head.

She opened the door but almost closed it again at seeing *The Three Musketeers* having sex with Saffron at the same time across the hall. Averting her eyes, she hurried to the bathroom to relieve herself.

*Three at one time? Jeez.*

Washing her hands, she then kept her eyes downcast on the way back to Moon's room. Inside, she closed the door behind her to lean back against it.

"What's going on in that room should be illegal." Fanning herself, she tried to cool her heated cheeks down.

Moon, who was still under his pillow, leaned up on his elbows, dislodging it.

She started to fan herself harder at the sexy display Moon was unintentionally giving her with the sheet only covering one masculine leg and his lower groin area. His other leg was bent and sprawled out on the bed in a decadent position, which had her wanting to crawl back in bed.

"What's going on?" Interest filled his expression.

"Saffron is having sex with *The Three Musketeers*."

Laughter glittered in his eyes. "They did say, 'All for one, and one for all.'"

"She's a better woman than me." She stared at him with

unbelieving eyes. "If I hadn't seen it, I would never have thought it was possible. I mean …" She raised her hands in disbelief. "How?"

She almost fled at the sexual grin he gave her.

"Come here, and I'll show you."

She shook her head. A herd of horses couldn't drag her closer to that bed. "No, thanks." She waved her hand expressively toward his body. "Besides, they have three … dicks; you don't." God, she hoped he hadn't been holding out on her, and he was some alien from outer space. Was that why they had nicknamed him Moon?

"Come here," he coaxed seductively. "I'll improvise."

"We should be going home." She braved a step away from the door, poking around for her shoes. She found one under Moon's sweatpants. Picking it up, she continued searching for the missing half.

"Looking for this?" he asked innocently, the shoe dangling from his fingertip.

"Give it to me."

"Come and get it."

Warily, she stood on the other side of the bed, holding her hand out. The next instant, she was getting hauled onto the bed.

"Moon, we should … go." Crawling on her knees, she halfheartedly fought getting drawn toward him. "I need to talk to you about something when we get home."

As Moon pulled her toward him, he started lying back on the bed. Unable to resist, her eyes went to where his cock was getting harder, her gaze inadvertently landing on the mark on the inside of his thigh.

Red-hot fury smashed through her skull, as if a nuclear explosion had been set off.

"You son of a rat, I'm going to kill you!" she screeched at him, hitting him with the shoe in her hand.

"Have you lost—" he yelled in surprise when she managed to land a whack before rolling to get away to avoid her flaying arm.

"Fuuuck!" he cursed when he became entangled in the sheets, sending him falling into the nightstand before dropping to the floor.

Vindicated, she crawled to the edge of the bed to glare down at the rat bastard.

Shoving the lamp off his chest, he glared back at her. "Woman, what in the hell has gotten into you?"

"I'm going to kill you!" she screamed at him. "The court will find me mentally incompetent because you have driven me insane!" Pointing the tip of the shoe at his thigh, she dangled half-on and half-off the bed, trying to hit the bite mark she had made when they'd had sex in the basement. "You made me think—"

Too late, she realized it was a mistake to get so close to the edge. Unexpectedly, his legs came up to pull her down to him.

"*Oof!*" Hitting him, she wasn't able to prevent him from pinning her under his body with her hands in his. "Get off me!"

Moon's hand covered her mouth, allowing only outraged gasps to escape. His scowling face hovered over hers. "Listen to me. I was going to tell you it was me when *you* told *me*. I'm going to remove my hand, but keep your voice low. I don't want anyone to hear," he muttered under his breath. Then, slightly lifting his hand, he allowed her to talk.

"I was going to tell you when we got home." She burst into tears. "You did that to pay me back, didn't you?" She turned her face away so he couldn't see how badly he had hurt her.

He forced her face back to his. "I had to for the votes."

The unexpectedness of his answer made her mouth drop open. "Huh?"

Moon raised his hand and closed it in a fist. "My vote, which you already had." He raised one finger. "Killyama." Another finger rose. "Train." Another finger rose. "Both said they would give you their vote for delivering their baby. Everyone believes it was Wizard in the warlord costume." Another finger rose.

"I only need two more, then?"

Moon slowly shook his head from side to side. "Not exactly. There are cameras in the basement, which are viewed in the security room. There were two Last Riders monitoring the cameras tonight. They gave you the last two votes."

Slowly understanding that he had deceived her to get the votes from The Last Riders, she felt better ... marginally. But at least she no longer wanted to kill him.

"At least it was dark, and no one could see. Who were they?"

Conflicting emotions crossed Moon's face. "The cameras are infrared."

His hand hastily covered her mouth when she parted her lips to scream at him again.

"They didn't see much, not where the cameras were situated. They mainly got sounds of us having sex. You have the votes now to be a Last Rider." Meeting her eyes, he removed his hand. "You cool?"

"No," she grumbled. "I wish you would quit doing that. I'll stop yelling." Then she told him in a furious whisper, "I'm so angry at you, but I'm going to restrain myself until I get you in the car."

"That's fair."

When she pushed at his chest, Moon warily lifted himself

off her. Clamoring to her feet, she ignored the hand he extended to help her up.

"I don't understand why you went this far for me to become a Last Rider. I told you—"

"You *had* to become a Last Rider." His face had turned into a mask of determination.

Quizzically, she stared at him as he sat on the bed. "Why?"

"If anything happens to me and you're not a Last Rider, they will check on you and do what they can, if you ask for their help."

"That's nice—"

Moon shook his head. "You'll basically be on your own … But if you're a Last Rider, they will watch over you. You will be protected as if I were there, and so will Jace."

"Ahh, now I understand. You want Jace protected."

"I wanted you *both* protected." His hand came out to pull her between his thighs. "One of The Last Riders will become my backup if anything happens to me. I want you and Jace to have that safety net. My life changed after my makuakane died. I won't leave my son unprotected the same way."

"Nothing is …" She wanted to assure him that nothing would happen to him, that he would see their son grow, but she couldn't. No one was guaranteed tomorrow, not even a Last Rider.

He slid the dress down over her hips. "I don't exactly drive the safest mode of transportation."

"You do have a car."

"Which I hate driving. I'm not meant to be cooped up."

She had to agree with him there. "No, you're not." Winding her arms around his neck, she didn't struggle as Moon lowered them back onto the bed.

She cupped his face between her hands as she stared into his eyes. Moon would never be an easy man to love. The more a woman sought to chain him down, the more he would struggle to be free. It not only pertained to women but to anyone who sought to claim his loyalty. The Last Riders even only took what he was willing to give them, nothing more. Anyone who attempted to push past the invisible line that Moon had set to keep himself isolated would find themselves grasping air.

The only one who stood a modicum chance in hell of getting past Moon's guard was Jace. That was why he was so overprotective of his son. Jace was his kryptonite.

Helplessly, she let him lure her back under his spell. In the last year, he had made concession after concession for her—buying a home, not attending the parties—and as far as she knew, he hadn't cheated on her, other than that kiss and one bike ride. He had even confided in her why he wanted her to be a Last Rider. It gave a woman hope that maybe, just maybe, he was starting to care for her … starting to love her.

Holding that hope to her chest, she let go of the last of her fears and gave him the final vestiges of love she had been holding back. Opening her soul to his … She'd worry about getting it back another day. Tonight, it belonged to Moon.

# CHAPTER SEVENTY-SEVEN

Hovering her hand over a glass on the shelf, Larissa asked Moon as he came around the counter, "Would you like me to make you a glass of juice?"

"No, thanks. I'm late."

Leaning back against him when he came up behind her, wrapping his arms around her, she gave in to the pleasure of his mouth nuzzling her neck.

"What time are you getting off today?"

"I should be done by twelve." She lowered her arm from the cabinet to link her fingers with his at her waist. "I thought I would give Mom the day off and run some errands with Jace; take him to the park for some fresh air. What would you like me to make for dinner?"

"How about you ask Kendra or one of your sisters if they'll babysit tonight? We could get dressed up and eat at King's, or splurge and drive to Jamestown. There's a nice restaurant there we could check out."

"Can we go on your motorcycle?"

She felt Moon pulling away before his arms did. Her throat grew tight as he moved to the fridge for a bottle of water. Blaming herself for pushing him to take her on a motorcycle ride when he had made it obvious several times that he didn't want to, she once again told herself that she had to learn to pick her battles with him, and this one, she wasn't going to win.

On the brighter side, she had been basking in the attention he had been giving her.

After arriving home from The Last Riders' party, they had spent the whole weekend alone with Jace, spending much of it in bed during Jace's naptimes.

Refusing to lose the glow surrounding her after the wonderous weekend they had spent making love, and what she had taken as them growing closer emotionally, she gave herself a mental nudge to just take it slow and not push Moon past his limits.

"We can do King's," she quickly gave in. "I love their appetizers."

He pulled her back into his arms, where he rewarded her with a passionate kiss that ended abruptly when her mother walked into the kitchen, placing Jace's empty bottle in the sink.

"Morning, Kendra," Moon greeted her mother cooly.

"Moon," her mother responded smoothly.

Giving Moon and her mother reprimanding glares at the insulting expressions they gave each other as they passed behind the counters, Larissa filled her glass with juice.

"I'm going to head out." Pausing beside her, Moon pressed a kiss to her cheek. "I'll see you around five?"

"Okay."

As she made a slice of toast, she was aware of her mother's watchful gaze. "What?" she asked, turning around.

"You seem particularly sunny today."

Smilingly, she buttered the toast. "Why wouldn't I be?"

Her mother's lips tightened into a thin line. "Oh, I don't

know … he shut you down pretty hard when you suggested going to Jamestown on his motorcycle."

"If I'm not upset, then you shouldn't be." At her mother's worried expression, she set her toast down to hug her. "We had a wonderful weekend, it's a beautiful day, and Moon wants to go out for dinner. I'm so happy, and you should be, too. Moon and I are getting along great, and Jace is a dream-boat. Nothing is wrong just because Moon doesn't want us to take his motorcycle tonight. Don't overanalyze it just because you don't like him."

"You're wrong there." Her mother surprised her by contracting her. "I like Moon. I just wish you would take up for yourself more when he acts like a prick."

"I will. I promise." Finishing her drink, she grabbed her toast. "I have to go, or I'm going to be late for my appointment. See you this afternoon."

Her mother still looked worried but dropped the subject. "Bye, darling."

---

The short drive was made in no time, and as she got out the car, she noticed Lana's car parked next to Priss'. She hadn't seen either sister since they had helped her get ready for the masquerade party on Friday.

Smiling, she locked the car door, thinking Lana had come by to talk about how the party had gone. Already deciding which parts she was going to leave out, she opened the office door to see both of her sisters talking at the reception desk.

"Good morning." Cheerfully walking toward them, she noticed neither smiled in return. "What's wrong?" She frowned. "I'm not late for my appointment, am I?"

"I asked Priss to reschedule your appointment." Lana rose from behind the desk. "We need to talk in your office."

"Okay …?"

Their grave expressions had fear knotting her stomach. Was there something wrong with Mom's health? Was one of them sick?

Apprehensively entering her office, she saw a pile of folders placed on her desk. Lana and Priss took opposite sides of her chair to stand when she sat down.

In her chair, her gaze was caught on the computer screen, which was on. She read the name on the top, then jerked her eyes up to Lana's. "What's this about?"

Lana's expression was one she was familiar with. It was the one she wore when giving life-altering facts to her patients.

"Larissa, when Bennett stole my money, I hired a firm to go over our financials. I was terrified he used his relationship with me to steal from both of you. Thankfully, he didn't. But I signed up for a two-year subscription in case he was biding his time."

Her fear eased a bit. At least nothing was physically wrong with any of their family. She almost cried in relief.

"For goodness's sakes, you two nearly scared me to death." Sympathetically, she grasped Lana's hand. "Don't worry. Whatever Bennett has done, we'll fix it."

Lana turned her hand over to hold hers instead. "Larissa, it isn't Bennett who we have to worry about."

"Moon?" Her mouth went dry in fear. "What's he done?"

"Did you know Moon is a contract lawyer?"

"You have to have the wrong man." Disbelievingly, she shook her head. "He' a factory worker for The Last Riders." She gave her sister an angry look. "You had him checked out?"

"He does more than work at the factory." Lana released her hand to point at the computer screen. "I did have him checked out on Friday, but only when the company I hired to monitor our business finances sent me an email."

"He's been stealing from me?" she choked out.

"No, Larissa." Lana gave her an anguished look. "He didn't have to. You've been giving everything away to him."

---

Numbly, she drove home, leaving Lana and Priss at the office. When she arrived at the house, she carried the folders inside that Lana had prepared for her.

"You're back early."

Forcing a smile to her lips, she carried the folders to the dining room table before going to the living room, where her mother was sitting on the couch, to stare down at Jace playing on the blanket on the floor. "I finished early. I thought I would save you a trip from bringing Jace for his feeding."

"Oh." Her mother stood. "Then I might call Lana and see if she wants to grab some lunch."

"You should. I'm sure she'd like that."

"You want to come and bring Jace?"

"No, Jace will be ready for his nap after I feed him. I don't want to disrupt his schedule."

"Okay, I'll go ahead and leave, then. Did you need me to babysit tonight for yours and Moon's date, or did you ask Priss or Lana?"

"I decided not to go out. I've got a headache. I thought I'd take a nap with Jace."

"Good idea." Her mother brushed a quick kiss over her forehead. "Are you sure you're okay?"

"Yes, thank you."

Carrying Jace into the bedroom, she fed him then laid him down for a nap. Once he was asleep, she got to work.

In much less time than she had expected, she left their bedroom and headed into the dining room, where she took out her cell phone to type out a text.

*"I need you to come home. Now."*

Sending the text, she sat down to wait.

# CHAPTER SEVENTY-EIGHT

"You think they'll go for it today?"

Moon shrugged at Viper's question. "We'll know when the truck arrives. We've set the stage; that's all we can do. Either way, they won't make their move until the truck gets here. You don't have to stay. I'll text you when it does."

"All right. I want them to see me walking to the club-house." Viper stood up, preparing to leave. "Shade, you staying?"

"Yes. I want to make sure the brothers are where we need …"

Moon's eyes went to his cell phone lying on the desk, missing what Shade was saying to Viper. When he picked it up, he frowned at the message Larissa had sent. What the fuck? She had never sent him a message like that before.

Glancing at the clock on the wall, he turned to Viper before he could leave. "Larissa needs me to come home. Can you send for Reaper to take over here until I get back? I should only be gone for an hour."

"You want to leave?" Viper scowled.

"Something's going on with Larissa. I need to go."

Viper gave him a reluctant nod. "Go, but hurry the fuck up. I'll stay until Reaper gets here."

"I'll be as quick as I can."

As he rushed out of the security room, he thought about calling Larissa, but if something was going on with the baby, he didn't want to distract her. She had never asked him to leave work in the time they'd been together.

Striding past Train and Rider as they worked on one of the bikes, he got on his bike without speaking.

He sped home, his mind going through scenarios of what could have happened for him to have to come home so urgently.

Jumping off his bike, he hurried inside.

He was about to head to the bedroom, when he saw Larissa sitting at the dining room table. The utter silence in the house sent tendrils of warning down his spine.

"What's up?" he asked, walking toward the table, noticing the pallor of her skin. "Are you sick?"

"No."

Moon came to a stop in the front of the table, seeing the pain-racking look in her eyes.

Larissa's hand came out to send the folders sitting in front of her skittering across the table toward him. "Can you explain the documents inside to me?" she asked in a voice void of all emotions.

Moon looked down at the folders then back to her. "It would be hard to do since I haven't read what's inside."

"Then look."

He took a step forward and opened the folder closest to him. He only had to read a couple of sentences. Leaving the folder open, he reached for another, then flipped open the remaining two. "What do you want to know?"

"How much is your fee? According to these files, I can't afford you."

"If you want to talk, we'll talk. But I'm not going to have you cutting snips at me while I am."

Moon winced at the bitter laugh coming from her lips.

"Only you would expect me to mind my P's and Q's after you've bankrupted me and my whole family."

"You're exaggerating."

"How am I exaggerating?"

The total lack of emotion in her voice made him wish she would go back to snipping at him.

"Listen, I know you're upset. I can explain this afternoon after work." Raking his hand through his hair, he gave a frustrated sigh. "I have to get back."

Larissa stood up and placed her hands on the table. "Why am I not surprised? Of course, you don't have time to spare to explain how I owe you thousands of dollars for rent not on this house but the one I thought you had bought. You have manipulated me from day one since I came back to Treepoint. God, how much you must hate me."

Moon moved down the table toward her at the broken sob she stifled with a hand over her mouth.

Seeing him coming near her, she raised a hand. "Don't you dare come near me. There's nothing you can say that's going to make this all right." Hunching over, she wrapped her arms around her stomach.

Moon took a couple of steps back to give her space.

"You must have laughed your head off at me with The Last Riders when I signed those papers."

"They don't know."

"Don't lie to me anymore. *Please.*"

His jaw clenched shut, giving her the opportunity to unload on him.

"I haven't felt this naïve since I talked my mom into

giving me permission to go home with one of the students from school."

"What happened?"

She sent him a tortured look. "Why should I tell you anything more about myself? So, you could use that against me, too?" Larissa sat back down as if she didn't have the strength to hold herself up any longer. "You know what told more than those documents did?"

"No," he clipped out. "What?"

"I packed your things before I texted you. Do you know how long it took me?" She didn't wait for his answer. "About three minutes."

Her bitter smile, which was so out of normal for the natural gentleness he always saw on her face, made him want to jerk her into his arms. Instead of doing what he wanted to do, he held back.

"I can't believe I missed it. Everything in this house, I brought here, except for what you bought for the baby."

"I didn't bring much crap, because I don't have much. I've never been someone who buys a bunch of useless shit to have it sitting around or in a drawer. I'm used to traveling light, going back and forth between the clubhouses. When I'm not there, the rooms are used by different brothers. I got in the habit of making do with what I need, and when it wears out, get something new. Me not having enough to fill a suitcase doesn't mean I don't consider this my home."

"Do you?"

Moon thought about lying about it, but she deserved the truth. "No. It's okay for now, but it's too small for me. I've been confined to small bedrooms at the clubs, and I want more space. That's why I want us to go out to dinner tonight —so we can discuss switching houses with your family now that Jace is getting older."

"You actually think I believe that?"

"Whether you believe it or not, it's the truth. It was the plan before I moved in here and your mother sold her house, remember? But I can't just be a jerk and make them move since there are more of them than us, which is why I've been putting it off."

"Did you really think I would go along with that after I found out about this?"

"You weren't supposed to know. I fixed this shit weeks ago." He swept his hand out, knocking the folders to the floor. "If the firm your mother hired was any good, it should have been in there that both mortgages have been paid in full, and ownership of both houses are in your name, free and clear."

"My mother isn't the one who hired them; Lana did. And it doesn't matter if you did or didn't fix anything. You did it in the first place. I bet you've hated every second you stayed with me … I looked through the paperwork; the balloon payment would come due around Jace's birthday. That's when you planned to leave me. Jace would be weaned, old enough for you to get full custody, with me without a home, and none of my family having a place, either. You planned it meticulously. God, I won't stand a chance in court with you, will I? You crossed every T and dotted every I. That's why you refused to be seen around town with me after Jace was born, why you won't take me out on your motorcycle."

"I haven't taken you out because …" He broke off, shoving his hands in his back pockets. "I don't know why, but I've become paranoid about Jace's safety. I can't explain it … this feeling I have," he admitted, feeling foolish. "That's why I stay on you about the sock when he's sleeping. It's worse when you take him out. A voice in my head tells me he's in danger. The only reason I let Kendra leave the house with Jace is because she's going directly to your office and back. That, and no one would dare mess with Jace around that bitch. She'd gnaw their hand off if anyone dared to touch him."

"Is that why you put cameras all over the place?"

"Yes. That way, I can watch him when I'm at work. I also put a tag on your and Kendra's cars so I know where you are when you do go outside with him."

Larissa nodded at him, showing she believed him. "Then you were telling the truth about not wanting to get in a wreck with both of us on the motorcycle?"

"Yes. The thought of Kendra raising my son without one of us gives me nightmares."

Neither said anything, and then Moon's cell phone ringing broke the momentary silence.

"Yeah?"

"The truck is ten minutes away," Shade informed him.

"I'm on my way."

Disconnecting the call, he picked the folders up off the floor and set them back on the table. "I have to go. I'll be back as soon as I can."

"I'm going out to run some errands and find a place for Jace and me to eat. I would appreciate it if you would come, take your things, and move back into The Last Riders' until my family can move in here. It shouldn't take long for them to get their things moved in. Tomorrow, I'll find a lawyer to come up with a custody agreement that we both can agree on. We've said all that needs to be said. I'll text you my lawyer's number tomorrow. Unless it pertains to setting up a time to see Jace, I prefer you not send me any further communication. In case you're not getting what I'm saying: we are over. I'm sorry to beat you to the finish line. You'll just have to be satisfied with succeeding in hurting me since that was your goal all along."

He raised his cell phone in order to call Viper and tell him that he was needed here when Larissa's expression broke.

"Please leave."

"Dammit. I'm going, but we aren't done talking, not by a long shot."

"Yes, we are," she stated firmly. "I'm done making concessions with you, Moon. Anything else, you'll have to fight for."

# CHAPTER SEVENTY-NINE

"Hey, Moon!"

Cutting his engine, Moon swung his leg off the motorcycle.

Saffron was sitting provocatively on Jesus' motorcycle while Jesus and Train worked on Pace's.

Moon kept his gaze focused on her body from the neck up. "Saffron. You keeping Jesus and Train entertained?" he commented with a hard glance in the brothers' direction.

Pouting, Saffron leaned forward between Jesus' handlebars, showing off her jutting, braless breasts. "I want a ride to the store, but I can't convince anyone to take me."

"They're working," he clipped out.

"How about you? Could you take me?"

Women using baby talk voices affected him as if someone was running a cheese grater down his back.

"No time. Running late. Back from lunch." Walking past Saffron, he stopped long enough to issue her a heads-up. "If Killyama sees you hanging around Train when she comes out from working out, that tube top you're wearing will be used for something other than making it easier for you to flash your tits."

"Moon!"

Paying no heed to her pretend wail of injured innocence, he continued past her.

"Brother." Moon caught Train's amused eyes as he neared the two men. "I would deal with that shit before Killyama does it for you."

Train straightened from being bent over the motorcycle, elbowing Jesus in the gut to give him space. "Look who's giving me advice," Train joked. "I know how to handle my woman. I'm not the one who got his ass kicked Friday night. You worry about your woman, and I'll worry about mine."

Moon's boot halted mid-stride at seeing Killyama coming down the path from the club. The way Train and Jesus were standing, neither man could see the bitch bearing down on them. "Your funeral." He gave Killyama a two-finger salute as she stalked toward her oblivious husband.

If Viper weren't waiting for him, he would have waited to watch Train get his ass handed to him. The brother was going to get his comeuppance. He'd have to make sure to save the video feed of the encounter.

He would give his left nut to stay and watch after Train had given him grief about the spat he'd had with Larissa. He wasn't about to share with the brothers how Larissa fucked liked a juiced-up succubus when she was riled up.

Not about to share that tidbit when he had no intention of sharing her, anyway, Moon looked at it as a public service. Larissa in the wrong hands could be dangerous. He was actually saving their lives, especially if any of the motherfuckers thought they could steal her away from him.

He was buzzed in through the security door and found Viper and Rider sitting at the control desk, their eyes glued to the monitor.

"Cutting it close, aren't you?" Viper's forbidding profile was the only hint he needed to know the brother wasn't happy.

Taking the seat next to him, he reached for a yellow pad of paper and ink pen. "Had some fallout to deal with."

His concentration on the monitor broken, Viper focused on him. "Who with?"

"Leave it to that woman to pick the worst possible time to try to break up."

Neither Viper nor Rider seemed surprised.

"Been there more than once myself," Viper said wryly. "What shocks me is it hasn't happened to you before. When you moving back into the clubhouse?"

"I'm not moving back. I'm going to change her mind."

That information did surprise them.

Viper and Rider shared a glance, as if silently asking, *Which one of us is going to tell him?*

Rider's sigh showed he had lost the battle of wills.

"That's going to be hard for you to do." Rider leaned back in his chair, hooking his ankle over his knee. "You might have getting women into your bed down pat, but when it comes to the hard stuff ... Mr. Sensitive, you're not."

Moon cocked an eyebrow in Rider's direction. "How in the fuck would you know?"

"I don't know ..." Rider drawled sarcastically. "Maybe me having to listen to countless women threaten to tattoo *'love them and leave them'* on your back more times than I can count."

"Then"—opening a roll of mints, Viper popped one in his mouth—"a week later, he's complaining he can't find a woman who's ready to get serious and have a bunch of kids with him." Viper shook his head in disbelief. "I'm still amazed none of them have taken you out in your sleep. Remember Lucinda?"

Rider's expression turned pained. "I do."

"You told her you loved Mexican food, so she started bringing you a fucking buffet every Friday night. Then, when you started dating her, she introduced you to her whole family, and you started hanging out with them, too. For a couple of months, you were at Lucinda's apartment more than you were at the club, except on Fridays, of course, and … let me tell you, brother"—Viper's expression turned just as pained as Rider's—"I count them some of the best Fridays I've spent. But what did you do? What you always do—you fucked it up. You invited the woman cleaning her house to come to a party right in front of her."

"I still don't get why that pissed Lucinda off." Moon rubbed the stubble under his chin reflectingly.

Balefully, Viper stared at him. "I don't know," he said snidely. "Maybe it was because the cleaning lady was Lucinda's sister-in-law. We had to post three guards at the club doors for a year because her brother tried to take you out no less than four times. The only reason he stopped was because he got arrested for arson when he set four of our bikes on fire."

"Don't forget the mayor who tried to put his ass in jail if they caught him, for taking his daughter's cherry," Rider reminded Viper.

Viper grimaced. "I try not to."

"She wasn't a virgin any more than I was."

Suddenly, Rider shot up in his chair to press a button that opened the garage door, allowing the transport truck entry.

"Here we go."

Laying the ink pen down when he stopped doodling on the pad, Moon folded his hands together as they watched the monitors.

As the three men watched, the last cart of the day was wheeled out of the factory. Moon looked at the employee identification number flashing up on a side screen to his left. "Gundy, that's number one."

They watched as Gundy rolled the cart to the appropriate number spot painted on the concrete then went to add his signature to the sign-in sheet. After hanging the sheet back up, he walked back to the cart as the factory door opened and another cart was rolled in by another employee.

"Howie, number two."

Observing, they noticed none of them talked. Their eyes went back and forth between the different monitors—one showing the two men by the carts, the other two cameras angled so they were able to see different views of the truck parking and the driver getting out to open the end of the trailer and lower the ramp.

Once the ramp was lowered, Howie rolled his cart down the sloping ramp to the truck. The driver didn't take his eyes off the inside, carefully watching the two men as they loaded the carts inside.

Gundy and Howie had loaded four carts when another employee wheeled another cart from the factory.

"Delaney, that makes three, plus the driver."

Viper took out another mint. "How many do you think are going to be involved? I bet a hundred it's just the three."

Rider shook his head. "Nope, not going to take that bet. I'm thinking the same."

"I bet a rack that there are five of them," Moon threw his bet in the ring.

"Brother, I'll take that bet," Viper accepted. "Rider, you in?"

"I'm in."

Viper started to tap his foot impatiently. "Fuck, is this going to be another dud? I thought for sure they would try it again. Don't tell me I wasted a shit ton of money on throwing the masquerade party to get the rest of The Last

Riders from Ohio to come down who haven't even been here since Pace's death."

"Be patient." Moon stole one of Viper's mints. Damn, he needed a fucking cigarette.

Moon's eyes narrowed on the monitor where Gundy started to struggle with one of the carts. The worker must have called out to Howie and Delaney to come help.

Moon tensed. "Here we go."

"You see that?" Rider pointed at the monitor with the trucker. He seemed to be pushing one of the carts inside, as if making room for another cart. "He's giving whoever's inside their signal."

A couple of seconds later, they could see a factory worker come out from behind the trucker, as if they had loaded a cart and was coming down the ramp to get another.

"Is that"—Viper leaned forward—"Charlie?"

"Yep," Rider confirmed.

"Damn, I liked Charlie." Moon made a moue of disappointment at the image on the monitor.

Charlie was short for a man, barely four-nine, and couldn't have weighed ninety pounds soaking wet.

"I was hoping it was one of the women. He's going to be hard to replace."

"And Gundy takes care of his mom," Rider filled them in. "That's why he always volunteers for overtime."

"That's not the only reason." Dispassionately, Moon continued to watch with the others as the rest of the carts were loaded into the truck. When they were done, the driver raised the ramp and closed and locked the door.

Rider picked up a headset and placed it on his head, positioning the mic near his mouth. "Rolo and Doom, get ready. The rest of you, stay where Shade has positioned you. Everyone keep eyes on Gundy and Charlie. You know what we're looking for."

"Have Widowmaker trail Gundy, and Silver on Delaney," Viper ordered.

Moon understood Viper's reasoning. Both bikers were in the tail end of their probationary periods. Viper wanted to test them while, at the same time, give them assignments that they could handle on their own without backup, leaving the more experienced Last Riders free.

Gundy, Charlie, Delaney, and Howie went through the door back to the factory area.

Viper's hands tightened on the arms of his chair, as if holding himself back from leaving the security office. "That's the last time those fuckers get away with that trick. After today, they'll have to key their employee identification entering and leaving the docking area."

Moon was just as pissed as Viper. "I still can't believe we didn't catch it sooner."

"I do. Usually, there are more employees out there. They would create a distraction while the one hiding in the cart slips out of the truck and blends in with the others. It's the end of the day; they're ready to go home. The workers inside are just wanting to get the job done and go. We were focused on the IDs going in and took for granted those inside having scanned their IDs."

"We also don't know if they've been using other methods, and this is the one the fuckers have used to circumvent our efforts to catch them. Hell, we don't even know why they've gone to these efforts to steal from us. With the amount of people involved, it wouldn't be worth them losing their jobs if they got caught."

"We're about to find out." Viper ordered, "Send them in, Rider."

Raising the garage bay door, Doom and Rolo walked inside. The driver, who was waiting for someone to come out of the security office to sign off on the load, was confronted with the two Last Riders who moved him away from the truck.

Rolo emptied the driver's pockets then left Doom to watch over him and went back to the truck to unlock it and lower the ramps. He went inside the truck and started rolling a cart out as Rider gave the all-clear.

That was when the wives started filing in, each of them taking a cart to unload and unwrap with the packages. Armed with box cutters, they laid the opened contents next to the packages as Rolo unloaded the last cart.

The three men in the security room left Rolo and Doom to oversee the garage while they continued watching the monitors for the men who had loaded the carts.

"It's going to be interesting to see what the motherfuckers have been doing." Moon stole another mint, waiting for one of the wives to find something that had no business being there. "Who do you think will be the lucky lady?" Moon scanned the women, settling on his bet. "I bet Diamond finds it. You see how fast she's opening those packages?" He whistled admirably. "I bet a grand on her."

"Is there anything you won't bet on?" Viper tiredly rubbed his eyes.

"Nope. It makes life interesting. Rider, you going to bet on Jo?"

"No. I'll take Killyama. That bitch is lethal with that box cutter."

Rider switched the screens to show the outside cameras as the men walked out with the rest of the employees leaving.

"You in, Viper?" His hand went out to swipe another mint, but Viper forestalled him by taking the last one.

"Put me down for Diamond. She's going so fast because she wants to go home."

Knox had offered Diamond's help, which Viper had initially refused until Knox told him he wanted the excuse to get Diamond out of the house. Since her attack by a deranged client, she had grown reclusive, only coming out of her withdrawn shell when Knox would take her and their children to their private island, which she and Knox had purchased when she had become convinced a zombie apocalypse was in the near future.

The bets settled, they all tensely waited for the results of their search while keeping their eyes pinpointed on Charlie and Gundy.

Gundy got into his truck and drove away while Charlie walked to his compact car. Neither of the employees had spoken since leaving the factory.

"I be a motherfucker," Viper swore as they watched Saffron call out something to Charlie.

With a casual wave, he motioned to his car, and Saffron got off the motorcycle and headed to the passenger side of the car, getting inside while Charlie got in the driver's side.

"She asked him for a ride to town," Moon filled them in at what he was positive Saffron had said to Charlie.

"Train and Jesus," Rider spoke into the mic, "stay where you are. Cash, Nickel, you follow Charlie's car. Report when Saffron and Charlie get where they're going."

Moon watched the monitor until Charlie's taillights disappeared from view. "What did I tell you?" Gloating, he linked his hands together to pop his knuckles. "Double or nothing, she's the one who pulled Pace's plug."

Viper shoved his chair back from the desk. "Poor fucker always did have a hard-on for a good pair of tits. You got this, Rider?"

"Yes," Rider answered, despite remaining focused on the reports coming in from Shade.

"You ready, Moon?"

Moon was already getting up from the chair before Viper could finish his question.

"You think she's going to pay him off for the drop?" Viper asked as they hurried out of the security room. The women were still working at unwrapping the packages as he and Viper hurried to the open garage door.

They had just walked through the door when Viper's name was called out. Rushing back inside, they saw all the women and Rolo had gathered around Winter. Willa and Beth moved to the side, allowing them to see what everyone else was staring at while Winter unwrapped another package.

"Damn." Moon blinked then started laughing. "That, I did not expect." Crouching down, he picked up two neatly packed bundles of cash.

"Real or counterfeit?" Viper snarled.

Moon peeled one off to take a closer look.

"Real." Killyama picked up one of the bundles, flipping through the bills. "Come to Mama."

Viper gave her a speaking glance. "Let's go, Moon. Rolo, have them finish opening the packages then put the cash in the security office. Ladies, thank you for your help."

"No thanks are necessary," Killyama told him magnanimously, separating the bundle of cash to tuck the two halves down her bra.

Keeping a straight face, Moon hastily left with Viper, who knew getting the money back was a lost cause.

"There was at least fifty grand there."

Viper's angry visage had Moon shutting his mouth as he got on his motorcycle. The Last Riders' president was fuming that their trucks had been used to transport cash. They still didn't know the source of the money and, until they did, everyone's lives could be in danger.

"At least we know why she wanted to hitch a ride with Charlie," Moon returned to what they had been talking about before Winter found the cash. "Saffron knew no one would take her into town this time of day. She'll be able to pay him off where no one can see. But what I'm really hoping for is Saffron, or one of the others, going to their source for more shipments now that they have resumed doing business again."

"If they don't, I'm past the point of waiting and watching to find out who's using us to transport their fucking money. If I have to beat the information out of all of them, I will."

"What if they don't know?" Moon asked. "I think Saffron is up to her eyeballs in it, enough to follow what orders she's given. But a mastermind, she isn't."

"Regardless"—Viper started his motorcycle—"Wizard won't show her any mercy."

They rode out of the parking lot and into town, pulling in behind the back of the hotel. Viper took his phone out of his jacket pocket and called Rider.

Impatient, Moon felt the anticipation rising in him, waiting for what was about to go down, or if anything would. Saffron could call for someone to pick her up, and the men just went home. If that was the case, Viper would send one of the brothers to give her a ride to the clubhouse and question her there. Glancing at his watch, he hoped it would be over soon. He needed to get back to Larissa. They had shit to straighten out. Viper and Shade would handle Saffron's questioning; he could peace out.

*Oh shit*, Moon thought, seeing Viper's expression.

Seeing Moon was watching him, Viper didn't lower his phone as he started repeating what Rider was telling him. "Charlie dropped Saffron off at the grocery store then went home. He lives next door to Gundy. Rider told Widowmaker to watch both houses. If one leaves, he'll call in for backup to watch the other house. Cash reported in that Saffron waited until Charlie left then took off walking."

Moon cocked an eyebrow at him, grinning. "Where's she

going?" He rested his arm on his thigh. She was meeting their source; he was sure of it.

A puzzled frown crossed Viper's forehead. "She went into the diner," Viper told him then went back to talking on the phone. "Tell Cash and Nickel to hold back. Park in the parking lot first; one then the other. Then act as if you're talking outside the window and see who Saffron is talking to."

Moon waited for Viper to feed him more information. He even motioned at him that he would ride his bike to the diner, but Viper gave him a wait signal.

"Nickel and Cash are walking toward the diner." Viper's voice broke off as he listened.

Moon's gut instinct kicked in at the same time Viper's expression changed, his voice becoming more urgent.

"Tell them to go inside and act like they're meeting her for dinner."

Moon frowned. "Why would they act like they're meeting Saffron for dinner?"

Viper signaled him to stop talking as he listened to Rider continuing to speak on the phone. "Tell them when they can to pull out and get them *the fuck out*."

Dread gripped his heart in a cold fist. "Viper?"

Viper met his eyes, holding the cell phone in the crook of his neck as he continued to listen. "Moon, they didn't have time to stop her before she went inside."

"Who?" he asked, though he already knew, his hands instinctively going to his handlebars.

"Larissa, and she has the baby with her."

# CHAPTER EIGHTY

They made the three-minute ride to the diner in less than two. Moon told himself Nickel and Cash would protect Larissa until he could get there. Shade and Reaper weren't far behind them. Saffron knew it would be her death warrant if anything happened to Larissa and Jace.

When he pulled into the parking lot attached to the diner, he felt Viper searching his face as they got off their bikes.

"You good?" Viper asked.

Moon nodded. Both men had worked together in dangerous situations before, so they moved in unison as they briskly strode toward the restaurant.

As they turned the corner toward the front of the diner, Moon saw Greer running out of the sheriff's office, starting to cross the street at a run.

"Heard gunshots!" Greer shouted.

Immediately, Moon and Viper removed their weapons and hurried toward the door. He wanted to rush inside, but his training held him in check. He would be no good to his family if his brain was blown out as he went through the door.

"Greer," Viper spoke once Greer made the sidewalk, "take the back."

Greer took off without arguing, his own gun at the ready.

Taking opposite sides of the door, Moon and Viper opened it, keeping their bodies to the side.

"Cash?" Viper called out.

"It's clear," Shade called back.

Rushing in next to Viper, Moon's eyes frantically searched for Larissa among the bloodbath that had taken place in the restaurant.

Nickel was covered in blood next to one of the tables by the door, and Shade was doing CPR on what was left of the bloody mess of his chest. Cash was lying on the floor with gunshot wounds on his side and shoulder, unconscious.

Seeing the tip of a woman's shoe, Moon rushed forward to kick a table aside that had been knocked over. "Larissa!" He rushed around the table to get to her but instead found Saffron's lifeless eyes staring up at the ceiling.

A sound in the doorway had Moon reflexively turning, but it was Train and Puck walking in through the door.

"Where's Larissa?" Moon shouted, heading toward the counter.

"She's not here." Shade scooted to the side so that Viper could take over Nickel's CPR.

"Cash was able to get out a distress call. I came in the front, Reaper was going around the back on his bike. When I came in, Cash and Nickel had already been hit. Larissa and the baby were gone. Saffron was behind the table; she was going to fire another round at Cash." Shade nodded to the table that had been overturned. "I don't know what in the fuck tipped them off, but they must have started shooting before Cash and Nickel could pull out their weapons. Because he had his phone out, talking to Rider, he was able to hit the distress call."

Greer came out from the kitchen door. "I saw Reaper take off after a black Camaro. Gundy Barber was driving. Charles Wells was holding the kid's car seat up as a fucking shield, or I would have shot both of the motherfuckers."

Moon rushed back to check on Cash. He pressed down on his side to stop the bleeding as Greer moved to stare down at Nickel, his hand going to Viper's shoulder.

"He's gone. Let him go."

Viper looked up at Greer, pleading, "You could …"

The sound of the ambulance from outside could be heard as it grew nearer.

Greer's face turned anguished. "Don't ask." His eyes went down to Nickel then Viper, who refused to stop giving him CPR. "It wouldn't make no difference if I did. Where he's gone, there's no getting him back." Greer stepped away to direct the paramedics to Cash, who had blood seeping from his side, and Nickel, who Viper still refused to stop working on. "There's another one out back. They locked him in the freezer. He's got a head wound."

Greer's hand went to his shoulder to key his mic. "I want an APB out on a black Camaro. It's Gundy Barber's. Reagan, get his plate number and send it out with an Amber Alert."

Moon moved to the side so the paramedics could assist Cash, urgency filling him to get to his bike now that Cash was getting help.

"Where are you going?" Viper asked, rising from the floor.

"To find Larissa and Jace." Taking out his phone, he wiped the blood off his hand and onto his jeans before pulling up the app he needed.

"Train, go to the hospital with Cash. Keep me posted," Viper ordered when Train came rushing in, answering Cash's distress call. "Call Rachel and tell her to go to the hospital. Then call Nickel's family and tell them that I'll call as soon as I can."

Finding what he wanted, Moon bolted for the door. "I've got them."

"How?" Viper clipped out, keeping pace with him.

"My fucking paranoia. I put an air tag on Jace's car seat."

Moon, Viper, and Shade bolted out of the restaurant and got on their motorcycles. The rest of the brothers, responding to the distress call, followed them at Viper's signal.

Holding his phone out, Moon followed the signal as Viper put the club on lockdown and sent Rider to check on Widowmaker after he failed to check in.

When Gundy's vehicle drove past the bridge to Jamestown, Moon swore to himself. Gundy wasn't taking any chances that Stud would be able to head them off from reaching the interstate. The fucker was going to hide in the mountains, and with Charles' help, they might succeed. Both were local boys, with Charles dividing his time between the restaurants he owned in Lexington and Treepoint. They moved in different social circles, so it was hard to imagine Charles being stupid enough to kidnap a child in broad daylight. He should have been smarter than his father, whose own crimes had been discovered, to the town's dismay. Charles' reputation had taken a hit, but as far as he knew, he had stayed on the straight and narrow.

Gundy, on the other hand, lived with his mother, and his redneck friends would hang out there, drinking until it was time to go home to bed. On his time off, he would go hunting on the weekends and would constantly come in Monday morning, bragging about going hunting, that he knew the mountains like the back of his hand, and what he had caught. Moon bet he wasn't lying about what he had bagged—several of the workers had constantly asked to go with him, who were also from town. They wouldn't ask if they didn't know for a fact that Gundy knew the best hunting spots.

What had him even more worried was the mountain they were driving on was winding and dangerous. Lumber trucks constantly traveled the road, as well as coal trucks. Parts of the mountain had closed mine shafts which could be used to ditch the car, providing Charles and Gundy a hideout. They could walk out through some of the old trails, and Gundy would never be seen again. Charles could make it back to Lexington and buy enough witnesses to swear he had been there the whole time, unless they lucked out enough to get him on tape.

Moon heard Viper tell the less experienced riders to slow down and ride at their own pace.

Moon let himself take a brief glance to the side, and then wished he hadn't. They weren't halfway up the mountain, and he saw the tops of pine trees far below them. What made it worse and what had Viper concerned was there was no guard rails. The only way he would feel safe riding across this mountain was if he were wearing a fucking parachute strapped onto his motorcycle.

He checked his rearview mirror; flashes of blue and red drew his attention. Farther back, lower down the mountain, Greer's patrol car was following behind The Last Riders.

Somehow, he felt better that Greer had come along instead of staying in town.

Tightening his hands on his handlebars, he had to fight the urge to increase his speed, imagining how terrified Larissa must be, and his son being at the mercy of two men who had nothing to lose.

As he neared a sharp curve, he didn't adjust his speed, sure he could easily take the curve at the rate he was going.

*Slow down!* a voice in his head yelled at him.

He gestured to Viper then his speed gage, and Viper adjusted his speed as well.

When he rounded the curve, he only had a second to react at seeing Reaper's motorcycle lying in the lane they were on.

Breaking with squealing tires, they saw burned tire marks on the road, leading into the dirt where Reaper was standing, looking down.

Getting off his motorcycle so fast the motorcycle fell onto the road, he ran to where Reaper was standing.

"No!" he screamed at what he saw.

Gundy's Camaro was wedged between two thin pine trees.

# CHAPTER EIGHTY-ONE

M oon started to climb down.

"Wait, Moon." Viper caught his arm. "Let Greer call for help." Viper pointed to one of the trees that was wobbling as Charles tried to climb out of one of the windows.

"Charles, stay still!" Viper shouted down. "You're going to knock the car loose!"

Charles didn't listen, continuing to try to shimmy out of the car.

Moon's mind was already made up. Charles panicking only cemented his decision. He crouched down, readying himself to go over the mountain.

"Moon ..." Viper started, taking off his vest.

"I'm going—"

"I'm not going to stop you. I'm coming, too."

"No." Reaper crouched down, sliding his legs over the edge. "I am."

"Charles, stop!" Moon yelled, sliding over the lip of the cliff, his heart catching in terror at Charles' frantic movements. "You're going to kill everyone!" Holding on to a tree

591

sapling hanging off the side of the mountain, he was able to scale down a couple more inches.

With his body halfway out, Charles grabbed the tree trunk to pull his lower limbs the rest way out of the car.

"If you don't move, I swear I'll get you out first!" Moon promised, willing to make a deal with the devil to save Larissa and Jace. "We'll let you walk away. Please, stop!" His voice cracked at hearing Jace cry. His son was alive! Blinking back tears, he climbed another couple of inches, Reaper keeping abreast of him.

With the way Charles' frantic movements were making the car rock, they were going too slow. He tried to go faster and nearly lost his grip. If not for Reaper throwing him back against the face of the mountain, he would have plunged right off the cliff.

Finding another handhold, Moon maneuvered himself downward, drawing closer to the car. He was within touching distance of the vehicle when Charles, seeing him so close, tried more frantically to shake his leg loose from inside of the car.

From the cracking sound the tree made, Moon knew another hard movement like Charles had just made, the stupid fucker, and the car would plunge down the mountainside.

"Larissa!" Moon screamed at the top of his lungs, wanting her to know he was there. "Larissa!"

As he called out again, he jumped as a gunshot rang out, echoing around the mountain.

Moon looked at the car and saw Charles slumped forward against the tree, no longer moving. Then, raising his eyes back up the mountain, he found Shade standing at the top, lowering the rifle to his side.

Taking a deep breath, Moon navigated his way around

the car enough to look inside the back window, seeing the top of Jace's carrier.

"Reaper, you get Jace." Moon delicately maneuvered himself around Reaper. "I'll get Larissa."

"I should get Larissa," Reaper argued. "I can hold more weight."

Reaper was right. They constantly worked out together; Reaper could bench press more weight than him. Still, *he* was going to be the one to get Larissa.

"Get Jace." Moon met Reaper's frowning gaze. "I'm trusting you with my son's life. I can't live without Larissa, and she doesn't even know I love her." His voice broke. "Would you trust me to save Ginny?"

"No, brother, I'd have to do it myself." Reaper started working his way toward the other side of the car.

On the opposite side, Moon was finally able to get an unobstructed view inside.

Larissa wasn't unconscious; she was holding on for dear life. The seat belt was holding her in place, and her legs were braced against the back of the seat in front of her, keeping her from flopping down into the seat below. One of her arms was outstretched, holding a red-faced Jace in his car seat.

Carefully pushing Charles' body back inside, Moon poked his head in. "Why didn't you fucking answer when I called out your name?"

Dazedly, she stared at him. "I was too afraid you'd start yelling at me for being in the car."

He never wanted to jerk her out of the car and into his arms more ... or spank her ass until she couldn't sit down for being so silly. But, from the damage already done to her face, he didn't think he'd ever be able to lift a hand against her, even when they were playing.

"Which of these motherfuckers did that to you?"

"Please stop yelling; it's scaring Jace. It doesn't matter which one hit me—they're both dead."

He couldn't argue that point. Gundy had a tree limb protruding through his neck.

Giving a nod to Reaper, he talked to Larissa as gently as possible. "Larissa, unfasten Jace's car seat. Reaper's going to catch him."

Larissa tore her gaze away from his to fumble with the car seat clip. Jace fell into Reaper's waiting hands.

"I've got him." Slowly, Reaper maneuvered his upper body out of the car.

"Reaper," Moon caught his attention before he could disappear from sight, "I was going to ask you this the other night and got distracted, but"—he gave a self-depreciating smile—"I guess no better time than the present. If I do …"—he didn't finish what he was going to say, not wanting to scare Larissa—"will you … raise my son as your own?"

"I'd be honored," Reaper promised, then moved away with Jace in his arms.

Having Reaper confirmed as being his backup was a load off his back.

With Charles' body practically blocking Larissa's way out, he was going to have climb to the other side and slide him over then come back and help Larissa out. It was going to be tricky, and he was already surprised the tree had held for this long.

He was about to pull his head out of the window when Reaper reappeared on the other side.

"Where's Jace?"

"Handed him over to Razer. Greer had a rope in his vehicle. Puck is coming down with a chain he's going to attach to the car. It might give us a couple of minutes."

"We could use them," Moon muttered.

"Larissa, when Reaper has moved Charles, and when I say *go*, release your seat belt."

"I'm going to fall." Frightened, she clung to her seat belt.

"I'm going to catch you," he promised. "Baby, we have to get you out of here."

"Okay."

Reaper pulled out a knife and cut a hole to deflate the airbag. Moon expected the car to plunge down the mountain at any second as Reaper then leaned inside to grab Charles, tugging his limp body toward Gundy enough that Moon could press the release to fold the front seat forward.

"Are you ready?" Moon gave her an encouraging smile. They were both aware of the perilous position they were in. "I'm going to get you off this fucking mountain. I swear."

"I'm ready."

Moon was proud at how calm she sounded. Bracing himself as best as he could, he prepared to catch her as Larissa's fingers went to the latch of the seat belt. With his heart in his throat, Moon then caught her by the waist when she dropped as the seat belt strap snapped free.

While the car started rocking dangerously, he used all his strength to pull Larissa out of the window. He actually thought they were going to make it when her feet cleared. Then horror filled him when the tree he had braced himself on gave a loud *snap!*

The tree splintered, breaking off into large pieces, which went tumbling down the mountainside. Dislodged, the Camaro went spiraling after the pieces of tree trunk. When he lost the tree's support, Moon grappled for something to hold on to.

He threw himself and Larissa to the side of the mountain and saw a rock poking out of the ground.

A scream came out of Larissa at the force of the landing. Holding her against him, Moon was unable to move with the air knocked out of him, gripping the rock like a lifeline, aware if it became loose, Larissa and he didn't have anything else to save them.

He gasped for air when he was finally able to make his lungs function again, and his eyes went to Larissa to reassure her, only to find her unconscious. Unable to determine if she had struck her head or had fainted, he started searching for a better hold.

"Let me take her," Reaper spoke from his side. He had managed to find an outcropping of rocks and was holding out his arms for Larissa.

Moon shook his head.

"Brother, listen to me." Reaper stared at him, determination on his harsh features. "Where you are isn't stable. Give me Larissa and grab the rope."

Moon stared at Larissa's pale face resting limply on his shoulder. "I can't."

"Brother, *trust me*. I won't let you down. You asked me to be your backup. Was all that bullshit? Trust me now. You can't save her alone; you're gonna get both of you killed. Give her to me."

It took everything in him to hand Larissa over to Reaper. Then, grabbing the rope, Moon felt himself being lifted upward. When he reached the top, Keller and Rider grabbed him by the arms and lifted him over the edge.

Greer had The Last Riders standing on the road, away from the ledge. Taking a quick scan, Moon saw Shade standing by the patrol car, holding Jace.

Finding Jace was in good hands, he went to the edge of the mountain, dropping to his knees and preparing to go back down to help with Larissa.

What he found humbled him, and any idea that he wasn't as important as any of the other brothers melted away.

Reaper had wrapped the rope around both Larissa and

him as Viper, Razer, Lucky, Puck, Jesus, and Knox pulled them up. What humbled him was the amount of Last Riders who had scaled down the mountainside so if Reaper lost his grip, there would be a Last Rider on each side of him to make sure they reached safety.

Moon didn't release his breath until Reaper's feet were on solid ground. Shaken to his core that they hadn't died, he held his arms out.

Reaper placed Larissa into his arms, then stepped away, as well as the other Last Riders, yet they remained standing close by.

Moon enfolded Larissa into his arms and buried his face in her neck. "I love you." His shoulders heaved with emotions. "I swear I'm never letting you leave the house ever again. It's too dangerous to let you out on your own." Tears fell from his eyes. "That's twice now you've taken ten years off my life. Only you could go out for a fucking hamburger and manage to nearly get killed."

"To be fair"—Larissa lifted her arms to circle his neck—"neither of those close calls were my fault."

Raising his head, he stared at the woman he loved more than life. "Did you hear me tell you I love you?"

She gave him a winsome smile. "Oh yes, I heard you, and so did all of The Last Riders and most of Treepoint."

"I was afraid I was going to lose you, and I wanted you to know in case we didn't make it."

She rubbed her cheek against his chest, and her arms tightened around his neck. "That's so sweet you wanted me to know you loved me before I died."

Moon shook his head. "No, that isn't why I wanted you to know."

A frown marred her brow. "It wasn't?"

"I wanted you to know, if you died, I wasn't going to let you die alone."

She looked at him in shock. "That's why you didn't want me to ride the motorcycle with you—in case you wrecked with me on it."

"I know my strengths and weaknesses. You're strong enough to survive without me, but I'm not strong enough to make it without you. I can't go back to a life without you. I love Jace, but we wouldn't be a family without you."

"If you wanted us to be a family, then why did you do everything you could to tear us apart?"

"Because I'm an idiot. I was so angry with you when you took off without telling me that you were pregnant. I wasn't going to have my kid living without me. What if you became involved with someone who hurt them, and I wasn't there to protect them? You wouldn't be the first woman who turned a blind eye to their child being mistreated by a new boyfriend or lover."

Sadness glistened in her eyes. "Like you were."

Moon nodded, acknowledging how the trauma of his childhood had spilled over to how he had reacted when Larissa had left Treepoint. "As much as I was beginning to care for you, I had to put Jace first. I wanted to have you under my control. Even if we shared custody, I would have no control over anyone you brought into his life the other half of the time. After Jace was born and I grew to trust you more, I realized how messed up what I was doing."

"That's why you wouldn't have sex with me?"

"Yes. I switched both houses into your name. You remember a couple of months ago when I had you sign the life insurance papers where I told you it was because I was increasing my life insurance coverage?"

"Yes."

"In the fine print, I deeded both houses to you, free and clear. I also had you sign where I can make deposits to your checking account. I repaid all the money that has been taken out of your account for the house payments. Lana should ask for a refund; the company she hired should have caught what was going on before the balloon payments had reached the point when they caught it. I have a much better company that I hooked The Last Riders up with."

From the way Larissa was looking at him, she wouldn't be letting him make any suggestions to any of her family members anytime soon.

"I love you," he reminded her, wanting to bring back the lovey-dovey way she had been looking at him before he'd started confessing.

Running his thumb over her bruised cheek, he used the voice she had a hard time resisting. "I had planned on telling you tonight. That's why I wanted to take you out to dinner. I was also going to ask you to marry me," he revealed.

Skeptically, she wasn't exactly swept away. "Before or after you told me what you had done?"

"Probably after we were married. I was going to try to convince you to have a quick wedding at the courthouse."

"I want a normal wedding, with a *long* engagement."

"A normal wedding, with a short engagement," he countered.

"How short?"

"Next week."

Lovey-dovey, she wasn't.

"Next month?" he conceded.

"I can go for that." Turning her cheek into the palm of his hand, she gave him the look he was waiting for.

A loud wail coming toward them made them look up.

Giving Shade a thankful glance, he watched as Larissa took Jace from Shade, settling him on her lap.

He held them both close to him, when he realized he no longer had that crazy feeling that something was going to rip Jace away from him. Unconsciously, the possibility of her finding out about his deception must have been the root cause of his fear for Jace.

Jace wasn't settling down, despite Larissa's attempt of soothing him.

"He's hungry."

Moon nodded as he helped her to her feet. "We'll ride to the hospital in Greer's squad car. You can feed him on the way. I want Lana to check you both out before we go home. You must have hit your head when I grabbed the rock."

"I didn't hit my head. I fainted," she admitted with an embarrassed look as Moon held the car door open for her then got inside with her.

Buckling in his precious cargo next to him, he pulled Larissa and his son back into his arms. It was going to be a while before he was willing to be farther away than arms' length.

As Greer pulled out onto the road, he looked out the window and saw The Last Riders getting back on their motorcycles. He would thank them all when they came to the hospital. He didn't even worry about leaving his motorcycle behind; one of The Last Riders would have his back. They always did. They always would.

Linking his fingers with Larissa's as she fed their son, he raised her hand to his mouth.

"Moon…"

"Hmm?" Moon pressed a kiss to the top of her head as Greer drove them down the steep road.

"There's something I feel I should mention about us getting married."

Moon jerked his head up worriedly. "You're not changing your mind, are you?"

"Oh no … It's just …" She hesitated then gave him a firm look. "I still want us to get married, just don't expect me to sign any prenuptial agreement."

# EPILOGUE ONE

Ginny walked inside the diner and took a seat at the counter. It wasn't long before Marty came lumbering out from the kitchen.

"I wasn't sure you would be open today."

"Should have stayed home. You're the first customer I've had today. Been closed for a week. Everyone knows what happened here. Customers are either going to come back, or they won't, regardless of how long I stayed closed."

Her eyes went to the stitches on the side of Marty's forehead. "How's your head?"

"Better. I don't feel as if it's going to explode anymore." Marty squinted, moving sideways to stand in front of her to avoid a ray of sunshine beaming on him from the window. "You want your usual?"

"No, thanks. I'm not hungry." She straightened the dull napkin holder. "Can I ask you a question?"

"I didn't take you for being a nosy shit, fishing for details about what happened."

Ginny searched the face of the man whom she had considered as one of her fathers. "Why, Marty?" she asked

601

him huskily. "When did money become so important to you it was worth more than a human life?"

Marty's eyes went over her shoulder to stare out the front window. "I'm surprised that husband of yours let you come in here to ask that question."

Remorse that she had befriended the man standing on the opposite of the counter had been eating away at her since Nickel's and Widowmaker's deaths.

Any hope that he would be repentant about the lives he had destroyed died at his unmoved expression.

"Gavin doesn't know I'm here."

"That doesn't mean The Last Riders aren't out there."

"True." Ginny met his gaze truthfully. "But they aren't. At least, not yet."

"What gave me away?" Marty laid an arm on the counter to support his weight. "Greer should go into acting. I thought he bought my story about getting locked in the freezer."

"None of them bought your story. They had to wait until they could have a church meeting to set your punishment. The whole Ohio chapter had to come down for the meeting to place their votes for Wizard to carry out your punishment, as you're the one who ordered Pace's hit."

"Figured that out, too, huh?" Marty straightened from the counter and started walking to the kitchen door without a backward glance toward her.

Sliding out of the chair, she followed him into the kitchen, watching him put hamburgers on the grill and drop fries into the fryer.

"Charles sent a text to Lily when he saw Gavin following them. He knew he wasn't going to get away and wanted her to know of your involvement." Ginny watched as Marty flipped the burgers. "Charles has loved Lily since they were kids. I guess he didn't want to take the chance she would one day be at the wrong time and place, like Larissa."

"They have their meeting?"

"This morning. They had to wait for Moon until he was ready to leave Larissa and his son long enough. It was traumatic, him coming so close to losing his family."

"The Last Riders here wanted Moon to carry out my punishment," he said matter-of-factly as he laid hamburger buns out on the counter and raised the fries from the fryer.

"No. They voted for Viper. As president of The Last Riders, it's his right to exact justice since Pace was a new recruit under Viper's protection. Moon had to be there so Viper could hand the responsibility over to him if he decided to ask. Because Viper and Wizard both had the right to be the one to administer what the clubs voted for, Moon was allowed to ask if he could administer the punishment because his rights superseded both Viper's and Wizard's."

"How?" Marty started placing the hamburgers on the buns.

"Because you're the one ultimately responsible for his woman and son nearly being killed. If you hurt one of their women, it's a death sentence."

"So, you know I wasn't the one who ordered Gundy to lose his shit and start shooting. I was in the kitchen with Charles when it went down. Gundy broke the rule about coming here. His mom is dying, and he wanted to take her on some big trip.

"We were arguing in the kitchen, and I told him to get his ass out of here and we'd talk about it later. When Gundy left the kitchen, he must have thought Larissa and the kid had been there the whole time. Before I could get out front, Gundy had already started shooting when the other two came in the door. I guess he thought she had called them."

"Would you have ordered him to kill them if she had, or would you have stopped him if you had time?"

"We'll never know, will we?"

"I guess not."

He might not have answered her directly, but with her blinders removed where he was concerned, she was able to discern what she had believed—him having a sarcastic attitude was for show. In reality, he hid an extremely callous person who was willing to do anything it took to remain in the background to protect his own interests.

Wrapping the burgers tightly, he started packing them into a plain brown sack.

"Why?" she asked again, heartsick that he had used their friendship as a cover to come to Treepoint to launder money.

If the workers he had recruited hadn't stolen merchandise, which had been logged as mail then replaced with packages of money to be retrieved on the other end, Marty would still be pretending to be a normal restaurant owner, not a criminal who didn't care who got in his way as long as his identity remained a secret.

"I could tell you it's because my ex-wives drained me dry and I needed the money for alimony payments, but I won't. I got greedy. It was too easy. I ran off the regular customers. Of those who did come around, it didn't take long to find out who was strapped for cash, willing to do anything for an extra payday. It's not like I was asking them to steal the Mona Lisa. Between the diner, Charles' two businesses, and my connections, we were making bank. I could keep track of everything right here, set up my cameras, and rake the cash in."

"Meanwhile, you had Megan and me telling everyone how bad of health you were in if anyone grew suspicious."

"I did." Dumping the fries on top of the packaged burgers, Marty folded the top down. "I took advantage of every opportunity offered to me. Where I screwed up was involving The Last Riders with transporting the money to Ohio. It was easy to reel Charles in; he goes back and forth to

Lexington. He's made more money with me than his restaurants make in a month. He warned me not to use The Last Riders' trucks. I should have listened."

"Yes, you should have. Why didn't you?"

"Stupidity." He shook his head. "I always knew a woman would be the death of me. Saffron caught Gundy stealing, and he told her. I let her convince me to funnel more money through some contacts she had in Ohio. Then, once we had enough put away, we could take off and live wherever we wanted. That's twice in my life I've let myself believe that bullshit."

Marty picked up the bag of food and handed it to her. "Goodbye, kid. Take care of yourself."

Tears welled in her eyes. Marty knew why she had come today. When she had left Nashville, she had gone by his restaurant to give him a goodbye present.

Taking the food, she had to swallow the lump in her throat. "I will. Goodbye, Marty." Blinking back the tears, she turned and left the kitchen. The front of the restaurant was still empty.

The tears were sliding down her cheeks when she went out the door, where Moon was waiting outside. When he saw her, he started to walk past her.

"Thank you," she said with a tear-filled voice.

Moon gave her a curt nod. "We're even now."

Unable to respond without breaking down, she forced herself to continue toward the parking lot. She rounded the corner of the diner and found Gavin leaning against the side of her car with his boots crossed.

"I had to say goodbye to him," she told him as she grew nearer.

"I know." Gavin raised his arms, spreading them open.

She walked into his arms and broke into tears. "I hate him so much," she sobbed as his arms closed around her.

"I know that, too." Leaning away from the car, he opened the door for her. "Get in."

He shut the door after she got inside, then went to the other door. Starting the car, he pulled out of the parking lot.

She looked at him when he didn't head in the direction of their home. "Where are we going?"

"I thought we'd go to the park and have a picnic."

---

Three Weeks Later...

Placing an arm around Winter's shoulders, Viper handed her a glass of champagne. He took a sip of his own champagne and smiled as the newly married couple danced, holding their son between them.

"It was nice of Reaper's in-laws to allow us to have Moon and Larissa's wedding reception here."

"They offered when Reaper told them we couldn't find a big enough space to have a party where both of the clubs could fit. The only other option was the state park," he joked as he continued to watch the couple.

A tap on his cheek had Viper turning his gaze to her.

"Be careful; he'll catch you gloating," she warned. "You're looking too proud of yourself. Just don't forget it was my idea."

"It was your idea to bring the girls to the club to set Moon up with one of them. May I remind you that you tried to set him up with the wrong one?"

"Because Lana was the one staring at him as if he were an ice cream cone on the hottest day of the year. I led the horse to the water. It wasn't my fault Larissa took a drink before Lana could."

"Need I remind you that I was the one who gave Jonas the

security tapes so he could slice out the parts where the women were there? I was also the one who had to convince the other brothers to go along with acting like Moon was making the whole thing up. Hell, the only reason I was able to convince them was because none of them wanted to go through another Christmas with Moon constantly whining about not having a family to share Christmas with like everyone else. I've never seen a man wanting to be in a relationship so badly, and then, when a woman gets serious about him, he sabotages it so they end up breaking up with him. The problem is he enjoyed the fucking chase more than the relationships."

"No, the problem was that women fell for him too easily," Winter disagreed. "They didn't make Moon work for it. My girl keeps Moon on his toes."

"Yes, she does," Viper had to agree with that assessment. "Moon and Shade have a bet going which woman will give them a heart attack first."

"Hmm ... I might need to put a couple hundred on that bet. Who has higher odds?"

Viper laughed. "Last I heard, it was dead even."

Winter burst out laughing at his pun.

Tightening his arm around her, Viper couldn't help but press a kiss to Winter's parted lips.

"What's that for?"

"For not being Lily or Larissa."

"You're forgetting I've given you your fair share of nightmares."

"Shh ... I don't like to think about it. You want to dance?"

"Yes, I do."

Setting their glasses down on the picnic table, they walked to where lights had been hung on the trees to create a magical glow for the dancing couples.

"You think you'll ever break and tell Moon we played

matchmakers?" Humor glinted in her eyes as he pulled her close, swaying along with Foreigner singing "I Want to Know what Love Is."

Viper watched as Moon and Larissa's mother traded skank faces at each other behind Larissa's back. "I'm not sure us playing cupid will be appreciated by everyone."

---

Strolling among the wedding guests, Silas unintentionally listened to all the conversations going on. When he was younger, being around so many people would have sent him into excruciating pain, as if his mind was about to blow into a million fragments. As he grew older, he had learned to lower the volume of the voices to a manageable level. Then, if he chose, tune into those he wanted to listen to. He had also learned the hard way to stay away from huge crowds.

He found a darkened spot under a tree a distance from the party but was still able to watch the festivities, and his eyes caught on the wedding couple. Making a slight gesture with his hand, he sent the evening breeze in Moon's direction.

*Relax. Be happy. Your son is safe. You don't have to be afraid anymore.* After repeating the thought a couple more times, Silas released the wind to go on its wayward journey.

Desolate, he watched the guests for a few more minutes, thinking over the last few months. His eyes went to his family members, seeing the same regret and self-reproach in them as he was suffering from not everyone having the same happy ending as Moon and Larissa had been blessed with.

They had learned a harsh lesson when Greer had his stroke. He had been walking a tightrope by warning Moon because the child's fate was in Moon's hands. If they had interfered in saving a life that was meant to be taken, the repercussions would be severe. They would have lost one of their own. He and his brothers had kept Ginny and Gavin in the dark until it was too late for their interference.

Shaking himself out the doldrums, Silas started walking to where his family had gathered at one of the picnic tables. Tonight was meant to share in the joys ahead, not the sorrows of the past. And there were so many joys ahead ... just waiting for a new day to begin, a new love to blossom.

# EPILOGUE TWO

Larissa threw herself down on the bed, staring up at the ceiling, too exhausted to remove her shoes. Thank goodness her mother and sisters were going to take care of Jace for the next two days.

Lifting one foot in the air, she wiggled it as Moon came near. "Please ... I'm too tired to move. Every bone in my body hurts."

Her new husband removed her shoe then took off the other before she had to ask.

"Do you mind if we have our wedding night tomorrow? The only thing that is going to excite me tonight is a shower and going to sleep."

"Really?" Moon massaged the foot he was still holding. "Nothing could excite you? Damn, I guess my wedding present can wait until tomorrow night."

Moon's tender smile turned mocking when she bolted up in bed.

Patting her fluffy wedding dress down, she raised her hands, wiggling her fingers. "Give me."

He didn't argue. He went to the closet and returned with a flat box.

Ripping the wrapping paper away, she opened the box and burst into laughter. She pulled out the *Warlord from Hell* costume, shoved the box off her lap, then went to Moon, throwing her arms around him and giving him a passionate kiss. "Thank you."

His arms circled her waist. "You can thank me better than that ..." he said throatily.

She always knew she was done for when he made that throaty sound that came from his chest. A woman could only take so much temptation, and when Moon used that sexy tone with her, it was like a laser hitting each of her girlie parts.

Jerking out of his arms before she went past the point of no return, she moved to her side of the bed, crouched down, and pulled a large box out from under the bed. "This is for you," she told him excitedly.

With a curious expression, Moon accepted the present.

She felt bad when he took his time, as if he wasn't used to opening a lot presents. Promising herself he would get so many from now on that he'd get sick of them, she waited expectantly for him to open the box.

"I see we were on the same track." He laughed, taking out the women's costume from *Warlord from Hell.*

Holding the outfit to her, Moon unashamedly nodded his head toward the bathroom and wiggled his eyebrows. "I will if you will."

Barely able to hide her excitement, she shook her head. "Since it is our wedding night, can I choose who we are tonight, and you can tomorrow night?"

Leering, Moon shrugged. "Baby, we can be whoever you want to be, as long as I get laid."

She moved to his dresser and took out her favorite pair of

jeans of his, then went to the closet to take out the ball cap she wanted him to wear. When she returned to his side, she handed them to him with a grin.

Moon's face cracked into laugh lines. "Seriously? This turns you on more than the warlord?"

She looked at him like he was crazy. "The warlord is sexy, but I like to see what I'm getting."

"You forgot the hula hoop," he reminded her.

She went to her nightstand and returned with a jump rope. "Wanna see if you can do it as good as him?"

"You're joking, right? Baby, there's no comparison as to who's better."

Larissa went to get her cell phone from where she had dropped it on the bed, pulling up the hula hoop video from the guy's account. Finding which one she had saved, she pressed *play*. "Can you do that?"

Moon's jaw clenched, looking at her more than what she was showing him. "How many times have you watched this?"

"Just a couple," she lied, not wanting to hurt his confidence. "So, can you?" she asked excitably. "Did I get the right jump rope?"

His eyes narrowed on her as he unwound the jump rope. "It'll do."

She excitedly ran to the bathroom. "I'll take a quick shower, then you can have the bathroom. I won't be five minutes."

Shutting herself in the bathroom, she took the fastest shower she had ever taken, then wrapped the towel around her and padded out of the bathroom. "It's all yours."

Moon's eyes slipped over her damp body. "You could have taken the time to dry off."

"I was afraid you'd get hungry, and you'd make yourself popcorn. You didn't eat much tonight."

When Moon moved around her, she could have sworn he

gave an irritated growl. Sure she was imaging it, she started drying herself off as soon as the door was closed behind him.

She went to the sound system and started the music she wanted before moving to the dresser to take out the white satin chemise. When she slid it on, she couldn't resist running a hand down the front, loving the erotic feel of the material on one side of the baby doll gown. The other side was a clear mesh, leaving that part of her body bare.

She had just finished brushing her hair when Moon came out of the bathroom, wearing the outfit she had given him.

Licking her bottom lip, she sat down on the side of the bed. Oh, my goodness … with the hat pulled down, he looked as good as the guy she followed.

"Is this what …?"

Larissa raised her hand to stop him from talking. "Don't ruin it. The best part is he never talks," she advised.

The sultry music playing in the background was "Lose Control" by Teddy Swims as Moon started jumping over the rope, making her heart beat faster. The way he twirled and twisted his body in different ways was magical.

"I'm curious … how good are you at push-ups?"

The jump rope went limp.

"Nevermind." She sensed that she was pushing her luck, " I think I prefer you jumping rope anyways."

She bit down on her lip as Moon rose and started jumping rope again, without missing a beat. This time Moon went faster, his tricks becoming more intricate as he jumped on one foot then switched to the other. Then he would double the rope to jump it sideways.

"You know, I'm wondering, I haven't seen you working out here. Do you work out at The Last Riders'?"

Moon gave her a nod.

"That's what I thought. Killyama showed me the equipment The Last Riders have at the clubhouse. It makes sense that you would work out there." Larissa noticed Moon's jaw getting tighter each time she talked. She must be messing with his concentration. "Do any of the other Last Riders work out with you?"

Noticing Moon was tilting his head back so he could look at her under the brim of his hat, she started playing with the pretty, pink bow between her breasts. She was saving the surprise for later that when the bow was untied, the chemise opened like a robe.

Seeing his slight nod, she ran her hand over her baby pouch which, in all likelihood, she would never get rid of.

"You know, I was thinking … maybe we could work out together? If you tell me when you and the other Last Riders work out, I could schedule my appointments around that time, and we can all work out together. I could get some tips from them …"

One end of the jump rope came swinging for her. With a frightened squeal, she jumped up from the bed and ran for the bedroom door.

Her hand was on the doorknob when the jump rope curled around her waist and she was tugged backward.

Gasping at what he had done without hurting her, she found, to her dismay, she wasn't able to dislodge the rope and was being pulled inexplicably within his grasp.

Feeling his heat behind her, she turned around to throw herself into his arms. "I was just joking." She batted her eyes at him as she wound her arms around his neck.

"I don't believe you."

"It's true." She gawked up at him as if he was the neatest thing since sliced bread. "None of The Last Riders could compare to you."

Doubt filled her at the wisdom of her playing into Moon's jealousies. She hadn't needed Winter's advice at the bridal shower about Moon being competitive. She had learned early in life the more intelligent a man was, the more competitive he'd be. When she became bored, she found other educational outlets to keep her busy. Moon, on the other hand, she surmised had used women to fill that competitive void. He was no dummy. The way he had drawn up those contracts was a masterpiece of cunning.

No, she hadn't needed Winter's subtle warning about Moon. He would constantly be looking over a fence to see if the grass was greener on the other side, but she figured, if she kept him so busy making sure his own grass was green and trimmed, his own roots would become too deep to be blown away.

Cupping her butt, Moon lifted her up to him and plastered her body against him. "None of them can do as many push-ups as I can," he bragged, carrying her toward the bed.

"Have you guys had a competition to see?" Biting back a giggle, she stuck an awed expression on her face.

"I win every time."

"Was Jesus there?" Larissa dared to ask.

"Yes." Moon ground out, remembering he told her it was her night to choose what she wanted, but it was obvious already that he had plans to pay her back tomorrow night for that comment.

The man was lying through his teeth, but she pretended to believe him.

As he set her down on the bed, her hands went to the opening of his jeans as he started unwinding the rope.

"The next time you guys compete against each other, can I come?"

Frowning, she wondered why the rope was suddenly becoming tighter around her.

"No."

"I promise to be completely unbiased," she not so innocently offered.

"I bet you will."

She wondered if he was aware how menacing his face now looked? Was he meaning to scare her? Somehow, she thought he was.

"Moon ... uh ... the rope is getting a little tight."

"Is it hurting you?"

"No ..."

"Then you're good."

She knew she was in peril when she realized too late that Moon had removed the rope from around her waist to wind it around her ankle then extend it to her thigh, winding it around before looping it just over her elbow before using the end of the rope to tie her hands together.

Running her tongue under her lip, she thoughtfully stared at his handiwork. The jerk had managed to tie her in an extremely suggestive pose.

"I see your skills with the rope extend to more than using it for jumping."

"I've had some practice."

"More than some from my position."

Jealousy was about to get the best of her until she saw him removing his jeans. Seeing his erect penis would have had her fanning herself but, thankfully, her hands were tied. She would be damned if she was going to let Moon win this round.

Using her tied-up hands, she patted the mattress next to her. "Come here."

Suspiciously, Moon climbed onto the bed to lie next to her. He ran his hand over the curve of her hip to slide it down to her groin. "Your sexy as fuck tied up like this," he murmured appreciatively.

"I'm glad you like it." Unable to do much of anything, tied as she was, it only left one option.

She relaxed and went with it.

"This isn't so bad," she commented. "This turns you on?"

"Fuck yes."

"Then we can do this from time to time, as long as it doesn't get too exotic."

"You still want the same safe word?"

"I'm fond of the word *stop*. I don't want to change it. Is there a purpose to me being tied in this position?"

Moon looked at her with half-mast eyes. "Don't take the fun out of it."

"I was just asking."

Climbing over her, Moon spooned her from behind, his hand coming around her waist to play with her clit.

"Wow. I learned something today. I like it." Laying her head on the bed, boneless, she let Moon stroke her passion. "I really like this ..." she moaned out. "This is much better than what I had planned for the rest of the night."

Moon's fingers stopped moving. "What did you have planned?"

"Hmm?" She had difficulty grasping any thought with Moon about to send her into orbit with his magical fingers. "Ah ... yeah, I remember. You remember when you told me you were going to do something to me which had never been done before? I was going to do the same for you."

Moon's head reared up over her shoulder to stare down into her face, as if searching to see if she was telling the truth. "For real?"

"Oh yes. I was ... except, I was going to make it romantic for you."

"I didn't make it romantic for you?"

"You made it hot for me. There's a difference. You're a man, so it's hard for you to understand the difference."

"Just because I'm a man doesn't mean I don't understand," he argued back. "I'm the most romantic man in the club."

Larissa stared at him in disbelief. "I'm sorry to disillusion you, but you're not."

"How am I not romantic? I bought you earrings when you had Jace. I bought you two houses. I bought you an engagement ring that needs an armed guard when you go out."

"I don't like necklaces; I feel like they're choking me. You bought me two houses *after* you were caught nearly bankrupting me with ballon payments. And the engagement ring is beautiful, but I would have been just as happy with something more modest. And last but not least, I have to almost die before you tell me you love me. Moon, I love you with my whole heart, but romance isn't in your wheelhouse."

Larissa felt the rope release with a twist of his hand.

"Woman, are you trying to piss me off tonight?" he complained.

She felt bad at seeing his sullen expression. "I didn't mean to. I'm sorry. Is there something I can do to make it up to you?" she said contritely.

"No, you might as well go to sleep. I'm not in the mood anymore."

Feeling terrible, she rubbed his calf, inching her hand higher, hoping to put him in a better mood.

Moon swatted it away.

"I'm hungry. If I'm not getting sex tonight," he complained, "the least you could do is feed me."

"What do you want?" She started scooting off the bed.

"Popcorn."

*Ugh*. She hated it when he ate popcorn. But after critiquing how romantic he wasn't, she wasn't about to complain about what he wanted to eat.

Yawning, she went into the kitchen and opened the cabinet where they kept their snacks. Open-mouthed, she stared at the contents before returning to the bedroom.

Moon was sitting up in bed, leaning his back on the headboard with his arms crossed over his chest.

"You love me."

"I told you I did," he said huffily.

"You bought me a whole cabinet of girl scout cookies."

"I did, and I even dared Kendra to touch them. I told her I'd find another babysitter if she touched one single box."

"That's so sweet." Walking back to the bed, she picked the rope back off the floor. "Here, you can tie me up again." She climbed back onto the bed and handed him the rope.

"Nope," he said curtly. "You haven't earned me tying you up again. You hurt my feelings."

"I'll make it up to you," she promised.

Moon's eyebrows rose, interest sparkling in his eyes. "How?"

Larissa straddled his hips, tunneling her fingers through his hair. Even with his ring on her finger, she still couldn't quite believe this beautiful man was hers.

Pressing a sweet kiss to his mouth, she disentangled her hands from his hair to lean slightly back, untying the bow between her breasts. Shrugging the gown back, she allowed Moon to see her body.

His eyes slipped downward, stopping over her heart. "That's where you snuck off to this morning," he said in a husky voice.

"It's a little sore," she confessed. "Killyama told me it's kinda tradition with The Last Riders."

"You didn't have to do it because—"

Larissa pressed her fingers over his lips. "I would have done it regardless. I did it to show you I belong to you. Only to you. I love you, Moon."

"I love you, too."

Her finger hovered over the tattoo of the moon. "The moon, of course, is you," she explained. "And the two stars represent me and Jace, so you know that, regardless of if you're full of light or swallowed up in darkness, you will always feel us by your side."

His hand curled around the nape of her neck. "You got it so wrong."

"You don't like it?" Hurt, she tried to look away so he couldn't see.

Moon's hand turned her face back to his. "It's not that I don't like it; you just got it wrong."

Confused, she frowned at him.

"You're not a little star. You're the Earth. We're a team. I give you gravity, so you aren't always stuck in your head." His hand hovered over the tattoo of the moon. "The Moon and Earth are constant with each other, neither straying from the other's orbit. I provide a shield when any motherfucker tries to take what's mine. I'm no Shakespeare, so know I'm not great at coming up with something on the fly, but one thing for sure is you're no fucking little star."

She blinked back tears, a tremulous smile playing around her lips. "I'll make another tattoo appointment," she told him. "But what about the other star? It won't have any meaning."

"Yeah." Giving her a sultry look, Moon arched his hips under her, showing he was still hard. "In nine months, it will, give or take."

Her husband might be the most romantic Last Rider after all. His words removed her fears of him not wanting more children. He was giving her everything she wanted.

"Hey, what's wrong? If you don't want another kid so quickly, we can wait—"

She shook her head. "I do. It's not that."

"Then why are you crying?"

"I don't know why you love me. I drive you crazy." She gave him a shaky laugh to hide she was about to burst into tears. "There isn't one thing you can't get from another woman who won't make you feel as if the apocalypse is imminent. One whose mother you might even like. Heck, I bet they would beg you to tie them up. Name one thing I do another woman wouldn't do better."

"I can." Moon tenderly tilted her face back so she could see how serious he was. "None of them can kiss me like you do." Lifting her mouth to his, he held their mouths a breath away. "As if your soul is telling me you love me."

"Does your soul say anything back?" she whispered.

"You want me to tell you a secret no one else knows?"

"Yes." What did this secret have to do with her question?

"You know I told you I kept hearing a voice telling me to watch out for Jace?" He waited for her to nod before continuing. "It wasn't the first time I heard that voice. When I was young and my makuahine told me we would be leaving Hawaii to move to Nevada, I was so angry that I ran away." Moon gave her a wry glance. "I didn't get very far. I heard the voice and ran back."

She listened to him raptly, her interest piqued. Moon credited the mental voice for saving Jace's and her life.

"What did the voice say?"

"She'll come to you in the dead of the night." Moon spoke as if he were quoting it verbatim, as if it had played in his head a million times. "You will spend many years alone before she comes. Many heavenly bodies will tempt you away from waiting, but hold fast. One cold winter night, across the sea, you will walk not on sand but frozen grass to find a true love as bright as the sun and everlasting as the heavens above.

"After that, I quit giving my makuahine grief about moving because I knew you would find me someday. So, when you kiss me, my soul tells me you're the one I was waiting for."

"That's so sweet, but you didn't have to make that up."

"I'm not lying."

Disbelieving, she shook her head. "Then why did it take you so long to convince yourself you loved me?"

Moon gave her an irked grimace. "I thought I imagined the whole thing happened as I grew older. I mean, it does sound hokey as fuck. Hell, you thought I made it up just now. But when I started hearing the voice warning me about Jace, it finally clicked through my hard head that I didn't imagine the first time I heard the voice when I was younger."

Her brow furrowed in thought.

"That's strange," she admitted. "And odd. It's so similar to the night we met. Could it have been your subconscious?"

"I don't think so."

"What do you think it was?"

"No clue, and I don't want to know."

"Why not?"

"Because …" Moon gave her a sheepish look. "The room you snuck into at the club where I was sleeping wasn't normally mine. I made a bet the night before and lost the bigger room, which had a bathroom, to one of my brothers. We switched that morning." Moon seemed pained as he made the admission.

Larissa gaped at him. Through a twist a fate, she had ended up in Moon's bed the night Jace had been conceived? She could have ended up with a different Last Rider?

"Whose bedroom did you switch with?"

Reluctantly, Moon finally answered.

"Jesus'."